INEZ

NEW YORK TIMES AND USA TODAY BESTSELLING AUTHOR

JASINDA WILDER

INEZ

CHAPTER 1

LA VIBORA HAS COME FOR BLOOD

INEZ

RAGE IS AN OLD FAMILIAR HEAT, FOREVER pulsating at the core of me. Some days it gutters like a candle flame, other days it is a bonfire casting long coruscating shadows within me.

Now, the fire of my rage has burst its banks like floodwaters cascading over the top of a levee. I see red—literally. My vision is narrowed to a hyper-focused tunnel, so the only thing I see is the doorway of the trucking garage. All else is red-tinged nothingness, my hammering blood pressure filling my eyeballs with a flush of blood, staining everything a hazy crimson.

In contrast to the nuclear heat of my hate, I also feel an icy calm. It is a jarring juxtaposition. I am not acting recklessly. My hands are rock steady as I check the load of my MP5, tap the mag home, charge the weapon, and snug the butt against my shoulder. I've got four spare mags in my pockets and vest, four frag grenades, and two flashbangs.

I stomp across the road toward the warehouse, but before I reach it, I hear an engine behind me, and the crunch of tires on gritty asphalt as yet another car enters the trucking yard.

I spin in place, drop to a crouch, draw a bead on the driver of the early-aughts Corolla. There is no thought, no intent, only instinct. Reaction, instantaneous and automatic.

CRACKCRACKCRACK!

My MP5 is not a silenced model, unfortunately. I'd rather have an HK416, but my contact down here couldn't get his hands on any—jolts my shoulder as the rounds crater the car's windscreen. I see the driver jerk in the split second before the interior is bathed in a spray of red—I must have gotten a headshot. The driver's foot mashes the brake pedal as his body catches up to the reality that he's dead, and then his foot slides off the brake pedal and buries the accelerator to the floor, sending the car squealing forward in a wide arc. I hear shouts in panicked Spanish from the other occupants. The car smashes into the side of a parked trailer, wedging under it; the shouting cuts off abruptly upon impact.

I feel Lorenzo behind me, but my rage leaves no room for him. And I know Lorenzo. He'll have my back.

Rickety old wooden steps judder under my weight as I ascend them, and the oppressive heat of the Mexican sun is abruptly replaced by the relative cool of the shade beneath the covered loading platform.

I should wait for Ren.

Fuck it.

I kick the door in, planting my boot beside the doorknob. The frame splinters and the door slams open. Shocked exclamations greet me, a sea of surprised faces turning toward me, guns leveled at me. I spray a burst blindly before my eyes have adjusted; I have no idea if I hit anyone, but a howl of pain tells me I did.

My eyes adjust as I enter. Within, the interior of the warehouse is dimly lit by yellowish, flickering fluorescent bulbs, casting dancing shadows on cracked concrete.

There's a split-second of doubt—but the rage overwhelms it. These men are being paid by Rafael. They do his bidding. They know who he is. They know what he does. Upon his orders, these men will murder children and rape their mothers. I've seen it. I have been that mother.

I have felt their hands holding me down. I have tasted their hands smothering my screams as they force themselves inside me.

Not these men, but men like them. Gutless, soulless, mindless monsters, all.

The murder in my heart takes over.

They're stunned, confused into inaction. A couple of men return fire, but they are panicked and their rounds go high and wide.

Just inside the door at an angle, forgotten, is a large, waist-height rolling tool chest. I duck behind it, pause for the space of two breaths.

Swivel out from behind the tool chest onto one knee and spray a long burst into the crowd, raking my barrel at chest height from right to left. I duck back behind the cart as screams of pain rattle against the corrugated metal roof overhead.

They're not confused anymore—gunfire erupts, rounds dinging off the chest, smacking noisily into the bay doors behind me. I glance right as a long shadow stretches across the floor—broad shoulders, lean hips, ball cap: Lorenzo.

His hand drops from the grip of his MP5, grabs something from his vest. He tosses the object a moment later and then vanishes from the doorway. The object clatters; I peek out and see the telltale shape of a flashbang, and swivel back behind the cart. I plug my ears with my fingers and squeeze my eyes shut just in time. The light and noise are tremendous, and even plugged, my ears ring; even with my eyes shut and hiding behind a solid object, I have to blink the flashes away.

The small army of thugs and mercenaries is disoriented, stumbling into each other, rubbing eyes, shaking heads.

I grab a frag from my vest, pull the pin. "FRAG OUT!" I shout, so Lorenzo will stay behind cover.

I release the spoon and lob the grenade underhanded into the midst of the men and then duck back behind cover myself.

BOOOOOOOM!

Smoke boils and shrapnel cracks, dings, and ricochets in every direction, leavened by screams of agony.

"Moving," Lorenzo says, entering the warehouse and standing tall behind me, his MP5 barking in rapid three-round bursts. Further along the nearest wall is a stack of semi-truck tires. I sprint for the relative cover of the tire stacks as rounds chew up concrete at my heels, and then the tires thunk hollowly.

I drop to a knee and drop a tango with a burst that craters his chest. Bodies lay in writhing piles. Lorenzo is reloading. I see an enemy trying to flank us so he can get a bead on one of us. I send a burst over Lorenzo's head—close enough that he jerks when the rounds buzz and snap.

We work in effortless concert, then, firing while the other takes cover.

Two, perhaps three minutes total have elapsed since

I kicked in the door, those handful of seconds elapsing in a stretchy, fast-slow wobble.

Death stinks.

Screams echo:

"*Ayuda me!*"

"*Mama!*"

"*¡Está La Víbora!*"

A door clangs open somewhere at the rear of the warehouse, and the sudden silence is deafening.

"Get them," I snap to Lorenzo. "No survivors. No prisoners."

He doesn't respond, only jogs across the warehouse while reloading. I watch him pause in the doorway, assessing the rear yard before trotting out after the escaping tangos. I hear his MP5 chatter once, twice, three times.

A wail of pain shudders off the ceiling; the penny tang of blood is thick in the air, the choke of leaking effluvia acrid and sour.

I cast my gaze across the warehouse floor, looking for the right victim.

I see him. He's trying to crawl away, leaving a snail trail of blood from mangled legs, one arm useless and dragging. His ears are bleeding.

I let my rifle dangle as I march toward him, kicking weapons out of reach. Crouch in front of him.

"*La—La Víbora—La Víbora. Por favor…*" His dark eyes are terrified as he babbles at me in Spanish. "Don't kill me. Please don't kill me."

I flick out my butterfly knife, touch the blade's razor edge to his lips. "Hush," I murmur.

He falls silent, except for the ragging, rasping pant of agony and exertion.

"You have a choice," I tell him, applying a touch of pressure so the blade digs in, a trickle of blood dripping from his lips. "Tell me what I wish to know and you'll die quickly and painlessly. Refuse, and you die slow, bleeding out, begging for your whore mother."

"Please, please," he whimpers, drooling bloody saliva. "I don't know anything. My friends say we will be paid a lot of money to go to the States and shoot someone. I don't even know where we were going or who the target is."

I assess the rapidly spreading pool of blood beneath his legs, the chattering of his teeth, the fading focus in his eyes. "I do not believe you."

Across the warehouse another man leans against a post, fumbling with a pistol and a magazine, his eyes flicking between me and his desperate, clumsy attempts to reload his pistol. I stand and pace toward him a few steps, letting my rifle dangle at my side by the strap. "Go ahead," I tell him. "I'll give you a chance."

Instead of raising the gun at me, he touches the barrel under his chin. His mistake is hesitation.

I draw and fire my sidearm left-handed, a skill I've spent hundreds of hours practicing until I'm nearly as fast and accurate left-handed as I am with my right. His hand disintegrates in a splash of red, the gun clattering to the ground. His belly is a mess of red, shredded by shrapnel. He might survive with medical attention, but it's not likely.

I cross to him and drop to one knee. "Who is the target?"

"I don't know," he grits out. "They didn't tell everyone."

"Who knows, then?" I ask.

His eyes scan the writhing bodies, the still corpses. He juts his chin at a man who must have dropped in my initial burst after I kicked open the door—he's near the front of the crowd. He's on his back, gasping short, shallow, whistling breaths, fingers scrabbling at the concrete, heels kicking, digging.

I cross to him, pistol in my left hand, blade in my right. Twin holes in his chest whistle, suck, gurgle.

"Target," I snap. "Who? Where? When?"

"C-c-c..." His mouth flaps.

I whip my balisong closed, pocket it, and scan the area around me—someone dropped a plastic wrapper on the ground. I tear it open flat and press the clean side to his sucking chest wound—the plastic creates the necessary vacuum in his chest so he can suck in a gasping breath. "Answer me."

"Club..." he wheezes in English. "Vegas."

He's older, late forties or early fifties, grizzled, scarred, tattooed, ugly. The look in his eyes tells me he'll tell me what I want to know as long as I let him die quickly.

"What about the border? How were you planning on getting a caravan of armed men across the border?"

"*El Jefe*...Mercado, he has a new friend. A powerful man. Italian. Mr. Pool or...or something like that. We are told he will make it so we can cross over—tomorrow... six...six at night."

"And your target was the club in Vegas?"

"Yes. Yes."

"The Arrows aren't even there. They're all hunting your boss." He doesn't answer, and I understand the truth: Myka, Terra, and the others are the target. Kill, kidnap, rape, torture—the purpose is a moot point. "Mercado. Where is he?"

This gets me a laugh—one laden with a death rattle.

"Not here. Who knows? Mercado tells no one where he goes."

I jerk my head at the room at large. "Is this it? Everyone who was going to attack the club?"

"No. We were to...to meet up with more who were all...already across the—the border. Not Mercado's men. The other."

"Fuck," I hiss. "Was Mercado ever here?"

"I told...you. I don't...I don't know. I do not see him. I do not speak to him. His orders come from Luis. It is the only name I have heard. He is...Mercado's number two, I...I think."

"Who talks to him? You?"

"He calls me." The fingers of his intact hand point at a dropped cell phone a few feet away. "On...that."

He's fading. Losing a lot of blood very fast, and even my makeshift patch can't keep air in his lungs. And nothing can stop those lungs from filling with blood.

"When is the attack on the club?" I ask.

"Two..." his eyes roll, droop. "Two...days...after—after border...crossing."

I nod, stand. "Now you may die."

"Wait." He looks up at me. Struggles to point at his hip pocket. "Give...one more...one more."

I crouch back down beside him and dig in the indicated pocket—a small bag of heroin. Lovely. "That's how you want to go out, huh?"

"Sí. Please. Please. I...I told you—what I...what I know."

"Fine."

I open my knife and cut the bag open, dump the poisonous contents out onto his leg. Scoop a big bump onto the flat of my blade and hold it to his nose. He snorts once, twice, hard—with that chest wound, it must have hurt like hell, but I suppose he's past caring about that.

Immediately, his eyes roll back in his head and he slumps.

I wipe my blade off on his sleeve and leave him to his end.

Go in search of Lorenzo.

I only have to follow the screams.

Lorenzo, when I find him at the far rear of the trucking yard between a pair of long-retired trailers, looks dangerously irritated.

He gestures at the crumpled bodies at his feet. "They didn't know anything," he says in English, "other than they were headed across the border."

"They're headed for the Club," I tell him.

He frowns my way. "*Your* club? In Vegas?"

"Correct."

"And Rafael?"

"He's not here," I answer. "I doubt he ever was."

"So now what?"

"They're going for the girls," I tell him; he hasn't met any of the women except Scarlett, but he knows of them. Long hours of travel means you get to talking, and I know he's grown particularly close with Solomon, after our adventures in South America and Europe.

"We've neutralized the threat, have we not?" he asks.

I shake my head. "According to my source in there—" I jerk my head at the warehouse, "this group was only half the plan. Rafael is working with Pugli, it would seem, and Pugli pulled strings to get the border guards to look the other way while this pack of assholes crossed over. The plan

was to meet up with another group already Stateside—
Pugli's men, I would assume."

"Any idea when?"

"Seventy-two hours," I answer.

"Back north we go, then." He sounds exhausted at the
prospect of the drive back north to Vegas—a journey of
more than fourteen hundred miles.

He scrapes a hand over his head, removing his faded
red, ripped-brim ball cap and scrubbing his hair until it
stands on end. A thin red line mars the stubbled skin at
his throat, a dribble of dried blood trailing down over his
Adam's apple. From me—my knife.

The rage has dimmed from a nuclear meltdown to a
mere inferno, and I have only a vague memory of pulling
my knife on him. I'd been sure Rafael was in here; I should
have known better.

I step closer to him, my eyes on that tiny ribbon of
red. I lock eyes with him and touch the cut. "I'm sorry,
Lorenzo."

He captures my hand—his is huge and hard, im-
prisoning mine in the cage of his fingers. "It's fine. I
understand."

"Ren," I murmur. "It's *not* okay. I just…I am so *angry*.
Not at you, just…"

He frowns down at me. "Of course you're angry, *meu
amor*. How could you not be? After all that you have suffered at Rafael's hands? I know you." He lifts my hands to
his lips and kisses my knuckles. "I am with you. Always.
No matter what."

I shake my head, hating the way his lips upon my
fingers makes me feel: soft, shaky-kneed and breathless,
warm-bellied and hot-blooded. "Ren. I…" I yank my hand

free of his, reaching for the anger that fuels me. "I cannot be her for you. Not yet."

"Who, Sophia?"

I whirl away, holstering my sidearm and reloading my MP5. "I cannot be Sofia for you, Ren. I cannot be…" I flex the fingers of the hand he kissed. "*That*. I have a job to do. I have an enemy to kill. My men left their women at the club assuming they'd be safe, but they're not. As much as I want to hunt down Rafael and bleed him out slowly, I must protect my people." I turn back to look at him. "I only wanted to say that I'm sorry I put my knife to you as I did. It was wrong and I should not have. I know you are with me." I have to swallow hard, clear my throat. "How could I not know?"

Lorenzo once more closes the gap between us, standing so close that my breasts brush his chest, his tall, broad frame occluding the world beyond us. His dark eyes search my face, and for a moment, I wonder if he's going to kiss me. I shake all over at the prospect—It has been such a long time, after all. And I am a woman, with a woman's needs and desires. They have been long suppressed, those feminine needs, but they're there. And the more time I spend with Lorenzo, the more they bubble up to the surface, despite my best attempts to keep them bottled up.

"Not yet," he murmurs, more to himself than to me, I think. He slides the pad of his thumb across my lips, his eyes following his thumb's path with a wistful expression. "Come. I'll steal a car with working A/C, this time."

CHAPTER 2

BENEATH A GOLEM'S SKIN

LORENZO

I AM SICK OF DRIVING. SICK OF THE ENDLESS MILES. I don't even remember when Inez first called me. It feels like a lifetime ago. But ever since then, whenever it was, I have been constantly in transit. All over Brazil, Ecuador, Colombia, Italy, Germany, and now the States.

We literally arrived here in Fresnillo earlier today after more than twenty-two hours of driving, and now, having been here less than three hours, we're going right back the way we fucking came.

I'd rather cut off my own dick than drive all the way across Mexico and the US yet again, but I love Sophia, so here we go.

I take first shift behind the wheel; Inez broods in the passenger seat, the seatback tilted to forty-five degrees, legs stretched out, her hands idly playing with her butter-fly knife—*snick-snick*, open; *snick-snick*, closed; *snick-snick*, open; *snick-snick*, closed.

While I drive, I consider the question of Sophia ver-sus Inez. It's confusing to me, her near-obsession with her name. To me, when I see the woman I love—and have loved for nearly twenty years—I see my Sophia. I see, still, the seventeen-year-old girl I met, at once coltish and curvy, already with steel in her eyes and ice in her veins, already feared and respected by her father's lackeys, minions, and thugs. I see her eyes, so dark brown they're nearly black, watching me from the shadows as I spar with one of Rafael's bodyguards. I see her hands, fluttering over my shoulders like wary, skittish birds the first time I took my life in my hands and dared to kiss her. I see her soft, sleek, nubile, caramel skin gleaming in the moonlight the night she gave me what is still the greatest and most precious gift of my life: her virginity. Her body. Her trust.

That is my Sophia.

But I also see Inez. I see Inez when I think of the moment I discovered what her father did to her—a plan I knew about and could not stop. I warned her. Told her to leave, to flee with me. She refused. Told me I was mistaken. Her father was harsh, yes, but he would never do *that* to her.

He did.

I'm keeping a secret from her, regarding that awful day; a secret and a lie. The lie is that I watched her marriage to Rafael through a sniper scope. I didn't; I watched it from a cell beneath Bruno's estate, a gun to my head so I would not close my eyes or look away. I was forced at gunpoint to watch, every second of every day for three days, as Bruno let his men rape his daughter. I was forced to watch as she was married to that vile, evil, despicable monster. That is the secret.

Bruno's men let their guard down after the so-called wedding, and I escaped. By the time I was able to return to Bruno's estate, intent on freeing Sophia, Rafael had already murdered Bruno and taken control of the drug empire, increasing security to the point that it became obvious rescuing her was simply flat-out impossible.

I remember my superior officer in the Brazilian spec ops team handing me a manila folder full of photographs of the carnage left in her wake upon her escape from Rafael.

Thirty-two people. A mad rampage, it was. Godawful. Horrific. The responding officers who initially reported to the scene vomited. No one—not in law enforcement, not in the Brazilian intelligence community, *no one*—knew the truth of what prompted the massacre. I could not tell them, either. I could only let them vilify her. Paint her as a psychopathic lunatic dead-set on murdering as many people as possible. They hunted for her all over Brazil, but they were looking for what they assumed was a serial killer or some kind of deranged maniac. They never found her, obviously, and they never could understand why or how she never appeared again, anywhere. She never killed anyone in Brazil ever again—or anywhere in South America. To the Brazilian government, the massacre of Rafael's entire estate staff was an inexplicable mystery.

It wasn't.

To Sophia—or more accurately, Inez—everyone who lived and worked on that estate was complicit in what was done to her. And to be honest, she was right, at least partially. They all knew who Bruno was. They all knew who Rafael is. They all knew the kinds of things both men did. You could not live or work on that estate and not know the evils that were done there. You could not avoid the blood, the corpses, or the screams.

They were paid well, and so they pretended not to know. But they knew.

They knew what was done to Sophia. They knew, and did nothing. Said nothing.

Complicit.

I do not make excuses or justify the massacre of thirty-two people, no matter the reason. But I understand.

Inez was born that day. She was birthed out of trauma. She emerged from the ocean of blood spilled that day, full-formed, with hate in her heart and death in her veins. Inez is fueled by a sun-hot rage, a fission of fury.

I love Sophia.

I'm not sure how I feel about Inez.

I fear her. Respect her. But do I love her? I don't think so. How can one love a creature like Inez? For, in my mind, Inez is not a person. Not a woman. Inez, to me, is a golem, a creature shaped by the hands of hate out of the clay of torment, fired in the kiln of killing, given life by the infernal magic of agony.

Somewhere within the destructive golem that is Inez, there is my Sophia. The girl who loved me. The woman who taught me to love. I will destroy that golem. I will free Sophia.

"Stop looking at me like that, Ren," Inez mutters, without so much as a glance at me.

"Like what?" I ask.

She shakes her head. "Just…don't."

"Why not?" I ask. "We're safe and alone for the moment."

"Lorenzo," she says, sighing. "You should give up."

"On what?"

"Me."

I bark a laugh at this. "Every single day from the moment I escaped your father's estate to the moment you called me to ask for help rescuing Solomon, I thought about you. I searched for you." I pause, but the truth emerges. "In São Paulo, there is a post office box."

I have her curiosity, now. She doesn't look at me or say anything, but the quicksilver blur of her incessantly flipping knife ceases and her body angles ever so slightly toward me.

"That post box is crammed full of letters," I say.

When I let the silence linger, she sighs. "Fine, I'll bite. Letters *to* whom and *from* whom?"

"From me to you."

"I don't have a post box in São Paulo," she says.

"No, but I do." I shrug. "They're from me to me, but they're letters I wrote to you. It was…a journal, sort of. It was the only way I could cope with missing you."

The knife resumes snicking open, snicking closed. "Ren," she whispers. "Don't."

"I needed to send them somewhere. The act of mailing out the letters…." I shrug again, shake my head. "It was…it helped me get the feelings out. I wrote you nearly every day for over a decade."

"That many letters wouldn't fit in a single box, Lorenzo," she says. "A letter a day for ten years? That's…" she pauses to do mental math. "Almost four thousand letters?"

I chuckle. "When it filled up, I went to São Paulo, emptied the letters into a bin, and started over."

"Where is that bin, now?"

"A storage unit a few blocks from the post office, along with some extra gear."

"What did you write about?" she asks, after a few minutes; her tone suggests the question is spoken begrudgingly,

as if her curiosity overpowered her reticence to discuss...
well, anything to do with our former romantic relationship.

"Everything," I answer. "I complained about work.
Superior officers. Missions. I wrote about dead friends.
How I missed you. What I'd want to do with you, if I
could see you. What I would say if I ever saw you again.
Everything. My life."

She doesn't answer for a long, long time. "Why keep
them all this time? Especially if you didn't know if I was
even alive."

"I don't know. Throwing them away seemed wrong. I
never imagined I'd actually see you again, though I never
stopped hoping." I sigh, shake my head. "I suppose...no.
I don't know."

"Say it, Lorenzo." She finally turns to look at me. "Say
what you were going to say."

"I kept them because some part of me always held
out hope that I would find you one day, and you would..."
I pause, clear my throat gruffly, hating the thick knot of
clogging emotion. "That you would perhaps want to read
some of them, someday."

"Ren," she whispers.

"I know. It's foolish."

She stares at me, her black gaze inscrutable, unknow-
able. "It isn't foolish."

I don't know how to answer that.

Her gaze rakes back to the window. "Maybe..." a hard
swallow. "Maybe someday, I will read them."

I don't know how to answer that, either.

I held onto the thinnest thread of hope for so many
years, hoping against all evidence that she was alive, that
she was out there somewhere. Hoping she was thinking

of me. Missing me. Trying to find me. To return to me. I dreamed of seeing her again.

Our reunion is not as my dreams portrayed.

She does not want me. She is not my Sophia.

I do not know how to reach beyond Inez's hardened clay golem skin to the Sophia at the core of her. I see glimpses of her, now and then, but I can as easily grasp a fistful of water as I can hold on to those fragments of the woman I once knew.

Long minutes of silence blossom between us, with only the roar of the engine and the hum of the tires.

"I'll never give up on you," I say, my voice low and rough. "I never have and I never will."

"The Sophia you once knew is gone, Lorenzo," she murmurs. "She died in that cell. She died along with the thirty-two people I murdered."

"I know."

"Then what is it you hope to find?" she asks, looking at me once again. "Who are you looking for, when you look at me the way you do?"

"Just...you."

"Why?"

"Because I love you." It is the only answer there can be.

"Then you love a ghost."

"No," I answer. I reach over, moving slowly and cautiously, and rest my hand on her knee; when she doesn't slice my hand off, I give her knee the gentlest of squeezes. "I love the woman you are now. Whatever name you choose. Wherever you are. Whoever you are. I have loved you since I first saw you and I have never stopped. I will never stop. I cannot."

She only shakes her head and resumes staring out the

window, brooding. "I say it again, because it is the truth, Lorenzo: you love a ghost."

"Then I love a ghost. So what? I have asked you for nothing, Sophia...or Inez. Whichever. I will walk beside you wherever our paths lead. I'll fight with you. I'll fight for you. I'll kill for you. I'll die for you." I squeeze her knee again. "I ask for nothing. I would love nothing more than to hold you. To kiss you. To make love with you. But if you cannot give me any of that, so be it."

"Why?" she asks. "You have a choice. You don't *have* to cling to these feelings. You can give up on me. You can let go."

"Of course I have a choice." I capture her hand and bring it to my lips. "I choose you. Loving you is a choice and it's one I make every day."

"Why? *Why*, Lorenzo? We shared, what? A few months of stolen moments, more than fifteen years ago? Closer to twenty, is it not? Why? Why cling to the bones of a dead woman, Lorenzo?"

"I don't know. A lovely, deadly seventeen-year-old girl captured my heart and never gave it back. Maybe I'm just a stubborn old fool, but..." I shrug, shake my head. "I don't know. I just know I love you, and I cannot, will not ever stop."

Her silence shifts, then. She tilts the seat all the way back and drapes her arm over her eyes. "I'm going to sleep for a while. Wake me up when it's my turn to drive."

My hand is still on her knee. That is a small but significant victory.

CHAPTER 3

BROKEN PIECES

INEZ

THREE A.M., SOMEWHERE JUST SOUTH OF THE border. We're at a gas station. I've been driving for the past five or so hours. Lorenzo is sprawled across the back seat, hat pulled over his eyes, snoring quietly. He stirred when I stopped at the fuel station, peered around, and went back to sleep.

My phone rings, an insistent buzz in my back pocket. I set the pump handle to dispense automatically and walk out of earshot before I answer. "Hello, sir."

"Inez." His deep, smooth, cultured voice washes across the line. "I apologize for the long delay. What's the emergency?"

After the attack on the trucking garage, I sent him our prearranged code indicating that I had an emergency and I needed to speak with him ASAP.

"We have a serious problem, sir," I answer. "Rafael was not in Fresnillo."

"That is unsurprising, and therefore not the emergency, I assume."

"Correct. I was able to get some information from the survivors."

"Survivors of what, exactly?"

"We tracked what we thought were his movements to a trucking company in Fresnillo. It wasn't him, obviously, but it was his men. A lot of them, massing for some kind of attack. Lorenzo and I…neutralized them."

"How many?"

"I don't know. Thirty or forty. We didn't have a chance to do an exact count."

"And?"

"And they were preparing to raid the Club."

His silence is telling. "*My* club?"

"Yes, sir."

"You neutralized the threat, you said."

"Pugli and Rafael *are*, in fact, working together. It was suspected, but now it's a verified fact. Pugli was going to make sure border guards let the caravan through. He also has a contingent of men on the US side of the border, perhaps even in Vegas as we speak." I pause. "We have to assume the raid is going to happen as planned, even though we eliminated Rafael's half of the attack force."

"So the women are in imminent danger."

"Yes sir."

"And my Arrows are out hunting, and you're… where?"

"Mexico, still. Not far from the border. We'll be back in the States by dawn, but it's still several hours from the border to Vegas."

"Do you know when the raid was supposed to happen?"

"The day after tomorrow, I think? It's hard to remember what day it is, to be honest, sir. We've been driving for so long I don't know where I am or even *when* I am."

"Get ahold of the women. Get them out of there. I'll arrange for a safehouse of some kind."

"They found Lorenzo at a safehouse."

"I am aware." A pause. "There is a penthouse at the Bellagio. I own it through a series of subsidiaries and shells. We will put them up there. Get to Vegas ASAP, Inez. I'll be in contact."

"Yes, sir." I wait, glance at the screen—he's quiet but still connected, so he has something else for me.

Another long pause. "I just received an update from a contact in law enforcement. Beatriz was found dead. Ren—Little Ren, I believe they call him, as opposed to your Lorenzo—is in our custody. He is safe and unharmed, but from what I am given to understand, he witnessed his…ahhh, Beatriz's execution at the hands of Roberto Pugli himself."

"Fuck!" I snap, and then follow it with a long series of the most vicious curses I know in Spanish, and Portuguese, and then revert back to English for the Boss's sake. "God*dammm*it, Boss. She was innocent. She was his fucking *mom*."

"I know, Inez. I'm sorry."

"Who is taking care of him?"

"An individual named Nicholas Harris and his wife, Layla. They are known to me. They own a security company, the best in the business. More to the point, they are wonderful, compassionate people, and grade-A operators themselves who employ a cadre of grade-A operators."

"You trust them to keep him safe? My son?"

"Nicholas Harris can field a fully armed F-16, and his men are the best of the best. I would hire them to protect me, if I didn't have you and the Arrows. You have my word of honor that your son could not be in safer hands."

"Good enough for me, sir." I scrub my face. "I need better intel. I need to know where Rafael is. I need someone to put a fucking slug in Pugli's goddamn skull, post-fucking-haste."

"Get to Vegas. Secure our people. By the time you do those two things, I will have something for you, if I have to leverage every contact, favor, and marker I have."

I let out a harsh sigh. "Watch your six, sir. Pugli has major reach. So does Rafael. Between them, even you cannot assume you're untouchable."

"The dead cannot die, Inez. But I take your point."

The dead cannot die? That's the first direct reference he has ever made to his past, which I have guessed at—in the privacy of my own mind, never out loud. I've long had suspicions as to his identity, but I respect his privacy and have not attempted to find out who he truly is.

He laughs, a quiet, amused chuckle. "You mean to say you've never tried to figure out who I am, Inez?"

"Sir?"

"Your silence is rather telling."

"No, sir. I have not. I would not. I, more than perhaps anyone, understand that one's past is one's own. You gave me a life, a future, a career, a home…and, I am coming to discover, a kind of family in the Arrows. I would not betray that favor by trying to discover your secrets. If you wished for me to know, you would have told me."

"Your loyalty is priceless to me, Inez." A soft breath. "Get to Vegas. We will speak again soon."

"Sir."

The line goes dead, and I pocket the phone. When

I return to the car, the pump has stopped and Lorenzo is awake, sitting in the passenger seat, gnawing on a stick of beef jerky. I slide behind the wheel and start the motor, but do not put it into gear, yet.

I look at him. Sigh. "Pugli murdered Beatriz. Little Ren is safe, and with some security contractor my boss knows, a man named Nicholas Harris."

Lorenzo nods. "I know *of* him—any operator, mercenary, or security operative knows of Harris. Alpha One Security is the top name in kidnap recovery, elite security operations, and off-book, white hat black ops."

"White-hat black ops?" I echo.

He nods, shrugs. "He's very particular about the work he accepts. Think of them as…paladins, of a kind, if you know what I mean." He eyes me, shrugs again. "I am not surprised you haven't heard of him. You have not worked in the black ops field, not really. It's a very small, very insular world unto itself."

"The Boss trusts him, and that's good enough for me."

Lorenzo eyes me. "Beatriz is dead?"

I nod. "Yes. Little Ren watched Pugli blow her brains out, apparently."

"Fuck," he growls. "I am sick of that man. Beatriz was no threat to anyone."

"I know."

"So…have our plans changed in light of this information?" he asks.

"No," I answer. "We go to Vegas as planned. We secure my girls. Boss says he'll have some kind of intel on Pugli, Rafael, or both once that's done."

"*Your* girls?" he says, eyebrow arched at me.

"Yes," I snap, silently daring him to push the point.

"*My* girls. Myka, Annika, Anjalee, Naomi, Terra, Tatiana, and Scarlett." I swallow hard, thinking of them. Of all they've been through. Their attempts to draw me into the social fold. How much they've improved the lives of my guys—my Arrows. "Anyone seeking to harm them will have to go through me."

Lorenzo nods, resting a big, strong hand on my thigh and squeezing. "Both of us, *meu amor*. You will never face anything alone again. *Eu prometo.*"

This makes my eyes burn. His hand on my thigh scorches my skin through the fabric of my black denim jeans.

"Lorenzo, I..." I shake my head, clear my throat with a hoarse, scratchy cough.

He runs his hand along my thigh from knee to hip crease. "You don't need to say anything."

I grasp his wrist as his hand passes up to my hip crease once more—where his pinky presses against the seam of my core. I squeeze hard, fighting for breath, for calm; his touch, there, allows neither. "Ren," I whisper. "It is hard for me to endure being touched. By anyone. At all. Ever."

He moves to remove his hand. "I'm sorry, Sophia... Inez. *Deus, meu amor*, I don't know which name to use."

I grip his wrist with all the strength I possess, eyes closed against the army of biting ants crawling under my skin at his innocent, affectionate touch. "I *am* trying, Ren. I know—I know what you want. What you need. I do not know if I can ever give it to you, but I swear, I'm trying."

"What I want and need is only you. Just you." He peels my fingers away from his wrist and mates our hands, fingers intertwined. "We can start here. *Sím*?"

I look at our joined hands. His is large, hard, and

scarred across the knuckles. A faded green-blue ink tattoo, long faded into unintelligibility, is smeared across the web of skin between thumb and forefinger. It was once an insignia of his particular branch of the Brazilian Army Special Forces. Now, it's little more than smeared, faded lines on brown, weathered skin.

I rub my thumb over the tattoo. "This, I can do."

I put the car in gear and continue north. I hold his hand, resting on my knee, for the next few hours.

For some reason, it comforts me.

———◆———

I wake to oppressive heat layered with cool-ish air from a struggling A/C system.

Lorenzo took over driving a while ago, and I took the opportunity to catch some sleep. I watch him through slitted eyes, not quite ready to admit to being awake just yet. His hat brim is pulled low against the blazing sun, mirrored aviators perched on his nose just beneath the curved brim. He hasn't shaved in who knows how long, his hard, angular jawline shadowed with the start of a beard. It suits him, though I prefer him clean-shaven.

He scratches that jawline, sniffs, rubs his nose. Adjusts his crotch.

I find myself wondering at his life, between escaping my father's enmity and me calling him for help.

Did he ever marry? Have a girlfriend? Or, like so many in his line of work, was he married to the job, the teams?

"You're awake," he murmurs. "Get some rest?"

Found out, I nod and sit up. "Yes."

He eyes me sidelong. "What?" he says. "You're looking at me like you want to ask me something."

I shrug. "Not really."

"Ask. I will answer, if I can."

I'm horribly uncomfortable with personal conversations like this. It invites questions. But this is Lorenzo, and he knows everything about me.

"Your life, after me," I start.

He nods. "What about it? I went into Spec Ops and then intelligence, and now I'm freelance."

"Not your work," I say. "Your...personal life."

"I didn't have much of one," he answers. "Drinks with my teammates. The occasional football game."

"Did you ever have...relationships?" I ask, the words stumbling and tumbling out of me awkwardly.

He glances at me. "Ahhhh. Well? Yes. I was no monk. I...there was someone, when I was stationed in Goiâna. Consuela. Sweet girl. Beautiful. Kind. Funny."

I feel a strange burn in the pit of my stomach at this news. "I see. What happened?"

A shrug. "I went on assignment, and when I came back, she'd moved out. Left me a letter telling me how to find her, if I ever wanted to settle down properly."

"You did not, obviously." I can't look at him. The ache in my gut won't let me. I'm not sure what this sensation is, but I don't like it.

He shakes his head. "No. I never saw her again."

"Why not?"

He's silent a long time. "Many reasons."

"Such as?"

He glances at me. "Do you really want to know?"

"I wouldn't have asked if I didn't."

"The more I thought about things, the more I realized that it wasn't the job or the time away from her that drove us apart. It was…well, it was you."

I feel as if I've been punched in the stomach. "Me? How?"

"I couldn't commit to her. I couldn't…connect with her past a certain point. I was holding some part of myself back. Keeping a distance between us, emotionally. And even physically, in a way." He takes off his hat and plucks idly at the loose threads of the brim's ragged edge, driving with his knee for a moment or two.

"And what does that have to do with me, Ren?"

He frowns at me. "You don't get it?"

"Lorenzo, how could I have come between you and this Consuela of yours when I was on a different continent entirely?"

He lets out a slow breath. "Because she wasn't *you*, Sophia. She could never *be* you. She could never understand me—she accepted the danger of my job, she accepted the time apart. But she couldn't *understand* me. It's the only way I can put it. And beyond that, as I said, she just wasn't you. I couldn't love her because I was still in love with you."

My eyes burn, and it makes me angry. "That's not my fault."

He shakes his head. "No, it isn't. I suppose it doesn't make any sense to anyone but me, but even though you were the reason, I never blamed you."

"You're right—that *doesn't* make any sense," I snap.

He looks at me with a heavy sigh. "Sophia—"

"I am NOT Sophia!" I shout. "Sophia is dead! The woman you loved is fucking *dead*, Lorenzo!" I slam the heel of my palm against the steering wheel as I all but scream the word *dead*.

"Inez, then—"

"You know *nothing* about me—about Inez. I may occupy the body of the woman you once knew as Sophia, but that person is gone. Inez is…I am…" I shake my head. "You cannot love Inez. I'm not…capable. Whatever thing it is inside of a person that lets us love and be loved…it died in that cell. My father's men raped it to death. Rafael raped it to death. And I…I finished it off, when I…all those people…"

I steal a look at Lorenzo and he's staring at the window, shoulders bunched around his ears, jaw tight, fists clenched so hard they tremble, white-knuckled.

The burn behind my eyes turns into a haze I cannot see through, and I pull onto the shoulder and brake to a skidding halt in the gravel with a swirl of dust.

Lorenzo is out of the car before I've put the shifter into park, hands knotting in his hair. I'm out and after him, memories of that awful, bloody night surging through me in a crushing cascade of gore-soaked nightmares.

Heads snapping back, brains spattering walls.

Stunned eyes going vacant as crimson circles bloom on shirtfronts, again and again.

The kitchen.

Maids' quarters.

Dining room. Cellar.

Stables.

Bunkhouse.

Spent shells trailing me like hot droplets of brass blood.

Bile stains the back of my teeth, presses against my lips. I stagger away into the scrub beyond the shoulder, fall to my hands and knees, and vomit until there's nothing left but strings of spit.

I feel him. He hands me a wad of gas station paper towels and a water bottle. I wipe my lips, rinse my mouth.

He pulls me to my feet, guides me away, and we perch side by side on the rear bumper. Bugs skirl and flutter in the beams of the headlights. "Tell me."

"I've never spoken of it. Not even to Jay—" I cut myself off before a dead man's name leaves my lips. "My employer."

"Of course not. But you have to get it out of you, *meu amor.*"

I look at him. "How can you still call me that?"

A semi groans past in a skirl of noise and wind. Silence returns. A gigantic moth flutters in front of me for a few moments, investigating me briefly before vanishing into the night.

"Sophia is gone. I accept that. But Inez…if that is the name you choose, I will honor that, because no matter the name, you are still you, and you are not dead. You went through a hell few could ever fathom, and you survived. I still see the woman I love whenever I look at you. I see your soul."

I shake my head. "I was never a very religious or spiritual person, you know that. But lately, thinking about…" I choke on the words. "When I face the fact that the blood of thirty-two innocent people is on these hands?" I examine my palms, turn them over to examine the backs, as if they are literally bloodstained. "I am beginning to believe in eternal damnation, Lorenzo. Because I deserve it."

"They weren't—"

"Oh, spare me the justifications, Ren!" I snap, pacing

away and whirling to face him. "They were all complicit in some way, I know. They knew the things that went on at that estate. Father's barbarity was no secret to anyone, nor was Rafael's. But does that make it okay? No one I murdered that day was directly involved with what happened. I just...snapped. I couldn't—"

Words fail me. I choke on them, like hot, bitter stones lodged in my throat.

"Tell me," he whispers. "Tell me everything."

"It's bad enough I have to live with what I did," I breathe, my voice bile-hoarse. "You shouldn't have to carry those memories, either."

"Tell me, goddammit," he growls. "You think you're the only one with innocent blood on your hands?"

I sit back down on the bumper beside him. "What is there to tell, Lorenzo? You know what happened."

"Yes, I do. But I don't know your perspective."

"My perspective?" I repeat, brow furrowing.

"Yes, Inez. Your perspective. Your feelings. Your memories. They're festering inside you like cancer. Get them out."

I shake my head. "I...Ren, I can't."

He takes my hand in his, threads our fingers together. "Try."

I shut my eyes. "Seventy-two hours after the wedding, I emerged from the shower to find Rafael with four of his men and a doctor waiting in my bedroom—I had one separate from Rafael. I was...well, you can probably imagine the state I was in. I'd been beaten and raped dozens of times, as you are aware. I was in so much pain I could barely walk. Emotionally, I was...well, at that point, I was too...I was in too much shock to know what I was feeling, and the physical pain overrode the emotional trauma, or I probably would have killed myself. Later, rage kept me alive, as it has done ever since." I swallow hard. "I froze, seeing Rafael and the men. They...they held me down on the bed and the doctor ripped the I-U-D out of me."

"Jesus," Lorenzo breathes, muttering something in Portuguese that I don't fully catch, something about a vile monster.

"He did give me another week to recover before he began...trying to impregnate me."

Lorenzo's head hangs. "Inez..."

"I won't speak of the things Rafael enjoys. I cannot. Not even to you—especially not to you. Suffice it to say, there were times I wished I was back in that cell instead of enduring the sick shit that twisted fucking demon did to me." I look at him. "Still want to know the rest?"

Head hanging, he nods. "I will bear witness to your pain, *meu amor.*"

A warm rush of...I don't know what...rushes through me. Gratitude? Something akin to gratitude, I suppose. "It took...god, I don't really know how long. My life then was a blur of agony and rage and disgust and horror and terror. Emotions too dark and awful to have names in any language. The kind of thing there just aren't words for. So it was all a bit of a blur. It was weeks of...him. Not every day, he was too busy for that, which was the one small mercy. Eventually, after a few months, I would guess, I began throwing up in the mornings. I never had a normal period after...after those days in the cell, but the morning sickness was a pretty obvious sign. He sequestered me in my rooms, locked from the outside with armed guards to prevent me from leaving. I spent the next nine months locked in those rooms. He didn't try anything with me once I was pregnant, which was another small mercy."

Lorenzo rubs his face with a hand. "Jesus. Jesus. Jesus." He paces away, muttering under his breath in Portuguese, and then comes back to me, listening.

"When I was near term, he brought a midwife in from…god, I don't even know. Some nearby village. She was a mean old woman. She was there against her will, and hated me for it, no matter that I was there against my will too. I went into labor. It was long. There were no drugs for the pain. I bore my son. I was alone. Where the midwife was, I don't know. She appeared after I birthed him. Took him from me. That…that's…" I shut my eyes, shake my head. "That's when I snapped. She took my son from me. Said it was *his* orders. I only remember certain things. I…" I look at Lorenzo. "This is ugly, Lorenzo. I warn you."

"I saw the photos."

"Photos," I say, huffing a bitter laugh. "The photos don't tell the whole story. I remember thrashing when the midwife took my son. She called in the guards to hold me down and cut the umbilical cord. The guard who cut it was just a boy, barely old enough to even have fuzz on his lip, but he was already one of them. I could see it in his eyes. He saw me suffering and he enjoyed it. He cut the cord with a pocket knife. I was all bloody. Naked. Still bleeding. I hadn't passed the afterbirth yet. But I…I watched the midwife tie off the cord stump on my baby's belly and take him away, and I snapped. I took the knife from the boy and cut his throat. I took his AK-47 and shot the other guard. I…I couldn't stop. My vision was this reddish-hazed tunnel. And I couldn't stop myself. I went room to room, shooting everyone I saw. I couldn't stop. I ran out of ammunition and found another rifle. The second-to-last person I killed was a stable hand. He was sleeping—he must have been drunk to sleep through all the shooting. I shot him while he slept. He never woke up. He didn't even have a beard. He was…simple, I think they used to say. He just liked the horses. Of everyone I killed that day, I regret his death the most."

Lorenzo says nothing. But he is looking at me, unblinking, unwavering. Bearing witness.

"I found the midwife trying to sneak out with my baby."

"Rafael wasn't there?"

I shake my head. "No. He was gone on business with most of his men."

"So you killed the midwife."

I nod. "I took my baby from her and I shot her. She was a mean old woman who hated me, but she didn't deserve to die. None of them did." I stand up again, breathing hard. "I know their names, Lorenzo. All of them." I face away from him. Slowly, I lift my T-shirt to bare my back. Peel up the strap of my compression bra.

"Inez," he whispers. "*Meu Deus*."

Thirty-two names are tattooed on my back, between my shoulder blades and over my spine, in the shape of a skull.

I recite each name in full, all of them—some of the names are extraordinarily long, as is customary, especially among older, more traditional families.

Lorenzo listens to each name. "You recited those names from memory."

"Every night, I say the names as I try to fall asleep. If I am home in my quarters at the club, I sometimes light a candle for them. Pray for them. I don't know why I do it. But I do." I pull my bra and shirt back down and sit with him once more.

"You have to forgive yourself," Lorenzo says.

I can only laugh bitterly. "If only it were so easy as that."

"How did you make it through the jungle to where I was?" he asks.

I shrug. "I don't really know, honestly. I don't even remember how I knew where you were. I don't remember much of any of that journey. I remember being in the jungle. Walking and walking for an eternity. My feet hurting. The baby crying. An old farmer gave me a ride, took me over a hundred kilometers, and gave me food and water. If not for him, I probably would have died in the jungle."

Silence reigns for a long time. I appreciate the fact that Lorenzo doesn't tell me how sorry he is, or give me a bunch of empty platitudes meant to comfort me. He's just there, and he knows there's nothing to say.

"What will you do about Reninho?"

I shrug. "I don't know. I can't even begin to think about that. I'm not…I can't imagine…" I shake my head. "I don't know."

"That is fair, I suppose."

"Let's go," I say, standing up. "We don't have time to waste on pity parties."

"Thank you for telling me all that, Inez." He holds me by the arms, gently.

My skin burns where his hands touch. The crawling of my skin that I usually feel when anyone touches me is… less. Or different. I don't mind his touch.

It even provides something like comfort.

I wrap my fingers around his wrist and hold on, breathing slowly as I try to put the memories back in their box.

It's funny, though…

The sharpness and the burn of the memories have faded, somehow. Dulled. As if…well, as if Lorenzo was right, and I did need to get it out.

It isn't some magic fix, some miraculous healing balm, but it's something.

"I don't deserve your love, Lorenzo," I whisper. I'm not certain I meant for him to hear, but he did.

"Deserve has nothing to do with it," he answers. "My love for you is a fact, Inez. Like the sun, or one plus one equaling two, or gravity. It just is."

"I thought you said it was something you chose?" I ask.

"I do. Because I tried not to. After you disappeared, I tried to move on. That's what my relationship with Consuela was. But it didn't work. I couldn't move on, so I stopped trying. And eventually, I just accepted the fact that you own my heart. Whether you are dead or alive, Inez or Sophia, guilty or absolved, I love you. I can't *not* love you. And now you're back in my life and I love you all the more. I choose to. I could…I don't know. Pretend not to. I could accept your idea that you're incapable of accepting or giving love. But I won't. I'll give you time. I'll be patient. But what I won't do is give up."

I look at him, meeting his dark eyes and seeing the truth in what he's saying written in them. "I don't know what I'll ever be able to give you, Ren. I'm broken."

"Then I will love all your broken pieces."

He lifts his hand from my arm, and I freeze, not even

breathing, as he ghosts his palm over my cheek, the barest brush. The contact makes me gasp softly.

I can't help nuzzling my cheek against his palm, just a split second, eyes closed, wondering why there seem to be moths fluttering at the pit of my stomach at his gentle touch.

He drops his hand. "I'll drive. You rest."

CHAPTER 4

MY NAME IS JAKOB

LORENZO

AH, THE LIGHTS AND GLITTER OF LAS VEGAS.
I fucking hate it.

I came here once a few years ago as part of an intelligence operation. Why anyone would plop a city down in the middle of the goddamned desert is beyond me. I hate the noise. I hate the lights. I hate the casinos. I hate the scent of desperation that somehow seems to permeate the very air.

I push that aside as irrelevant as I follow Inez's directions to the club. It's a massive, imposing black block of a building, the name "CLUB SIN" spelled out in mammoth blood-red letters on the side over the covered front entrance. It's located in a remote industrial area, tucked away behind warehouses and office buildings and manufacturing plants, hidden behind a snaking line of jagged-edge hills. It sits on a plot of several acres of blacktop parking lot—clear sightlines in every direction, with one way in to the lot and one way out.

It's nearing noon, so the lot is empty, save for a row of Mercedes G-Wagens parked on the west side near an inconspicuous black door.

Inez directs me to park our stolen car beside the expensive SUVs. She's out of the car before I've shut off the motor, marching for the door. She inputs a six-digit code into the keypad above the knob; a green light flashes, and she yanks open the door. Fluorescent lights illuminate a staircase leading down.

I follow her down the steps—the floor at the bottom is pale gray epoxy with blue flecks; a long hallway extends away from the stairs, featureless, unnumbered doors on either side.

Voices echo, chattering excitedly, coming toward us—female voices.

"Boys? Is that you?" A woman calls, with a slap of bare feet on the floor. "We hadn't heard anything in a few days so—"

A woman appears from the other end of the hallway, her words cutting off as she sees it's not who she was expecting. She's gorgeous—blond hair, blue eyes, beautiful body. She's wearing tiny black skin-tight workout shorts and a black sports bra, and she's sweating, panting.

"Sorry to disappoint, Myka," Inez says. "Gather the others in the common room. Now, please. We have a situation."

"Inez?" The woman—Myka—queries. "Who's your…friend?"

We're standing close, Inez and I. Hip to hip, the kind of close contact you share with someone you know very well. Inez doesn't put space between us.

"His name is Lorenzo," she answers. "No questions. Just gather the rest of the girls for me. Who is on duty upstairs?"

"Toro is in the security booth," Myka answers, "and Taj and Fonz are roving. Should I call them?"

"No. Just the girls, for now."

Instead of doing Inez's bidding, Myka takes a few steps toward Inez, one hand outstretched. "Inez, your face. And you're limping."

A series of expressions crosses Inez's face—confusion, surprise, irritation, and something like wonder or stunned amazement. "Hazards of the job. I'm fine."

Myka shakes her head. "Inez. Don't bullshit me."

Inez's lower lip actually trembles—it's very subtle, but I saw it. "I was Rafael's…guest, briefly. It wasn't pleasant, but I've been through worse. I promise, I'm fine. I appreciate your concern, however."

Inez's face has actually healed remarkably fast since we sprung her from that basement. Bruises still shadow her face in florid greens and blues and yellows, and her lips bear the scabs of having been split. But if Myka had seen Inez even after we got her cleaned up, she would have known that what Inez went through was far, far worse than merely unpleasant.

Myka, judging by her expression, seems to understand that Inez is still downplaying the whole thing. "Is one of the guys hurt?"

Inez shakes her head. "No, everyone is okay. But time is of the essence, so let's get going."

She breezes past Myka, and I follow her. The hallway opens into a common room—an open floor plan kitchen and den. It's industrial but homey, somehow.

Two other women are seated on a large black leather sectional in a U-shape around a coffee table and a massive flatscreen TV—a reality show is playing, and the two women are facing each other on the couch, painting each other's toenails. One of the women is Indian—or from that part of the world, at least—and the other is very tall, athletic, and red-haired; a walking cane, intricately hand-carved into a helix with a sharp, hooked, beak-like handle, hangs off the back of the couch by the handle.

I hear Myka knocking on doors and murmuring. A couple of minutes later, A few more women pour out of the other rooms: another fairly tall woman, perhaps the same height as Myka, with long, jet-black hair, wearing a knee-length skirt and tank top; a short and very curvy woman with scarlet hair; a medium height woman, willowy, with auburn hair and a shy, observant manner.

They all gather in the common room, finding seats on the sectional; they sit in a tangled cluster, an intimacy of proximity despite the size of the couch. I lean against a pillar at the center of the room as Inez stands with her back to the TV.

"Hello, ladies," Inez says, her voice low and quiet. "I trust you are all well."

The Indian woman speaks. "We are all quite well, thank you." Her voice is lilting and musical. "It seems you have received some manner of violence. Are you alright?"

Inez's face goes carefully blank, and her eyes shutter closed. She opens them again after a moment and smiles—it's a rare thing, to see her smile like that. It lights up her face, softens the icy mask she wears. "Yes, Anjalee, I am fine. I..." she looks at me, swallows hard, seeming to hunt for courage. "I may as well tell you, I suppose. You are all aware of the general outlines of the situation, I hope?"

The willowy woman with auburn hair speaks up—her voice is so soft and quiet I can barely hear her. "I would not object if you explained things a bit. If…if you don't mind."

Inez's smile holds as she regards the speaker with open affection—an expression I don't know if I have ever seen on her face before. "Of course, Naomi."

A long pause as Inez gathers her thoughts.

"To be honest, I don't really know where to start. It is very complex. I suppose I must give you some context so you can understand the present situation." She looks to me for courage again, and I smile; she lets out a breath. "I have not spoken of this at all for many years, so please forgive me if the telling is difficult. Inez is not the name I was born with. I was born Sophia Bruna Santos de Silva. Legally, my name is Sophia Bruna Santos de Silva Sousa. Sousa is the surname of my husband—Rafael Sousa."

"You're *married*?" The question is blurted, shocked, by the woman with scarlet hair. "Holy fuckin' shit!"

Inez rolls her eyes. "It's not what you think. It was not a love match. Nor was it my choice. There are details which…I…" she trails off, glancing at me for support.

I move to her side. "Ladies. I am Lorenzo Oliveira Araujo. I have known Inez for…well, a very long time. Her father was a Brazilian warlord and crime kingpin, and she was raised to be his successor. That was her role and purpose in life, whether she liked it or not. She and I…developed an attraction for each other. It was forbidden, since I was the hired help and she was the boss's daughter—as good as a princess, in that part of the world. She was betrothed to her father's right-hand man—as she said, it was against her will. Her father gave her a choice—an ultimatum. Marry Rafael Sousa, or face the consequences."

The willowy woman, Naomi, pales. "What...what were the consequences, if you don't mind me asking?"

Inez lifts her chin, expression hardening into the icy mask of venomous indifference she has shown the world for so long—her armor against the pain within. "I refused. Rafael was...is...a vile, disgusting, evil, depraved...*thing*. A creature of...of...utterly unspeakable..." she shakes her head, trailing off. "Sorry, I..." she lets out a breath. "I refused to marry him. My father locked me in a cell, chained me to a bed, and had his men rape me. It...I..."

I jump in. "It lasted three days. I was...unable to stop it." I clear my throat. "She was married to Rafael after that."

Silence boils in the room as the other women process what was just said.

"*Inez*," the woman named Naomi whispers. "No. No."

"Your own *father*?" Myka asks, her voice shaky. "He...he allowed that to happen?"

"*Allowed*?" Inez barks a laugh. "He *ordered* it."

"Be glad you cannot fathom the evil some fathers are capable of, Myka," Naomi says, her voice low, her tone indicating a personal knowledge of what she says.

Inez and Naomi share a long look—this Naomi has been through her own hell, I would guess. After a moment, Inez sighs. "I was forced to conceive and birth a child. My husband, while I was recovering from what was done to me before the wedding, murdered my father and those loyal to him and took over his empire. I..." she drops her eyes, fists clenched at her sides. "What I must tell you next is very difficult for me. As you can probably imagine, I was…not in the most stable headspace at that time."

The scarlet-haired woman lets out a sarcastic laugh; she has what I believe to be a Boston accent, though I am no expert on American regional accents. "No shit? I can't imagine why. I'd have been pretty murdery."

"Murdery," Inez echoes, her voice faint. "Yes, Terra. *Murdery* is a pretty damned apt way of describing me."

"What you must know is that she was trained from the time she could walk to be a killer." I glance at Inez, and she gives me a small nod to continue. "She was her father's executioner when she was as young as sixteen or seventeen. I mean that literally. She was, and is, as competent an operator as any of your men."

"I gave birth," Ine says, taking over. "It was long, agonizing, and traumatic. I was…broken. Mentally, physically, emotionally. After I gave birth, I…had a mental break. And I…" A sigh, a touch of her hand to mine for courage. "I went on a rampage and killed everyone who worked on the estate compound owned by my husband, formerly belonging to my father. Everyone. Innocent people. Women. Teenage boys. *Every*one."

Silence once more.

Slowly, the red-haired woman levers to her feet, snags her cane from the back of the couch, and crosses to Inez. She pauses a foot or so away, leaning on her cane, and then gently, gingerly gathers Inez into her embrace. Inez is stiff, arms at her sides, eyes closed as the woman embraces her.

Naomi moves in, next, and then the others, one by

one. I move out of the way as the women, all seven of them, surround Inez in a huddle.

No one says anything. I hear a sniffle, a shuddery breath—Inez fighting for calm.

"Let—let me go," she hisses. "I can't—I…let me go. Let me go."

A soft voice whispers something I can't make out.

"No—I can't—I can't," Inez says. "I won't be able to—"

Another whisper.

"*NO!*" This is a ragged screech from Inez.

I can't see her inside the huddle of women, only a flash of black hair.

Abruptly, the whole cluster seems to sag, and then collapse as Inez crumples and the women catch her, help her settle onto the floor.

Her shoulders are shaking. Six heads angle toward hers, arms wrap around shoulders.

A scream rips out of Inez's throat, and this is a primal sound of raw agony, grief and horror, rage, and sorrow. This is a scream long denied finally emerging. It becomes a wail, shuddering and awful, and my heart breaks all over again for her. The wail tapers off into a sob, and I hear murmurs from the other women, whispering support, encouragement, understanding.

I can only watch, and feel as if I'm somehow intruding on something sacred, viewing an ancient ritual of feminine trauma at the hands of men.

I do not belong here; I should not be watching this.

I turn away, find a doorway with stairs leading up. The door at the top of the stairs opens into a large, open, dark room—the main nightclub. It's silent and empty. I find a nearby bar, pull out a stool, and sit.

I lean my forearms on the edge of the bar, wishing I had a drink.

That scream…it still shudders in my soul. It is a sound I will not soon forget.

I hear footsteps approaching, feel a presence nearby. "Lorenzo." The voice is deep, dark, smooth, and powerful.

I frown in the direction of the voice. "You have the advantage," I say. "You know me, it appears."

"I am…a friend of Inez's."

I snort. "No, you are her mysterious employer, I think."

The answering silence is confirmation enough.

"Why are you up here?" he asks me.

"Inez and the women." I shrug. "They're…talking. I was in the way."

"Talking, are they?" His tone suggests he knows more than he's saying.

I peer into shadows, but all I can make out is a vague outline—tall, broad-shouldered. "Yes. Talking."

"You are careful. I like that."

"Imagine my relief." It's more than a little sarcastic.

He huffs a laugh. "I care about her," he says after a moment. "And I respect her."

"Good."

"What are they talking about?" he asks. "Rafael?"

If he knows that name, then he probably knows everything.

"Among other things," I respond. "She's giving them…context."

"It's good she's opening up to them. I have often wished she could have done it much sooner, but she had to find the courage to do so on her own."

The shadow moves, and I hear glass clinking, liquid pouring. Glass thunks on the bar and slides to me. "*Na zdravi,*" he says.

Dim light reflects off of glass.

I take the glass in front of me, sniff—excellent scotch. "*Saúde!*" I say in answer, touching my glass to his.

I sip—the scotch is world-class, very, very expensive. "Thank you."

"Don't give up on her, Lorenzo," he says, after a few moments of sipping in relatively companionable silence—as companionable as it can be when you are both in shadow. "She needs you. She loves you. She just… doesn't know how."

"It sounds like you know her well," I say, instead of answering his statement.

"I do. As well as anyone can, perhaps. She was the first, you know."

"First what?"

I see a long arm slide through shadows, gesturing in an expansive sweep. "All of this. The Broken Arrows. She was the first."

"I don't know much about it. There is a brand. They cannot kill. They live here. They're all operators."

"It's not important at the moment," he says. "Only that I have known Inez for many years. We built this together, she and I."

"You love her." It's not a question.

A long pause—the longest yet. "Yes. As… a sister, perhaps. Not as you love her."

"She is difficult to love."

A bark of laughter. "Yes, that is very true. But you must not give up."

"Give up? Senhor, I do not know your name. I don't care what it is. But if you know Inez as well as you say, then you at least know *of* me. And if you know anything about me at all, you know I will not give up on that woman. Not ever. I have loved her since I was eighteen years old. I have loved her across the years in which I thought she was dead. I have fought for her. I have bled for her and killed for her."

Another lengthy silence, broken by the sounds of sipping and swallowing.

"Those women down there. They've all been through hell. Worse than hell."

"I sensed as much. The one named Naomi in particular."

"Indeed." His accent is impossible to define. There is a vaguely Eastern European hint to it, at times. Other times, it is almost accentless—educated, sophisticated, articulate, and blank of origin.

"Rafael and Pugli must not be allowed to harm them."

"I would die first."

"Good. But better you lived. Inez needs your love."

"Getting her to let me is proving difficult, as I said. And with reason, as I'm sure you're aware."

"Quite aware. Those reasons are exactly why she needs you."

"You say nothing I do not already know."

"Sometimes the obvious bears stating."

A digital chime cuts through the moment—it

sounded like it came from a watch. A small swath of light illuminates sharp, hard, masculine features and dark, quick eyes. "They approach." Those eyes find me. "Go. Toro, Taj, and Fonz will assist."

I toss back the last swallow of the syrupy scotch. "And you?"

"I will be tracking our quarry. I came to meet you in person. A man who could claim the heart of Sophia Silva de Santos? I had to see you with my own eyes."

"Your name? Since you know mine?"

A pause; I hear him swallow, the hollow echo of a breath captured in the bottom of a raised glass. "My name is Jakob."

CHAPTER 5

THE SCENT OF DEATH, CORDITE, AND BLOOD

INEZ

I HAVE NEVER BEEN ENTIRELY COMFORTABLE IN THE company of women—not that I've had many opportunities. I understand men, as much as anyone can ever truly understand the opposite sex. I have spent my life around men, and violent men at that.

I have never had a female friend. Not until Scarlett—a kindred spirit, if ever there was such a thing. I find myself missing her company, and in particular the way she understands me. We are women who have spent our lives spilling blood. We have been used, abused, violated, and traumatized. We have been steeped in violence. I don't need to explain it to her. She simply understands.

These women are...different.

They understand trauma. They know pain. They have suffered abuse.

They have survived.

They are me.

Every bit as much as Scarlett, they are me.

They hold me as I shatter.

Anjalee murmurs in my ear in soft Hindi, which of course I do not understand, but the tone is soothing.

Naomi is praying, her whispers so quiet I cannot make out the words.

The others just hold me, squeeze my arm, my leg, my shoulder.

I am weeping.

I cannot stop.

Something broke inside me. The dam holding back the ocean of tears I have spent a lifetime refusing to shed—that is what has shattered within me. I hear myself keening, screaming, wailing. I rock back and forth, and they hold me through it. They don't shush me. They don't tell me it will be okay. They're just…here. They get it.

I could not give this to Lorenzo. Yes, he loves me. He accepts me as I am. He knows the darkest truths which define me, and still he loves me. This is a priceless treasure, I know, but he is a man.

He may sympathize, but these women empathize.

Mostly.

I don't know of anyone who can empathize with the guilt I carry for the thirty-two names tattooed on my back.

The flood of my tears flows, ebbs, and then subsides into shaking shudders. The heat of bodies and breath is overwhelming and I cannot breathe, all of a sudden, but before I can say a word, they all pull away and get to their feet. Naomi is last, and she takes my hands in hers and we stand up together. They surround me, they're all still touching me in some way, and I find it…acceptable. Comforting, even; I have not been able to tolerate physical contact from anyone in years. Not since that day.

I close my eyes, breathe. Wipe my face. Steady my breath. Examine myself—the state of my soul.

What I feel is nearly impossible to explain, even to

myself. Weightlessness? Not quite. It's as if…as if I have carried a burden on my back and suddenly that burden is gone. The weight I didn't know I was carrying has suddenly been removed.

I suppose Ren would probably liken it to taking off your pack after a ten-mile ruck through the mountains.

I open my eyes and look around at the women, and I cannot find it in me to be embarrassed.

Only pathetically grateful.

"Ladies, I…" words fail me, then. "I do not know how to—" so shaken am I that I only realize I was speaking in Portuguese when several brows furrowed in confusion.

I am a bit too accustomed to being around Lorenzo, Solomon, and Scarlett, all of whom can switch between languages as easily as I can.

I let out a breath, smooth my hands down my thighs, and try again, this time in English. "Ladies, I would like to thank you. For…for…" my voice quavers, dammit. "For allowing me to…without…" I shake my head, hissing in frustration as words continue to dry up in my throat. "Fucking hell. Sorry."

Terra wraps an arm around my shoulder and squeezes. "Girl, we *got* you."

I've never been gotten, before. It makes my eyes burn all over again.

"This is not why I came here," I say, after clearing my throat a few times. "I cannot bring myself to regret the wasted time, even though we have very little to spare. I am here with you now because you are in imminent danger. My enemies—*our* enemies—are coming here, now, to harm you, in an attempt to bait your men."

"What do we need to do?" Naomi asks, her voice soft but steady.

"Wait a second, though," Terra interrupts. "Can we talk about Lorenzo, though? Just for a second. Because girl, he…is…*fine.*"

I cannot help a small smile from stealing across my face. "Lorenzo is…" I blink hard, and dammit, I *hate* feeling so emotional. "He's…"

"You're still figuring it out, huh?" Annika asks. "We get that, for sure."

I frown. "I'm not sure that's it, exactly. I've known him most of my life—since I was sixteen. He…" I lick my lips and look at the ceiling. "He was my first everything. And the last. Not counting…you know…what happened. And Rafael. I don't count that because I didn't choose it."

Naomi's silver gaze searches me. "But you aren't ready, are you?"

I shake my head. "No. And I'm afraid I never will be. I am afraid that I can never give him that part of me."

"Which part, Inez?" This is Tatiana. "Sometimes we have to name our deepest fears out loud before we can fight them."

"My body," I answer in a whisper.

"Does he love you?" she asks.

"Yes."

She holds me by the arms. "Then it'll work out. It may not be easy, but it will."

Naomi, soft and sweet and shy but with a core of pure titanium, kisses me on the cheek—I'm so stunned by the unexpected affection that my cheeks flush hot. "It really will." She cups my cheek. "You know what I endured. It isn't…" She trails off with a huff. "I'm not comparing.

When I went there with Silas, it was frightening, at first, but it was worth it, Inez. So worth it to find something as beautiful as my relationship with Silas. You are strong. And Lorenzo seems very kind. Be honest with him. Be brave. If he loves you and you love him, you will find your way together."

"You make it sound so simple," I say.

The door leading up to the club opens and Lorenzo appears in a rush. "They're here. They're coming."

Instantly, everything vanishes—all that's left is the icy calm that is my customary emotional armor. I glance at Lorenzo, and I can tell something has happened—I can see it written in his features.

I lean close. "Are you alright?" I ask in Portuguese.

He smiles down at me, touching a soft, delicate kiss to my forehead. "Yes."

"Something happened, though."

He puts his lips to my ear, whispering. "I met Jakob."

My world rocks on its axis. "You...*what*?"

"Up there. We had a glass of scotch and talked for a moment. He's gone now, I think."

"You *saw* him? You spoke to him?"

He nods. "It was dark. I couldn't pick him out of a line-up, certainly. He has a very recognizable voice."

"And he told you his name?"

He frowns. "You seem shocked."

"I am. My employer is the most secretive man I've ever known, and I include Rafael." Of everyone in my life, Lorenzo would be the last person I'd think Jakob would show himself to. "What...what did you talk about?"

He juts his chin at the hallway and the exit sign at the end. "Talk later. Pugli's thugs are approaching and I've got…" he produces his pistol from the back of his jeans, ejects the mag, counts rounds. "Eleven rounds left."

"Come." I lead him at a run back up the stairs through the dark, empty club—I catch of whiff of the cologne Jakob wears.

We reach the security booth. A rack of servers with their array of blinking lights stands on one wall, encased in glass. I open the case, reach my arm inside behind the bank of servers—which give off an incredible amount of heat—and hunt around with my fingers. After a moment, I find what I'm looking for: a small button, slightly concave, along the back left corner near the top. I press it, and something clicks, something else hisses, and then I step away as the entire case rotates away from me, revealing a recessed space about the size of a telephone booth. It is lined on three walls with racks of weapons and ammunition: assault rifles, submachine guns, pistols, and shotguns, with boxes of ammo for each and empty magazines, as well as pre-loaded mags.

"Now we're talking," Lorenzo says, his face lit up like a kid at Christmas…or so I imagine. I've never experienced such a thing as anyone would consider a "normal" Christmas.

"Jakob and I are the only ones who know this is here," I tell him. "None of the guys know."

"Why not?"

I stare at him. "They're operators. They'd be up here all the time wanting to get out the guns."

He snickers. "Oh. True."

He selects an HK416 and I do the same, stuffing our pockets with magazines for those and our sidearms; I grab three more and a spare mag to go with them, and then

I close the case once more. I snag several radios as well, and we head back down to the common room. I select the channel we use in the club and key the radio. "Toro, Taj, Fonz. This is Inez. Come in, over."

Toro's voice crackles across the line. "Go for Toro."

"Tangos inbound," I say. "Converge on the common room in the Arrow quarters ASAP."

I get three affirmatives and a couple minutes later, Toro, Taj, and Fonz emerge from the stairs. They take in the women, wide-eyed, and then Lorenzo and I—loaded down with rifles, pockets bulging with magazines.

Toro is a somewhat unlikely looking fellow: he looks like a cartoon caricature of a strongman, with a chest as thick and shoulders as broad as Chance's, or nearly so, tapering down to a hard, lean waist, creating an upside-down triangle of a torso. He is not tall, but he is mammoth—Lash's build but with twenty-five pounds more muscle. His jet-black hair is slicked into an elaborate pompadour, and he wears a neat, precisely trimmed Van Dyke goatee. He is very vain, but his operator resume is spotless and impressive: four years with the Spanish Army's GOE, their version of Green Berets, and then four years with a classified black ops team operating primarily within UN peacekeeping parameters. He doesn't know it yet, but he's on the very short list of successors who will make up the second phase of Jakob's Broken Arrows plan.

Beside him is Taj, an Indian national with ten years in the Indian Army's Para SF unit—an elite airborne unit. He is quite tall—taller than the Cabot boys but not as tall as Rev—clean cut and clean-shaven, with glossy black hair and a quiet, reserved manner. Only Jakob knows his history.

Fonz resembles his nickname's sake, the character from the old show *Happy Days*. His outgoing, charming, class-clown persona hides a deep internal darkness stemming from both his childhood and his years with LAPD SWAT's D Platoon. Even though he's not technically military, he's seen as much if not more action than some of the Arrows, as the D Platoon in particular ran hundreds of operations every year, and Fonz was the type to volunteer for every mission he could.

I pass around the rifles and magazines. "Today, gentlemen, is your baptism by fire into the order of the Broken Arrows." I meet each pair of eyes in turn. "This is our home." I gesture at the women. "This is our family. Need I say more?"

"No, Señora, you do not," Toro says in his booming, Spanish-accented voice. "I believe I am speaking for my brothers Taj and Fonz when I say we are prepared to fight unto the death for this home and la familia. *Sí, mis hermanos?*"

Taj nods once, thumping his fist into his chest.

Fonz grins, winks at the ladies. "Never fear, the Fonz is here."

Toro rolls his eyes. "You are an idiot."

"Eyyy, you're just pissy cuz you couldn't charm water out of a fountain, big boy." He passes his hand over his carefully coiffed hair.

I clear my throat. "Not the time for witty banter, gentlemen. Our enemy is at the gates. Toro, Taj, take the roof and pick them off. Fonz, you guard this room and these women. Lorenzo and I will do the rest. Ladies, it's best if you lock yourselves in the gym. It's bullet- and blast-proof, and locks from the inside."

"We can help," Annika says. "None of us are exactly fainting daisies anymore."

"No, you certainly are not. But you are the targets of this operation. They seek to use you as bait to capture and kill your men—*our* men. You are all strong, capable women. You are survivors. But you do not have the training the rest of us do. I don't know how many enemy combatants we are facing, but it is a certainty that we are outnumbered. You will be safest in there."

Terra looks at the gym, and then at me. "I don't know how much I like the idea of sitting in there on my fat ass while the rest of you risk your lives for ours."

"That is the path we have chosen for ourselves, Miss Terra," Taj says, his voice low and quiet and gentle, with the same lilting accent as Anjalee.

"Facts, babe," Fonz says. "It's what we do. It's who the fuck we are."

"I agree with my comrades," Toro says.

"Enough talk," I cut in. "Positions."

Toro and Taj head for the stairs, clipping radios to waistbands and threading earpieces under their shirts.

Fonz guides the women to the gym and waits while they lock themselves in, and then takes up a position with his back to the door, where he can monitor the stairs and the exit to the outside.

Lorenzo and I head for the exit, emerging squinting into the blinding sun and blazing Vegas heat.

"Let's create defensive positions with the SUVs," I tell Ren.

He nods, and we pull the G-Wagens into a half-ring around the side door; the main entrance is well-nigh impregnable by design, so this side entrance is the only possible way in for attackers. We park the SUVs in staggered formation, so there isn't a straight line to the door.

We take up positions in the first line of vehicles, crouched behind tires, waiting.

"Jakob got that notification several minutes ago," Lorenzo says. "I was under the impression that that meant they were a hell of a lot closer than this."

"We have an early warning system. Anyone approaching the Club during the day passes through a series of laser sensors that trigger video cameras," I explain. "Those cameras use algorithms to determine speed and formulate an ETA." I gesture at the hills. "We have them up there, as well—laser trip wires along the paths in the hills, so we can't be flanked without warning." My phone chimes, then. "Speaking of which, we have contact in the hills."

I pass the message along to Toro and Taj.

"Too bad we don't have a sniper," Lorenzo says. "It would be nice to have oversight up there on the roof. They could put a rifleman up in those hills and pick us off."

I eye him. "A good point." Another chime from my phone—the nearest set of cameras shows a caravan of black Tahoes approaching at breakneck speed; I count five. "We'll hold them off here. You go take out that contact in the hills. I'm only seeing one, at the moment."

Lorenzo nods. "On it." He leans in and kisses my cheek. "Don't die."

My cheek burns where he kissed it, and I have a sudden, powerful, and inexplicable urge to kiss him. Before I can second-guess myself, I'm wrapping my hand around the back of his neck and pulling him down to me and my mouth is fusing to his and my tongue steals against his lips and I'm moaning low in my throat at the lush feel of his mouth. He growls, hunching over me, clutching my jaw in one strong hand, sucking my tongue into his mouth.

We part after a too-brief moment, both of us panting.

"You either," I whisper.

Brow furrowed, chest heaving, Lorenzo peers down at me, shocked and aroused. He opens his mouth to speak, but I shove him roughly away. "Don't," I breathe. "Just go."

He stumbles backward a few steps, easily catching his balance. He nods. "*Eu te amo.*"

He doesn't wait for an answer he knows isn't coming, but turns and jogs away toward the hills, picking up speed rapidly until he's running flat out across the baking oven of the blacktop parking lot. His figure dwindles into the distance, becoming hazy in the shimmering heat waves. His pace only slows slightly as he begins ascending the hills.

When he is out of sight, I wait with my back to the tire.

"Contact," Taj's quiet voice says. "Two hundred yards. Five vehicles. If each carries eight men, we could be facing up to forty tangos."

"Affirmative," I answer. "Don't fire until I give the order."

"Roger," he says. "One hundred yards. Fifty. They're stopping. I count…seven in the first vehicle. Vests, rifles. These are not untrained thugs, I believe."

I twist in place and rise to peer over the hood. The tangos have parked in a single file line and are exiting their cars and forming twin lines on either side of the vehicles. They jog toward the entrance, rifles raised. I let them approach until the last man has cleared the cover of the SUVs, and then I give the order. "Fire at will."

I tuck my rifle butt tight against my shoulder, peer

through the reticle, putting the dot on the lead tango. *POP!* The freakily quiet HK416 jolts my shoulder with a click of the bolt, and my target drops, a red hole in his forehead weeping crimson down his nose. Pink spray bathes the man behind him, momentarily stunning him. I thumb the fire selector switch to semi-auto and squeeze off a trio of rounds, dropping the tango behind my first target and raking the line of my fire further back, squeezing off burst after burst. Above me, Toro and Taj are firing as well—I can't hear their rifles, but I see targets dropping one after another.

At least half a dozen tangos are down within the first few seconds of contact—the element of surprise at work. They haven't even gotten off a single shot, yet.

CRACKCRACKCRACK! An M4 barks from their side and something hot whickers past my ear—too damn close for my comfort. I twist and drop to my ass, let out a harsh breath, and then pop back up. *CRACKCRACKCRACK!* Their rounds whizz over my head as I find a target—a short, powerfully built Hispanic man with a bandana across his mouth and nose, a backward ball cap on his head. He's aiming at the roof. I drop him, swing bead to the next target, drop him. In my peripheral vision, I see men in the other line dropping with sprays of red.

The tangos are getting organized, now, however. They're pouring suppressive fire up at Toro and Taj, and now rounds are whipping, whickering, buzzing, and snapping around me, forcing me to drop down as the Mercedes' body thunks with incoming rounds.

I bolt for the next nearest SUV, feeling something catch at my braid. I scramble behind the SUV, panting; I grab my braid and examine it. A round neatly severed it about an inch above the tie. "Bastards," I mutter to myself.

I remove the hair tie, re-wrap it above the point of damage, and use my balisong to slice away the dangling remnants.

Movement in my peripheral vision catches my attention—Lorenzo sprinting across the parking lot as rounds chew up blacktop at his heels. He reaches the relative cover of the rear of Club Sin, dropping to a knee and ripping off a series of bursts intended more to suppress than to kill, although he does drop at least one tango. He's in motion again almost immediately, sprinting hard for the doorway. He grunts in pain as he nears the SUV a few feet away from the one I'm taking cover behind, stumbling and tripping into a tuck-and-roll, skidding to a halt on his back and then scrambling behind the wheel, gasping raggedly.

"Motherfucker," he pants in English. "They shot me in the ass." This is in Portuguese.

"Show me."

"I'm fine. Grazed it. Not to worry." His nose is bleeding and his shirt is cut at his belly, a thin red line slicing across his navel.

"And that?" I say, jutting my chin at him.

"He was well fucking hidden," he answers, pauses to pop up and fire off a burst. "I stumbled over him, literally. Ended up a hand-to-hand fight, and he had a knife."

"You won, clearly."

He grins. "Please, *meu amor*. I was winning knife fights before I had fuzz on my lip ."

I know for a fact he isn't kidding or exaggerating. Growing up a street rat in the violent favelas of Rio, his life was one of violence from the time he could walk. We

spoke of these things at length in the brief, beautiful delir-
ium of teenage love, whispering to each other in stolen moments, sharing dreams and nightmares and histories with
the wide-eyed wonder of youthful, wild, hormone-fueled
desperation.

We take turns popping up and firing, dropping down
and reloading, but the numbers are against us, and no matter how many we drop, they keep progressing closer to us,
pouring withering suppressive fire at us as they make their
rush. I hear a shout from above—a sound of wounded
male rage.

"Who's hit?" I demand over the line.

"Toro," comes the reply. "My arm. *No es anda.* I am
alright."

"Sounded bad," I answer.

"I do not enjoy being shot," comes his answer.

"Pussy." Fonz says, "It's my favorite fuckin' thing."

"Because you are a strange little man."

"Enough chatter," I snap.

"They are getting very close," Toro says. "You should
fall back to the door or you will be overwhelmed."

Lorenzo pops up and fires, drops back down. "He's
right," he says to me. "Fall back. I'll cover."

My instinct is to argue that he should go first, but I
swallow it—now is not the time to bicker. I sprint for the
door, yank it open—rounds bite into the wall inches from
my face, spraying me with stinging flecks. I slip down a few
steps and drop prone with my rifle barrel on the top step. I
fire beneath the SUVs, and at least one man falls, gripping
his ankle. I lock eyes with him for a moment, and then my
next burst erases his face.

"Go!" I snap. "Now!"

Lorenzo creeps backward, firing, blindly trusting me to stop him from toppling down the stairs. He has a bloody red line creasing his ass horizontally across the middle. I stop him with a hand on his back when he reaches the lip of the stairs.

"You have a second ass crack," I say as he slips down beside me.

"Don't tell the others," he mutters back. "They will give me some stupid nickname like Double Crack or Two Butts."

I cackle at this, and he glances at me with an odd expression.

"What's that look for?" I ask.

He snipes a tango as he passes between two SUVs, and then we both have to worm down further as return fire snaps over our heads. "You. You have smiled *and* laughed in the last hour." He grins at me, and then pops up to crack off a burst. "I like it."

I frown at him. "It isn't so strange." I take his place as he ducks down a few steps; the number of leg pairs still milling beyond the rings of SUVs is concerning. I key my mic. "How many are left, topside?" I ask.

"Perhaps twenty," Taj says. A pause, and then his voice, frantic. "Flashbang! Take cover!"

Lorenzo and I both scramble down the steps and away from the opening—just in time, too, as a cylindrical device clatters to the top step, rolls, wobbles at the edge, bounces, bounces, and then—

BANG!

Even with my eyes shut and my fingers plugging my ears, I'm disoriented and blinking and my ears are ringing. A hand yanks me backward with such unexpected force that both feet leave the ground; I'm airborne for a heart-beat and then my ass hits the floor with enough of an impact that the breath is jarred out of my lungs.

I blink away the rotating, flashing, coruscating lights to see Fonz on one knee in front of me, rifle at his shoulder, firing burst after burst up the stairwell.

Bullet holes pock the floor where I'd been had Fonz not yanked me backward.

Sucking in a breath, I make my feet and assess. Lorenzo is tucked against a bedroom door, pressed as flat as he can get, wincing as he blinks and shakes his head to clear the effects of the flashbang.

A barrage of rounds pepper down the stairs, chew up the doorframe next to Lorenzo's ear, divot the floor between Fonz's knees. Throwing himself backward, Fonz hits the floor on his back as another flurry of bullets craters the floor where he'd been.

He fires up the stairs from his back, and I hear a gurgling cry, thumping, and then a bleeding body topples to a stop at the base of the stairs.

"Them bitches almost had my number," Fonz mutters, eying the floor where he'd been.

For a moment, all is deafeningly silent.

And then...

A clatter of something hard bouncing off a stair, another. The something is small and round...

"GRENADE!" Fonz shouts, twisting to his hands and knees and lurching into a scrambling run.

Lorenzo is moving, too, a blur of shocking speed. His arm slams into my middle, just when I'd finally regained my breath from the last time, and I'm airborne once again, this time carried in Lorenzo's arm, ass up and belly down like a toddler having a tantrum being carried out of a restaurant.

He throws me bodily around the corner of the hall-way's end where it opens into the common area and then his body is surrounding mine, a hot solid envelope of masculine brawn sheltering me from the explosion.

The detonation shudders the walls and floor, rattles the droptiles of the ceiling, sending several of them fluttering to the floor. Shards and shrapnel whizz through the air and pepper the walls and floor and ceiling.

Silence, abrupt and total, except for the ringing in my ears I fear will be permanent.

Lorenzo staggers to his feet and hauls me to mine; I hold on to his arm as I struggle to catch my breath yet again, coughing as acrid smoke billows. Emergency lights flash. Electricity arcs and sparks in the ceiling over the blast site, blue-white light obscured by smoke.

Shadows move in the swirling smoke, lit in strobe effect by the sparking of electricity and flashing emergency lights.

"Contact!" Lorenzo shouts, rifle crashing to his shoulder and jerking as he fires into the eddying smoke.

Coughing, gasping, wheezing, I drop to a knee beside and behind him, aiming high. Between bursts, I hear a low groan.

"Fonz?" I call. "Report!"

"It ain't great, boss-lady," he grunts, his voice tight with pain. "Shrapnel to the leg."

"Gym," I snap. "Now."

"I can fight, boss. Just gotta tie this bitch down."

"Gym—*now*!" I shout, and then devolve into hacking as smoke fills my lungs all over again.

"Fuck," I hear him growl. "Hurts like a motherfucker." A moment later, he grunts again. "Oooh, nice, I'm bleedin' like a stuck pig. Very cool, love that for me. Yeah—gym. Gym sounds good. Pretty ladies to play doctor for me. And away…we…go!"

Lorenzo pauses and glances at me as he reloads. "He is always like that?"

"Yes," I answer. "Wildly inappropriate humor is his default setting for every situation."

"We heard an explosion," Toro says across the radio. "Report, *por favor.*"

"Grenade," I answer. "Fonz took shrapnel to the leg but he's mobile."

"Mobile may be a bit of a stretch. Don't ask me to run any hundred-yard dashes," Fonz says over the radio. "But I ain't gonna die—ow*FUCK*, woman, Jesus. No, tighter. *FUCK!*"

Lorenzo's rifle chatters beside me again, and I add mine to the fray as more shapes glide through the smoke.

The scent of death, cordite, and blood is rife and thick and pungent.

Our rifles fall silent when no more shapes appear in the eddying, arc-lit pall of smoke.

"Moving," Lorenzo says.

I put my hand on his shoulder and follow him forward. Grit crunches under my feet. My toe hits something soft yet solid—a body. I glance down; sightless eyes stare at nothing. I slip in a pool of blood, and Lorenzo's hand flashes out to catch me, steady me. Another body. Another.

"Parking lot is clear," Toro says.

Moving slowly and cautiously in a crouch, barrel sweeping side to side, Lorenzo precedes me through the haze, stepping over rubble and bodies. They're piled at the base of the stairs.

"*Jesus Cristo*," Lorenzo mutters. "What a clusterfuck." He peers up the stairwell, but there isn't much to see: the explosion partially caved in the stairwell. "Clear down here," he says.

"We will have to exit through the club," I say. "Rendezvous at the SUVs ASAP. We need to get out of here in case there's a second wave."

CHAPTER 6

ONE IMMUTABLE FACT

LORENZO

TORO IS WINGED, A THROUGH-AND-THROUGH TO his left tricep—which is a whole shit-ton of meat, so it could have been worse. Taj took a grazing round to the side of the neck, which bled fucking buckets, bathing his entire upper torso, making it look worse than it was. And Fonz, the lunatic jokester, took a sharp, jagged chunk of metal to the back of the thigh. It's embedded deep, too risky to remove, so we wrap it in a makeshift bandage. Toro and I support him as we move through the club.

We emerge into daylight again and make our way around the giant building, Inez leading the way in a tactical crouch, rifle sweeping this way and that, pivoting mid-stride to assess every possible angle. We reach the array of Mercedes SUVs—most of them are so bullet-riddled as to be useless, the glass shattered, tires flattened, bodies full of holes. Three of them, however, are driveable, with only a few dings and dents from ricochets marring the bodies. We pile everyone into the two vehicles; it's a tight fit as these aren't the most spacious of trucks, despite their exorbitant price tag.

Annika, behind the front passenger seat, grunts in pain as she uses her hands to force her knee to bend the right way. "This thing was not built with a six-foot-three giraffe-woman in mind," she grumbles.

Inez scoots the seat forward until her knees touch the dash. "Better?"

"Yes, much, thanks," Annika answers.

Inez snickers as she buckles. "You ought to see Chance trying to shoehorn himself into these things."

Annika splutters, and then dissolves into cackles. "Ohmygod, I'd pay money to see that!"

"The amount of cursing and bitching is unbelievable." Inez drops her voice into a remarkably accurate impression of Chance. "'What is this, a car for *ants*?'"

"Where to, *meu amor*?" I ask, glancing at Inez. "Also, I think that was your first joke."

She glares at me, but the ice is melting and the daggers have dulled. "Why do you keep pointing out whenever I laugh or smile? Are you trying to make me self-conscious?"

I reach a hand out and rest it on her thigh. "No, just the opposite. To see a smile on your face, to hear you laugh? *É linda, meu amor.*"

Terra, wedged in the middle between Annika and Anjalee, leans forward between the two front seats. "Um, wait, hold on. Inez…he called you 'amor.' And, y'know, I don't even speak English all that well, but I'm pretty damn sure that means 'love.'"

Inez meets my eyes, and then glances at my hand resting on her thigh, and then turns to look at Terra. "It is… complicated. We have a long history."

I sigh. "Our history *is* complicated, I suppose. What is not complicated, however, is the fact that I love her."

Inez opens her mouth to protest, but I speak over her. "I know, I know. You aren't ready for that. It's alright. I am a patient man."

Rather than answer, Inez turns her attention out the window. "The Bellagio," she murmurs, after a moment.

The Bellagio is in sight when Inez's phone buzzes with an incoming message. She reads it, pockets the phone, and glances at me. "Go to the service entrance. Arrangements have been made."

Finding the service entrance turns out to be the trickiest part. Once we arrive at the rear of the building—after a lot of circling and wrong turns—a ramp leads down to a loading dock where several tractor-trailers are docked, supplies being unloaded. A burly bald man in a tailored suit, the curly wire of an earpiece trailing under his collar, directs us to park off to one side of the loading dock next to a white catering van and a few Bellagio groundskeeping fleet pickups. Toro and Taj assist Fonz out of the Mercedes—he spent the drive here on his belly in the back seat in what must have been a truly awkward and uncomfortable position—necessitated by the shrapnel's location. Inez and the security operative lead the way through a maze of service hallways. None of the staff we pass seem overly shocked to see a cavalcade of armed operators bathed in blood helping each other limp along the corridors, coated in dust and grime. Makes you wonder what they must see in a normal day that they wouldn't bat an eye at the spectacle.

Inez murmurs a question to our guide—I can't hear her question but I hear his response: "Our staff is entirely discreet, ma'am, you have my word. Your presence here will remain a secret. Only myself and a handful of hand-picked staff know of your arrival. No one here at the Bellagio will speak out of turn."

A freight elevator takes us up, we get off, transfer to an express elevator dedicated to a penthouse suite which, apparently, is our destination. It turns out that a significant percentage of an entire floor has been converted into a single suite with multiple bedrooms, bathrooms, and a kitchenette. The girls all ooh and ahh at the luxurious accommodations, while Inez, Toro, and I do a sweep. Taj helps Fonz lie down on his belly on the couch.

Our Bellagio security liaison, Bradley, says a private doctor has been contacted and will be here soon to see to Fonz's leg and any other injuries. He addresses Inez and I separately, then.

"The owner of this suite made separate arrangements for you two—they actually own the entire floor." Bradley hands us each a heavy black keycard. "The elevator to this floor cannot be accessed without these keys—and these are the only two. I will be posted in the lobby near the elevator, and more of my men will be monitoring the stairwells."

Inez stares at him. "Separate arrangements?"

Bradley nods. "Yes, ma'am. This way, please."

He leads us out of the suite into a lobby or foyer area featuring the emergency stairwell and elevator, a floor-to-ceiling window overlooking Las Vegas, the double doors to the primary suite, and another set of double doors. Our keycards, he tells us, work for the elevator and both sets of rooms.

The secondary suite is a fraction of the size of the primary, with one bedroom, one bathroom, the living area, and no kitchenette. After ushering us in, Bradley waits at the door while Inez and I do our sweep and return to him.

He hands us a business card with his first name and a phone number. "That's my direct line. Call or message me at any time, for any reason. I am your sole contact here at the Bellagio, so if you require room service, additional amenities, or anything at all, contact me, *not* hotel staff."

"Understood," I answer, and shake his hand. "Thank you, Bradley."

He nods, and takes the elevator back to the lobby, leaving Inez and I alone.

Inez, standing with her back to the still-open French doors, scans the suite with a puzzled expression. "Why would he do this?"

"I don't know," I answer. "Ask him?"

She glances at me, nods, and slides her phone from her back pocket. Hits a contact from her favorites—the only entry, as a matter of fact—and puts it on speaker.

It rings twice. "Inez." It's Jakob—his voice is unmistakable.

"Sir. We've arrived at the…safehouse."

"This line is secure, Inez. And I had that entire floor swept for surveillance before your arrival. You may speak freely."

"Very well, sir. You are on speaker, and Lorenzo is beside me."

"Hello again, Lorenzo."

"Jakob," I say.

"I trust you understand that my identity is a secret which I guard rather aggressively. Inez is one of two people on the planet who have seen my face or know my name."

"And I do not know your surname," Inez adds.

"My point is that in telling you my name, in speaking to you as I did, I extended my trust. Please do not violate that trust by revealing that name to anyone."

I consider my response for several moments. "As a former intelligence operative with my country's highest security clearance, sir," I say, "I believe I am more than capable of keeping your identity to myself."

"I would not have spoken to you in person as I did if I didn't believe that, Lorenzo. But some things should be made clear so there is no possibility of error."

"Of course."

Inez sighs. "Jakob, why do we have a separate suite?"

You can hear the amusement in his voice when he answers. "You and Lorenzo have much to work through, Inez. You require privacy for that. You have been run ragged the last several weeks, and you in particular have endured... well, it doesn't bear discussing. I thought you might enjoy some privacy in which to recuperate and refresh yourselves before the next phase of our operation."

"Do we have a next phase?" Inez asks.

"Indeed. I am working on it. I have several resources working on a location for our quarry, and the men are closing in on Pugli, I believe."

"The situation at the club..." Inez starts.

"I am surveying the damage now. I'll have to close down for awhile so my engineers can assess the structural damage. Everyone made it out alive, however?"

"Yes, sir. Fonz took a serious injury to his leg, and Toro to his arm, but considering the number of opponents we faced, we came out remarkably well."

"You had some of the best shooters on the planet at your side, my dear friend. Of course, you came out on top.

I'd expect no less. If Pugli thought a pack of amateurs could take out La Víbora and Lorenzo Oliveira Araujo, then he is stupider than I imagined."

"We wouldn't have made it without Toro, Fonz, and Taj, sir," Inez states.

"I am aware."

"What about Rafael, sir?" Inez asks. "Do you have any leads on his whereabouts?"

"He is nearly as elusive as I am," Jakob says. "But my sources are making headway. Stay ready, but take time to recover."

Inez looks at me as if she's trying to decide something, or figure something out. "Sir, I—"

"Inez," Jakob interrupts.

"But sir, I—"

"*Sophia.*" It is spoken softly, gently, but somehow still manages to crackle with authority. "Things are changing. For all of us. You have spent the last several years merely existing. As have the men. As have I. Now is your turn to reach for more."

"I do not know how, Jakob," she whispers.

"I know. Believe me, dear friend, I know." He clears his throat. "Try. The man beside you knows all there is to know. Don't be afraid."

"I'll try," Inez says.

"That's all anyone can do," Jakob answers. "Ah, one of my sources is calling. I'll be in touch."

The line goes dead and Inez pulls it away, stares at it as if it holds some answers to life's questions.

She looks shaken.

"What?" I ask. "What is that look for?"

"Jakob, he..." she shakes her head. "He is behaving

strangely. Revealing himself to you. The things he just said? It's all very strange."

"He cares about you," I answer.

"He called me dear friend," she whispers. "Twice. And Sophia—he called me Sophia. He has never done that before."

"Walls are tumbling down everywhere, it seems," I say.

"I was comfortable with my life," she whispers. "My job. The Arrows. The Club."

"A comfortable existence is not the same thing as a fulfilling life." I shut the doors, lock them. Toss the keycard on the narrow table near the doors, take her hand and lead her further into the room. "He wants more for you than that. So do I."

"And *you* are that more, I suppose?" She asks, her tone wry, looking at me with an arched eyebrow.

"Yes. I believe I am." I look down at her—her face is gray with dust from the explosion, dotted with gritty smears of pink and red. He hair has come almost entirely out of the customary braided bun, now hanging loose and tangled and filthy around her shoulders. "But if you were to decide you didn't want me in your life, I would honor and respect that. It would break my heart all over again, I admit, but I would do it."

Her eyes close, and her lips press together. "Lorenzo... I—I feel..." she shakes her head. "I don't know."

"Tell me how you feel, please. Whatever it is."

"Weak," she breathes. "Afraid. Emotional."

"Afraid of what?" I step closer to her, so less than a foot separates us.

She shakes her head again. "I don't know."

"Yes, you do."

She puts her hands up, palms out, so I can't draw any closer. "You."

"You are afraid of me?" I ask.

"You *see* me, Ren," she whispers, so quietly I must strain to hear. "You know my every secret. You...I feel almost naked around you. As if I have no armor. No walls. No protection. You, more than anyone, can hurt me, Ren. Rafael...he hurt my body. I can take that. I know pain. I am comfortable with pain. But you, Ren. You...you can hurt my soul."

"But I *won't.*"

"I don't know who I am anymore." Her deep, dark eyes lift to mine, fraught and wet with emotion—shocking to see in the face of my indomitable, unshakeable warrior queen. "Sophia, Inez...neither fits anymore. Sophia Bruna Santos de Silva Sousa...that part of who I am died in the cell, and then again in childbirth and the horror that followed. Inez? She was all that was left. I chose a name at random when I left everything else behind. Now, my past as Sophia has been resurrected and is haunting me. Inez was a shell, and that shell has cracked open. What is left of me, Ren?" She lets out a shaky sigh. "What is left of me?"

I don't have an answer for that. "We don't need to have all the answers right this second, meu amor," I tell her. "Let's get cleaned up and go from there. You take the first shower while I check on the others."

She nods, eyes distant, tired. "A shower sounds good. I don't remember the last time I was clean."

I cup the side of her face. "Take the longest, hottest shower of your life. I'll be here when you get out."

I watch her head for the bathroom and then go next door. The women have settled in front of the TV, watching some old rom-com on cable. The room phone rings—I hear Toro answer it, murmur quietly, and then he appears from one of the bedrooms.

"The doctor is here," he says. "We must greet him in the lobby and escort him up."

"On it," I answer.

I take the elevator to the lobby; Bradley is waiting with an older man dressed in a sleek, bespoke suit, salt-and-pepper hair in a short, neat, classic side-part, a large rolling suitcase at his side. Nothing about him says doctor, which is a discretion I appreciate. I accompany him up and bring him to Fonz.

No introductions are made—the man kneels at Fonz's side, unwraps the makeshift bandage, examines the wound, and nods once.

"Deep, but I don't think it has done any significant damage. It is good you didn't remove it, however."

"None of us are rookies, Doc," Fonz says. "But I'd be happy if you could get the fuckin' thing outta me. And if you got any happy pills to take the edge off, I'd be grateful."

"Certainly. Give me a few minutes to get set up."

I watch him lay down and unzip his suitcase, revealing a precise, orderly array of medical supplies. He begins preparing what he'll need to remove the shrapnel and close the wound.

I feel a soft tap on my shoulder. "Mr. Lorenzo?" The voice is delicate, shy.

"Naomi," I say, smiling down at her. "Call me Lorenzo, or just Ren. We're all friends here."

"Is Inez alright?" Naomi asks, her eyes full of concern.

"I think so. Or, she will be. She's strong."

Naomi frowns. "She...I don't mean to speak out of

turn, but she went through quite a breakdown, and then a gunfight and an explosion."

"She's taking a shower right now," I tell her. "I'm headed back over once I'm sure things are settled here." I lead her away a few feet and speak in low tones. "I am glad you ladies were there. She needed that breakdown—it was a very long time coming."

"It seemed that way to me. I just...I know from experience that such breakdowns can leave one feeling empty and exhausted. She will need support."

"And she will have it." I give her shoulder a gentle pat. "I appreciate your concern, and I know she does as well."

"Inez, she...the first time I ever spoke to her, I was being pursued by people who wished to kill me. She talked me through it. I wouldn't be here if not for her." Naomi's eyes are misty. "I've felt a connection to her ever since. She hides a beautiful soul behind all that toughness and coldness."

"She does, doesn't she?" I smile at her again. "We just have to convince her it's safe to let the rest of the world see what we do."

"Only you can do that, I think," Naomi says.

"I guess we'll see, won't we?"

I watch the doctor for a few more minutes, assessing his work with the experienced eye of someone who has seen more than my fair share of battlefield triage. He works carefully, efficiently, and skillfully. Satisfied that the man is a qualified medical professional and not a secret assassin, I turn to leave. I lean close to Taj, who leans a shoulder against the wall near the door, watching the room silently and attentively. "Watch him, yes? I trust no one, at this stage."

Taj searches my face, then returns his attention to the doctor. "Of course."

I head back to the other room, locking it behind me. For the first time in I don't know how long, I feel safe to set my firearms aside and remove my boots—I have had them on for nearly a week, at this point, I believe, though the days and nights of endless travel have warped my perception of the passage of time.

My socks smell abysmal, as do the boots, so I leave them by the door. I curl my toes into the thick pile of the rug under the couch and sigh at the glorious sensation of simply not wearing boots and socks.

I flop onto the couch, groaning—now that I have a moment to tune into myself, I realize I am exhausted beyond all comprehension, and the various injuries I've sustained in the course of this mad, wild adventure ache something fierce.

I stretch my legs out, let my head sink back into the couch, close my eyes...

◆

It's a scent that wakes me. Shampoo, soap, wet hair, and lotion; the unmistakable, indelible scent of a freshly showered woman. I open my eyes to see her perched on the edge of the couch beside me, a thick, fluffy white towel wrapped around her torso. Her hair is loose and wet, slicked back over her scalp to hang down her neck, sticking to her shoulders. The towel hem is hitched up and bunched beneath her buttocks, leaving the curve of one leg bare from toe to hip, an alluring expanse of flesh. She has a complimentary bottle of lotion balanced on the arm of the couch beside her and she's rubbing it onto her leg. I watch for a few moments.

She doesn't look up from what she's doing when she speaks to me. "I used all the hot water, I believe. I'm sorry."

"Don't be. How are you feeling?" I ask, unable to tear my gaze away from the lovely view of her long, bare leg.

"Better," she says, still not looking at me. "Being clean is a wonderful luxury."

I lift one foot and wiggle my toes. "That's how I felt when I took off my boots and socks."

She wrinkles her nose. "Is that what I'm smelling?"

I laugh. "Could just be me."

Her skin beckons me. Smooth, caramel, and olive, warm. I swallow hard as a visceral memory of the first time I saw her naked sledgehammers through my brain.

I was on guard duty outside her quarters—it's how we met. She passed me every day, and I thought she was the most beautiful creature I'd ever seen, and could never stop myself from staring at her whenever I saw her. Well, one day she didn't pass by. She stopped and struck up a conversation with me. It was innocent enough, just idle chit-chat, but it felt like a gift from heaven to be close to her, to speak to her. We shared more conversations, after that, and eventually it became a daily habit. And then we began meeting in secret, late at night after the compound was asleep—except for her father's guards. Those late-night meetings were the highlight of every day. I spent those conversations staring at her lips, of course, wishing I was brave enough to kiss her.

She kissed me first.

Eventually, it was clear we both wanted to be

somewhere more private than a shadowy corner of the compound where we could be together.

The day in question, I was on duty outside her father's cash room—a bank vault built within a bombproof chamber below his bedroom. She waited until I was off duty, arranged to make sure we passed each other, and secreted a note into my hand: *stables at midnight,* it said.

I found her hiding in the back corner of the hayloft, sitting cross-legged on a quilt, wearing a pretty white sundress adorned with pink flowers. Her hair was down and loose in a wild black cloud.

My heart had pounded in my throat at the sight of her sitting there waiting for me, as visibly nervous as I felt.

We'd kissed awkwardly for a while, and then less awkwardly as passion and lust and hormones took over. I had stolen a condom from one of the other guards, and I remember distinctly the way it felt in my back pocket—as if it weighed a thousand pounds, searing a circle in the back of my leg.

We'd stood up together, and I had peeled my shirt off, shucked my jeans. I'll never forget the moment she shrugged her dress off, letting it pool at her feet; I'll never forget the way my dick had hardened at the sight of her, standing there in the harsh light of the electric lantern she had brought. She wore a matching bra and panties set—scarlet lace and silk that hid and accentuated her curves at the same time.

She held my eyes as she reached behind her back and unhooked the bra, drew it off, and revealed her breasts for me. Shimmied out of her panties. Stood utterly naked for me, bold and unafraid, eyes hungrily raking over my body, and the obvious evidence of my arousal.

I knew then, as I took in the lush wonder of her beautiful body, her bright eyes, her smooth skin, that I would never want anyone else but her.

"Why are you looking at me like that, Ren?" she asks, bringing me back to the present.

I shrug one shoulder. "Just…looking at you," I say. "You're beautiful."

She smiles at the compliment, a shy curve of her lips that brightens and livens her features. "Ren," whispers. "Stop."

"Never. I will be telling you how beautiful you are when we are both old and as wrinkled as raisins."

Her dark eyes search mine. "That isn't what you were thinking."

"It is," I counter. "It's just not *all* I was thinking."

She closes the lotion cap with a click. "Tell me. Please."

"I was remembering the first time I got to see you naked," I answer. "That night in the hayloft. The white dress with pink flowers. Red underwear and bra. You were so fucking beautiful I couldn't think straight."

Her chin drops to her chest; it's hard to tell with skin like hers, but I'm pretty sure she's blushing. "You wouldn't let me touch you for the longest time. I was so frustrated."

"Because if you'd so much as brushed my dick, I'd have exploded."

"I know that now." She smooths the towel over her thighs. "You still remember what I was wearing?"

I bark a laugh. "Of course, *meu amor*. How could I forget the best day of my life? I remember every detail."

"The best day of your life?"

"To this day, yes. I felt like I could fly. I was the luckiest boy who'd ever lived. You, the princess of Rio, the most beautiful girl I'd ever seen, in real life or on television. I was obsessed with American TV and I thought you were more beautiful than…well, anyone. And you…you wanted *me*. You chose me—*me*, a gutter mouse from Rocinha. A nobody who barely rated a gun for guard duty. When you let that dress fall to the floor and I saw the red bra and panties? My god, Sophia. I could have died a happy man in the moment."

"You were so handsome, Ren." Her smile is…soft with remembrance. It is a sacred thing, that smile. Rarer than any gem or precious metal, and more priceless to me than either. "I remember thinking how cool and different and exotic your name was. I would walk around saying it—Lorenzo. It doesn't sound Brazilian. Because it's not, I suppose. But it…it just rolls off the tongue differently. You were a little older than me, of course, and you had a man's body. Big and hard and muscular." Her eyes drop from mine. "That was the best day of my life, too."

Silence stretches between us, laden with a million unspoken thoughts and feelings.

"You are even more beautiful now than you were then," I say. "You are still so beautiful to me that it is sometimes hard to breathe."

She shakes her head. "You're ridiculous. I'm not. I'm covered in scars." She gnaws on the corner of her lip, looking away from me, one hand covering her belly over the towel. "And stretch marks. Reninho was a *very* big baby."

"Sophia—"

She glares me into silence. "If you give me some shit about tiger stripes, I'm going to stab you."

I sit up and angle toward her, my knee touching hers.

"Do you really think a few scars and stretch marks can make you any less beautiful to me, *meu amor*?"

She shrugs. "I don't know, Ren. I...I haven't felt..." she tips her head back, blinking. "Dammit."

I touch her chin, turn her face to mine. "I am not afraid of your emotions. You shouldn't be, either."

"I have spent the last fifteen, almost twenty years keeping my emotions locked away in a box, Ren," she says, fiddling with the corner of the towel. "Trying like hell not to feel *anything*. It meant I couldn't feel happiness, perhaps, but what was there to be happy about? Nothing. It meant I didn't have to feel the shame of what was done to me, or the horror and guilt at what I did. It isn't so easy to just... let it all come tumbling out."

"It did back at Club Sin," I prompt. "With the other girls."

She sighs. "I can't put how that made me feel into words. I felt...connected to them. To every woman who has ever come before me—because we've all suffered something like that. We all know how it feels. And they... they let me..." she shakes her head. "I don't know. I feel lighter. They took a burden from me. Like I've been walking around with rocks in my pockets, and suddenly...I'm free." Another head shake, another sigh. "But now all of those emotions are out of their box and I can't put them back in and everything is too fucking much, Ren."

I put my hand on her knee—her bare skin is hot and silky smooth. "Not for me. Nothing you are is too much for me."

At the touch of my hand, she sucks in a sharp, hissing breath and tenses all over, still as a statue. "Ren, please."

"Please, what?" I ask, whispering.

She's panting, short, frantic breaths. "Don't touch me. It's too much."

I remove my hand.

She drops her head and exhales in relief. "I'm sorry. I know...I know what you want."

"No, you don't."

Her head jerks up with a derisive snort. "Of course I do. You're looking at me and remembering the first time we were together. You're remembering an eighteen-year-old virgin. I was eager, back then. Free of all this..." she shakes her head, tipping it back again and blinking, sniffling. "Free of all this fucking trauma. I'm not that person anymore, Ren. I want to give that to you. I haven't been touched or wanted for so fucking long. I haven't...I haven't felt like... like a *woman* in so fucking long. But I don't know how..."

I touch her lips with one finger. "Hush, my love. It's alright."

"But what if I can't ever go there with you?" She whispers, her voice shaky and breaking. "What if I can't give you...*anything*?"

I take her hand in mine, kiss the knuckles. "Then I will still love you."

"You need..." she swallows hard, licks her lips. "You deserve a woman who can give you sex, Lorenzo."

"I haven't been with anyone since Consuela, and that was nearly five years ago."

She frowns at me. "So you haven't..."

"I have not touched a woman in that way since Consuela. I tried to. I...well, I hired a girl, to be blunt about it. But I couldn't...perform. I couldn't so much as kiss her. So I paid her for the full hour and left after about ten minutes."

"And what about your…needs?"

It's funny—she's a warrior. She can drop a man with a bullet to the face without blinking. She can stab a man and watch the life drain from his eyes. But she can't speak of sex in direct terms.

I shrug. "I have a hand." I meet her eyes. "And some very vivid memories."

"Lorenzo!" She hisses. "You don't mean—"

"I do."

"No!"

"Yes."

She looks away from me, and now I can see that she is indeed blushing, hard. "You—you think of *me…when* you—"

I turn her palm and kiss the center of it, holding her gaze. "Sophia, my love. Listen to me. I am not ashamed or embarrassed, and you should not be either. We shared something special and incredible, and those memories have sustained me throughout my life."

"Stop," she whispers.

"No, I will not." I bring her palm to my cheek and nuzzle it. "I am going to go take a shower now. I'm going to take my clothes off and get in the water, and once I'm clean, I'm going to close my eyes and remember. I'm going to remember you and me together in that hayloft. I'm going to remember you taking your dress off for me, taking that bra off, and your panties. The way you looked, naked and perfect and all for me. I'm going to remember kissing you. The way your skin felt the first time I got to touch your breasts. The way your hand felt wrapped around my cock."

She whimpers softly. "Ren, stop. Stop. Please. I can't—I can't. I can't."

I nuzzle her hand again, whispering. "I'm going to re-member that night, and I'm going to touch myself while I do. I'm going to come, thinking about you. How beautiful you were—how beautiful you *are*." I drag the pad of my index finger from her kneecap to the towel's edge at her upper thigh—goosebumps pebble her skin. "I'm going to fantasize about you as you are now, Sophia. Picture you, as you are now. Naked. Perfect. Scarred and stretch-marked and tattooed and powerful and perfect. And mine, Sophia. You are *mine*. You have always *been* mine. You will always *be* mine. I will never ask you to do anything you are not ready for. But I will think of you, and in that way, you still give me what I need and want, and that will be enough, even if that's all of you I ever get."

I rise from the couch and sink to my knees in front of her. She presses her knees together, stiff and tense. Staring at me, eyes wet and wide and black. searching. Searing. I cup her face in my hands, lean in ever so slowly.

"Ren," she breathes.

"Trust me," comes my answering breath.

"I do."

I touch my lips to hers in a delicate ghost of a kiss. Barely a touch. "I love you, Sophia." I do it again, another whisper of a kiss. "I love you, Inez." Again. "No matter your name, I love you. I *see* you. I *know* you. That will never change. It cannot. It is…*imutável*. I can't think of the word in English for some stupid reason."

"Immutable," she murmurs.

"Yes, exactly." I brush her cheeks with my thumbs. "Like the sun and the moon and the stars."

"But stars die."

I laugh. "Everything dies. Don't be obtuse. You know what I mean."

"You know the English for 'obtuse' but not 'immutable?'" she says, with a wry grin.

"You scramble my brains with your eternal beauty." I stand up, reluctantly. "I'm not asking anything of you except that you let me in, Sophia."

"I am trying," she whispers.

"Then that's all I need."

CHAPTER 7

FIRST TOUCH...AGAIN

INEZ

I CAN'T BREATHE.

My body is locked in place, frozen and tensed as raw panic shears through me, searing my lungs with icy, tightening bands.

My mind is a coruscating madhouse of swirling thoughts, exploding desires, and conflicting fears.

I need him.

I want him.

He touched me—touched my bare thigh, so close to a part of me no one has touched for so, so long.

He kissed me.

Twice.

He fantasizes about me.

He...pleasures himself while thinking about me.

Rusty metal bit into my wrists as I thrashed, screaming. Papa stood over me wearing a white linen suit, a black silk shirt unbuttoned to his diaphragm beneath the jacket. His hands were shoved casually into his pockets, as if he was here to discuss the weather or the terms of a business deal.

"Last chance, Sophia," he said. "This isn't what I want, but you're forcing my hand."

I snarled at him like a trapped wildcat. "Then let me go! I won't marry him. I won't. He's a vile pig!"

"You **will**, my daughter. It has been decided. He is the heir to my empire. We must make it official, which means you must marry him. He really isn't so bad. Perhaps some of his tastes are…questionable, but then, this isn't a love match. He'll have his…playthings, and if you're discreet, you can have your own." A pause, a tip of his head to one side. "Once you've produced an heir, of course."

I thrashed again, harder. "I knew you were a monster, but this? Papa, this is sick even for you."

"The moment you say two words, it all ends, Sophia. Say the words. 'I accept.'"

"**Never!**"

He looked genuinely displeased. "I really would rather you didn't make me do this to you."

"Then don't, Papa, please." I hated the tears in my eyes, the quiver in my voice, but I was terrified. "Please, Papa. Pick someone else. Anyone else. Please. Please. Don't. Please don't."

He lunges across the cell, bends over me, and grips my jaw with agonizing power. "Then **agree**, Sophia. All you have to do is agree." He released me and stepped back. "You will marry him one way or another. After you've endured this, or… agree, and all will be well."

"All will be well?" I screeched. "He beats women to death and fucks their **CORPSES**!" I screamed the last word so loud and so hard my throat felt shredded and bloody.

"That is an exaggeration."

"I heard him bragging!"

"Then you must have misunderstood."

I sobbed, knowing there was no way to win this sick game.

"I didn't. He is a sick, depraved, evil monster. You are marrying me off to the devil himself, Papa."

He stepped away, sighing sadly. "You won't relent? You would rather this," he swept a hand at me, chained spread-eagle, naked, to a cot in the middle of a subterranean cell, "than simply marry a man you don't like?"

I couldn't stop a sob. "Please, Papa."

"So be it." He strode out the door and didn't look back. "You may begin."

One of Papa's men, a grizzled, sweating middle-aged man with tobacco-stained teeth, swaggered in as my father exited. The man, a laborer in Papa's fields, grinned savagely as he fumbled with his belt buckle. The jingling of that buckle has been imprinted on my mind forever, the sound of what innocence I had left being eradicated.

He climbed on top of me. He smelled awful. An actual flea jumped from his skin to mine as he mounted me; and I could not flick it away. I could not do anything.

The rusty manacles flayed my skin at wrists and ankles as he entered me.

He was not quick.

None of them were.

Eventually I stopped thrashing…but only because I was weak from blood loss.

That was the last time I saw my father.

My hands tremble violently as the memory wracks me, and I suck a ragged breath into my screaming lungs.

That breath turns into a sob through gritted teeth.

I look at my wrists—the scars are faint. You'd have to look for them to notice. The same scars adorn my ankles.

I close my eyes again, and immediately the memory threatens to return. I had nightmares for years. Nothing helped. I tried sleeping pills, alcohol, meditation, canna-bis…only with time did the nightmares subside—and even now, I'll still have one on occasion. I even tried talk therapy, but in three hour—long sessions I was unable to speak a single word of what happened.

I open my eyes again, focusing on the sound of the shower. I call up a different memory—that first time with Lorenzo. I remember seeing how obviously nervous he was, as he climbed up into the hayloft and approached me. I'd felt bold and daring as I dressed in my lingerie—cho-sen and purchased with this night in mind, with Lorenzo in mind—and carried the quilt and lantern to the hayloft. But then he'd appeared, dressed in faded, dirty jeans, a plain black T-shirt, and threadbare work boots. He was so handsome. I remember thinking that. I remember my desire—I remember that feeling.

Looking at him as he peeled off his shirt to reveal the hard, lithe, lean body of an eighteen-year-old—not quite a man, but neither a boy—and I remember how my hands itched to carve over his hard abs and broad shoulders, how curious I was to see his erection. I'd seen penises before, of course, and I knew perfectly well the details of sex. But I'd never wanted to *do* it with anyone until I met Lorenzo, until I tasted his kisses and felt his hands on my waist, until he dared grasp my ass, caress my breasts over my shirt.

My breath comes fast as I delve into the memory, and the emotions and sensations that accompany it. Lorenzo standing there in a baggy pair of boxers, erection bulging against the fabric, his eyes fixed on my cleavage; I'd stood up and shrugged out of the dress, and his erection had, improbably, seemed to grow. I slipped off my bra, shak-ing all over, a little scared and a lot excited, feeling like a woman for the first time as his eyes hungrily fixed on my bare breasts. We had both removed our underwear at the same time, standing naked in front of each other. I'd fought the instinct to cover my vagina, and the way he clenched his fists at his sides told me he was fighting the same urge to cover himself.

He took the first step toward me, and I'll never forget the searing heat of his hand as he placed it on my hip, a hesitant touch. That searing heat slid toward my bare bottom, and I'd sucked in a breath. His hand had flown away from me, worried, I think, that the hiss of breath was a protest at his touch. I had put his hand back on my bottom, and touched his as well.

It was a questing, awkward time, then, as we explored each other's bodies—bottoms, breasts, stomach. He slid a finger over my seam, and my legs had nearly given out. But when I went to grasp his erection, he'd stopped me, grabbing my hand, pulling out of reach.

He touched me, then. Explored my sex, delving a finger inside me, watching rapt as I panted when he discovered my clit. I'd shown him how to make me feel good—I had been masturbating regularly for years by that point.

Finally, we'd lain together side by side on the quilt and kissed and touched. His erection had slid against my belly, smearing leaking wetness all over me. I remember being on the verge of orgasm so many times as we'd writhed together, kissing, grinding.

He'd pulled away, snagged his jeans, and produced a condom from his back pocket. I remember the fascination I'd felt watching him roll it onto himself, and I remember wishing I could have done that. I wanted to know how a cock felt in my hand. I'd heard the maids discussing sex on any number of occasions when they thought I wasn't listening, and I remember distinctly a specific conversation where one girl told another about giving her boyfriend a blowjob. I'd been shocked, confused, and even a little disgusted at the time. But in that moment, watching Lorenzo put the condom on, I'd known I wanted to do that to him, too.

I remember clearest of all the moment he hovered over me. His cock had bobbed above my sex with each breath, one of his hands braced beside my ear, the other fondling my breast. He'd finally let me grasp his cock, just long enough to nudge him at my entrance. He'd waited, watching me carefully as he slowly slid inside me.

I had gasped at the alien sensation of being penetrated. It had hurt, at first. Especially when he broke my hymen. But then, slowly, gradually, the pain subsided and I grew used to the feeling of him inside me, and I had wanted more. Needed more.

He gave me more.

So, so much more.

He came quickly, and I could tell he was embarrassed about it.

He made me come with his fingers, a bit awkwardly and clumsily, but eagerly and thoroughly.

God, I had loved him, then. I began craving him after that night. My hunger for him was relentless and all-consuming.

I want it back.

I want to feel his hand on my flesh and not experience it as razor blades slicing me to pieces.

I want to kiss him and lose myself in that kiss.

He's in that bathroom right now, naked and wet, wanting me, and thinking of me as he touches himself.

I find myself on my feet, hand on the bathroom doorknob before I know what's happening. I pause and examine myself—terrified and full of panic, yet determined.

I can do this. I can go in there. I can sit on the toilet lid and watch him shower. I can look at his naked body and not flee. I can watch him pleasure himself.

I don't think I can take off my towel, but I can take this one tiny step toward regaining my sexuality…

My sense of self.

I twist the knob and push the door open. Steam envelops me, and I close the door behind me. The bathroom is a wonderland of marble and glass. The shower is on the left, hazed with steam, revealing Lorenzo's brown skin and hard muscles rippling with brawny power as he stands beneath the rainfall showerhead, face tipped up to the water, scrubbing lather out of his longish black hair.

A splat of water hits the marble under his feet, and then he scrapes his palm down his face and blinks. His gaze happens to flick my way, and his hand slowly lowers from his face.

"Sophia," he murmurs.

I swallow hard. "I can't—I can't go in there with you, Lorenzo. Not yet."

"That's okay," he answers.

"But I…" I step toward the glass separating us, trying to find the courage to say what I want. "I wanted to… to see you."

He turns to face me, and my eyes rake over his body— heavy pecs, thick arms, bulging thighs. His abs aren't shredded, but rather are a hard, flat anvil of powerful muscle sheathed in skin, a thin layer of body fat, and a spattering of curly black body hair. I see the various injuries he has sustained on my behalf, in varying stages of healing—scabbed and pink, raw and red and angry.

His cock hangs thick and heavy between his thighs, swaying slightly from the momentum of his pivot.

I swallow hard—I haven't looked upon a naked male form in a very, very long time, and not voluntarily since my last lovemaking with Lorenzo all those years ago.

He is beautiful. No longer a boy barely on the cusp of manhood, Lorenzo is a huge, hard, powerful specimen of virile masculine beauty, intensely fit, covered in scars—burns, cuts, bullet holes, and who knows what else.

My mouth is dry as I look at him, and I cannot swallow, can't draw a breath.

I touch the pads of my fingers to the glass at chest height, searching his eyes, his face, and then letting my gaze slide over his body once more—catching, inevitably, on his manhood once more.

He just stands there letting me look. No quips, no jokes, no invitations, no innuendos.

I square my shoulders. Meet his eyes. "You are more handsome now than you were twenty years ago."

"I'm glad you think so," he says.

"Have you already…" I trail off, glancing at his penis again.

"No."

"Oh."

I inhale deeply, my chest swelling—I feel the towel, wrapped around my torso and tucked in at my breastbone, loosen with the breath.

Determination to conquer my trauma wars against the unreasoning panic boiling in my gut.

I'm breathing hard, suddenly, and the towel loosens with each panted breath. My heart pounds in my chest and my palms go clammy. The towel slips, the tucked-in portion sagging free. Lorenzo's eyes remain fixed on mine.

"You don't have to do *anything*, Sophia," he murmurs. "You have nothing to prove to me."

"I have something to prove to myself," I answer.

I lift my chin and hold his gaze as I feel the towel sag, droop, and then flutter free to pool at my feet, leaving me naked in front of Lorenzo, the only man I've ever loved.

It's that night in the hayloft all over again, but now I'm a woman and he's a man, and I'm terrified and fighting the urge to flee.

I don't.

I stand with my chin lifted, hands at my sides, teeth gritted as I refuse to cover myself. Tears pool.

"Sophia," he whispers. "So beautiful. So brave." His eyes are fixed on mine, unwavering.

"Look at me, Lorenzo," I say, willing my voice to be firm; it isn't.

He swallows hard, and his gaze stutters down to my breasts; I'm not the slender, nubile girl I was the last time he saw me naked. I carry extra weight in my hips and breasts. My curves are generous. I hide my curves in my everyday life with compression garments and tailored clothing. But now, I'm bared to him. Exposed. Vulnerable. My breasts are large and feel heavy, swaying pendulously with my breathing. My nipples go hard, pebbling under his gaze. My belly isn't flat or hard; I have a little pooch of a belly that I can't ever get rid of, no matter how I exercise or diet. The stretch marks from my pregnancy wrap around my stomach to my sides, down to my hips. I've always been a little bottom-heavy, and that's only grown more true as I age.

I feel his gaze finally leave my breasts, flitting down to my belly, to my sex.

He drags his eyes to mine. "Sophia," he whispers. "You're perfect."

His cock is unfurling, hardening. He could lie with his words—he could tell me he thinks I'm beautiful without meaning it. But that? The hardening of his cock juts from looking at me naked. You can't fake that. He does like what he sees.

The fierce, desperate urge to cover my privates with my hands fades the longer he looks at me, the harder his cock gets as he rakes his hungry gaze over my nude form.

He swallows hard again, and his tongue slides over his lips. "Sophia, my god. I…" he closes his eyes, hands tightly fisted at his sides. "You are *incredible.*"

His cock is fully erect, now. It stands straight up against his belly, thick and veiny with a dark wreath of closely trimmed fuzz at the base. The head is broad and plump.

"Do it," I breathe. "What you said earlier."

His right hand drifts up to curl around the base of his huge, hard manhood. My breath lodges in my throat as he grips himself, squeezing.

"Tell me what you're thinking about, Ren," I whisper.

"You." He slides his grip upward, plunges it down. His jaw tightens at the movement, his belly hardening.

"Me, what?"

He closes his eyes, shakes his head. "I don't want to scare you."

"Too late. I'm terrified. But I'm not running away, Ren." I hold his eyes. "I want to know. Please."

He opens his eyes, and they go to my breasts. He strokes himself again. "Touching you. You're in the shower with me. Your skin would be wet. Slippery. I…" he lets out a slow sigh as his strokes find a slow rhythm. I'm rapt, watching that plump dark round head sprout over his fist. A quick but vivid memory sears through me:

Ren and I are in our hayloft. We'd been meeting there almost every night for months, having sex. But that night, I had decided I wanted something different from what we'd been doing—that being kissing, stripping each other naked, fondling each other until he's hard, and then fucking. No, this night, I wanted to experiment. Touch him. I told him what I wanted, and he tentatively agreed.

He let me get him naked, and by the time I was naked with him, he was hard for me. I'd gripped his cock in my fist, giggling nervously as I touched him that way for the first time. Well, not for the first time, but the first time he'd let me touch him just to…touch him, rather than as part of the act of feeding him into my sex.

His jaw had gone tight, his abs hard as I caressed his length. The more I caressed him, the faster his breathing became, until he was gasping and groaning at each slide of my fist from tip to root. His knees had begun dipping, as if they were about to give out.

He'd tried to stop me, but I kept going.

He came with a soft grunt that turned to a quiet gasp and then a low growl, a stripe of viscous white fluid spurting out of him and coating the backs of my fingers. I had laughed in shock—that part was a surprise to me. Having sex, when he was finishing, he'd grunt and go still, shuddering, and then roll off me. I hadn't realized that was what was going on...inside.

"Sophia?" His voice brings me back to the present. "Are you alright?"

I nod. "Just...remembering."

He's stroking himself slowly, still. "Remembering what?"

"The first time I..." I nod at his moving hand. "Did that to you."

"Do the words make you uncomfortable, Sophia?"

I nod, shrug. "Yes."

"You jerked me off," he says, trying to shock me, I suppose. "You gave me my very first handjob."

"I'd wanted to touch you like that from the moment I first saw you naked, but that was the first time I had the courage to say so—to do so."

"I couldn't believe how lucky I was," he says. "I still think of that when I do this. I imagine it's your hand on my cock."

"Is that what you're thinking about now?" I ask, a thrill of boldness taking over, if only for a moment.

"Yes. That...and other things."

"Like what?"

"Your mouth."

"Tell me."

"Laying in bed with you. You kneeling astride me. Moving down my body. Hair trailing over my skin as you kiss my belly. Your hot, tight mouth wrapping around my cock..." he trails off with a quiet groan, his grip speeding up. "*Fuck*, Sophia."

He dips at the knees, and my lungs seize and my

breasts ache and my sex pulses. Dampens, slick with desire for the first time in nearly twenty years.

Lorenzo's fist blurs on his cock, and my hands clench at my sides. The ache in my sex is spreading like wildfire, heat building, sending desire sluicing through me, dripping out of me as I watch Lorenzo pleasure himself.

I can almost feel him in my hand, sliding and stuttering.

"Fuck, Sophia." I meet his gaze, find his hot and wild and fierce and hungry. "With me?"

I know what he's asking. "I…don't know if I can."

"Try, my love," he whispers. "Touch yourself. Watch me. Come with me."

Biting my lip, eyes sliding closed, I cover my sex with my hand, fingers wedged between my thighs. I slip my middle finger against my seam. Panting, afraid the nightmares will erupt all at once and ruin this beautiful moment, this experience with Lorenzo, I drag my finger up the seam… press the pad of my middle finger against my clit.

I gasp.

Lightning sears through me at the touch and my knees shake.

"Yes, Sophia," Lorenzo growls. "Perfect. So fucking gorgeous."

"Lorenzo," I breathe, forcing my eyes open so I can watch him, watch his hand blur on his cock, watch his knees dip and his stomach curl in with his gasps and groans. "Oh god."

"Does it feel good?" he asks.

I swirl my finger in a circle, and sensation rips through me—heat, wetness, desperation. "Yes," I answer, between gasps.

"Don't stop. I want to watch you come."

"You first," I say.

"I wish it was your hand," he breathes. "I wish you were in here with me. That would be my hand. Better yet, my mouth."

"Oh god, Ren," I breathe.

"Talk to me."

I shake my head, because I have no words, not with the heat and pressure building inside me. It's been so long since I've felt pleasure like this that it may as well be the first time—it's overwhelming and intense, and tears pool in my eyes and a sob hitches in my throat, and the edge of orgasm slides out of reach once more.

I close my eyes, frustrated and embarrassed. I hear the water shut off, hear the shower door open. Tears pool in my eyes—my emotions are at the surface all the time now, ever since I broke down with the girls. I hear fabric rustling. I turn away, shoulders shaking in anger at myself—at everything that's caused me to be so hung up.

I feel him behind me. I'm drawing deep, hard, slow breaths of panic and embarrassment and frustration.

His hands settle on my shoulders. I jolt at the touch, but then...instead of razors, I feel...him. Calluses and heat.

It's wonderful.

"Okay?" he whispers, lips near my ear, the words hot and hissing.

I nod. "Yes." I reach up and touch his hands with mine. "I am now. I'm sorry."

His lips touch my ear. "Don't apologize. All I want is to make you feel good. Anything that's not good, you stop."

"I'll try," I whisper.

His hands ghost down my arms, and goosebumps

cover my skin. I lean back a little, and feel his hot, wet, hard chest against my back. I give him more of my weight, and he accepts it, tucking his chin against my shoulder. I reach up and back, clasp the back of his head. His hands descend to rest on the upper swell of my hips. Each touch is slow and deliberate, giving me time to stop him.

I don't.

I don't want to.

I don't need to.

As long as I'm focused on Lorenzo, I can manage the fear and control the panic.

I grasp his wet hair, fingers dimpling into his scalp as he brings his hands around to flatten on my belly.

"Lorenzo," I murmur, squirming. "Don't. Not there. The skin—I'm not—it's not—I don't like it."

His lips brush my ear. "Hush, my love. *This*—" he dimples his fingertips gently in the skin of my belly that never returned to its former tautness, "created life. It is a beautiful thing, to me. There is no part of you that isn't perfect and beautiful and sexy."

I rest my head backward against his shoulder. "I'm so scared, Ren."

"Of what?"

"I don't know. Everything. That—" I hiccup a sob. "That I won't *be able* to feel good like that ever again. That I'll panic. That I'll have a flashback. That I...that I'm broken."

His hands slide down from my belly to my thighs— which I press tightly together, crossing one thigh over the other. I whimper, and his hands rise up to my waist once more.

"It's—" I force my breathing to slow. Force my eyes

open. "It's okay. Just…" I let go of his head and drop my hands to his, covering them as they rest on my hips.

I guide his hands back down to my thighs, leaning back against him so I'm off-balance, forcing myself to trust him. His hands splay open and he grips my thighs, dragging his touch up to my hipbone and then back down. His fingers drift inward, slipping between my tight-shut thighs.

I exhale shakily and relax the tension in my legs.

"Okay?" he whispers.

I nod. "Good."

He turns us so we're facing the mirror—it's a large mirror in front of a rather low sink, so our reflection reveals my body down to mid-thigh.

Where his hands are.

Mere inches from my sex.

He's behind me, cheek to my ear, chin to my shoulder, arms around me. My breasts hang heavy, my nipples pebbled and hard, silver-dollar-sized areolae darker than the rest of my flesh.

I look at his hands. Press mine against them and guide his touch back up to my belly, and then to my diaphragm, and then higher, until they're brushing the undersides of my breasts.

"Your tits are incredible," he murmurs.

His praise makes me flush. "Ren," I whisper.

"May I?" He breathes, the words felt against my ear as much as heard.

I can only manage a nod, dropping my hands from his. I reach back to clutch at his thighs, fingers digging into hard muscle as his hands flatten against my diaphragm, hesitate, and then score a hot path upward until he's cupping my breasts.

"Fuck, Sophia. Do you have any fucking clue how many times I've dreamed of getting to do this?"

"How many?" I ask.

"A million. A hundred million." A groan of delight as he fills his hands with my flesh. "They're even more amazing than I'd fantasized."

His touch is pleasure, not the pain I'd feared. The panic is still there, but the amazed wonder I feel at his touch occludes it. Especially when he flicks my nipples, sending a searing line of heat from breasts to sex.

"Ren," I breathe. "I…that feels good."

"Watch, Sophia." He releases a breast to touch my chin, and I open my eyes. "Look."

He scoops my aching breast into his hand again, and his thumb scrapes my nipple—I jerk, squealing as the sharp sensation shocks me. His hands are huge and sun-darkened and scarred and weathered and rough. They scrape against my sensitive, soft skin. His touch is gentle, but I can feel the titanic strength in his grip.

"Ohhh," I breathe, shaking as he fondles my breasts, tweaking, twisting, pinching, and caressing my nipples until I'm panting with the pleasure of it.

Yet the frustration still burns in my belly, boils just behind my sex. I know what I want, but I'm too frightened to ask, too embarrassed.

I'm a grown woman, but I'm terrified of saying what I want. Terrified of…

Myself.

My past.

My dreams.

My long-ingrained trauma response to everything—to being touched.

Yet this whole time, every touch of Lorenzo's hands has felt good. Nothing I've been afraid of has happened. No flashbacks. No panic attacks.

It's because it's him.

My Lorenzo.

He knows my heart. He knows the substance of my nightmares. He has fought for me, bled for me, killed for me.

He loves me.

He loves me.

And with that knowledge inside me, I can find the courage to let him help me fix the broken pieces of me.

I let the tension in my legs slacken, and then gradually let my stance adjust until my sex is exposed.

I meet his eyes in the mirror. "Ren," I whisper. "I…I want…"

"You're sure?" he asks.

"I…yes."

"Sophia, my love, there's no hurry. No pressure. I want to make only you feel good, however that looks."

I grab his hands and guide them down to my belly, hesitate, and then lower—just above my pudendum.

I'm panting—more nerves than fear, now, although I am afraid. The fear is part of me, I think. But *I* am in control.

Me.

No one else.

I trust him. I know him.

I am not chained to a cot in a cell.

I want this.

My fear does not rule me. My past trauma no longer defines me. I am a woman, with a woman's needs and

desires. I can trust Lorenzo to be gentle. To give me pleasure without pain.

I press my hand over his and guide his touch down
until his fingers cover the triangle of my sex. My eyes
squeeze shut at the intimate heat of his hand, the rough
sandpaper of his touch. My breath catches. He does nothing else, just waits.

"Soph?"

"I'm alright. Just..." I force my eyes open yet again
and look at his hand, covering me. He's searching my face
in the reflection, concerned, cautious. Ready to pull me
into his embrace the moment I show any sign of distress.

"I'm alright," I whisper. "Thank you for being so patient, Ren."

His other hand palms my cheek, turns my head toward his. His lips ghost over mine. "I love you, Sophia.
Whatever you want, whatever you need. I am yours. I'm
here for you."

I whimper at his words, the undisguised passion in
them like a bolt of heat to my heart, setting it to pounding,
making my stomach flip with desire, my heart crash with
love. "Kiss me?" I breathe. "Please?"

"God, yes," he growls.

His kiss is slow and gentle and delicate, his lips soft
and wet and warm. A surge of intense emotion floods my
system—an emotional response to the kiss.

Desire.

That's the feeling.

Need.

Desperate need swells within me—exactly as I

remember feeling for him when we were kids first discovering sex together in the hayloft by the light of a stolen lantern.

I let my tongue steal over his lip. Lean further back against him, wrap a hand around his nape and pull him down to me. Break, panting. "More."

He growls his desire, and gives me his tongue. I take it, taste it. Our kiss deepens, becomes a fury of mated mouths and panted breaths. I shift my legs apart to give him more access, and he takes it as the invitation it is.

His middle finger swipes up my tender seam, and I gasp into his kiss, break but don't pull away, panting against his mouth as he uses just the pad of his middle finger to pet my seam.

I inhale, a deep filling of my lungs, turn away from his mouth to look into the mirror; as I watch, Lorenzo slides his finger inside me.

I release my held breath on a whimper. "Ohhhh… god!" I cling to his neck as my legs shake.

"So tight, Soph. So wet."

I can't respond—I can barely catch my breath.

He delves inside me, exploring my depths. Withdraws, drags his now-glistening finger up…and touches my clit.

"Oh god!" I cry. "Ren!"

"You're so responsive, my beautiful one," he says, and I realize belatedly he's switched to our shared native language.

"More," I whisper.

He plunges his finger back inside me, withdraws it and smears my essence against my clit. My legs jerk, threaten to give out.

He cups my breasts in his other hand, teases my

nipples, tweaks and twists one and then the other, and smears my essence against my clit. I cry out, and my legs shake and turn to jelly, and he sets a slow, building rhythm. Slow circles at first that make me pant in time with his touch. And then faster, and faster, and now my hips start to writhe and gyrate, pressing into his touch as I pant and gasp.

"Ren," I whisper, his name a plea—for what precisely, I'm not sure.

"I've got you, my love," he murmurs. "Just let go."

Let go?

Of what?

How?

I am holding back, I realize, as I tune in more carefully to my body and my physical sensations—a word that cropped up more than once in my short-lived attempt at therapy was "disassociation." As in, I disconnect my mind from my body. It's not hard to figure out why: in order to mentally and emotionally survive that awful, endless nightmare, I had to go somewhere else in my mind. I had to disconnect from my body, and I have never really reconnected.

Until now.

Aware, now, of the physical disconnect, of the fact that I'm holding myself back from truly feeling and releasing, I can take steps to correct the situation.

Panting, knees shaking, teetering on the cusp of release but unable to reach the other side, I reach up and cup the side of Lorenzo's face, turn his face to mine, whispering. "I need to lie down, Ren. I don't think I can do this standing up anymore."

He scoops me into his arms like a groom carrying his

bride over the threshold and carries me out of the bathroom to the bed. With exquisite gentleness, he sets me
on the bed. For a moment, he stands beside the bed, bent
over me, and touches his lips to mine. I whimper, needing
more—I don't recognize myself, the sounds I'm making,
the need I feel; most unrecognizable of all is the softness
Lorenzo's attentions have engendered within me. I have
survived this long by virtue of unyielding hardness, hiding
my brokenness inside a shell of ice as hard as any diamond.

Lorenzo has shattered that shell, melted the ice.
Revealed my soft, broken center.

My only choice is to trust him with those pieces. To
yield that softness into his care.

I clasp his nape and pull him to me, deepening the
kiss. I part my mouth for him, accept his tongue, his breath,
his heat. The kiss sets fire to my veins, makes my stomach
surge and flip.

He slides a leg over me and then he's above me, strad-
dling me, one hand punched into the pillow beside my
face, the other tenderly caressing my cheek.

I pull away and look up at him—the onslaught of
panic is abrupt and punishing. A scream lodges in my
throat, trapped behind the breath I can't draw, can't release.

"Off!" I manage, the word choked. "Off, off. Please,
please—get off get off getoffgetoff*getoff*!"

He rolls away at the first syllable out of my mouth.
"I'm sorry, Sophia, I should have known—I should have
known. I'm so sorry, my love—I didn't think."

I shake my head, grab his hand and squeeze hard,
breathing through my nose to force my breathing to slow.
"I'm sorry, Ren. I just—the second you were above me
like that, I…I saw—*them*. Felt them."

He nuzzles my cheek. "I should have known. Forgive me."

I shake my head. "No, you couldn't have. I didn't know I'd react like that myself until it happened." I turn my face to his, brush my lips against his. "I don't want to give up, Ren."

He sighs, sadly, softly. "We can take a break. It's not giving up."

I shake my head again, turning toward him. "I was so close. I'm just—tense. Holding back. Or holding on to…" I sigh, struggling to find the words. "To everything. I want to let go, I just don't know how."

"How can I help you, my love?" he asks, sliding his hand from my shoulder down my arm to my hip.

"I wish I knew, Ren. It felt good, you touching me. I want to be able to let go. I want to be able to orgasm. To… share myself with you. I just…" I squeeze my eyes shut, fighting to properly and accurately express my inner turmoil. "I'm afraid—not of you. Never of you, Ren. I trust you with my life, with my body, and with my heart, I truly do. But the fear is…it's got deep roots, Ren. It's irrational, but that doesn't make it any less…"

"Real," he finishes for me. "Anything you want. Anything you need. I am here. I am for you. I am with you. Nothing is too much to ask."

The sweetness is almost too much, and my eyes burn again with a fresh wave of stupid, absurd, suddenly ever-present tears. "My god, Ren. How can a man like you, a warrior, a fighter, a killer…how can you be so sweet? So perfectly, wonderfully sweet?"

"I love you, Sophia. I don't know how else to answer."

Side by side, facing each other, I shimmy closer to

him, until our hips touch and my breasts are crushed between us and his manhood is a hot slack ridge low against my belly.

I let myself touch him—explore him. I caress his broad shoulder, his thick, hard arm. Pet his pec, trail my fingers up his abdomen, palm his hip. Scratch his back, and then soothe the scratched skin with a slow slide of my palm.

Heart pounding, I cup the taut, iron-hard bubble of his ass.

"I like being naked with you, Ren," I breathe.

"The way you touch me, Soph, it's…" his eyes close, and I could be mistaken but it almost seems like he's close to tears himself. "It's heaven."

"I'm sorry I can't give you more yet," I say.

He touches my lips. "No. None of that. No more apologies. Not ever. Whatever you feel comfortable with is all I want or need. I'm perfectly content just like this. But if you want more, you have only to ask."

"Maybe…" I lick my lips, letting out a nervous breath. "Maybe just kiss me? But…like this. Not…I don't think I can be on my back just yet."

He nuzzles my mouth with his. "I could kiss you for the rest of eternity, my darling."

I open my mouth to his, bury my fingers in his damp hair at the back of his head.

I lose track of time, then. It begins slowly. Delicate and subtle, tender and soft and hesitant. It builds slowly. From a series of lip-touches with the occasional questing tongue, it becomes a slide of mouth on mouth, tongues tangling as we battle for breath. And then it becomes hungry and wild, frantic—on my part at least. I am frantic for him, for the intimacy of kissing him, as if I can find the release I need simply by kissing.

I can't, however.

I need more.

I want more.

I pull my hips away, clutch his hand, guide it down between us. "Touch me, Ren. Please. I want to try again."

He brings our hands back up, presses my hand to his lips. His eyes are dark and deep and burgeoning with love as he presses my hand to his face and then drives his down between our bodies. He holds my eyes with his as he feathers a ghostly brush of a fingertip over my seam. I gasp, my eyes going wide. This gets me a hot grin.

"I've barely touched you, and you're gasping for me," he murmurs.

"It feels good."

"Guide me," he says. "Tell me what you like, what you want. Teach me how to pleasure you, Sophia, so I can make you weep with ecstasy unlike anything you've ever felt."

He drags that one thick, clever finger up my seam, and down, and up, and down, again and again, and each time he fits it ever so slightly deeper between my nether lips. With each pass, my breath comes quicker, until I'm panting rapidly as his finger finally, finally delves deep into my pulsing, drenched channel.

"You're wet for me, Sophia," he murmurs. "Wet and tight."

"Oh god, Ren, the way you touch me. It's so good." I close my eyes, feeling the tension in my shoulders, in my belly, in my thighs. I focus on his touch, will my muscles to relinquish their tension.

I start with my toes, my feet, my calves. Imagine them

melting into the bed. My thighs. My hips. My belly. Hands, arms, shoulders—melting, dissolving, disappearing.

There is no me. No past. No trauma. Only Ren, only his touch. Only the pleasure of his finger swiping deep inside me, slicking out and smearing my wetness over my hard, sensitive little clit, buried within the hood of soft, tender skin.

Now, I lose myself.

I knot my fingers in Ren's hair and pull him to me. Gasp against his mouth as heat and pressure build inside me, ratcheting with each swipe, circle, and delve of his finger.

I'm panting and whimpering now, and my hips begin to lift, to press into his touch as my climax at long last shudders through me. Or, the beginnings of one, at least.

It is merely a tremor, at first. My breath hitches, and my hips spasm, bucking up against his touch. He devours my mouth, his tongue insistently driving against mine as he drives his finger inside me, withdraws it to circle my clit faster and faster and faster until I'm trying desperately to fuck his finger.

The heat and pressure inside me become unbearable, the need to reach release all-consuming.

"Ren!" I cry. "Oh god, oh god, *Ren*, I—I need…"

"What, love? Tell me so I can give it to you."

"I need to come but I can't!"

He slows his touch but doesn't stop; he pulls back so he can meet my eyes. "Do you trust me?"

I nod—no hesitation. "Yes, Ren. I trust you."

He captures my mouth with his in a slow, gentle kiss, his lips sliding against mine and his tongue mating with mine, demanding more heat from me, pouring gasoline on the inferno of my trapped need.

Moving slowly and carefully, he pulls me onto him. Our bodies are flush, and I feel the hard press of his cock against me, digging against the seam of my entrance.

"Ren," I whisper, fighting panic. "I—I can't—"

"Trust me," he whispers. "I know. Just breathe. I've got you."

I squirm, feeling him pressing against my opening— the slightest movement and he'd be inside me. The thought doesn't terrify me as much as I thought it would. I'm not ready for that, but I can see myself being able to find my way to it, and soon.

Just not now.

I should have known better, though. Ren wouldn't do such a thing if he wasn't sure I was ready and that it was what I wanted.

Instead, he slides me up his body, dragging my sex up his belly, over his chest. He wriggles down while gripping me by the hips and guiding me further upward, until I'm sitting tall on my knees over his face.

I gaze down my body at him. "Ren, what are you doing?"

He grins up at me. "Hold on to the headboard, my goddess."

I grab the top of the headboard. "Okay, but what—?" His mouth meets my pussy, eliciting a ragged, shrill, shocked gasp from me. "Ren!"

I know of such things, of course. I've just never experienced it; Ren and I were too young and naive and inexperienced back then to know of things like this.

Once again, he begins slowly, merely kissing my

nether lips as if kissing my mouth, and then I feel his tongue swipe up the seam, once, twice, a third time. And then his tongue presses against my clit, and lightning strikes my core with sudden, nuclear heat. I scream, head thrown back, breasts arched to the ceiling as my hips spasm to shove my pussy against his questing, kissing mouth.

"Oh god! Oh my god!" I cry, tears of shocked wonder leaking down my face as the trapped heat and crushing pressure pulsating low inside me shudders, shivers. "REN!"

His big, strong hands frame my ass and pull me against his mouth, guiding me into motion—ride his face, he's asking. Grind on him. Take my pleasure from him.

His hands crush my ass as I close my eyes and start slowly, nervously, and hesitantly rocking back and forth, and he growls low in his chest as if lost in thrall to the taste of me. I find a rhythm, gradually, as I tune into my body.

I feel his tongue driving against my clit, a soft wet pressing thing that sends wave after wave of pleasure through me, and I feel his hands gripping my ass, and I feel the muscles in my legs working powerfully to provide movement; I feel my tits swaying and bouncing, aching and heavy, my nipples tight and hard and beaded into diamond points, begging for touch. I feel my core pulsing, feel heat billowing through me, feel the pressure growing and growing until I almost fear something inside me might crack, or break.

And then Ren slides one hand up and finds my breast, cupping the weight of one and rubbing his palm over my nipple until I shudder and gasp, and then does it again with the other. This gets a quiet wail out of me as the added attention sends the pulsing, cracking pressure into a new peak of frighteningly intense crescendo.

His other hand cups my ass for a moment, pulling
me against his mouth even harder, pulling me to ride him
faster, to let go. Let myself break. He'll catch me and put
me back together. That hand drifts around and he wedges
it under his chin, and then I feel his fingers teasing my sex,
trailing over my pussy—my legs are spread wide, and I'm
split open for him, bared to him, nothing hidden, nothing
closed. He drills one finger into my channel, and I whimper at the intrusion, gasping as his mouth devours my clit
with renewed intensity. It's not enough. But he knows—I
don't have to ask. He adds a second finger, and now I'm
almost full, and it feels…fuck, *so* good.

And now, with coordination that defies belief, Ren
plays me like a violin—he thrusts his fingers in and out of
my pussy, fucking me with them in slow, gentle rhythm;
he strums my nipples, too, twisting and tweaking, flicking
and pinching, cupping and squeezing the heavy globes
of flesh, worshipping, playing; he suckles my clit past his
teeth and flicks the tight bundle of nerves with his tongue.

White heat smashes through me and the pressure
swells and swells until I can't breathe and my belly is taut
and I'm lost to the rhythm and sensation, glutted on the
myriad sensations he's giving me. I reach down and clutch
at his head, pull him hard against my pussy, and I ride his
face, and I'm weeping and sobbing and laughing and groaning all at once as my orgasm finally, finally, finally shatters
through me.

I lose track of everything. nothing exists but Ren
and his fingers and his mouth and my climax, which
rips through me like a hurricane, and I don't know if I'm
screaming or crying, if I'm speaking Spanish or English or
Portuguese or some fucked up pidgin of all three.

I know only the ecstasy my lover is giving me.

It is ecstasy like nothing I've ever felt, like nothing I could ever conceive of.

I have absolutely no clue how long my orgasm lasts—I only know that when it finally subsides and releases me from its titanic grip, I'm shaken to the core, wrenched limp.

I have no strength left—none at all. I collapse onto him, and Ren slides me down his body, shifting me off so I'm tucked against his side with my head on his chest. I hear his heart beating—*bumBUMbumBUMbumBUM.*

He kicks the blanket out from underneath us, lifting his ass so he can whip it out and drape it over us both.

Still gasping for breath, shaking like a leaf and wracked with tremoring aftershocks, I press as much of my body against Ren's as I can. I need more of him. I need to get closer. His skin, his heat, his hardness, his muscles—I need him. I need the shelter of his body.

I throw a leg over his legs and I feel the soft give of his testicles against my thigh, and shift my leg over his cock. It's hard and thick and long. I remember being shocked at how big it was, the first time I saw it erect. The only penises I'd seen up until then had been slack and soft...and small.

With a quiet huff of need, Ren drives his hips up, grinding against my thigh in search of relief.

"Oh, Ren," I breathe.

At the sound of my voice, he drops his hips back to the bed and pushes my leg down. "My love."

I whimper as an aftershock makes me shudder. "Ren, that was..." I tilt my face up, kiss the underside of his jaw. "Thank you, Ren. *Thank* you."

"What else could I ever want but to give you pleasure?

Nothing, Sophia. Nothing. The sounds you make while coming for me are the sweetest music."

I huff a laugh. "When did you become a poet?"

"I'm not. I just want you to understand how you make me feel."

"Ren, I…I want…"

He turns his face down to meet mine, kisses me. "Tell me, my love. Anything."

"I want to make you feel good, too."

"Don't think about me. I don't want or need anything but you. Just like this. Whatever needs I may have can wait."

I search myself yet again.

The fear is still there—I don't think my fear of sex will go away all at once. But I can face the fear. Lorenzo gives me the courage—I know if I try something I'm not ready for and have to stop, he won't be upset, won't make me feel guilty.

He is my safety. My shelter from the storms of my trauma.

"I love you, Ren," I whisper. "And I want to try."

His breath hitches at the first part of my statement. "Soph," he says. "I said anything, and I meant it. But whatever you do, do for you. Not for me. You stop when you need to stop. You don't explain or apologize—not for anything, no matter what. Promise me that."

I nuzzle my nose against his jaw, the fullness of my heart a soft swelling tenderness for this man. "I promise."

He rests his hand on my hip, tucks his nose and mouth against the top of my head, and inhales my scent. "Then do with me as you will, my love. I am yours."

CHAPTER 8

THIS LITTLE BUBBLE

LORENZO

DESPITE MY REASSURING WORDS TO SOPHIA, I ache with the need for release. I would never put any kind of pressure on her to do anything, but in my secret heart, I cannot help but hope she is able to touch me. It feels selfish, but I am nothing if not honest with myself, if I don't always burden her with truths that would only overwhelm her, make her feel guilty, or pressure her into something she's not ready for.

I close my eyes and let my heart hammer in anticipation, holding absolutely still. I have the generous curve of her hip under my hand, the other stretched out beside me over the blanket.

Her hands are tucked between us. For a few moments, she just lays partly on me, head on my chest, thigh draped over mine, breathing. And then she rests her hand on my chest, over my sternum. She explores my chest, palming my pecs, thumbing my nipples. Then my abs, my ribs, my sides. Her touch moves in a circle, stomach to waist to chest, opposite side to stomach and back to my chest again.

A pause, her hand resting on my stomach.

I hear her swallow. Feel her take a deep breath, hold it.

She lets it out slowly, shakily.

"You're the only one," she whispers.

"The only one what, darling?" I ask.

"The only one," she repeats. "Anything good I have ever felt has come from you." She sighs, the sound shaky, emotional. "I'm sorry I'm such a weepy, pathetic mess."

"I told you, no apologies. I don't want them, I don't need them." I cup her cheek, brush my thumb over her lips. "I *want* you to feel. If you must cry, then cry. If you want to laugh, then laugh. Scream. Get angry. *Use* me, Sophia. Take everything you want and need from me. I want *all* of your emotions. You've had everything you are and everything you feel locked away inside that icy box for so long. You had to, I understand that. But you don't have to anymore. So give me all of your emotions, whatever they are. Trust me with them."

She shudders, sobs. "I'm trying to find the courage to touch you, but I—"

"Soph, I told you—"

She covers my mouth with her hand. "Hush, Ren. Let me speak." She exhales slowly, starts over. "But I have to...I have to understand what I'm feeling. I have to talk it out, I think. I don't mean to tease."

"I know."

"I just have this big tangled knot of fear inside me. It comes from everything that happened, I think. The... those days in the cell, all those men doing what they did. Then being drugged. Married off to a monster. Rafael using me as a receptacle so he could get his son. The birth. The massacre. Crossing the jungle, alone, bleeding, barefoot." She shudders a half-sob. "There was pain, and anger, and shame. But more than any of that, I was *terrified*. I have lived with that fear ever since. The ice queen thing? That was to try not to be afraid. To not show it."

"That makes sense."

She roams my stomach and chest once more, slow, delicate circles with her palm, and then light scratching trails with her nails. "I am afraid of men. Of being touched. Of touching—Rafael, he made me…" she shakes her head. "I can't speak of it."

"You don't have to."

She's quiet for a long time, stroking my chest and stomach all the while. "I won't be afraid anymore. It's not a fear of anything specific, just this leftover mess inside me. I hate it. I want it gone."

"It may just take time."

'I know," she says. "But being with you…it helps, Ren. I trust you, and that's precious to me. I trust the Arrows, of course, and now I also trust the girls. But it's different with you. You know all of me. You know who I was and how I became Inez. You have known my body. You have never wavered in your love for me, even after years of not knowing if I was alive. You never even got upset that I'd stayed away from you, that I hid from you for so long."

"I always understood why you left and why you hid."

She nuzzles my jaw. "I know. And I am grateful for that. For all that you are, Lorenzo." She sighs again. "But now, I…I have to face this fear of touching you. I guess… it's complicated. I *want* to. For me—to know that I can. I want to have my sexuality back. Those men and Rafael stole it from me. But it's *mine*. Letting you touch me, letting you see me naked…that was a big step for me, Ren."

"I know," I say. "And that's why I would understand if you need to take a break."

"I don't want to," she says, shaking her head. "I face things head-on. I always have. Right now, this irrational fear of intimacy is the enemy, and I *will not* let it rule me anymore. I'm not afraid of you. I'm not afraid of being with you. I'm not afraid of touching you. The fear is trying to tell me that something bad will happen if I don't run away and hide from anyone and everyone who could possibly hurt me. It's trying to tell me that if I touch you, I'll end up back in that cell, chained to that cot. I know it's false. Letting you see me naked was terrifying, but you made me…you make me feel beautiful. Letting you touch me was scary too, but now I feel…incredible, Ren. Free…or somewhat more free, at least. Lighter. It's like…like having that breakdown with the girls opened the floodgates and now I have to just bulldoze through all this."

I chew on all that for a few moments. "I really do understand, my love. My commitment to you remains the same—whatever you need, I am here to provide, as long as it's within my power to do so. If you need to wrestle with your demons, I will fight them with you. Even if that's just lying here and letting you find your way to touching me." I huff a laugh. "Which will be no great hardship, let me assure you."

She laughs. "I hope not." She goes serious, then. "I just want you to understand that I don't know how this will go. I may have to stop. And I don't want you to think it's you, or that I don't—"

I touch her lips. "I *know*. Even if I'm about to come, Sophia, if you need to stop, you stop. Spare no thought for me. Only for yourself."

"You are the most amazing man I've ever known." She shakes her head. "I love you, Ren. So much."

I choke on my emotions, a thick swirl of them lodged in my throat. "The sweetest words I could ever hope to hear, my love."

She lets out a breath, a slow, shaky exhale through pursed lips. Nuzzles her nose and lips against the side of my chest. Her short, blunt fingernails trail down my centerline from breastbone to navel; even the hint of a possibility of her touching me has my stomach curling inward in anticipation. I have to force myself to relax, to breathe.

I can't help that I'm already hard as an iron girder, aching with desperation to have her hand wrapped around me.

Sophia tilts her head to look at me. "Ren, I'm—"

I touch the underside of her chin with my finger and kiss her—softly, sweetly, lips only. "No explanations, no apologies. Anything you have to say, I will hear. But there is nothing that needs to be said, in this moment. Take your time. Whatever you need to do, however you need to do it. I'm here, I'm yours."

She kisses me back, a quick, soft peck. "I know you must be feeling...a lot of things ."

I nod. "Yes, of course. But this is about you right now, Sophia. Not me."

"But I don't want our whole relationship to be about me."

"It's not. It won't be. But this moment is. It has to be. I *want* it to be. I can't make everything all better, no matter how badly I want to. If I could fix the things that have hurt you and made you feel broken with a snap of my fingers, I would. If I could take your pain into myself, I would. If all I can do is lie here and be supportive and understanding as you work through this, then that's what I'll do, gladly and willingly."

She huffs. "But you're still not telling me what you're feeling."

"Do you want me to?" I ask. "I would not complicate things by inserting my silly feelings into a situation that isn't about me."

"Your feelings aren't silly, Ren."

I kiss her again. "No, I suppose not. But they're not important right now. And if I'm being honest, I think you're trying, perhaps subconsciously, to make this a conversation so you can avoid the thing you're afraid of."

Her brow furrows as she considers this. "Fuck. You're right."

She pulls away out of kissing distance, her head on the round of my shoulder, searching me with her dark eyes. I hold her gaze, smiling, hoping my expression conveys patience and understanding and love.

Her gaze flits away from mine after a moment, dancing over my chest to the edge of the blanket resting an inch or so above my navel. She stops breathing, swallows hard—a heartbeat passes in silence. Another. And then she peels the blanket down, exposing my ramrod-stiff cock inch by inch, until the blanket is at my knees.

She sucks in a sharp breath. "You're magnificent, Lorenzo. Do you know that?"

I shrug. "I am pleased you think so, *amor*."

She hesitates, clutching the blanket down near my knee so tightly her knuckles are white, and then releases her grip, flexing her fingers as if to release the tension. Her palm settles on my thigh. Drifts up, up, up to my hipbone. Lifts, hovers over my erection…and then drops back to my hip.

She buries her face in my chest, making a frustrated whining sound. "I'm sorry. I'm sorry."

"No apologies, remember? As long as you need. Or we just rest for now and you try again another time."

"I want to, though, that's what's so frustrating. You made me feel so good. You gave me my first orgasm in I don't even know how long. Since the last time you made me come, I suppose. I *want* to touch you. I *want* to make you feel good."

"Holding you—"

"Oh, *stop*, Lorenzo," she snaps, a hint of the old Inez peeking through. "Be real for a second. Be selfish."

"Never. And I *am* being real." I sigh. "But, yes, Sophia. I want you to touch me. Very, very badly. I've dreamed of it and daydreamed of it for so long. But it has to be *right*. It has to be in *your* time."

She swallows noisily again, staring at me. "Kiss me, Ren. Please. Kiss me..." she trails off, closing the distance between our mouths, so her whisper huffs hot on my lips. "Kiss me like you want me."

I tighten my grip on her hip and cup her cheek, touch my lips to hers, tease her with my breath, flick my tongue against her teeth. She pushes her mouth to mine, whimpering a soft gasp of desire when I pull away, teasing, teasing, and then slash my tongue into her mouth. "Ren!" she hisses. "Please."

I growl my need for her and crash my mouth onto hers, giving her the kiss she wants—hot, hard, aggressive, and full of my raging desire for her. We kiss this way for a moment or two, heads angling this way and that as we battle for supremacy.

She pulls away first, panting. "It gives me courage when you kiss me like that, Lorenzo."

I slowly allow my hand to drift from her hipbone to

the small of her back, and then down to her ass. Her eyes fly wide and she sucks in a breath, holds it.

"Okay?" I ask.

She nods jerkily. "Yes. I...yes. It's good."

"Thank god, because this ass of yours," I squeeze it. "It's fucking marvelous."

She blushes, turning her face into my chest. "I'm not good at compliments."

"That's alright. I'll give them until you are, and then keep on giving them."

She kisses my chest, and then turns and tilts her face down, staring at my manhood, and her hand on my thigh mere inches away.

"I can do this," she breathes, more to herself than to me. "I want to. I will. I am."

Jerkily, hesitantly, she moves her hand inward on my thigh, and then upward by millimeters. Halts with her thumb nearly touching the bottom of my balls. I can't breathe, the anticipation too intense.

She lifts her hand as if to grasp me, and then her fingers clench into a fist and rest on my thigh again. "Fuck."

"It's alright. It's okay, Sophia."

She rolls her head on me in a negative shake. "It's not. I'm stronger than this."

"It's okay if you're not."

"There's just this...barrier. I feel my desire for you, my need for you. But there's the fear, the stupid, irrational fear." A pause. "I'm not afraid anymore. You are mine and I am yours. You love me. I love you. You're my man and I want to make you feel good."

This is to me, but more so to herself. I don't feel like

she needs a response, so I just caress her ass, her hip, her thigh, and kiss the top of her head.

She grips my thigh in strong fingers, reaches up with her other hand and forces my head down. Claims my mouth with hers, lips parted, tongue seeking.

I don't tease or toy this time—I meet her desperation with my own. I groan in delight at the taste of her mouth, the wild hunger in her kiss.

My groan is the thing that sends her over the edge, I think.

She buries herself into the kiss, all soft, wet lips and seeking tongue, fingers dancing over my cheek and temple and stealing into my hair and clutching it, knotted and grasping tight, keeping me a willing prisoner to her kiss.

My desire swells and my cock throbs with need, and I turn toward her, hitch her higher and tilt her toward me, gripping the sweet, lush swell of her beautiful ass, palming the weight of it, exploring the generous fullness of it as I've dreamed of doing for so, so long.

Sophia breaks the kiss with an exhaled whimper, presses her forehead to my lips…

And cups my balls in her palm. A raw groan escapes me, and my cock twitches. Her breath catches in her throat on a choked gasp.

My fingers dig into her ass, clutching a thick handful of flesh as she simply holds me like that for a long moment.

I'm not breathing; I don't dare.

Her touch edges upward…slowly, so slowly. Finally, after what feels like a thousand years, she wraps her fingers around my cock.

A low, rough, ragged groan rips from her lips as she clutches me at the base, turning her face into my chest and inhaling deeply, her breasts swelling against my ribs. "Oh god, oh god," she whimpers. "I forgot."

"Forgot..."I have to clear my throat and try again. "Forgot what, *amor*?"

Her fingers, curled loosely around my shaft, slide upward. "How much I love the feel of your cock in my hand." She grips the head, squeezing, and then returns her hand down my shaft again.

"I haven't forgotten how good your touch feels, my love." I cup her cheek and tilt her face up to mine and kiss her. "It feels like heaven."

She palms me again, cupping and fondling my heavy, tight, aching balls until my erection throbs, and then caresses my length again. Her mouth moves on mine. "Ren, am I...is it..." she gasps as I thrust into her hand. "Do you like it?"

I grunt a tense laugh. "Like it? Sophia...fuck. I don't remember anything feeling this good, ever."

She pulls her face away from mine and looks down to watch as she begins stroking my length in slow, gliding caresses. Occasionally, she glances up at me, as if to assess my reactions—I let my face show everything. Every stroke, every twist, I groan, gasp, grunt, mouth hanging open, brow furrowed. My stomach hollows inward as she strokes my pulsating erection, and now my thighs begin to bunch, my heels to dig into the mattress, scrabbling for purchase as she caresses me in unhurried rhythm. If anything, the longer she caresses me, the slower she goes, and the raw, adoring affection I both see and feel in her touch is the most sensual and erotic thing I've ever experienced.

"Soph," I whisper, arching fully off the bed as she changes it up, giving me short, shallow, twisting jerks around the head of my cock. "Oh fuck. *Fuck*, honey. *Fuck*, that feels so good."

She watches my face as she plunges her fist down my shaft, a shy smile playing on her lips as she sees my unaffected ecstasy arrange my features into an awed, desperate grimace.

"Ren," she breathes. "You're beautiful, my love. So beautiful. I could touch you like this forever."

"Y-yeh—" I gulp around the broken attempt to answer. "Yes—yes, please."

She laughs, a soft, breathy giggle. My Sophia—giggling, girlish, and aroused. "Are you going to come soon? I want you to."

"Uh—unnhhh!" I can't even manage an affirmative grunt as she releases my cock to squeeze my balls again. "I—fuck—oh fuck, Soph. *Please*—oh god. Ohgodplease—"

She touches her lips to my cheek, mouth open in a grin, nuzzling me with her. "Please what, my handsome warrior?"

"I don't want you to—to stop," I admit. "Feels—ohhh god, Sophia...It feels too—"

I break off with a long, ragged groan as she strokes my length from root to tip and then clutches my cock around the head in a loose, soft grip, slowly pumping there in short little caresses that have me arching off the bed again with a guttural snarl.

She gasps when I make the raw, animal sound of need.

My eyes fly open and I drop to bed. "I'm sorry, I didn't mean to scare you," I say.

"You didn't," she answers, "I liked that sound. I liked knowing I made you make it."

I search her face and see only the truth written there.

My worry that I'd frightened her with my feral, aggressive growl pulled me back from the edge—which means I get to let her bring me back there all over again.

"Did you imagine this, Ren?" she asks, watching me as she rhythmically strokes my length. "Me touching you like this?"

"Yes," I answer.

"Did you touch yourself while you imagined me doing it?"

I nod. "All the time."

"Tell me what you pictured me doing, Ren."

"Exactly this."

"What else?"

"Everything, Sophia."

"You can tell me. I want to hear everything and anything you fantasized about me doing to you." She pauses to caress my balls again, spends a few moments there, watching me as I react to her touch. "I want to know. I may not be able to do all of them yet, but I want to know."

"Your mouth," I murmur, trusting her to know what she's asking. "I imagined you taking me in your mouth and stroking me with your hands. I imagined you beneath me in the bed jerking me off until I come all over your big, perfect tits."

She gasps. "Ren!" It's a gasp of shock but not disgust.

"Just a...just a fantasy, Sophia," I mutter, and then groan low in my throat as she slides her fist up to my tip, twists there, and then plunges down to my root, pumping and pumping and pumping there faster and faster. "I would—oh fuck, oh fuck, Soph! I'd—fuck! I'd never ask you to—ohhhh fuck."

"Why not?"

"It's just a fantasy. I would never want you to feel…" I pause, swallowing hard and gasping to catch my breath as she abruptly stops pumping and resumes slow caresses from root to tip.

"To feel what?"

"Disrespected or…or degraded. Used."

"If I chose to make you come on my chest, you would not be disrespecting me." She turns her face to mine, kissing me as she leisurely strokes my cock. "You think my breasts are…perfect?" There's a note of delicate, hesitant, hope in her voice.

I roll into her, gently easing her to her back while being careful to not move above her, but rather angle toward her. I see a hint of fear flash over her expression; she closes her eyes, momentarily squeezing me as she works through the moment.

"Breathe, my love. Breathe."

She inhales sharply, a deep gasp as if surfacing after a free dive. "Okay," she pants. "I'm okay. I'm okay."

I rest my hand on her belly, hold her eyes as I slide my touch upward. "Stop me at any time."

She shakes her head. "No. I won't. It's you."

"That's right," I whisper. "It's me. I'm touching you. You're touching me. We're sharing this, *amor*. It's beautiful, isn't it?"

She nods, eyes hazy with emotion. "Yes. Beautiful."

"Just like in the bathroom," I tell her. "I'm gonna touch you—touch your breasts."

She nods. "Please."

I cup a breast, rolling her nipple beneath my thumb; she exhales slowly, shakily, her eyes cutting from mine to where her hand is slowly stroking my length. "Perfect," I whisper. "Absolutely perfect."

I kiss her mouth, and then wrap my lips around her nipple, flick it with my tongue. She jerks, gasping shrilly, her grip on my cock pulsing tight.

"Ohmygod! Ren!" She pants.

I stretch over her torso, bring her far breast up toward me and suckle her pert, tight nipple into my mouth and suck hard on it. Her gasp is loud and wild, and she jerks against me, squeezes my cock again, and then remembers herself and resumes stroking.

This time, her caresses are greedy and needy. She whimpers as I move back to her other breast, arching to press herself into my mouth, and her fist tightens around my erection, carving down my length and blurring back up, faster and faster. I manage to keep control over myself for a few more moments, shifting from one breast to the other, licking and kissing and suckling on her perfect, delicious little nipples.

But then I can't function anymore, not with the need rising in me like magma swelling up into the mouth of a raging volcano, threatening to overflow. I rest my face against her breast, gasping soft grunts as she pumps my cock.

"Ren?" she breathes.

I can only manage another grunt, my abs contracting as I start to buck into her fist.

"Are you gonna come?" She breathes. "I want you to come for me. Please, Ren."

"I—" Whatever I was going to say is lost in a ragged groan as my climax rises, rises, and I—lying on my side angled toward her—try to thrust into her touch. "Sophia, oh god. Oh god—don't stop. Please."

She lifts up and wriggles higher, closer to me, presses her body against mine so her breasts crush against me and her thighs press against mine and her hand shifts between our bodies as she continues to stroke me. Her mouth meets mine, and then all of a sudden it's not just a kiss but a mating of our souls through our mouths, tongues dancing and tangling, all breath and wet lips sliding and turning and seeking more.

I think nothing of it when she tips me sideways so I have no choice but to straddle her hips, so lost am I in the drowning joy of our kiss, in the wild ecstasy of her touch, now gone slow and sensual, delivering long soft caresses of my length, twisting and pumping and then stroking again. She grabs at my ass, clawing her nails into it and pulling at me, encouraging me to move, to buck, to thrust. On my hands and knees above her, I groan into our kiss, gasping a growl when she sucks my tongue into her mouth, lifting up to press harder into me. Her grip on my ass releases, becomes a soothing petting caress of one side and the other, of my hamstrings, and then back to my ass for a moment before retreating to grip my cock in both fists. She pumps my length like that for a while, until I'm thrusting into her fists with rough, animal grunts.

"Oh fuck, Soph!" I snarl. "Oh fuck. I'm gonna come, sweetheart. I'm—you're gonna make me explode, my love."

She palms my balls in one hand and pumps my length with the other, squeezing my balls until I grunt in near-pain, and then releasing. She does that in time with her strokes, then—squeeze and jerk, release, squeeze and jerk, release. I've lost all control, now. There's no way to kiss her, or speak, or hold back. There's only her touch. Only Sophia, giving me pleasure. Taking it from me. Finding her freedom from the past in me.

"Ren," she whispers. "Now, sweetheart. Let go."

I have no choice but to obey. Her order is the catalyst for my release; her words are accompanied by a renewed frenzy of hard, fast, pumping strokes of my length with one hand, the other gently fondling and massaging my balls, and her lips touch my chin, my jaw, the corner of my mouth, my cheekbones, my closed eyes. I'm rocking on my hands and knees, bucking wildly into her fist, grunting like a caveman as my climax boils in my balls and burns up my erection.

"Soph—Sophia—fuck—fuck…I'm…oh god, Soph, I'm coming, I'm coming!"

"Watch, Ren!" she cries. "Watch! I want us both to watch me make you come all over my tits."

My eyes fly wide as I realize I'm on top of her, above her, kneeling astride her—I couldn't stop or move in this moment if there was a gun to my head, and I see nothing but arousal in her eyes. Her big, brown, smooth, lush tits jiggle hypnotically as she jerks my length.

"Fuck, Soph," I snarl. "Your tits are fucking perfect."

"They're all for you, Ren," she murmurs. "Paint them with your come, my love. Show me. Show me your fantasy."

"Better—" I grunt, losing my train of thought as I hold back, not wanting this to end. "Better than—oh fuck, I can't—I can't stop it, Sophia."

"Come for me, Ren," She pleads. "Show me, show me how good I'm making you feel. Fucking *give* it to me, sweetheart."

"Tell me—" I gasp, fucking her fists. "Tell me you—oh fuck, I'm—it's—oh fuck. Tell me you love me, Sophia."

Her teeth seize my earlobe, and then her breath huffs hot in my ear, and her words bathe my soul. "I love you with all that I am, Lorenzo Oliveira Araujo." She cups and squeezes my balls and speeds the slide of her fist down my length to a wild blur that leaves me breathless and arched and frozen as my orgasm reaches the point of no return. "Now—*please*, my love, I beg you—*come*. Come on my tits. Bathe me with your love."

I wrench my eyes open, soak up the sight beneath me: my Sophia, her hair loose in a wild black cloud around her shoulders, eyes burnished and blazing with love and erotic need and sensuality, her big perfect tits jiggling for me as she jerks my cock to completion, mouth open, eyes wide and fixed on my cock.

I fuck into her fist once, hard, and then my climax erupts out of me, ripping a guttural, broken gasp out of my throat. A hot white rope of cum ribbons out of me and lays in a thick stripe across her heaving chest, and she gasps, giggles breathlessly.

"Ren, yes, more! More!" She uses both hands, then, pumping me as fast as her hands can move.

I jerk into her fists, spurting another stream of seed over her breasts. She lets go of me with one hand and cradles her tits together with the other and arches her chest up high and proud. She slows her touch, then, going soft and loving and sweet and affectionate, her eyes hungrily watching my cock. I come hard, again, and the ribbon of cum lays across her tits, coating one nipple and dribbling down the plump round curve toward her diaphragm. Another spasm wrenches me, another hot line roping out of me—this one with far less force, trickling over her knuckles. Her expression is one of wonder and joy and arousal, pure and unadulterated and transformative. This is a Sophia I've never seen—free, full of life and love and joy, radiant and nearly divine, to my eyes.

She continues caressing my cock, pumping my length to milk every last droplet out of me, until her hand is coated and dripping with my seed. Gasping and shaky, I drop heavily to the mattress beside Sophia.

She has a dreamy smile on her face as she holds up her hand, watching my come slide slowly down over her knuckles. She turns her head to look at me, the dreamy, happy smile on her face. "Ren, that was…" she shakes her head. "Incredible. So hot."

I laugh. "You cannot know how amazing that felt for me, Sophia."

She arches an eyebrow. "I had not orgasmed for… well, I don't even know how long…until a few minutes ago, Ren. I think I *do* understand."

"True," I murmur. "But I got all the pleasure out of that."

She returns her gaze to her hand for a moment or two, and then looks at me once more, the smile fading a little. "I'm…actually a bit shocked at how much I enjoyed doing that," she whispers, her gaze darting away in embarrassment. "Seeing you lose control, knowing I made you feel that way? It's not a sexual enjoyment, it's…I don't know how to explain it, Ren. I…" she's remembering, and becoming mortified. "The things I said…I don't know who that was."

"Hey," I say, touching her chin to turn and face mine. "Don't go away."

She frowns. "I'm not."

"No, I mean…the you who said those things, did that to me—*for* me—don't go away. She's a new version of you, and I have to stay, I really, *really* like her."

She grins. "Truly?"

"Absolutely." I lean in and kiss her, soft and sweet. "And not just because of how it felt—which was, I kid you not, the most incredible thing I've ever experienced." I cup her cheek, hold her gaze. "You were radiant, Sophia. Full of light and joy. I've never seen you like that. I want to see you like that all the time."

"Radiant?" she breathes.

I can't think of the word I want in English, so I switch to my native language. "Luminous. Free and happy and…" I shrug, go back to English. "Like you could fly."

She shudders, lets out a shaky sigh. "Being able to do that, to share that with you, to experience sexual intimacy again, Ren…you don't know what it means to me. You just don't—you *can't*. I feel…" she sniffles, wipes at her eyes with her clean hand—the other is resting on her belly. "Like a new woman…like a woman, period. Beautiful. Worthy of desire. Worthy at all—of anything." The last sentence is whispered.

"Ohhhh…Sophia. My sweet, beautiful Sophia. You *are* worthy. So, *so* worthy."

She lets out a long sigh. "Thank you, Ren. For…well, everything. For loving me the way you do. For being patient with me."

"You said it first, darling: you're the only one."

She smiles at me—a sweet, soft, shy smile unlike any I've seen on her face in all the years I've known her. "I'm gonna go clean up."

"Let me," I protest.

She shakes her head, leans over me, breasts brushing my chest, and kisses me. "No. Stay, please." She rolls out of bed and traipses for the bathroom.

"Gotta admit I enjoy the view," I say, admiring the violin curve of her back and the swell of her hips and the taut, round bell of her heart-shaped ass. "A whole hell of a lot."

She grins at me over her shoulder as she enters the bathroom. She twists on the faucet, but before she rinses her hand, she looks at me, at her hand, and then in a darting movement, she touches her tongue to the mess on her hand. She makes a surprised face, laughing. "Oh! It's…" another tiny taste. "Not what I was expecting."

I laugh. "You're crazy."

She shrugs and washes her hands, and then wets a washcloth and wipes down her chest. Her return walk from the bathroom to the bed is a sexy, alluring saunter. All swaying hips and bouncing tits, pussy playing peekaboo with each step, her eyes on me—hungry, eager.

And exhausted, beneath all that.

I hold out my arm, and she crawls onto the bed and snuggles up against me, pressing her soft, generous curves against me, sighing happily.

"This may just be my favorite place in the world," she whispers, wriggling against me until we're tangled up like cords in a drawer. "Right here, just like this."

"Me too."

I let the silence breathe around us, then.

But I become gradually aware of a change in her breathing—not into sleep, but into panic.

Faster and faster, and her shoulders heave.

"I'm—I'm s-s-sorry," she says through hiccuping sobs. "I d-don't know why I'm—c-crying. I'm so happy, and I…"

I wrap both arms around her and kiss her crown. "Let it out. It's alright. Just let it all out, Soph. Happy, sad, overwhelmed, confused—just feel it."

"I'm so s-s-s-sick of c-c-crying!"

"You've got a lot of overdue crying to get through, I think."

She nods, shaking and shuddering against me.

She cries for a long time—not wracked, violent sobs this time, but soft, quiet tears and delicate shudders.

How long? An hour? More? I don't know, don't care.

I have my Sophia in my arms. She loves me. We've found our intimacy. Our physical expression of our love.

All is right in the world.

At least, this little bubble of it.

CHAPTER 9

VOCÊ SENTE...

INEZ

WAKING UP IS A GRADUAL AFFAIR. THIS IS unusual for me—I always wake up suddenly, fully awake at precisely 5 am. You can set a clock by that, usually.

This time, all is confusing and disorienting. I don't remember falling asleep. I don't remember where I am. I'm hot. I'm not in my bed at the club.

Where am I?

I open my eyes—hotel room. Hotel?

My eyes are gritty with sleep. The blinds are open, revealing the glow of Las Vegas at night. Horns honk. Lights flash and strobe and coruscate on the ceiling.

The bed beneath me moves.

It's not a bed—it's a male body. I'm not just laying in bed with him, I'm fully *on top* of him, draped on him like I'm his blanket. My head is on his chest, my hands tucked over his big, hard shoulders. His hands are splayed possessively on my ass. I feel his cock wedged against my hip. My breasts are flattened against his chest.

Panic rifles through me—I'm hazy with sleep, disoriented, confused. I don't know where I am or who this is beneath me. I can't breathe, and I'm frozen in terror. A keening whine seeps out of my tight, hot throat.

"Mmmmm?" The man beneath me stirs, grunts a wordless query. "Soph?"

His voice is instantly soothing, but I'm caught in the grip of a panic attack. Tears squeeze out of my eyes, and I want nothing more than to crawl away, to get away, to hide in the corner.

I can't. I'm frozen.

The man senses it. "Hey, hey, hey—" his voice is soft and soothing and deep and reassuring and calm. "You're okay, Soph. You're safe."

Safe. *Safe?*

I'm not safe. I'm never safe. He's out there and Lorenzo—

"L-Lor—" I can't manage the rest past the teeth-clenched panic.

"It's me, sweetheart." His hands skate upward and roam my back in calming circles. "It's me. You're with me. We're at the Bellagio, in the penthouse."

"C-c-can't—br-bree—bree—breathe."

He does a sit-up with me in his arms, and suddenly I'm curled against his chest, sitting on his lap with my knees beneath me and his heart beating under my ear and his hands roaming, soothing.

His lips touch my ear. "You're okay. You were deep asleep. You just woke up confused. You're okay. You're safe. I've got you." He lifts my hand, puts his palm to mine. "Look at our hands. This is real."

Flashes: *the cell. Dirty, sweaty, evil, leering, drooling faces. Grunts. Violation. Rafael—locked in his room. Drugged. Used. Rewarded for cooperation—made his whore.*

Things I've still never spoken of.

"R-Rafael," I chatter.

"We're gonna catch him and you're gonna put a bullet in his fucking skull. But for right now, he's nowhere near us. We're safe. No one but Jakob knows where we are."

I shake my head—but that knowledge does ease the panic. "When I...when I told you what happened. After the wedding."

He goes still, hands tensing on me and then immediately gentling. "Yes, my love."

"I wasn't...entirely truthful."

"Okay. You can tell me anything."

"I made it sound like I got pregnant with Little Ren soon after. I didn't."

He doesn't answer right away. "I know, Soph. The timeline you gave never added up."

"I couldn't conceive. Not for...a long time. Years—I don't know how long—I was allowed to recover from what was done to me. Rafael allowed that. For his own selfish reasons, not out of care for me." I swallow hard. "Once I got my strength back, physically, it took a long, long time for me to..." I shake my head. "I was all but catatonic for a time. Could barely eat. I weighed less than a hundred pounds at one point."

"Fuck," he hisses. "*Soph*."

Telling eases the panic, somehow. It's been locked inside me for so long, eating away at me like battery acid corroding a terminal.

"Rafael didn't so much as enter the room with me for over a year. I heard gunfire at one point soon after the wedding—a lot of it. Rafael murdered my father and took over in a violent coup. He sent a doctor in, a psychologist.

A therapist. The doctor tried to touch me so he could examine me, and I snapped his neck." I shake my head. "I forgot about that until now. He didn't deserve it."

"No need to add to that list, Soph."

I shrug at this; perhaps, perhaps not.

"I came out of it on my own, very, very slowly. And as I came out of the catatonia, the…horror, the trauma, it sort of…crystallized. Hardened. Into…hate. Rage."

"Understandable."

"I got my health back. That took a while, too. It was… oh, nearly two years after the wedding before I left the room I was in. Before I even saw Rafael again. I had blocked out the wedding. Forgot. Or chose to forget. But then he… he visited me."

Lorenzo sighs. "Ah *deus, meu amor.*"

"It didn't start right away. He…he knew better than to just come at me, after what I went through. But I knew. I knew what he wanted. What he expected. And he knew I was dangerous. He drugged my food. I knew it after the first time, but I had to eat. My hate and anger were too great to allow me to hunger strike. So I ate. It was a sedative, mild enough that I remained conscious but powerful enough that I was helpless.

"And he…he would visit me, after it took hold. At first, he would just…touch me. Innocently. My arm, my leg. I couldn't stop it. He really was trying to restrain his… more violent and disgusting urges. Credit where credit is due, I suppose."

He opens his mouth to speak, but I touch his lips. "Let me get it all out."

He nods, swallowing hard. "I'm listening."

"For months, it was just that. As long as I ate the food

so he could visit me and do as he wished, I was otherwise left alone. I had a TV, books, puzzles, workout equipment, and a balcony where I could get fresh air. The room was locked and guarded." I close my eyes, but I see him again, and open them. "Then he stopped drugging my food. He visited me. Touched me. I was…confused, so I allowed it. He tried to grope my chest, and I hit him. Broke his nose. He sent six men in to beat me. When they were done, he sat beside me once more, and cleaned away the blood and told me that if I cooperated with him, I would not be hurt. And if I cooperated well enough, I could go outside. I could take walks under guard. I had not been outside other than the balcony for more than two years, remember."

"*Jesus Cristo.*"

"He left. I was not fed again for nearly three days. He came back. Told me to take my clothes off." I dig my nails into Lorenzo's chest. "And I did. I…I was weak. I didn't want to be beaten again. I wanted to be able to eat. So I took my clothes off."

"That's not weakness—"

"I—was—*WEAK*!" I scream, sudden and piercing. "I was weak! I gave him what he wanted. And…and I kept giving it to him. Whatever he wanted, I did it. All of it, no matter awful or disgusting or depraved." I shudder, choking back bile. "I refused one day, about six months after that first beating. I'd had enough. I hated myself. I hated him. I hated the things he liked. So I refused. I was beaten unconscious, electrocuted. Beaten again. Starved for almost a week."

"Fucking hell, Fucking *fuck* me," Lorenzo snarls, his voice shaky and wet. "Sophia…my Sophia."

"He came back once I was somewhat recovered. He

demanded, and I let him. He rewarded me with a week of freedom—from him. I was allowed to go outside whenever I wanted. A woman came and did my nails." I look at my hands. "I haven't had a manicure since, actually. I was given food. Wine. Cannabis. A massage. Rewards for behaving."

"He broke your spirit." Lorenzo's voice is just that—broken.

"No!" I hiss. "Not broken. Not entirely. Only...almost." I pause, thinking. "He was very busy running his empire. Things settled into something like normal. I stopped fighting him, stopped refusing. He was gone quite frequently and for long periods, so it...it wasn't so bad. For the most part, I was the mistress of the estate. I could ride wherever I wanted on his fine Arabians. With guards, of course. The men—his men he left there to guard me and his estate, they came to fear me. I was...cruel. Any man who crossed me in the slightest way, I killed him. If they stood too close, or spoke in a way I didn't like. Rafael knew this, of course. He allowed it. He liked it, I think. He thought I'd become what he wanted: a wife. Someone like him. But I was..." I shake my head. "The hate was festering. Growing. Everyone I saw around me, I hated. They looked at me, and I could tell they knew. They *knew* what had been done to me by my father. They *knew* what Rafael did to me. Sometimes, he would...he would lose control and hurt me. That's what he likes. He's a sadist. The sickest, most twisted, vilest, most perverted and disgusting sadist imaginable, and I truly hope you cannot imagine the things he enjoys."

I lapse into silence, and Lorenzo remains quiet, just holding me.

"That's how I became the kind of...of *creature* who

could do what I did. But it wasn't a year or two or three or whatever you may have thought. It was almost ten years that I was his...*belonging*. His pet. For *ten years*, I was Senhora Sousa. *La Víbora*, the Spanish-speaking workers called me—Rafael liked to hire Spanish-speaking laborers so they couldn't understand him when he spoke of business around them. *La Víbora*—The Viper. *La Reina de Hielo*—the Ice Queen. I earned those titles. I am not proud of who I was in those years. As bad as my father, as bad as Rafael. I was cruel and vicious and wicked and violent."

She lapses into silence for a while.

"And then...Rafael came home from a business trip, and he wanted what he wanted, and he got it, as always. And he...he was violent. Very, very violent. The details of that night will go with me to my grave, like the details of my time in that cell. Some things cannot be spoken of."

"I know," he whispers.

"I was left a ruin again. It took weeks to recover. Maybe even months—time is hard to measure when you're delirious from agony. The pain...such pain, Lorenzo." My eyes burn as I try to force away the memories. Instead, however, they roll through me. I see the things he did, and I let them exist.

I wallow in them.

I am wracked with sobs so violent I nearly vomit.

He holds me through it all.

Eventually, I recover enough to continue. And I feel....lighter, yet again. As if the ocean of acidic nightmare within me is reduced yet again, dwindling with each exorcism until it's nearly nothing.

"He impregnated me, that day. Neither of us realized it until I missed three periods. My cycle was never the same after the rapes. I still had them, they were just irregular. But when I missed three, and when I started getting sick at the sight of certain foods, I knew. I didn't tell him. I didn't tell anyone."

I sigh, swallow, continue.

"He came to me a few months later, after being away on business for a very long time, and I was...big." I make a rounding motion over my belly. "That earned me a reprieve from his attentions for the rest of the pregnancy. I relished it. And...plotted. The hate was so...*much*, so hot yet also so cold. So vicious and dark and powerful that I couldn't...I couldn't live with it anymore. And I knew the birth would be the end of the reprieve. I couldn't go back to taking his vile abuse. And the staff...the pity when they saw me waddling around the estate...the laughter, the disgust. They didn't understand how I could let a man like Rafael have me. They thought I...they didn't *know*. But I didn't see that. I was blinded by hate and rage."

"Sophia, my love—"

"Almost done, Ren." He kisses my crown, and I let the rest tumble out. "I came to hate the staff as much as I did Rafael. I planned to escape with the baby, and I was willing to do whatever I had to in order to get away. I didn't plan what actually happened. I went into labor early. I wasn't ready. The midwife wasn't there. My water broke and there were no drugs. It was just me alone on the bed, screaming, in agony, terrified that my child would die, or turn into Rafael, or...or be taken away. That I'd die before I could murder Rafael." I choke, swallow. "As a man, you cannot fathom what it feels like. I don't know if you have ever witnessed a woman giving birth, but we are not always exactly...rational...under the best of circumstances. And I was far, far from rational. The midwife showed up when I was about to actually give birth. And thank god for her, or I would have lost him. He was twisted, and she…she knew what to do." I shake my head, sniffle. "I regret her death, too, even though she was a mean, spiteful woman. Hers and the stableboy, most of all."

A brief silence.

"I was so…*mad*, so crazed, with rage and hate and pain and the hormones of birth….I don't know. I just snapped. I've told you the rest." Another pause. "I was eighteen when my father put me in that cell, and I was twenty-eight when I slaughtered Rafael's staff."

"Sophia, I…"

I turn in his arms so I can wrap my arms around his neck and bury my face in his throat, feel his pulse thrum against my nose. "There's nothing to say, Ren. That is who I am. I spent the next ten years hiding from all of that. Letting it all harden inside me like…" I shake my head. "I don't know."

"I have heard of a rare medical condition," Lorenzo says. "A woman becomes pregnant, but it isn't…*viável*."

"Viable," I offer the English word.

"Yes, viable. I am upset for you and….yes." He sighs, clears his throat. "Instead of miscarrying, the dead fetus stays inside the woman and fossilizes, essentially. It hardens into this thing. Calcifies, I think the word is. It makes her sick, after some time. I think that is what you mean."

I nod. "Yes. Exactly like that. And I had to get it out. With the girls. With you."

"Thank you for sharing that with me," Lorenzo says.

Silence for a while then. My eyes are heavy, and I feel

Lorenzo's breathing grow slow and deep. "Are you still awake?" I ask.

"Mmmm. *Um pouco.*"

"Earlier," I whisper. "What we did. What I…wanted you to…to do."

He stirs, clears his throat, coming more awake. "Mmmm-hmmm?"

"Was it…was I…" I swallow hard. "I don't know how to say it."

"You feel self-conscious," he guesses.

I roll a shoulder, answering in English because it's what comes easiest, at this point. "I…yes, I suppose so. I don't know what came over me." I can't help but snort. "Don't say it."

He chuckles. "I don't think I need to." He's still talking in Portuguese.

"I just…I don't know who that woman was, Ren. Saying those things, doing those things. It was almost like an out-of-body experience."

He's quiet for a while, considering his response. Or just trying not to fall asleep. "Sophia, that was…so fucking sexy." His half-asleep brain is drifting back and forth from one language to the other at random. "I know you have to be Inez, still, at times. But in private with me? Be *that* woman, the Sophia from yesterday. Don't be embarrassed or self-conscious. Nothing we do together can be wrong or bad or disgusting, as long as we both want it and enjoy it. I love you. I am honored that you trust me so much as to offer your body to me. Your heart. Your past. Everything you are, you are trusting to me. That is the most precious and priceless gift I could ever receive."

"Can I ask you a personal question?"

He laughs. "Sophia, I have no secrets from you."

"Have you ever done that? What we did?" I clear my throat. "The part where you...you know. On me."

He curls me closer and kisses my temple. "No. That was a first for me. It's not something I would normally think of doing."

"Why not? I'm just curious."

"The few other lovers or partners I've had aside from you—and they are very, very few—things were more geared to getting to actual sex. The occasional handjob, but that was just to get me ready for sex. Or a blowjob, sometimes just for the sake of it and other times as part of foreplay."

"Ren, I promise I will get there. I just don't know—"

He cuts me off with a finger over my lips, leans over me, eyes glittering in the gloom. "Hush, my love. What has come before for me is irrelevant. I have no expectations, truly I don't."

"But you have to want—"

"You. I want you. I want to share my life with you. I want to share my body with you. I want the intimacy of sex with you. But if intercourse isn't possible—if it is too frightening, too triggering, I will be perfectly and utterly happy with anything you are comfortable with." He sighs slowly. "To put it bluntly, ejaculation feels great, yes. But if all I wanted was to ejaculate, I would just jerk off, as I have done for years. What I want, what I care about, is sharing experiences with you. I'm not overly concerned with whether I come, or how, or where, really. And to be honest—because this can only work if we are both honest—yes, I do hope you become comfortable with intercourse. It is the deepest source of intimacy, the closest connection two people can share. But Sophia, my love, if we get there at all, it will be in your time and in your way. Just communicate with me. Tell me or show me what you want and what you need. If you can't find the words, if you are too nervous or scared to say it out loud, that's okay. Find a way to show me. All I want is your love, however you feel comfortable giving it to me."

My eyes burn and my heart threatens to swell and crack beyond the confines of my ribcage. "My god, I love you so much."

"That's all I need."

I nuzzle his jaw—some small, bitter, cynical, absurd part of me feels ridiculous and self-conscious at showing that kind of affection—at all, to anyone. It scares me nearly to panic being so vulnerable with him, showing him the softness in me. I've had to be so hard and so cold for so long, it's hard to relinquish the impulse to protect myself by walling off and controlling my emotions.

As if to prove to myself that I can conquer those demons, too—the ones that demand isolation and hardness and icy self-control and emotional rigidity—I dive deeper into softness, into affection. Into femininity. Not that softness, gentleness, or affection are the purview of women only. It's just…alien to me.

I nuzzle his jaw with my nose, my lips. Palm his cheek and caress his beard, scratch delicately with my fingernails. Press ghost-soft kisses to his cheeks, his nose, his upper lip, his brow, his ear, his chin.

He rumbles, a low, happy growl. "Soph…" his voice is tight with emotion. "Love that. So much."

I bury my face in the side of his throat, let my eyes

grow heavy, let them shutter closed. Focus on the safety of Lorenzo's arms around me. On the love between us.

I fall asleep again, and there are no dreams, no panic.

◆

When I wake again, gray pre-dawn light bathes the room. I'm spooning Lorenzo, his big, broad back curved against my belly and breasts, my knees tucked against his. I drowse like that for a while, basking in the feeling of happiness. Eventually my bladder drives me out of bed, but I hurry back as quickly as possible, resuming my position behind him. I curl my arm over his waist, under the heavy weight of his arm. Unable to fall back asleep but unwilling to leave the bed and the warmth of Ren's body and the soul-filling contentment of simply holding him, I find my mind wandering back to yesterday.

Specifically, to when he made me come with his mouth. God, that was good. Bizarre at first, but incredible. I feel my sex grow hot and damp at the visceral memory, and I squirm behind him as arousal builds low in my core.

I can't believe that was me last night, that I let—that I *begged*—Ren to come on my breasts. While I didn't derive any physical, sexual pleasure from it myself, the intensity of the situation was its own reward. But more so, Ren's pleasure was my reward. My freedom in being able to do such things with the man I love is its own reward.

I had him above me, and I didn't panic.

I *enjoyed* it.

I liked his weight over me, his presence surrounding me. Rather than oppressive and triggering, it was comforting and safe and…arousing. He makes me feel small and delicate and beautiful. I can show him what I have long thought of as weakness, and I can trust him with it. With all of me.

My hand rests on his belly, low, below his navel. Arousal burns in my veins, creates a pressure inside me— not a need for release, but a desire for him. I crave him. I crave his body. His heat, his weight, his power, his aggression, his need. I crave his touch. I crave his body—I need to feel his hardness in my hands.

I imagine Ren above me, his dark eyes piercing mine. I picture his mouth on my breasts, his hand between my legs. His cock in my hands. His hips between my thighs. His erection at my entrance. Filling me. Entering me.

Instead of terror and panic at the image, I feel… arousal, a hot pulsing pressure swelling inside me. Need for Ren.

Ren stirs, grumbles sleepy, wordless noises. His hips shift, tilt. I let my hand drift lower, and I encounter him waiting for me, a curled comma of manhood drooping against his thigh. I cup him, wondering at the strangeness of the fact that, like this, I can fit all of him in my cupped hand, yet when he grows to full erection, I need both hands to grip his entire shaft.

He exhales heavily, groaning quietly, and his hips tilt again; I feel his cock stir under my hand, thickening, hardening, growing. I palm his heavy soft warm balls, enjoying the feel of him, letting myself feel possessive of him.

He is *mine*. His body is *mine*. Just I am his, my body is his.

Slowly, his cock unfurls in my hand, becoming a hot, silky, rigid shaft in my fist. I stroke him, resting my cheek on his back, smiling to myself at the joy I feel in simply being able to do this. To touch him without fear, to enjoy his body without flashbacks or triggers.

"Soph?" Comes his low, rough, sleepy rumble. "Feels good."

He rolls to his back and I drape myself half on him, nuzzle his cheek and caress his big, beautiful cock.

"Good morning, my handsome lover," I whisper. "I woke up wanting you."

He turns his face to mine but doesn't kiss me. "I woke up with your hand on my cock. Can't get any better than that."

I grin against his jaw. "Hmmm. Maybe if you woke up in my mouth?"

"That would be pretty amazing," he agrees.

For another few moments, he simply lays on his back, eyes closed, a smile on his face, letting me caress him.

And then he rolls into me, forehead to forehead, his fingers diving between us to my clit. I let my hand drift down his length, not trying to make him come, just touching him for the pure joy of it—he, however, is trying to make me come.

And he succeeds, quickly.

A few circles of his fingers over my clit, and I'm a gasping, writhing mess, needing more. "Ren," I whisper. "I need you."

His answer is to roll to his back, taking me with him. His hands grip my hips as I straddle him, sitting on my shins with my body pressed against his, my hands burying in his hair. He palms my ass, growling a sound of pure male appreciation.

"Fuck, you've got a great ass," he murmurs. "You know that?"

"I do now," I whisper.

He starts to lift me up his body. "C'mere. You need to come for me."

I resist his pull, sitting down on his belly. My heart hammers in my chest as I let my true need grow into a rolling boil within me. "I don't want that right now, my love," I breathe, lips brushing his ear.

He squeezes my ass. "No? What do you want, then?"

Swallowing hard, nerves jangling in every cell—but just nerves, not fear—I reach between us, grasp his erection. Notch the broad plump tip against the seam of my pussy. "This," I whisper.

"Sophia, are you sure?" He cups my cheek, gazing into my eyes, searching me.

I stroke his length, keeping him pressed against my seam. "Yes," I whisper. "I'm sure. I want you. I woke up wanting you. Needing you. Needing *this*."

"Then show me," he growls.

I capture his mouth, grip him, panting into his mouth as I press his tip against my clit, eliciting a sharp gasp. His fingers claw into my ass, and I feel his muscles tense beneath me. Anticipating. Craving.

Abruptly, Lorenzo stills, grabs my wrist. "I'm not wearing—"

I kiss him quiet. "Unnecessary. All I'll say right now is that the birth caused what's called secondary infertility. I can't conceive again. And obviously, considering our respective situations, we are both free of any possible STDs."

"If you're sure," he says. "I won't put you at any kind of risk."

"I've had three different ob-gyns confirm my

infertility. We're safe." I rest my cheek against his. "And I don't want anything between us. I want to feel all of you."

He guides my face away so he can search me. "You aren't afraid? No panic?"

I smile at him, my heart melting all over again at his concern for nothing but me. "I'm not afraid. I just want you. I want to be one with you."

He releases my wrist and brushes the wild, inky cloud of my hair away from my face, and then roams his hands down my back to take hold of my ass once more. "I am yours, my love. Do with me what you will."

In my time, he means. He won't move until I tell him he can.

I'm in control.

I caress his length again, once, twice, and I feel him respond, hips tipping to push his cock into my touch. I rest my forehead on his and lower my hips—just a touch. Press him against my opening until the fat, thick head of his cock splits my lips apart. My heart, despite my claims of a lack of fear, starts to hammer madly, and my breath comes in shaky, gasping pants.

"Soph?" he whispers, concerned.

I cover his mouth with one hand for a moment. "I'm good. I'm okay. Just…try not to move. Please."

He runs his hands up my back, soothing over my shoulders and down my spine to my ass, repeating that circuit in comforting circles. "I won't. Not until you say so." His voice is tight, however, and I know it's costing him to hold still when I imagine all he wants is to bury himself inside me.

I keep hold of his cock at the root, eyes closed tight as I feel him splitting me open. I whimper as I lower my hips another inch, taking more of him; he's inside me up to his glans—I stroke his length until I meet my own flesh, and I feel him pulsing in my hands. I already feel so full, stretched open and aching with him, and he's barely inside me. I let go of him, rest my arms on his chest and grip his shoulders, head ducked, panting and whimpering—nervous, scared now, yes, but also aching with need for him, ready to take all of him, to be full of him, to be one with him, heart, mind, soul, and body.

I feel him shaking with the strain of holding so absolutely still when I know every fiber of his being must be screaming at him to move, to take me, to drive the rest of the way in.

I sink lower, take more of him—my mouth drops open and a shrill gasp escapes my throat as he fills me with another inch of his immense, hot cock.

I hold still, letting my body grow used to him, letting my sex stretch around him. I feel every last centimeter of him inside me, and I want more. I want all of him.

I pant breathlessly, mouth hanging open and shuddering against his throat. "Ren, you feel—oh god. Oh god, *Ren.*"

His grip on my ass tightens to the very edge of painful, and his answering growl is rough and ragged and raw. "Sophia, my sweet Sophia."

"Sweet?" I echo, huffing a laugh—the laugh makes me squeeze around him, and he jerks in response. "I'm *any*thing but sweet."

He tilts my face up to his. "Kiss me."

"I have morning breath."

"I don't care. Kiss me."

I slide my lips against his and part my mouth for his

tongue and kiss him, letting my love and need and desire and affection and passion and desperation bleed into the kiss, infuse it with wild hunger.

He pulls away after a moment, just enough to whisper. "See? Sweet."

"Only for you." I brush my mouth against his ear. "I'm ready for all of you, my love."

"Soph—" he starts.

I drive my hips slowly down toward his, and I let out a shrill, breathless cry as his huge, hard cock sinks into me, inch after inch of thick, hot manhood splitting me, stretching me, filling me to glutted, aching fullness. He's so big and it's been so long that it truly hurts at first, and I have to go still, trembling above him, whimpering as my pussy stretches to accommodate him.

"Oh god, Ren," I gasp. "You're—god, you're so much *bigger* than I remember."

"I'm not…" he trails off, groaning and trembling, and starts over. "I'm not hurting you?"

I can't answer—the painful burn of him fully impaled in me is rapidly morphing to something else.

Still a burn, still an ache, still a stretch, but…

A good kind of burn. A delicious ache. A glorious stretch.

"No," I whisper. "Not anymore. Now you just feel…" I knot my fingers in his hair and give an exploratory rock of my hips, and fireworks detonate inside me, heat and pressure and need burgeoning in every cell of my being. "Oh god, oh god, oh god—*Ren*."

I feel him respond to my testing movement, his hips involuntarily trying to drive up to meet me—it's a partial movement, a thrust restrained. "Sophia…*ah meu deus, meu amor, você se sente tão bem…*"

My arms wind around his neck and I cling to him, shaking. "My Ren, my love."

I tilt my hips to pull away, and his cock slicks and stutters through my tight, pulsing sex, and I cry out, gasping, head hanging to press my lips against his chest. I hesitate, drawing out the moment until I'm half-mad with the need to have him inside me—now that I know the wondrous beauty that is having him buried within me.

I nip his earlobe, breathe my request. "Ren, I want—I need you to…" I chicken out, and words fail me.

"What, my love? Anything."

"Take over, please. I need you to take over." The words tumble out, and now that they've been uttered, I feel free to be more bold. "Take me, Ren. Love me."

He cups my face, brushes my hair away, fingers diving into my hair, tilting my mouth to his, and he claims a kiss. "Yes, my love."

He kisses me and kisses me, all tangling tongues and sliding lips and gasps for breath, I have his cock wedged just inside me and I ache emptily for him to fill me, to take me, to bring us into union again. He scours the expanse of my back, palms sliding over my spine, and then he has a double handful of my ass and he grips me, hard and tight.

"Ready?" he breathes into my ear.

I nod. "Yes. Yes, please, yes, Ren."

"You'll tell me if—"

"It won't hurt, and I won't be afraid or panic. But if I do, I'll tell you." I cling to him, shake above him, gripping his hips with my thighs. "Now…take me."

He pulls me down his cock, thrusting slowly up into

me, and he groans a long, ragged sigh of ecstasy and relief as he buries himself to the hilt inside me. My cry is guttural and gasping, and I clutch his neck so hard I must surely be choking him, my face in his throat, his pulse a soothing, rapid stippling against my nose and lips.

"Again," I rasp. "Please. Again."

He drags me up his shaft and then immediately draws me back down, thrusting up into me again, and now we both groan in unison, and our mouths find each other instinctively.

"Ren!" I cry. "Yes—yes, my love. Again. Don't stop."

"It's good?" he asks.

"So much more than just good," I answer, lifting up to brace my hands on his pecs. "You're the best thing I've ever felt."

It's true. I burn with the ache of him as he gives me what I asked for—another slow stroke, lifting me up his cock and dragging me back down, thrusting so deep I feel him penetrate my very soul, ripping a ragged choking gasp of ecstasy from my lips.

Nothing has ever felt this way. Nothing—never. I hold his eyes as he sinks into me until my ass settles and squishes wide against his hips and thighs; he pulls my ass apart and drives deeper, and I cry out again, head hanging with my chin to my breastbone.

"More," I whisper, and then find my voice. "More!"

He groans at my demand, and his hands slide up my belly to gather my breasts, and he drives up into me, pushing deeper without pulling out first. "Oh fuck, Sophia—fuck, you feel...oh god, my love. How are you mine?"

I shift forward, putting more weight on my hands, still braced on his chest. "I am—I'm yours. All yours. All for you." I rock forward as he pulls back, and when I feel him start to thrust, I drive my ass down to meet him.

A high, breathless scream tears out of me, and I feel my thighs shaking, feel my core blossoming with expanding heat, pulsating with hot, detonating fury—an orgasm swelling low and deep.

"Soph," he groans, "Oh god, my love. You feel—fuck, fuck—"

"How?" I gasp in his ear. "Tell me, please tell me."

"Like home. Like heaven. You feel perfect." He squeezes my tits, thumbs my nipples so I judder and gasp, and then grips the crease of my hips and pulls me down while spearing up into me, and now he's shaking, his thrusts uneven and slow and shallow—holding back, desperately restraining himself.

I know what he needs. I search myself, and know I'm ready to give it to him.

I need it as much as he does, I discover.

"Ren, sweetheart." Terms of endearment come effortlessly, now, when once it felt strange to hear and impossible to say. "You can let go. I can take it."

He shakes his head. "I . . . I don't want to—"

I fall forward and frame his face in both hands and kiss him until we're both gasping and breathless, and I rock on him, my ass sliding against his thighs with his cock buried inside me, and I show him that I can take it.

My lips move on his, my plea so soft I don't know if he can even hear me. "Fuck me, Ren. I want it. I need you."

He groans, a raw, shaken sigh of desperation and relief. "Sophia, *meu amor*, I need—oh god, I need to . . ."

"I know," I whisper in response. "Give it to me. Don't hold back anymore." I rock on him some more, faster now, panting as he fills and withdraws. "I know what you need, my love, and that's what I want. Right now. More than anything."

He growls through gritted teeth, his hands raking blunt fingernails down my spine, making me shudder on top of him, and then he fills his hands with my ass and grips me tight. As I continue rocking on top of him, he drives up to meet my thrusts—slowly at first, tentatively, gentle and shallow.

"Yes," I gasp. "Harder, darling. Please."

He's panting, now, teeth gritted, and his grip on my ass is painfully tight, but it's a delicious twinge, registering more as pleasure than pain. His next thrust is perfection— he draws me up and away until he nearly falls out of me and then yanks me down hard, fucking beautifully into me.

"*YES!*" I cry, dig my nails into his chest and rock against him, take him deeper, squeeze my inner muscles as hard as I can. "*Again*, my love. Do that again." I press my lips to his ear. "Don't stop."

He moans long and low and ragged and gives it to me again, slamming me down onto him while bucking up into me. "Tell me it's good, Sophia," he demands.

"It's good, Ren, *so* good, so fucking good."

Again.

And again.

"Yes!" I pant in his ear, gasping my encouragement. "Again, Ren. Harder. Harder!"

He obeys.

He thrusts harder, rocks into me, and with every subsequent thrust I feel him lose more and more of his control, and I feel my own ebbing away as well.

"Touch your pussy," he breathes. "Touch yourself,

Soph." He lifts me upright, cupping my breasts as he digs his heels into the mattress, heels drawn toward his ass so he can thrust into me. "Come while I'm inside you."

I obey him, crying out as I press a finger to my throbbing clit. Instant, volcanic pressure shears through me, ripping a full-voiced scream from me as he thrusts up into me, hard, making my tits bounce wildly. "Oh god! Ren! FUCK! Oh god, oh fuck oh godoh*fuck*!"

He grips my waist and we find our rhythm together— he drags me down onto his thrusts and I use my thighs to lift up, balancing precariously on him while fingering my clit.

The sensations are overwhelming, and he adds to them, pinching my nipples so hard I gasp in shock, and then soothing the ache with a rolling thumb, and he's driving into me and I'm glutted on his thick, hot, sliding cock, and drenched with arousal and my bouncing tits ache and he pinches my nipples and twists them and cups the heaving weight of my breasts and my finger flies around my clit and orgasm bursts within me with the heat of a thousand suns and the smashing force of an earthquake.

"Ren!" I pant, as we rock together in frantic, frenetic rhythm, his cock pounding home in perfect, delicious, wickedly hard strokes. "Oh fuck, my love, I'm—oh god, oh god, REN! REN! REN!"

I can't even call it an orgasm. It's something else.

Something more.

I can't balance any longer, can't stay upright. I collapse forward onto Lorenzo and roll my hips into his thrusts, each tilt and pump of my sex a desperate, sinuous, liquidly rolling movement, and then the orgasm shatters me, and I realize I wasn't really even coming before, I was only in the precursor tremors, and now he's fucking me in earnest, and I hold his eyes and I know I've never ever been loved this way, so fully, so perfectly.

I scream and scream until I have no breath left in my lungs and then I can't even scream anymore, and I can only keep coming and coming and coming as my Ren fucks me with abandon, and my climax is fierce and wild and potent beyond all belief or description, and I can't move or breathe or scream or do anything but tremble and shudder and shake as everything inside me, everything I am as a human being and as a woman shatters and dissolves and leaves me helpless and weeping and wild.

He pounds into me as I come, and I feel my pussy spasming around his slick, hard, sliding cock, clutching and clamping until his thrusts slow as my orgasm finally subsides into wracking, shuddering aftershocks, each one a mini-orgasm unto itself.

He slows his thrusts until he's stopped, buried deep. "Sophia," he breathes. "My *god*."

I can barely manage a breath. "R-Ren…" I cling to him, shaking all over. "You—you didn't—" a full body shudder leaves me gasping. "You didn't come."

"No," he admits, kissing my temple. "Not yet. This isn't about me—it's about you."

I lift up, brace a hand in the pillow beside his face, cup his cheek with the other. "Lorenzo, this is about *us*. I *want* you to come. I *need* you to come." I hook my heels under his thighs and roll over, hauling his huge, heavy body with me; he allows me to bring him on top. "It's your turn."

"Soph, I—"

I feel him inside me, thick and hard and long, and I see

the tension in his jaw. I claw at his ass and pull him against me. Groaning, he acquiesces, starts to move into me again.

I grip the hard, taut bubbles of his ass and jerk him against me, curl my legs around his thighs, pulling with my legs as well, and I rock my hips against his, encouraging him with my entire body. "Please, Ren," I beg. "More. Harder."

"Sophia," he groans, head dropping to my chest as he drives his hips against the cradle of my thighs. "You feel— ah god, *meu deus, meu amor, você sente*…fuck, you feel so fucking good, *meu amor*, so tight, so wet."

I hook my legs high around him, cling and clutch and pull, my hands digging into his hair and clawing at his back as he strokes into me. "Everything I am is for you, Ren," I whisper in his ear. "I'm yours. Take me. Claim me. Mark me. Fill me."

His teeth sink into my flesh where neck meets shoulder and he growls, spine arching and hunching with his increasingly desperate thrusts. "*Amor*—Sophia—I—oh god, my love, I'm—oh god, Sophia, I can't stop it…"

"Yes, Ren, yes! I want it. I want you. Come inside me, my love. Come for me." I rock with him, cling to him with arms and legs, chanting my encouragement in his ear as he rocks into me hard and fast, fucking me with wild gasping grunts of exertion that is the sweetest music I've ever heard.

I feel his thrusts falter, lose their rhythm and speed, becoming staccato and hard as his climax starts its detonation. His hand curls around the back of my neck and he presses a trembling, gasping kiss to my open mouth.

"Sophia!" he breathes. "I'm coming!"

I push his face away so I can meet his gaze. "Look at me, love, look at me. Look at me. *Olhe para mim, meu amor.*

Não desvie o olhar, my love, my mate, my everything." I cup his face and go still, legs hooked around his backside, gazing up at him as he pounds into me, his eyes radiating love and blazing with passion, wide-eyed and fraught and almost in disbelief. "Come for me, Ren. Come inside me."

He drives deep and shudders, jaw dropping open as a breathless gasp escapes him, shock and wonder and ecstasy playing across his face as he finally releases. "Sophia…I— oh god, oh god—fuck! Fuck, my love, my Sophia…"

I feel him unleash inside me, feel him flood me with his cum, and it only requires a swift circling roll of my fingertips against my clit to join him in climax. "Yes! Oh god yes, Ren! Yes!"

When I come around his pulsing cock, his entire body wracking with a jerking spasm, and then he thrusts into me with renewed frenzy, pounding into me all over, groaning and grunting, and I feel his cock pulsing against my walls and sliding through me and filling me with his hardness, and I feel him coming, still or again, gush after gush spilling his hot seed inside me.

My own orgasm is fast and hard and intense, stars bursting behind my eyes, my pussy clenching and clamping around his cock with unbelievable force.

Tears pool in my eyes as we rock through our climax together, and I meet his gaze and see his eyes are misty as well, and I kiss his eyes, one and then the other, tasting salt as we move in synchronicity until there's nothing left in either of us, until we're limp and panting forehead to forehead.

I frame his face in my hands, cradling his hips in my thighs, and brush my thumbs over his damp eyes. "I love you so fucking much, Lorenzo."

He seems unable to speak. Just shakes his head, overcome by emotion. "Sorry, I—sorry. I can't—I don't—"

I kiss his eyes once more, tasting the salt of his emotions. "This is nothing to be sorry for, Ren. It's beautiful." I love this sense of self I have with him—this freedom to be soft and loving and delicate. "Sharing this kind of emotion with me, Ren, it's…it's so beautiful. It is strength. It's trust."

"I love you," he whispers, his voice low and shaky. "I love you. I love you."

I guide his weight down onto me, gather his face to my breasts and breathe in his scent and luxuriate in the shelter of his big body wrapped around and draped over mine, and I just hold him.

After a time I couldn't possibly measure, he rolls to his back, reversing our position so I'm laying full on top of him with his cock still buried inside me, his arms around me, hands on my ass.

I fall asleep the way I woke up that first time—my Ren beneath me, around me, holding me.

CHAPTER 10

BODIES; ARMOR

LORENZO

WE WAKE TANGLED AND SWEATING, BATHED in the full bright sun of late morning.

Her eyes are bright as she rests her chin on my chest and stares at me. "I wish we could just stay here forever."

"Me too," I say. I search her face. "I didn't expect…" I can't find the words. "I've never known anything like that. I didn't think you were ready, I wouldn't have…" I groan in frustration. "Soph, tell me the truth. Did I hurt you?"

She rolls her head from side to side. "No. Not at all. Not even a little." Her grin is heated. "I'm a bit sore, but I love it. You were perfect."

"I lost control," I mutter, angry at myself for it. "I should have been gentler."

She slithers higher on my body, gaze serious. "No, you should *not* have," she says. "I absolutely fucking *loved* every single second of making love with you like that, Ren. I wouldn't change a thing. I *wanted* you to lose control. You gave me exactly what I needed. You were patient while I got used to how fucking gigantic your cock is." She grins at me. "And baby, it…is…*huge.*"

I may blush a little. "You sure know how to stroke a man's ego."

"I'll stroke more than just your ego," she says, giggling. Serious, again, then. "For real, honey. I mean it. You were gentle when I needed gentle, and you fucked me like you couldn't get enough when I needed that."

"You're sure?"

She nods. "I am."

I run my fingers through her hair. "How are you feeling about everything?"

"Emotionally you mean?" she asks, and I nod. "I don't know if I'm awake enough yet to know. I need coffee and breakfast."

I grab a handful of her gloriously full ass, give it a shake and a soft slap. "Get a shower while I order us some food."

Her grin is lopsided. "You may need to do that next time we have sex."

"Do what?" I ask, giving that ass another gentle clap. "That?"

Her eyes heat and sparkle. "Yes. That."

"You're sort of shocking me, you know," I tell her.

She tips her head to one side. "Oh? How so?"

I roll a shoulder. "I guess I didn't expect you to…I dunno. Be as…into it, as you are. I thought you'd take longer to get over things to the point that you'd be able to…" I shrug again. "I don't know how to put it."

"I know what you're trying to say," Sophia says. "And I'm kind of shocked myself. I guess. I don't know, Ren. I guess once I broke the seal on everything, it was a purge of—of everything. Talking about it, telling you the things I've kept secret all these years, facing the things I've been afraid of…it's been wildly cathartic. I don't know if I've fully processed it all yet, to be honest." She dots a quick, light kiss to my lips and wriggles off the bed. "Shower for me, breakfast for us, shower for you, and then we check on the others."

I watch her sashay into the bathroom until she's out of sight, and then I use the number the security guy gave me to order a breakfast spread. That only took a few minutes before I got a confirmation text from him with an ETA of thirty-ish minutes for the food.

Leaving quite a bit of time to kill before the food arrives.

I go into the bathroom and lean against the counter to watch Sophia in the shower. She's wet and naked, black hair plastered to her scalp and neck and shoulders, head tipped back as she scrubs her chest and belly with a soapy washcloth.

God, she takes my breath away.

Her voice startles me. "You gonna just stand there or are you getting in?"

I don't need a second invitation. She lets me get under the spray with her, and soon we're entwined together, kissing, hands sliding on slick skin.

We spend as much time kissing and groping as we do getting clean. I get out first and dry off, and then wrap her in a towel, sink to my knees and take my time scrubbing her dry. And, since I'm on my knees already, I use the opportunity to take her pussy with my mouth. This time, there's no hurry, no desperation, no hesitation or concern. I take my time bringing her to a shuddering, panting orgasm, her ass against the counter, hands in my hair.

When she comes the first time, I hike her up onto the

counter with a folded towel under my knees and I devour her all over again. She arches backward, hands reaching up and back to press against the mirror, heels tight against her ass, knees splayed wide apart, pulsing her pussy against my greedy mouth as she comes, and the sounds of ecstasy she makes for me burn into my my brain, into my soul, the panting whispers and gasping pleas and hoarse cries of delirious release.

I'm about to go for a third when a sharp trio of knocks announce the arrival of our breakfast.

I tuck a towel around my waist and leave Sophia spread out on the bathroom counter, slumped back against the mirror, panting, bleary-eyed and stupefied. I close the bathroom door after myself and head across the suite, making sure the towel is secured.

I hear the shower turn on a moment later, and I grin to myself at the thought of Sophia trying to stay upright in the shower on shaky legs.

Feeling pretty pleased with myself, I have my hand on the knob, the other on the lock, but some faint instinct jangles in my gut. I hesitate, hungry enough to ignore it.

Long years of training and experience, however, mean I know better than to ignore my instincts.

I throw myself to the side, away from the door. A deafening blast leaves my ears ringing, and the door explodes inward in a storm of splinters—a shotgun. I hit the ground on my ass and roll backward to my feet. The towel droops off me, and I snag it, crouched and waiting. I have a split second to glance across the room at the rifles and pistols, uselessly lying across the room on the couch.

A black combat boot kicks the ruined door inward— it flies open and slams against the wall, shuddering halfway back toward the frame. The boot's owner steps through, a massive Binelli sweeping across the room. I still hear the shower running, but there is absolutely no chance Sophia didn't hear that blast.

I have no time to think about anything else, then. The breacher is pivoting my way in his sweep of the room. I whip the towel at his face, and in his attempt to bat it away, he gets the shotgun tangled. I lash my foot out in a front-kick, my heel slamming into his gut. He doubles over, gagging, and I snag the shotgun, towel and all, out of his hands. I slam the butt as hard as I can into the side of his skull, and I feel it give with a wet crunch. I drop to a knee and find the trigger, tug it through the towel. The fluffy white fabric disintegrates as the slug rips through it, and I yank the towel away and toss it aside. My first slug left a giant hole in the wall just outside the door but didn't hit an enemy. It did buy me a few seconds, though.

The second tango steps through sideways, aiming where I would be if I was on my feet; he fires a burst as he crabwalks through the doorframe, but his rounds buzz over my head and chew up the floor just behind me.

My slug slams into his chest and sends him flying backward into the frame, blood spurting from his mouth; his body armor stopped the slug from penetrating, but the sheer blunt force trauma of the ultra-close-range blast caused some sort of severe internal damage.

Another burst rips through the doorway, a buzzsaw of bullets intended more to keep my head down and me from moving across the opening than to harm me. A flash-bang rolls with a clatter across the marble floor. I react on instinct, using the butt of the shotgun like a golf club to whack the explosive back toward the enemy, and then curl over the shotgun and clap my hands over my ears, face buried in my thighs.

The blinding light and concussive noise is a sensory assault, leaving my already ringing ears ringing even worse. I surge to my feet, blinking away the blurring, coruscating, flashing afterimages, butt tucked against my shoulder, and step toward the doorway, firing blindly into the opening. After my first blast, I dart sideways and fire again, shoulder slamming into the far side of the frame. I fire a third time, jerk the barrel to my left a touch and fire a fourth time. I'm still firing mostly blind, as the afterimages still dance across my vision and the ringing in my ears leaves me off-balance and nauseated.

I hear an assault rifle chatter in a burst, burst, burst, and then feel a small soft hand on my left shoulder: Sophia, HK in her hands, as naked as I am, moving past me in a tactical crouch, firing off burst after devastating burst into the foolishly clustered group of tangos. They're all wearing body armor, so most of her shots that do hit don't kill, but leave them momentarily out of commission.

My sight is clearing and the ringing is abating now. I go for lethal headshots, putting slugs through skulls—the mess of gore painting the foyer is unbelievable.

The door to the other suite crashes inward, and Toro fills the opening, rifle *crack-crack-crack*ing; he steps through diagonally, and Fonz follows him, limping so badly it's more of a one-legged hop. His aim is unaffected, however, and in short order every tango is down, either dead or badly wounded.

Toro, once the gunfire has been silenced, eyes the moaning, bleeding survivors with a cold glare, mutters to himself in Spanish, and then whips his rifle back up to his shoulder and double-taps those who aren't dead yet without moving from the doorway.

"I guess we know what you two were up to, eyyy?" Fonz says, grinning at me.

Sophia seems unaffected by both her nudity and Fonz's off-color joke. "Is anyone hit?" Her gaze flicks to me, rakes over me. "Ren, you're okay?"

"Yes, *amor*, I am unharmed. If I had hesitated another moment, I wouldn't be."

Toro saunters back into the foyer from our suite, where he'd been finishing off the last survivors. His gaze rakes over Sophia with brief but blatant appreciation, and then he shakes his head like a dog and whips around, facing away. When Fonz doesn't immediately follow suit, Toro yanks him around by the shirt, keeping hold so the injured man doesn't topple over.

Naomi's face peeks around the doorframe, eyes going wide at the godawful mess of gore bathing the walls, floor, and ceiling, and then fixing on Sophia's naked form, and then mine. I don't miss the way her eyes linger on certain portions of my anatomy before she squeezes her eyes shut, blushing. She vanishes, and reappears with a bathrobe in each hand, proffering them to us. We both gratefully shrug into them.

"We need to move out ASAP," Fonz says, uncharacteristically devoid of humor. "If this bunch found us and gained access, you can be sure more baddies are inbound. You lovebirds get your shit on and we can get scarce."

"Fonz is correct," Sophia says, her tone and expression once more hard, cold, and unforgiving—purely Inez, now. "Dress, gather whatever is necessary, and we will all meet in your suite in five minutes so we can plan our next move."

She turns on her heel and glides back into our room, an incongruous sight with her sopping wet hair sticking to her neck, wrapped in a thick, fluffy white spa robe, assault rifle in her hands, bare feet flashing beneath the too-big robe.

She vanishes into the bathroom again, slamming the door behind her with a resounding crash. I take a moment to drag the bodies out of our room so I don't have to look at them while I get dressed, and then close the door to the suite behind me.

My phone is buzzing—it's Bradley, our liaison. I answer it, ready to rip him a new asshole. "How the *fuck* did they get up here?" I snarl, by way of hello.

The voice is not Bradley's. "Mr. Araujo, my name is Bruce, I'm the assistant head of security. Bradley was my immediate supervisor. They, uhhh…tortured and killed him for access. I don't know how they got into the Bellagio in the first place without being spotted, but rest assured we're on high alert. The authorities have been contacted, obviously, since the noise was reported by multiple guests. The owner of those suites is one of our most important VIPs, so as a courtesy, I'm giving you a heads-up so you can make your exit before law enforcement arrives."

"I appreciate it, Bruce. We'll be gone in a few minutes. I'm sorry to hear about Bradley."

"Me too, Mr. Araujo. He was a good man. He didn't give up the information easily."

"I don't doubt it. Goodbye." I end the call and then head for the bathroom.

I tap on the door and then let myself in. Sophia is hunched over the sink, slowing her breathing. "I heard the shots," she whispers, "and I thought—I thought you…"

I pull her into my arms, turning her to face me. "I'm okay. I'm fine. Not a scratch."

She nods against my chest, letting out a shaky breath. "I need to…" She pulls away, straightening, lifting her chin, hardening her features. "Sophia needs to go away for now, I think. I can't be her out there."

I pinch her chin and tip her face up. "I know. But first…" I take her mouth, kiss her breathless.

She pulls back, panting softly, gazing up at me with a soft, loving expression. "Ren," she breathes. "I wish we had more time. I had planned on returning the favor. My legs are still a little shaky from those *three* orgasms you gave me."

I kiss her again. "Only if you want to, *amor*. There's no score, no keeping track, no returning any favors. I do that because I like to. Making you come is more than pleasure enough for me." I run my thumb over her lips, silencing her protest. "I know. I know. And if you want to, I will very gladly let you. But if that's a trigger, then you need to know down to your very soul that I will *never* feel deprived if you can't do it."

She smiles up at me, searching my face with such love and gratitude that my heart feels incapable of absorbing the blinding beauty of it. "Ren, my sweet love. Your compassion and understanding are…" she shakes her head, shrugs. "Such a gift. One that a part of me says I don't deserve." It's her turn to speak over my protest. "I know, Ren. I know—I do deserve it. Just as you deserve the love I have to give you. I just…I can only hope that it's….that I'm enough. That it's balanced, between us."

"You're enough and more than enough. Especially when you look at me like that." I dip down and kiss her once more, soft and sweet and quick. "Now, as much as I hate to see Sophia go, it's time for you to become Inez again. We need that part of you if we're going to get ahead of these assholes and put a slug in Rafa's fucking skull."

"Rafa," She snorts. "If only you knew how much that man *hates* being called Rafa." She scratches fingernails down my beard, gives me a peck on the lips, and then steps back. "All the more reason to call him that, I suppose, eh?"

I watch the transformation with fascination—her posture stiffens, her chin lifts, her eyes harden, the smile vanishes. Any trace of softness and warmth is utterly gone as if it never was.

We dress quickly, gather our gear. I remove body armor from one of the less messy corpses, find the breacher and stuff my pockets with slugs for the shotgun, and clip a few flashbangs to the vest. By the time I've finished this, the rest of our group has gathered in the living room of our suite.

Inez faces them. "I thought we were safe here—how our enemies knew we were here, I don't know. I'll be contacting my employer for an explanation when we're en route. For now, we're simply going to get out of this hotel and out of Vegas while I figure out our next destination, which hopefully will be Rafael's location so we can end this once and for all."

My phone buzzes again—Bruce. "Law enforcement is in the lobby. I have a pair of Suburbans for you at the loading dock, but you need to get down there *now*, or I won't be able to keep them from detaining you."

"Understood. Heading down now. Thanks." I hang up and address the group. "We're out of here, now. Law enforcement is in the building and we do not have time for that. And with Pugli involved, we can't trust law enforcement anyway."

———————— ◆ ————————

Forty minutes after the assault, we're a caravan of two heading west toward LA. Toro and Fonz are in the Suburban behind us with Annika, Anjalee, and Myka. With me and Inez are Naomi, Tatiana, Terra, and Taj.

Inez has called Jakob no fewer than six times in the last forty minutes, and it's obvious she's becoming concerned.

She tries him again, letting it ring until it goes to voicemail with a digital female voice: "We're sorry, the voicemail box you're trying to reach is full. Please try your call again later."

She tosses the phone into the cupholder with a hissed curse in Portuguese . "He has never not answered, Lorenzo. Not once in the decade I have worked for him."

"Decade?" I ask. "That long?"

She nods. "After I left the base in Goiâna, I made my way north. You gave me several thousand dollars, a fake passport, and a Beretta."

"It was all you would accept."

She nods again. "I desperately wanted to stay with you. But I knew Rafael would be looking for me, once he returned and discovered what I'd done. I couldn't risk putting you in his crosshairs." She inhales deeply, holds it, lets it out slowly. "It's why I stayed hidden so long. I knew the second I reappeared in the wider world, I'd end up on his radar, and if I were to approach you, you'd be in danger. I just couldn't do that. It seemed better to remain invisible."

"I understand. I would have accepted the risk to be

with you, but I also would have made the same choice—
to protect you—if the roles had been reversed."

She nods. "I took a bus from Goiâna to Manaus, and
another to the Colombian border. One of my father's business associates whom I knew rather well lives—or lived—
in Medellin, so I took a chance on him. He remembered
me, and more importantly what I was capable of. I worked
for Vicente for two years, under the assumed name you put
on the passport. Only Vicente knew my true identity, at
first. But a few of his lieutenants knew me too, and eventually it became an open secret that Bruno de Silva's daughter and Rafael Sousa's wife was working for Vicente, and
rumors of *La Víbora's* return to cartel operations began to
spread. Unfortunately for me, I didn't realize the danger
until it was too late. I thought Vicente could protect me.
He was always like a kindly old uncle to me, ever since I
was a little girl, and I had faith in him. I underestimated
Rafael, however."

"This is all new to me," I tell her.

She shrugs. "It isn't a secret, nor very traumatic. Just...
context. Timeline. Anyway. Vicente sent me to finalize a
deal for American-made fentanyl. It wasn't very popular
on the streets back then, so it was a risky move for him."
She waves a hand. "Unimportant. Rafa—as I shall now call
him, just to piss him off even in spirit—found out that I
was supposed to be doing the deal. He laid a trap, and I
walked right into it. Only through dumb luck did I survive,
and only just barely. I was hit several times, and hid until
they left, and then crawled away. I patched myself up as
best I could and..." she hesitates, remembering, and then
continues. "I hijacked a private plane at an airfield and
made them fly me into Mexico. I nearly bled out before

some weird, crazy old man found me wandering around, bleeding, in the hills near the Benito Juárez park. He put me in his truck, took me home, and nursed me back to health. He didn't speak a lick of Spanish, Portuguese, or English, just Zapotec or whatever. He wouldn't take my money when I left. Just pointed me north and slammed the door in my face."

"Something similar happened to me, once," I say. "Except it was a Guarani woman."

She's quiet for a while, and then resumes her story. "I walked across most of the rest of Mexico. Hitched rides when I could, walked when I couldn't. Thankfully, I'd managed to keep hold of the briefcase of cash, so I had plenty of money."

"Why not buy a car?" I ask.

She shrugs. "I wasn't thinking clearly. I'd lost a lot of blood, and the old Zapotec guy only did enough to prevent me from bleeding out. I left his hut before I was really ready to go anywhere, and I developed an infection. I was just…stumbling around, I suppose. It's all a hazy blur. I remember reaching a river in the middle of the night and running into a group of migrants. One woman recognized that I wasn't in good shape and stuck with me. She helped me cross. I wasn't even aware that that's what I was doing—crossing into the US. I just had this drive to keep moving. If I kept moving, Rafa couldn't find me, I thought. I was terrified of him finding me. Petrified. I'd have panic attacks about it all the time. Just keep moving, keep walking, keep going north, no matter what—that's all I could think about in my fever state."

"Understandable, I'd say."

She nods. "Yes, I suppose so." A pause, a wave of her

hand. "Border Control hit the group after we reached the US side, and I ended up in a detainment center and interrogated, especially in light of the fact that my passport was discovered to be a fake, I had a handgun on me, and had three not-exactly-healed gunshot wounds. I couldn't exactly give them my real identity or I'd be in even worse trouble, so all I could do was pretend I didn't speak English *or* Spanish. It took them a while to find a Portuguese translator, but by that time the infection had left me so delirious I was incoherent. They put me in the infirmary under armed guard, handcuffed to the bed, which as you can imagine did real wonders for my state of mind. I was in and out of consciousness and coherence for who knows how long."

"Barbarians," I mutter.

She shrugs. "I was obviously not an average migrant, Ren. I was *absolutely* the threat they assumed me to be. I just wasn't a threat to *them*. They had no way of knowing that. I don't blame them for how I was treated. I do not excuse their treatment of others who are innocent of everything except trying to flee the horrors of home and enter the US illegally, but me? I *was* dangerous. Their precautions were logical and understandable."

I growl. "Perhaps. I have not had the best of experiences with that organization, personally and professionally. Perhaps I am biased."

"Believe me, I understand completely. I am only saying that in that particular situation, they were not wrong to treat me as a threat. Regardless, I was the unwilling guest at that detention center for several weeks, hovering on the brink of death from infection. It turns out that swimming across the Rio Grande with open, already-infected wounds isn't the best plan. I developed multiple, severe infections. I remember very little but faces and noises and pain and being so, so thirsty."

"God, Sophia. That sounds awful."

She nods. "It wasn't fun. There are much worse things one can experience, however, and I remember being thankful that at least I was safe from Rafael. Even he couldn't get to me in the middle of an American detainment center." A pause; she looks back, remembering that we aren't alone and that she has an audience. "The man who became my employer, however, could."

"That's where he found you?" I ask.

She nods. "I remember his face above me. He was speaking to me, or maybe to someone else. I don't know. I was uncuffed, transferred to a wheelchair, and brought out of the facility. To this day, I still don't know how he knew who I was, since I was listed as a Jane Doe in the official records, with my fake passport name as an alias. But he knew, and he got me out of that facility, brought me to LA, got me healthy, gave me a new identity, a new life, and a job."

"This was before the Arrows, I assume," I say, "so what was the job, back then?"

"Personal security. He was…reorganizing, shall we say, and made quite a few enemies for himself. Keeping that man alive was a full-time job for a while, there. The rest of how I became Inez as you know me and how the Arrows came into existence is not my story to tell."

She picks up her phone and stares at it as if willing it to ring. "I am very worried, Lorenzo. This is highly unusual. What if Rafael or Pugli got to him? He can handle himself well enough, but he's not an operator."

"I'm sure he's alright, just unable to answer the phone."

She glares at me, knowing as well as I do that my answer is bullshit. "I will keep trying every fifteen minutes."

And so she does, and every fifteen minutes, the call goes to voicemail.

Two hours later, she's dozed off, head against the window, phone wedged between her thighs. Everyone has either dozed off or nearly so, leaving me to my thoughts as I drive.

I'm startled into cursing in Portuguese when her phone abruptly jangles with the shrill, jarring trill of an old-fashioned landline handset ringer. Inez jolts upright with a snort, fumbles the phone, and stabs the answer button.

"Pull over!" she snaps at me. "Pull over, now!"

I jerk the wheel and mash the brakes, skidding and fishtailing to a halt on the gravel shoulder. Inez is out of the car before it stops. "One moment, sir."

I exit as well, gesturing for everyone else to stay put. She glares at me as I join her, but she doesn't otherwise protest. "You're on speaker with me and Lorenzo, sir," she says.

"Lorenzo, Inez." Jakob's voice is strained. Quiet, as if he can't risk speaking at full volume. "The situation has changed. You warned me that I could not assume I was safe from our enemies, and unfortunately your warning has proven true."

"Are you okay, sir?"

"I am…well enough. I find myself, ironically, in a situation rather similar to those our Broken Arrows have all recently experienced—that being hunted by a numerically superior foe, with an innocent life at stake."

Inez coughs in surprise. "Sir?"

"No time to explain. I'm sorry to have worried you, but I simply couldn't answer. I can handle this situation well enough on my own for now. I'm calling because I've finally heard back from my contact at the CIA. I have a definitive location for Rafael. And better yet, he's planning on meeting up with Pugli in the next twenty-four hours."

"When and where, sir?"

"Los Angeles. Precise time and meet location are both unknown. All I know is they're meeting somewhere in LA in the next 24 hours. Contact Solomon and have everyone rendezvous in LA as soon as possible. This may be our one chance at eliminating both players."

"I should send someone to you, sir," Inez says.

"No. I...no. Focus on Pugli and Rafael. I want photographic proof of termination, Inez. No prisoners, no mercy. Not for them."

"Sir, with all due respect, Lash could—"

"Sophia, I said *no*. You will need everyone you can get. They won't be alone, you know that. I may not be an operator, but I'm far from helpless."

She hisses her profound displeasure. "Understood, sir," she snarls. "I disagree with your decision, but I respect it."

His tone is amused. "If I find I need help, I'll ask. You have my word on that. Just...kill Rafael Sousa and Roberto Pugli. Their deaths will ensure my safety. In the meantime, while I may be in danger, I'm finding the experience so far to be...not entirely unpleasant."

"The innocent life, I presume," Inez says, her tone wry.

"Quite."

Inez slides her braid through her fist, flips the end up to examine the place where a bullet took off the last inch or two during the firefight at the club. "Jakob...You're not just my boss. You're my friend. Other than Lorenzo, you've known me the longest. I owe you everything. Please, sir. Stay safe. Stay alive."

Jakob clears his throat. "My, my. An emotional outburst from the great Sophia Bruna Santos de Silva, *La Víbora* herself. What is this world coming to?" Before Sophia can respond, he sighs, continues. "I tease, my friend. In truth, I'm touched. And amazed. I think you may be a miracle worker, Lorenzo. But a month ago, such a declaration from Inez would have been less likely than winning the lottery, twice."

"I am no miracle worker, Jakob," I say. "She has done the work to face her demons. The credit for her transformation goes entirely to her."

"Transformation may be a bit of an exaggeration," she mutters. "We can stop talking about me at any point."

"I have to go anyway," Jakob says. "I assure you, Sophia, I will be fine."

"Until later, sir."

A pause. "I think at this point, we can dispense with the 'sir.'" Jakob says something that is muffled and inaudible. "I have to go. We'll speak again soon. Hopefully, so you can report that Pugli and Sousa are dead."

"It will be done, sir—Jakob."

"I don't doubt it. Goodbye for now, both of you."

The line goes dead, then.

Inez looks at the phone with a curious expression, then at me. "He's met someone."

"I agree," I say.

"You don't know him like I do," she says. "So you can't understand how strange an idea that is. Until recently,

Jakob and I were two peas in a pod. Meaning, cold, distant, isolated, prickly, difficult, and often flat-out mean."

I smirk at her. "Armor, protecting your hearts. I hope for his sake whoever he's with can see through it to whoever the man is, or can be, beneath it."

She frowns thoughtfully. "I hope so, too. I get the sense that he's been that way for far longer than me. He may not know who he is without it."

"Did you?" I ask. "Do you?"

She shrugs, head tipping toward her lifted shoulder. "No. Not really. And I don't know that I would have been able to face everything if I didn't have you, so in a way, you *are* the miracle worker he said you are." She exhales sharply, and I sense the conversation is over. "Enough of that, for now. I have to trust Jakob to take care of himself. We have a mission to complete."

CHAPTER 11

PDA

INEZ

I HAVE A MESSAGE OUT TO SOLOMON, ASKING HIM TO contact me as soon as possible. We keep heading west, and are approaching downtown LA when my phone finally rings.

"Solomon," I say by way of greeting. "Sitrep?"

"Hello to you too, Inez," he answers, his tone amused. "No, no, we're all good, thanks for asking."

A former version of me would have ripped him a new asshole for the sarcastic insolence. "What do you think I mean when I ask for a situation report, Solomon Cabot?"

"Oooh, the full name. Spicy."

"Are you high?" I ask. "Since when do you have a sense of humor?"

"Back at ya, boss-lady."

I sigh. "You're spending too much time with Saxon and Chance, I think. Now. Enough nonsense. I have an important update, but I would like to know your situation first."

"Fine, fine. No appreciation for a new page having been turned in the book of Solomon."

"There is already a book of Solomon, I believe," I say.

"It's the *Song* of Solomon, actually." He speaks over anything I might have said. "*Any*way, you asked for a si-trep. We've tracked Pugli and his minions to Los Angeles. There was some chatter about an op in Vegas, but the one lackey we managed to capture and, um, question, didn't seem to actually know anything concrete about anything happening in Vegas."

"When did you question him?"

"Say hello to *La Víbora*, shitstain." There's a wet, raspy gurgle. "He says hi."

"Enhanced interrogation?"

"Nah. Just a good old-fashioned face-pounding."

I sigh. "You may as well let him go, Sol. The reason he doesn't know anything about a Vegas op is because it happened already."

The line goes ominously silent. "What op already happened, Inez?" His voice is deadly cold.

"Calm yourself. They hit the club in force in an attack in broad daylight. Forty-some men, either mercenaries or cartel soldiers, I'm not sure. The women are fine—we're all fine. Fonz took shrapnel to the back of his leg and Toro took a hit to the arm. Our employer put us up in a pair of suites at the Bellagio he owns through shells and subsidiaries, and they found us there, too, but only a half-dozen or so. We took care of them in short order, no casualties on our side."

"They hit the fucking club? With our women in it?"

"Everyone is unharmed and accounted for. But yes." I pause. "And that isn't all."

"Fuck me running, what else?" Sol asks.

"They've put Jay—our employer—on the run."

"That's the second time you've almost said his name, Inez."

"I know. I think it is likely that he will introduce himself to you when this is all over, but I cannot and will not reveal his identity before he's ready to do so himself."

"And I'd never ask. He gave all of us a second chance when none of us felt like we deserved one. We all respect his need for privacy, but hopefully he—and you—know we'd never reveal anything we may know about him to anyone else beyond the circle of Broken Arrows. And I include the women in that circle, obviously."

"I do understand, Solomon. It's just not mine to reveal."

"Understood. So. Anything else?"

"Yes, actually. He—our employer—received word from a CIA contact that Pugli and Rafael will be meeting in LA in the next 24 hours. We—meaning everyone, the women, Fonz, Toro, and Taj as well as Ren and I—are approaching downtown LA. We'll need to put out feelers so we can figure out when and where the meet is happening so we can end this fucking bullshit once and for fucking all."

"No shit. That makes sense. We've been focusing on Pugli as instructed, but my own contacts tell me they've had word of someone fitting Mercado's M-O being in LA."

"Elaborate," I say.

"Well, my contact is in the ATF, and they've been tracking the movement of a stolen shipment of small arms. It was jacked out from underneath the Army or some shit a few months back, but I guess the ATF had a lead that it was gonna be hit, so they put trackers in the cases, and they've got it sitting in a container at a warehouse in the Port of LA."

"And how does this connect to Mercado?"

"The hit was surgical, with overwhelming numbers. The squads assigned to guard the shipment had no chance whatsoever. One of them did manage to record and send a video before he ate a round himself, and it shows a figure who no one can identify inspecting the arms. I saw the video and it is one hundred percent your boy Rafael."

"A few months back is hardly proof that he's in LA right now, though," I point out.

"Right, but the ATF tried to get agents close enough to the container to verify that they didn't just find the trackers. The agents vanished. Yesterday, all three of the missing agents were dumped outside the LA field office."

"Dead, I presume?"

"Tortured. Beaten, electrocuted, and eventually given Colombian neckties."

"Not definitive, but that speaks to Rafael's favored torture practices, the electrocution thing in particular." I steel my voice so it doesn't shake. "He devised a process that is…quite effective. It is extraordinarily painful, but unlikely to result in even accidental death." I can't suppress a shudder. "It took some experimenting before he arrived at the system he uses now. Many of his victims died as he tried to figure it out."

Solomon is quiet for a moment. "Personal experience, eh?"

"Indeed." I clear my throat. "That's an excellent indicator that he's here in LA, but not proof. Where are you all?"

"We've been in LA for a few days. Let's rendezvous and put together a plan."

We agree on a rendezvous point and time, and end the call.

An hour and a half later—because LA traffic is its own form of hell—we're all together again, finally. We've met up outside an abandoned warehouse in the port—a location provided by Fonz, who is LA-born and -raised, and who spent his entire adult working life here.

It warms my cold, dead heart to see the way the girls greet their men. Car doors are flung open before the vehicles have even stopped and the pairs run to meet each other with an exuberance that would make you think it's been months rather than days.

Lorenzo, Fonz, Taj, Toro, and I stand together to one side, watching the couples whisper and kiss and act like love-sick teenagers.

Fonz spits on the ground at his feet. "Jesus, these people. Get a goddamn room or something, fuck. I gotta piss." He hobbles off, muttering under his breath.

I watch him go, and they glance at Toro and Taj in turn. "What's his problem?"

Toro answers. "He despises the idea of love. He won't speak of it, but I think he experienced some form of betrayal at the hands of someone he loved, and it has made him bitter and angry."

"And you?" I ask.

Toro rolls one broad, heavy shoulder. "I would like to find love for myself, but it does not seem to wish to find me. I am unlucky in love."

"Taj?" I ask.

He shrugs. "Love is a not needed thing. My parents and grandparents were arranged marriages and have much happiness. I, too, was married this way."

"You are married?" I ask, surprised.

He shakes his head. "No. Not anymore." He goes to

the back of the Suburban and busies himself loading bullets into magazines—conversation over.

I notice his gaze flicking occasionally to Anjalee, and I see a wistfulness in his expression. I join him loading magazines.

"I see the way you look at her," I murmur. "Anjalee."

His movements become jerky and unnecessarily forceful, answering in the same. "She resembles my… wife—ex-wife."

"Ah."

He snorts. "No 'ah.' You do not know."

"No," I agree. I don't."

He glances at me. "It isn't in some dossier somewhere?"

"The outlines, yes. The context, reasons, and fallout? No."

"I am not in love with Anjalee. I do not look at her in that way." He glances at me. "I do not wish to discuss this any further, if you please."

"Of course. But if you wish to, you have friends here, now. Brothers. Sisters."

"I am not a Broken Arrow."

"But you fought for us. And…there may be room in the circle for additional members, soon."

He nods. "Perhaps." He juts his chin at Anjalee, who is very busily and thoroughly making out with Kane, whose hands are buried in her ass. "Such a life is not for me."

"Why not?"

"I am Dalit."

"I admit, to my shame, that I know very little of the caste system of your country."

He shrugs, shakes his head. "It is not mattering. Not anymore. I am not there. I shall never return."

"Then—"

He grunts, irritation cutting through his normally placid demeanor. "Enough, please. Just...leave me be. Brand or no, I will be loyal to the brothers and these women. That is all anyone must know."

I hold up my hands. "I don't mean to pry, Taj. I have been...aloof, in the past. I am trying to be more of a friend and less of a boss or authority."

He nods, not looking at me.

I leave him and return to Toro's side.

Toro glances back at Taj, and then at me. "Discover anything about our silent comrade?"

"A bit. Not much. Mostly that he doesn't like being asked questions."

Toro snorts. "I have worked with him for a while now, and you got more out of him in that conversation than I ever did. He is truly a very closed-off person."

"So was I, at one point," I answer.

Toro grins, eyeing Lorenzo, who is in conversation with Solomon and Scarlett. "Lorenzo loosened your tongue, did he?"

I laugh. "Something like that, yes."

I let the reunion carry on for a few more minutes and then give a long, sharp, two-fingered whistle to get everyone's attention. Conversation cuts out and everyone gathers around me in a semi-circle.

"So, here we all are. This is the endgame, ladies and gentlemen. Intel suggests both Pugli and Mercado are here in LA. There's a shipment of arms somewhere in this port that is tied to Mercado, and the fact that the authorities can't seem to find it suggests that Pugli is using his influence and wealth to make sure no one is looking. We need to use every contact, every favor and marker, every resource we can all leverage to pinpoint the time and location for the Pugli and Rafael meeting. Whatever they're planning, we can assume it isn't good, and is likely directed at us and the man who employs us all."

Fonz lifts a hand. "I know some people who might be able to help. Let me make a few calls." He hesitates. "They ain't exactly workin' on the right side of things. Just so you know. The intel would be solid, though."

Solomon answers for me. "We aren't the police, and we aren't interested in due process or evidence or any of that shit, Fonz. I don't give a fuck if these dudes are serial killers. If they know where this meet is, or if they can find out, I'll deliver a dump truck full of cash to their door."

"Can I quote you on the dump truck full of cash?" Fonz asks. "Because these guys? Money talks *real* fuckin' loud."

I answer for Solomon, now. "If their intel proves solid and leads us to the meet and the deaths of our enemies, I will personally pay them a hundred thousand dollars each."

Fonz nods. "That'll do it."

"Just…make sure they know the cash only happens if the intel proves out and they don't double-cross us."

Solomon chips in, here. "And Fonz, make it crystal fucking clear that we aren't playing by the rules either. We're not cops. If they even think about double-crossing us, they'll die slow, painful deaths."

Fonz nods, digging his phone out of his pocket. "No problemo. Be back." He swagger-limps away, scrolling through contacts in his phone.

A few minutes later, Fonz returns grinning. "My contacts have heard some chatter. They're gonna look into it and get back to me. These two are seriously connected in the criminal underworld of LA, so if anyone can get a bead on what's going on, it's them. And better yet, Pugli and this Rafael-Mercado cat throwin' their weight around like this? It's makin' some people pretty damn unhappy. LA is all kinds'a carved up, know what I mean? Everybody's got their turf, and no one really wants out-an'-out war, so they tend to color inside the established lines, for the most part. These two dickbags show up with a container full of guns stolen from the US Army, push around local authorities, get ATF sniffin' around everyone else's shit? No one likes that kind of attention."

"Your point, Fonz?" I ask.

"My point is that the folks I know in the game want to see Mercado and Pugli eliminated, or at least taken off the board here in LA. So they're willing to play with us if it means shit goes back to normal."

"Excellent." I think for a few minutes. "Sol, Scarlett, Lash—do some recon in the Port while we wait for further intel. Sol, did your contact give you an idea where the container is located?"

Sol shakes his head. "No, but I can find out."

"Do it, and check it out. But be careful—we know all too well that these guys aren't playing games."

"On it." Sol paces away, phone already to his ear. He returns a couple minutes later. "I've got a location for the container. The most recent satellite imagery shows multiple contacts in the area, heavily armed, forming a perimeter around the area. We'll have to proceed with extreme caution, but I think we can put eyes on it and, see who's who and what's what."

"It is of the utmost importance that you're not spotted," I say. "We don't want to tip our hand that we're here or that we know what's happening."

Solomon grins. "They didn't call me Wind Walker for nothing, you know."

————— ◆ —————

Fonz happens to have a deck of cards with him, for reasons unknown, and a game of poker—played for bullets—ensues. Those not playing sit and talk, nap in the back of the vehicles, or merely lounge idly while we wait for the scouting party to return.

Three hours pass before Sol, Scarlett, and Lash return.

Sol gives the report. "We counted a dozen tangos armed with long guns. They've set up trip-wire alarms and motion sensors at every ingress point, as well. Whatever they're hiding in there, be it guns or Rafael himself, they're damned serious about keeping people out. They never opened the container, so we've got no clue what's inside. My feeling, however, is that it's not just a load of guns in that container. You wouldn't post twenty-four-hour armed guards with laser trip wires and motion sensors for that. They know damn well that at least the ATF knows the container is there, so if they were worried about it being taken back, they'd move it. The container being *there*, specifically, is important, for some reason."

"Ambush for us?" Chance asks.

Sol shrugs. "Maybe. But as far as we know, they don't know we're here. And for this crew, a dozen shitheads with

M16s is barely an ambush, and doesn't pose much of a threat to us. Five of you successfully defended the Club against forty. They know we outclass them so their only hope of succeeding against us is sheer numerical superiority. A dozen tangos ain't that."

"It is my feeling that Rafael is hiding in that container," Lash says. "Pugli would have to come to him, which fits with Rafael's sense of superiority. It also fits with his paranoia."

"I agree," Scarlett says. "The container is positioned in the middle of a stack, with containers on all sides. It would be a fairly simple matter to create a connection between the surrounding containers. With the right ventilation and some creativity, you could make a small living space for one person. Or, if not a living space, somewhere Rafael can hide in relative comfort with zero possibility of being spotted by anyone."

"That is something Rafa would do," I say. "So now we need to nail down the time of the meet, and whether it's in that container."

"Too bad we can't get thermal on that container," Sol muses. He glances at Fonz. "You don't happen to have a line on a helo with thermal capabilities, do you?"

Fonz tilts his head to the side and eyes the sky. "Maybe? Putting an LAPD chopper in the sky is a bit of a bigger ask than getting some lowlife thugs to spill the beans on a rival's activity."

"Chopper," Kane says, snorting. "A chopper is a motorcycle, buddy."

"A chopper is a motorcycle, buddy," Fonz mocks in a mocking, wheedling, whining tone. "Fuck you, meathead. You know what the fuck I meant."

"Fuck me?" Kane growls. "Fuck *you*. I'll turn you into a pretzel, needle-dick. A really fuckin' greasy one."

"Gentlemen," I snap. "Your penises are both massive, I'm sure. We don't need to measure them at this time, however, so please, attempt to rein in your egos."

Scarlett snorts in an attempt to suppress her laughter, but her snort sets Annika to cackling, and then in short order, everyone is howling…except Fonz and Kane.

"You've got jokes, Inez," Saxon says, grinning devilishly. "You must'a gotten some." I stare him down until he looks away, squirming. "You're not ready to *take* jokes yet, I see. Got it."

Lash raises a hand. "During our joint operation with Alpha One Security, I acquired a rather exceptional military-grade sniper rifle with thermal imaging capabilities. It was a gift from their sniper, Anslem See. I've not had a chance to use it, yet, and this is a perfect opportunity. I can monitor the container from a safe distance, and hopefully confirm whether or not there is a heat signature in the container. The rest of you can position yourselves to assault the container when I spot movement, and then I can provide sniper support."

"I like it," Sol says, nodding. "Inez?"

"It's as good a plan as any. An LAPD helicopter circling the area isn't exactly the height of stealth, anyway, even if Fonz could arrange it."

Fonz lifts his phone. "Messaged my buddy who's a pilot for the department and he says no-can-do. Off-book flight operations are a strict no-go. And yeah, it'd certainly let our friends know someone is watching them, which we don't want."

"That's the plan, then," I say. "Lash, get your new toy and find a spot. Girls, we're gonna need to find you somewhere less visible to wait it out. And we'll need someone to stay and guard them."

Fonz lifts his hand. "Got it, Boss-lady. I ain't gonna be able to keep up with you guys with this hole in my ass cheek." He jerks his head at the warehouse outside of which we've posted up. "There's bound to be a nice defensible position in there, somewhere. I'll take a gander."

"Excellent," I say. "Let's go over our equipment and prepare for action while Lash and Fonz get into position. This could very well be a case of hurry up and wait, however."

Rev, silent up till now, chuckles. "We're all ex-military, Boss-lady. We're used to hurry up and wait."

Lash comms us that he is in position. At the same time, Fonz hobbles back out.

"Found a good spot," he says. "One of those dinky little warehouse offices up on a catwalk. One entrance, so it's defensible, but there's an emergency exit right below it in case we gotta scram-a-lam lickity-split."

Silas frowns at Fonz. "Do you ever speak normal English, or do you have a disability?"

Fonz flips him off. "It's called having a personality, jackass, you should try it sometime. Having you around is like having a pet tree. You've got all the chutzpa of a fencepost."

"Ohhh snap, brother," Saxon says, cackling. "You gonna take that burn?"

"From a Muppet?" Silas responds. "Yes. He's the most unserious person I've ever met. "

"Yeah, well...look at you making up words,

Professor Tree Stump. Unserious he says. You're a real chucklehead."

Silas arches an eyebrow. "Unserious *is* a word. Which you'd know if you could read anything more complicated than *Green Eggs and Ham*."

"Dr. Suess is a literary genius," Fonz says. "*Fox In Socks* is a work of art. An' I'll have you know, I have a degree in criminal psychology. Do *you*?"

Silas doesn't answer, because he does not, in fact, even have a high school diploma. Not that I'd ever think less of him for it, since neither do I, although I was educated by a private tutor.

"What I thought, dick-for-brains," Fonz mutters.

"Hey, guy?" Saxon says. "Careful which tree you bark up. Jokes are all good and well, and we can all take 'em as good as we give 'em, but you gotta know when to shut your goddamn mouth."

Fonz just laughs. "Yeah, well, when God was puttin' me together, he forgot that part. Like when you take apart an engine and have a few leftover bolts, you know?"

"You're saying you're short a few bolts?" Saxon asks.

Fonz nods, chuckling self-deprecatingly. "Fuck yes. More than a few. But, look, *guy*, we all are, yeah? I mean, we all chose careers where people are shooting at us on purpose. No sane motherfucker is gonna do that if he ain't short a few bolts."

Chance laughs at this. "He's got a point."

"Degree in criminal psychology, my ass," Silas finally mutters. "From where? Cracker Jack University?"

"Took you a while to come up with that one, did it?" Fonz says. "Tip for ya, buddy—gettin' into a battle of wits when you're unarmed ain't a good plan. Stick to the rivers and lakes that you're used to, na'mean?"

Saxon slugs his brother in the shoulder. "I think you may be outmatched, here, brother."

Annika cackles. "He just called you a scrub."

Silas frowns. "A what?"

"Scrub? You know, the TLC song?" Annika sighs, shakes her head. "My god. How do you not know this song?"

She taps at her phone for a second, and then holds it up so the song can play for everyone to hear.

When the song ends, Silas is still frowning at Fonz. "I don't see the relevance, and you're still a Muppet."

Fonz just laughs. "Insult-based humor is where I live, son. Level up a bit and come at me again. I'll take it easy on you, promise."

Saxon claps Silas on the shoulder. "Good try, though, man."

Lorenzo watches all this from his place beside me, and then looks at me. "They're an interesting bunch."

I nod. "They are. All these out-sized personalities shouldn't get along, but they do, somehow."

Lorenzo laughs quietly. "I think Silas is still figuring out which things were insults."

"Probably. He's always been the most serious of the Cabot brothers. It's good to see him try, but he should have started with a less deadly opponent, in this case."

"His name. Fonz. Is it a nickname or his real name?"

"It's a nickname, a reference to a character from an American sitcom from the seventies. Our Fonz over there rather strongly resembles the actor who played the character, and there is a certain similarity in mannerisms, as well, from what I understand. Jakob had to explain it to me, too, when we first considered hiring him into the Club."

"Fonz. Hmm. It's a strange name."

"I believe it was short for something Italian. Fonzarelli, or something along those lines."

We're leaning side by side against the hood of one of the Suburbans. Lorenzo abruptly pivots, grabs me by the hips, and pulls me around flush against him. "Hi," he says, grinning.

I pull away from his grip. "Ren, not now."

He keeps hold of me. "Why not? You embarrassed to be with me?"

"No, but—" in the interest of preserving my dignity, I stop fighting his superior strength and instead go stiff and rigid. "It isn't the time for PDA."

He gestures around us—Chance has Annika leaning back against his chest with his mammoth arms draped over her shoulders, crossed over her chest; she has her hands hooked over his forearms, and appears to be rather happy about the position. Saxon and Terra are strolling along the edge of the pier, hand in hand, chatting quietly. Silas is sitting on the ground with his legs stretched out, ankle-over-ankle, hands braced behind him, with Naomi laying perpendicular to him, her head on his lap, while Silas idly strokes her hair. In fact, everywhere I look, the couples are in some degree of affectionate, intimate positioning.

I sigh. "You have a point, I admit. I just..." I chew on the inside of my cheek. "It's a significant step, Lorenzo. I'm still getting used to being with you—to being happy. Allowing others to see it is...difficult."

"Happiness is not weakness," Lorenzo says.

"I know that, in my mind," I say. "But reality is different. I wish it were that easy."

He gently tugs me flush against him once more, and this time, I let him. I close my eyes and just breathe, focusing on the comforting, pleasing sensation of Lorenzo's arms around me, his strength surrounding me and cocooning me. I feel…safe, like this. It bolsters the resolve within me. Provides a shield around the soft, vulnerable parts of me—but a shield which Lorenzo is on the inside of, rather than the outside. I rest my cheek against his chest and loop my arms around his neck, breathing him in.

Gradually, I become aware of that specific sensation of being watched—the feeling of being the center of attention.

I open my eyes to see everyone staring at me. Saxon, quite literally, is open-mouthed in shock.

"Something you'd like to share with the class, Saxon?" I ask, not moving from my comfortable position.

"You—you're…" His mouth clicks closed.

I smile at him. "Trying out this whole…happiness… thing."

Saxon blinks at me for another moment, and then makes a dramatic pantomime of shading his eyes and scanning the sky.

I arch an eyebrow at him. "If you're looking for your balls, they're in her purse." I turn my gaze to Terra, smirking.

Saxon flaps his mouth again. "No, I was looking for flying pigs."

"She burned you *again*, Sax," Sol says. "I think you've forgotten the face of our father."

Sax turns his uncomprehending stare at his brother. "What does that fuck-face have to do with *anything*?"

"'The man in black fled across the desert, and the gunslinger followed,'" Solomon says.

"What the *fuck* are you talking about?" Saxon seems ready to have an apoplexy.

Solomon looks around at the group, but everyone else is staring at him just as confusedly. "No one has read that series? My god, a perfectly good joke wasted on a bunch of literarily-stunted poltroons."

Fonz, yet again, surprises everyone. "Nah, I've read it, it just wasn't as funny as I think you think it was."

"You've read *The Dark Tower*?" Sol asks, sounding as surprised as I feel and everyone looks.

Fonz frowns at the group. "Wow, okay. So you all assume I'm some uneducated dumbfuck who's only good at shootin' shit?"

Chance, Kane, and Rev all speak in perfect unison. "Yes."

Fonz cackles. "Nice. Then my plan is working perfectly."

"Your plan is to make people think you're stupid?" Annika says. "Sounds...I dunno, kinda stupid."

Fonz taps his temple. "Ah, but it ain't. See, if people *think* you're dumb, they count you out. Ignore you. But if you ain't really stupid *or* uneducated, it works in your favor, because then when you bust an intellectual nut in their face, it's even funnier."

"Bust an intellectual nut in their face?" Silas echoes. "What does that even mean?"

"Dunkin' on a motherfucker," Fonz says. "That's what. Proving that not only are you *not* a dumbfuck like they assumed, but you're smarter than them, and then suddenly *they're* the dumbfuck. It's beautiful."

"Or, and I'm just spitballing ideas here," Saxon says, "you could just act as smart as you are?"

"Pffff," Fonz says, dismissing the idea. "Where's the fun in that?"

We're saved from further nonsense by Lash's voice from the comms. "Contact," he murmurs. "Caravan of SUVs approaching. I count six."

"Suburbans?" Sol asks.

"Affirmative," Lash asks.

"If they're each carrying eight, that's forty-eight," Rev mutters. "Lotta tangos."

Kane rolls a shoulder. "Yeah, but are eight full-grown adult males in body armor and wielding rifles gonna all fit, even in a Suburban?"

"Not comfortably," Chance answers. "But it don't fuckin' matter, does it? We got a mission to carry out no matter the odds."

"Enough chatter," I snap, leaving—regretfully—the comfort of Lorenzo's arms. "Fonz, take the girls to your position. Everyone else, we split up and come at them from multiple angles at once. Nicolai, keep us informed. We need confirmation that Pugli is in fact in that convoy."

"We pick our teams or do you wanna?" Solomon asks me.

I scan the group. "Scarlett, Sax, and Rev, you're Alpha team. Ren, Chance, and Kane, Beta team. Myself, Solomon, and Si are Charlie team. Toro and Taj, you're Delta. Alpha, you circle around come from the north.

Beta, west, Charlie, we take east, Delta, you take south. Delta, if for any reason Fonz calls for assistance, you two will be the closest, so you respond. Any questions?"

Silas raises his hand. "Yeah, are we trying to bring anyone in alive or...?"

I let my expression grow cold, summoning the icy brutality of Inez. "No prisoners. No questioning. If you see Pugli or Rafa and you have a shot, you fucking take it. And remember—this isn't over until I have visual, in-person confirmation of death for our two primary targets. The soldiers I don't give a fuck about, live or die. Rafa and this arrogant Pugli character are our targets." I scan the group once more. "Those of you who have taken the oath against killing, your vow still applies. Be strategic. Be smart. Work together."

No one has anything to add or ask, so I clap my hands once. "Move out and get into position, but wait for my signal. I want us to strike in synch. Nico, updates?"

"The convoy is approaching the target zone." A pause; the teams have jogged off in their respective positions; I join my teammates and we're moving east. "The convoy has reached the target zone. Stopping. Each SUV has at least six, and two of them have seven. They're fanning out to join the men already in position. Hold...I see Pugli. He's got body armor on. He's talking to someone—whoever down there is in charge of Mercado's security, I believe."

"Does it seem like he's going in, or is Rafa coming out?" I ask.

"He is going in."

"Damn. Figured that's how it would work, but a girl can hope for the easy way."

One by one, over the next couple minutes, the teams report in as they reach their positions—within sight of the target zone.

"All teams, confirm go," I say.

"Alpha team, go."

"Beta team, go."

"Charlie team, go," I say.

"Delta team, go."

I hesitate, let out a breath. "This is it, everyone. In a few minutes, this can all be over. No heroics. We all go home." I let another heartbeat pass. "All teams—go!"

CHAPTER 12

CLOSE BUT NO CIGAR

LORENZO

I'M POINT, WITH KANE BEHIND MY LEFT SHOULDER and Chance behind my right. We're spread out a few feet while we navigate the maze of containers; Solomon was able to call in a marker and get us a satellite shot of the container yard, allowing us to create predetermined routes. We follow this memorized, predetermined route now, as fast as possible, jogging the echoing, shadowy channels between towering stacks of containers. Red, blue, yellow, black, and green containers are stacked five high in some places and up to seven in others, creating walls fifty and sixty feet high. A cough, a sniffle, a heavy step, every sound echoes and carries and dopplers back to us—if you don't know exactly where you're going, you could end up lost in this place for days, as each next path between stacks looks identical to the one before. One wrong turn, and we'll end up who knows where and miss the cue, miss the entire fight.

Thus, I recite the order of turns under my breath as we jog: "left, left, right, right, right, left, right, left, left, right." But don't get the order wrong. Don't forget a turn.

"This fuckin' place, man," Kane murmurs as we pause at a three-way intersection. "Creepy and confusing."

I ignore him, chanting the turns loud enough to make my point—*don't fucking distract me*.

Chance slaps a hand on Kane's shoulder. "Unless you want to get lost, brother, shut the fuck up."

Kane goes silent. I slow the pace as we near the target zone—voices can be heard now, low, idle chatter and the occasional bark of laughter. Kane and Chance hold onto my shoulders, pulling our formation in tight. We make a left, jog straight down the corridor, another left; the voices sound like they're around the next turn, and we slow to a creep, approaching the last turn.

"...Y la puta intentó pegarme, como si no se lo pidiera..." *...And the bitch tried to hit me as if she wasn't asking for it..."*

"Le diste una lección?" *Did you teach her a lesson?*

"Si'! Si!" *Yeah, yeah.*

Fuck that.

I hold up a fist to call a halt and then inch forward so I can peek around the corner; a pair of armed guards—Rafael's, I would assume, judging by their Spanish conversation, and the vile subject matter—loiter a dozen feet down the corridor, AK-47s dangling barrels-down as they share a cigarette. The scent wafts me to me, and it's semi-sweet and skunky—not a cigarette, then. Even better.

"Beta team in position," I breathe. "Ready."

A moment later, Alpha and Charlie report in ready almost in unison, followed by Delta.

"Lash?" Inez asks.

"Pugli is still inside. The men seem to be settling in for a long wait. I cannot be sure that Rafael does not have a way out that we cannot see. Who knows how extensive his preparations might be. We risk losing him, is my point." Lash hesitates, sighing. "We either wait for Pugli to exit, or we attack now while they're inside. There are risks either way."

"Attack," Inez says. "We're as close as we've ever been. On my mark. Three—two—one—*MARK*!"

I swivel out from behind the cover of the corner, dropping the two guards in rapid succession—*TAKTAK!TAKTAK!* They drop to the ground, limp, boneless, and leaking brain matter.

Kane and Chance trot past me the second the rounds have left my barrel, reaching the next corner. Kane peers around, and then returns. "We missed a turn or something," he mutters.

I take a look as well—there should be a large group of soldiers around the corner, but there's not.

Just an empty corridor.

"Fuck," I snap. "Kane, look right, I'll go left. Chance, watch our six."

"Moving," Kane says, and jogs past me toward the right-hand turning while I go left. Chance stays where he is, watching our back-trail. Kane and I peek, pop back.

Kane signals that there's no one over there, and my side is empty too. Using hand signals, I indicate I'm moving forward and that he should do the same.

I round the corner and trot down the corridor—I hear voices again, echoing and tinny, their origin masked. Another corner; another peek.

A resounding *CRACK*! shivers the air, the sharp report of Lash's rifle. Gunfire erupts, then, and shouts, curses, orders, in a jumble of languages. I hear running footsteps behind me and whirl just in time to see a tango round a corner behind me—the light and shadows and angles made it seem like a dead end when it wasn't. I drop to a knee and fire off a trio of rounds. He never even saw me, the unlucky bastard. My rounds take him in the chest and knock him backward—he's wearing a vest, however, and he only drops to a knee, gasping, and manages to crack off a single shot that sizzles past my ear with the buzz of an angry yellow jacket. I fire again, and his face explodes in a pink mist.

Chance appears beside me, and his rifle chatters—round thunk and rattle against the side of the container inches from the skull of another tango. He skids and wobbles in his attempt to throw himself out of the line of fire, trips and goes down to one knee, firing wildly. His rounds go high and wide, not even hitting metal; mine do not miss, and he joins his comrade on the ground.

CRACK!

CRACK!

CRACK!

"The container is opening!" Lash snaps over comms. "Move in, move in!"

"Kane, back to me!" I shout.

"I'm—a little…" I hear him over comms, broken up by the crackle of his rifle, "busy at the moment."

"Got it," Chance mutters to me. "Hold your position."

"Fuck that," I snap. "I'm moving in. You two catch up. I am not losing this motherfucker again."

Chance whacks me on the shoulder as he moves out. "Fine. Just don't die—I'd never hear the end of it from Inez."

I snort a laugh and jog forward. Gunfire echoes from

every direction, overlapping and confusing. It's impossible to tell where any of it is coming from.

Something hums overhead, and then another yellow jacket buzzes past my ear, and then something hot slices past my knee. I throw myself to the side, shoulder slamming against the container so hard my arm tingles, partly numb; my momentarily weak hand means I miss my return volley, but it keeps his head down and gives me time to shake out the tingles, sprint forward on a diagonal to approach the corner wide. My mark is on one knee taking cover behind the corner; he wasn't expecting me to run toward him, and my rounds catch him unaware. His skull rocks backward, and he slumps heavily against the container. I hear an engine roar and tires squeal.

"Pugli is escaping!" Lash shouts. *CRACK! CRACK!* His rifle barks. "Driver down. He's running for another automobile. We are going to lose him!"

Cursing floridly in Portuguese, I sprint forward. A tango rounds the corner and I drop him. Another. A third. I'm reacting automatically, operating on instinct. I reach the corner, gasping, panting, pause for a split second, and then pop out, rifle up.

I bump into a body—surprised brown eyes meet mine. I jam my barrel into his throat as hard as I can, and he stumbles backward, gurgling and gasping, clutching his bloody throat; I fire from the hip and take him in the vest. His eyes are wide and blinking and terrified. I grab him by the vest and frog-march him backward, hunkering behind him as the sound of automatic weapons fire grows louder and more confusing. I reach the end of the corridor; my unfortunate prisoner-slash-living-shield is scrabbling at me and his throat, in which my rifle barrel tore a nasty hole. He'd be fine with medical attention, but his fate is already sealed.

I round the corner to a barrage of gunfire that whips past me on both sides and overhead, stippling the man I've shoved backward. He jerks and thrashes, blood dribbling down his chin as a dozen rounds slam into his back, shoulders, and neck. I tossed a flashbang the second I shoved him away; I bolt back around the corner and cover my ears as the device detonates. Confused, pained shouts ring out, and I pivot out, toss a frag, roll back. *BOOOOOM!* The shouts become screams.

"Havin' all the fuckin fun without us, Ren?" Chance says, appearing through the streamers of smoke blown back to me by the currents of wind swirling through the maze. Kane is with him, bleeding profusely from a long, ugly cut slicing from his forehead diagonally down the bridge of his nose and past the corner of his mouth. "Not as bad as it looks," he growls. "Just bleedin' a lot. Have a wicked new scar, though. C'mon, fuckers, let's dance."

He doesn't wait for an answer, rolling out from the corner and raking rounds across the corridor. I hear them clang off metal, whining as they ricochet, and I hear at least one thunk into something soft. Smoke swirls and clears, the dirty white smoke of the flashbang mingling with the darker gray smoke of the frag. Moans overlap as we jog through the mess—men lay bleeding from a myriad of wounds, others lay dying or dead.

CRACK! CRACK! CRACK! Lash's rifle speaks in threes.

The roaring engine cut off abruptly when Lash took out the driver, and now a new roaring sound bounces around the corridors.

"He's heading east! Beta team, intercept!" Lash punctuates his words with a rapid trio of shots.

I hear tires squealing and the engine groaning. Something crunches against metal. I catch a glimpse of black and silver and glass as the Suburban rounds the corner, partially obscured by the still-swirling pall of smoke.

Tires thunk over bodies.

"LINE ABREAST!" I shout.

Kane and Chance lurch into position on either side of me, and we open fire at the SUV. The glass pocks and splinters and spiderwebs, and then shatters. Red sprays. The vehicle squeals and fishtails to a halt. The driver is slumped dead over the wheel, but the passenger doors fly open and men disgorge, firing back over the hood. One of the men is Pugli, who wields a subcompact machine gun, spraying rounds indiscriminately as he hides behind the massive black SUV.

"We have Pugli trapped!" I snap over comms.

Chance and Kane pour suppressive fire at the SUV, switching mags in smooth, practiced alternation while I wait and watch, hoping Pugli shows his face.

One of his men pops up over the hood and I drop him with a lucky shot. Another SUV rounds the corner and rakes to a halt at an angle, windows down, starburst muzzle-fire flashing. This buys the enemy enough time to force us back behind the cover of the corner, and I hear a door slam.

"No!" I shout. "FUCK!" I lurch, foolishly, out from cover, firing from the hip.

Bees buzz past my face. Something sharp and hot slices my cheek, scrapes my scalp. A powerful hand snags the back of my vest and yanks me backward—this is my salvation. I feel the quick sharp hot blaze of rounds skating millimeters over my nose as I topple backward. Chance yanks me like a sack of seed, one-handed, and bodily tosses me to safety while Kane rips off a long suppressing burst.

"You fucking *dick*!" Chance shouts. "Getting your dumb ass killed won't help us!"

I struggle to my feet and rush forward again. "He's getting away!"

Tires squeal and Kane keeps firing. I hear glass shatter, hear shouts, but then Kane drops back with us. "Fucking got away."

"Anyone have eyes on Rafael?" I shout over comms.

"No sign of him," Lash answers. "The container door is open but he never appeared."

A sudden barrage of gunfire echoes, followed by an answering fusillade.

"I'm going in," I hear Inez say. "Si, with me."

"Inez! Wait!" Silas shouts—I hear him on comms and as an echo.

"Fuck," I snarl, and scrabble into a sprint.

Gunfire blasts and rounds whip past me, but I'm beyond caring. I feel Kane and Chance on my heels, hear them firing, but I have thoughts only for Inez. That open door has "trap" all over it, and I fear her determination to see Rafa dead will override her caution.

"Dammit, she went in," Sol says over comms. "Si is with her."

"It's—maze—bolthole—escape—following—" static breaks up her words as the metal blocks her radio's signal.

"A Suburban just flew past us," Toro says over comms. "Pugli has escaped—I saw only him, however. He is alone, and it looked like he was bleeding."

"With any luck, he'll bleed out," I hear Rev say.

I ignore this, sprinting as hard as I can around corners and down corridors. I must have badly miscalculated our route for us to be so many turns away from the target zone. Guilt and rage and shame ripple through me—I fucked up and compromised the mission.

Pugli escaped.

Rafa is escaping with Inez on his heels—and who the fuck knows what nasty surprises that snake has cooked up in that rabbit warren inside the containers.

"Inez!" I shout. "Come in!"

"Ren—on him—not letting him—away."

"Sophia!" I shout. "It's got to be a trap!"

Something flashes in the corner of my vision, and I drop and whirl on instinct—a round bites through my skin at my hip, glancing painfully off my hipbone at an incredibly lucky angle. It leaves me bleeding and in serious pain, but in no real danger. I return fire, taking my target in the groin. He stumbles, sags, drops to a knee, rifle lifting for another burst. A barrel chatters at my left ear, and I feel the heat of the barrel on my skin.

"You're hit, Ren," Chance says. "C'mon, man, let's get you to safety so I can patch you up."

I jerk out of his hold. "It's nothing," I snap, "fuck off or follow me."

"Don't speak Portuguese, my guy," Chance rumbles. "But I take it that's a no to safety."

"These fucking bastards won't fucking die!" I shout, still in Portuguese, not caring who understands or who doesn't.

I lurch forward, my injured hip screaming in pain, blood trickling hot down my leg. My previous leg wound is screaming from overuse as well—my whole body is a mass of pain from the various places I've taken wounds, major and minor.

No fucking matter. Inez is all that counts.

A body appears, starburst flashing. A round whickers overhead, another past my left elbow. A third slices along the outside of my thigh. I drop him. And his buddy, who follows him around the corner. Kane drops the next two with bursts to the vests, and I double-tap them as I pass.

Now we're in the thick of things, with Lash's rifle blasting in the distance, taking out targets only he can see, and there's Sol in the doorway of a container, trading bursts with someone inside. Rev has his back to Sol's, Scarlett is off to one side firing at a target running along the tops of the containers while Saxon kneels nearby, firing in different direction.

We're surrounded and outnumbered, and they're closing in.

"I've got tangos inbound," I hear Fonz say. "Six of 'em, on foot, moving my way. I don't think they know we're here, though." A pause. "They see our vehicles. Fuck. I've gotta do something. Girls, stay put. Here's my side piece—"

I tune him out, focusing on reaching that doorway where Sol and Rev are, where Inez went.

I hear gunfire in the distance, hear Fonz in my ear counting dropped tangos like he's keeping score in a video game.

"Do you require backup, Fonz?" Taj asks in his soft, lilting voice. "We are not far away."

"Nah, I got it…" he trails off and I hear a burst echo in concert over the comms and from the distance. "…All… wrapped…up. Fuck you, dickhead, think you can hide there? Take a bullet to the earhole, fucknuts. Yeah, bitch, how you like them apples?"

"Am I as annoying as he is?" Saxon asks.

"Not hardly, brother," Sol answers. "You're far more annoying."

"Oh, fuck you."

"Inez is in there alone!" I shout, sprinting across the open space. "Cut the fucking jokes!"

Solomon rips a burst into the container and then pivots behind cover as a return volley scorches the air where he was. Lungs burning, wounds pulsating agony so potent it leaves me snarling with each searing gasp, I don't so much as hesitate as I barrel into the container at full speed.

Only pure stunned shock saves me; Rafa left a handful of men behind to delay pursuit. I'm among them before I know what's happening. I drop my rifle to hang by the strap and lash out with an elbow, catching something hard that gives way with a crunching thunk. I draw my sidearm and fire it blindly at an upward angle in the general direction of the man I elbowed. The noise of the shot rings in my ears. I spot movement out of the corner of my eye and strike behind with my foot, catch him in the belly and leave him doubled over and gasping; I fire again, and he drops. Now I'm surrounded and fists are slamming into me. I turtle, taking the blows to my back and ribs, and then I hear punches and scuffling and grunting, and then a series of single gunshots.

The blows stop and I lurch into motion, limping as fast as I can, grunting through the pain of each step.

I hear a shout from ahead, but it echoes and distorts. I hear a female shout of anger.

"*INEZ!*" I scream. "I'm coming!"

I hear feet behind me but spare no thought or time for who it may be. I don't care.

A gunshot rings out, echoing weirdly.

I turn the first corner—the container that was open was more of a foyer, just an empty container with a few metal barrels overturned to create a firing position near a doorway cut through the walls. Here, the ambient light from outside isn't enough to cut the gloom, and I bring my rifle up and turn on the under-barrel flashlight attachment.

Here I see the evidence of Rafael's presence: the metal walls are covered with rugs to absorb sound and soften the harshness of the bare metal, and another rug covers the floor. On the rug is a couch and coffee table, with a battery-operated camping lantern providing harsh white lighting. A stack of paperback novels rests on the table, one of them propped open on its spine. A cigarette smolders in an ashtray near the open book and a green glass bottle of wine stands half-empty, a red Solo cup near it. The smoke twists up to the ceiling and vanishes through some cleverly hidden ventilation.

I take all this in as I pass through, hurdling the couch on my way to the next opening cut through the walls. The next container/chamber contains a porta-potty, the smell from which is truly awful, being trapped inside the container.

I hear another shot, a third.

My light beam sweeps the next opening—blood is smeared on the wall from someone bouncing off of it. A puddle of blood turns the floor slick and slippery, and I see a heel mark skidding through it, and another footprint directly in the middle of it—this gives me hope that the blood belongs to Rafa rather than Sophia.

A fourth container is empty but for a ladder leading up through a hole in the floor/ceiling; the rungs are coated in blood. The dull copper of a spent shell glitters in the beam as I sweep it across the container, still half on the ladder. Another casing rolls lazily toward me.

I hear feet clomping on metal directly above me, and then Inez's muffled voice.

A gunshot.

Inez's voice is silent.

"No, no, no," I snarl under my breath, hauling myself into the chamber and sprinting forward; the path now is a straight line following the long axis of four containers, an eighty-foot stretch that I sprint down, gasping raggedly, doggedly ignoring the excruciating pain in my hip.

At the end of the fourth container is another ladder up, which I ascend recklessly fast, intent only on catching up to Rafael and Inez.

I emerge in yet another empty container, hobble through it to another ladder leading up. Here, however, daylight spears down in a circular spotlight. Scrambling up, I emerge blinking into daylight. A hundred or so yards away, at the end of the containers, the waters of the Port of LA glitter and ripple and glint. I'm just in time to see Rafael dodge a vicious swing of the long black blade in Inez's fist. His left arm is bathed red, blood dripping from his fingers as he dances lithely away from Inez's wild swings. She's screaming in a mixture of Spanish and Portuguese, an occasional curse in English sprinkled in—she's almost incoherent. Gone is Inez's legendary icy calm. This is a creature born of her unleashed rage and hate.

My hip and leg are both ready to give out whether I will it or not, so I hobble-hop-limp from container to container, pistol in my hands as I try to draw bead on Rafa. Their fight is messy and chaotic, leaving me no clear shot.

Rafael spots me first, grinning evilly through a split lip and bloody nose. He's weaponless but far from help-less—Rafael is no stranger to combat, armed and unarmed. Normally, he'd pose no real threat to someone like Inez, but she's not in control anymore, and her left leg is bathed in blood. She's slowing, shaking her head as if disoriented or concussed.

She swipes at Rafael with her knife, catching him across the belly; she opens his skin and looses a ribbon of blood down his front, but it's no mortal wound.

And it's a mistake.

Rafael surges inside her reach, slamming a knee into her gut, grabs a fistful of hair and shirt, spins, and hurls her bodily into space.

"SOPHIA!" I shout, forcing myself into a run again.

I'm too late.

Always too late.

Rafael throws himself after Inez. I have less than thirty feet to the edge, and I cross it in quick time considering the state of my wounds, but it's too late, too late, too late.

A boat snarls to life. I stumble to the edge, pistol held in a Weaver grip, aimed down at the Zodiac seventy feet below, bobbing in the waters of the port. Rafael is clam-bering over the side, panting. The driver of the boat grabs him by the waist of his jeans and hauls him in one-handed. Rafael grins up at me as he reaches down and yanks Inez's head up to show me her red-bathed face, unconscious and bleeding.

I fire at the boat, but my shot goes low, slicing into the water behind the speeding away rubber craft. I'm in motion, leaping off the container—only to be jerked back by a powerful hand.

"I don't think so, bro," Rev's voice rumbles in my ear. "You ain't catchin' that fuckin' thing, especially not with that wound."

"Sophia," I whisper, sagging against Rev's hold, suddenly exhausted beyond comprehension, my aches and injuries catching up to me all at once.

"They're going to that yacht," Rev says—not to me. His voice is in my ear again. "We'll get her back, brother. Promise."

My knees hit metal and darkness swells behind my eyes. The rubber boat bounces across the water toward the mid-sized yacht anchored half a mile or so out—in the middle of the shipping lane, of all places.

I watch as it reaches the yacht, slows. Hands roughly pass a small figure up into the yacht, and then Rafael's figure follows on his power, although even from here I can tell he's badly hurt and moving slowly.

CRACK!

The driver of the Zodiac abruptly flinches, wavers, and topples backward over the motor into the water. Distant shouts float across the water.

CRACK!

CRACK!

CRACK!

Splashes announce Lash's accuracy.

"Fuck," Lash snarls across the comms. "The cowardly dog is using our Sophia as a shield. I cannot shoot for fear of hitting her."

The yacht rumbles to life, twists in the water, and

lurches into motion, angling away from the port and toward open sea.

"Sophia!"

I failed her.

He has her…again.

I cannot see her surviving him a third time.

Woozy now, I hear Rev's voice, Solomon's, Silas's.

Hands lift me, and I try to find my feet, but the darkness drags me under.

CHAPTER 13

THE UNPLEASANT TRUTH

INEZ

PAIN ROUSES ME. I REMEMBER THE PRECEDING events with awful clarity before I even open my eyes: pursuing Rafael into the bowels of his elaborate, extensive container hideout. Trading shots with him. I hit him first, a glancing slice to the ribs. His shot sliced the outside of my left thigh. He ran out of bullets, and so did I. I remember daylight. I remember the rage, the hate, and the pain. My knife swinging wildly, red clouding my vision. Hurtling through the air.

Water.

Choking. Drowning. Darkness.

Nothing.

And now, I'm waking up in pain; my thigh screams, a hot throbbing pulse of pain in time with my heartbeat. I assess before opening my eyes or moving—I hear engines, splashing water chucking against a hull. A voice, somewhere overhead. I smell coffee and cooking food—bacon and eggs and rice. My leg is the only source of real pain. It's bad but tolerable, and I don't feel feverish yet, so hopefully there's no infection.

My hands are bound behind my back, cinched

painfully tight by hard plastic ties—the tightness is a good thing, as it means I'll be better able to snap them later. My ankles are also bound. Less helpful.

I listen, but the groan of the engines and the slap of water against the hull are the only sounds. I open one eye to a slit, peer around, close it again: I'm in the cabin of a boat, obviously, and as far as my first glance can convey, I'm alone. I wait a few moments, listening. Nothing. So I open both eyes and take a better look. The cabin has been stripped of everything except the bed frame and mattress—the frame is wooden and attached to the walls and floor, and the mattress is bare. There's a 5-gallon bucket on the floor in the corner, orange with a white snap-on lid, in which I'm meant to relieve myself.

I just love pissing in buckets.

I'm on my side, facing the room. There's a small round window showing that I'm just above the waterline, and there's no land in sight on this side of the boat.

I hear boots squeaking on the floor outside and then the lock thunks—apparently, the door to this room has been retrofitted to lock from the outside. I shut my eyes and force my breathing into a slow, deep rhythm, faking sleep.

I hear the door open. Smell food.

"Leave it on the floor, José," I hear Rafael snap. "Keep your distance from her."

"But chief," the other says—they're conversing in Spanish, "she is bound hand and foot and asleep."

"Oh, she's awake."

"But how do you know?"

"With that one, you only assume wrongly once. You must treat her like the serpent which you all have named her after—the viper. Even bound hand and foot, I imagine she can find at least three ways to kill you."

Inside, I'm pretty proud of this. Good to know my husband is still afraid of me.

He should be—I shall kill him with my bare hands before this is over. A bullet from a distance would have sufficed, and would have been the swiftest end to this ridiculously drawn-out game of cat and mouse, but far less satisfying. Watching the life bleed out of him will be far more enjoyable.

I hear boots on the floor and then the rattle of plastic as José leaves the tray on the ground. I feel him hesitate, feel his stare. I snap my eyes open and meet his with the iciest, most vicious glare I can summon, the kind of glare that would flay him to the bone, were mere looks able to kill.

I wish.

He yelps and scrambles backward, topples to his ass, and then crab-walks backward out of the room. Rafael, arm bound in a sling against his ribs, lounges outside the room, watching amused as his lackey stumbles to his feet and runs, muttering under his breath about "the fucking witch."

"It's impossible to find good help these days, don't you think?" Rafael asks, his tone casual and conversational.

I roll to my back and sit up, and then swing around to perch on the edge of the bed, eying the food; my stomach rumbles at the smell of it, and I realize I have no idea when I ate last.

Rafael grins at the sound. "Hungry, eh?"

I ignore him. I know better.

He saunters in—well, limps. I only remember hitting him in the ribs, but it appears I injured him in more than one place, but I don't remember. I glance down and see that my leg has been bound in bandages.

"Here we are," he says, stopping a safe distance away, "together again. Our last session together was rather rudely interrupted by your friends. I doubt we'll have that problem this time."

I ignore him. Mainly because I have nothing to say, but also because it pisses him off like little else. He's paranoid out of necessity, but deep down, he craves attention.

He snarls. "Look at me, *whore*."

I don't.

He is afraid of me. Even when I'm bound hand and foot and injured, he still won't approach me too closely. As if I'd waste an escape attempt on something so foolish and useless as merely causing him pain, as delicious as that would be.

Oh, no. When I make my move, it will have been planned, rehearsed, and executed with intentionality. When I strike, he will look into my eyes and see his death at hand.

For now, I sit perched on the edge of the bed, eyes on the floor, spine straight, shoulders back, head high, pulse calm and steady.

He sighs, as if disappointed. Crouches on the floor just out of reach of my feet, should I decide to try and kick his teeth in; he draws that ridiculous gold-plated hand-cannon of his and angles it in my general direction.

"I *will* have my son, Sophia Sousa."

I lift my eyes to his. "My name is Sophia Bruna Santos de Silva. I am not your wife. I am not your anything. I never was and I never will be. And that child will never know who you are. To him, you will only ever be the villain responsible for his mother's death."

He seems genuinely puzzled. "But you are not dead yet."

I laugh at this. "Not me, you idiot. Beatriz. That pompous fool, Pugli, murdered her in front of him."

"Which means I did not kill her."

"It was at your behest, and he knows it." I don't know if this is true, but I'll see that it is. "He doesn't know who I am either, Rafa." I meet his dark, cruel, vicious stare. "And so it will remain. Do your worst. There is nothing you can do to me which I have not already endured. You cannot break me. Torture me, beat me, set your thugs upon me—I have survived it. I survived my father's worst. I have survived *your* worst. I will survive this, too."

He shakes his head. "I have no wish to harm you. I just want my heir."

"He is not your heir. Find a woman who wants you, Rafa. There has to be some brainless, greedy tramp out there stupid enough to let you violate her into having your sick whelp. The child you seek will never, *ever* belong to you. He will never, *ever* know your world. He is innocent and he will remain so, no matter what you do to me or any of us who have been caught in your twisted web of vengeance and greed."

"Sophia, you leave me little choice. I was hoping we could resolve this with some civility."

"We can, Rafa. Go back to Brazil. Run your pathetic criminal empire as you wish—I could not care less what you do, as long as I, my employer, my men, and their partners are left alone. And the boy, obviously. Forget us, Rafa. Leave us alone."

He stands up, paces away, and then abruptly whirls on me, jamming the gun barrel into my wound, ripping a cry of pain from me, despite my best effort to remain silent. "I *will* have my son, Sophia."

"No, Rafa," I growl through gritted teeth, meeting his furious stare with one of my own. "You will *not*."

He jerks the gun away, bizarrely calm once more, the fury buried as if it never was. "You have never called me Rafa. You know I dislike it." He spins on his heel, pries my jaw open with cruelly strong fingers, and shoves the cold, hard barrel of his gun into my mouth. "I should kill you now and be done with it."

I gag against my will, but my stare is as cold and calm as ever. I lift my chin, daring him to pull the trigger.

After a beat, he yanks it out of my mouth and paces away again, pistol dangling at his side. "That would be too easy. Too fast. Perhaps I've been going about this wrong. Perhaps you need a different kind of motivation."

"I don't know where he is, Rafa," I say, truthfully. "I don't know, and I can't tell you what I don't know even if I wanted to."

He tips his head to one side, ceding the point. "Perhaps. But you know how to find out. "

"Just have another child, Rafa," I repeat. "One you can twist and manipulate into your evil little clone."

"You are missing the point, Sophia. I do not *want* a different child. I want *him*. He is cartel royalty. He is *my* son. He is *your* son. He is the grandson of Bruno de Silva."

"He is none of those things. He is the son of an innocent Colombian woman named Beatriz. He is just a boy." I lay down and turn away from him, facing the wall. "Do as you wish, Rafa. I have said all I will say. Just know that unless you forget this silly, petty, childish vendetta, you will die, soon, at my hands."

He hisses in disgust. "I really fucking hate you, do you know that?"

I turn my head enough to make it clear he's gotten my attention back for a moment. "I spent a long time hating you. I have resolved to waste no more of my life on the emptiness of hate. I will kill you because you require killing. Because I made a vow ten years ago as I bled my way across the jungle that you would die at my hands, and that is a vow I intend to keep. But I no longer hate you. I have freed myself from the bondage of hatred."

He snorts. "A pretty speech, Sophia. Very inspiring." He crosses the room slowly, leans over me, and whispers softly in my ear. "We shall see how your resolve holds up against what I have planned."

Fuck.

That doesn't sound good at all.

Three days pass in a haze of stultifying boredom, hunger, thirst, and pain. I am fed once a day, allowed to drink once a day, and, obviously, am given nothing for the pain of my wounds, not that I want or need it.

I hear a helicopter approach around midday on the third day since waking up. It lands, idles for a few minutes, and then departs. Someone getting on or off, I imagine.

Moments later, I hear feet. A key in the lock, the door opens. I remain as I am, hands still bound behind my back—they cut my hands free while I eat under the cold eyes of three armed guards, guns pointed at me, fingers on triggers, and then re-bind me when I've finished.

The door opens.

"Sophia." Rafael's voice is curiously eager. "I have someone I'd like you to meet."

Fuck.

I sit up and turn to face him; a woman of perhaps twenty or twenty-five stands before him, shivering, tear-tracks on her cheeks. I don't know her. But I know what's next: I talk, or he tortures her in front of me.

I sigh, and lift my eyes to hers. "English?"

"No English," she mumbles. "Español."

I address her in Spanish. "I will tell you the unpleasant truth. He is going to hurt you very badly to try to get me to tell him information." Her eyes shimmer wet with fear. "Do you have a child?"

Rafael watches and listens, curious, letting this play out.

She nods. "A son. Alejandro. He is three."

I search for the ice and the steel that have gotten me through so much, and I wrap myself in it. I am *La Víbora. La Reina de Hielo.* "I have a son, too. He is ten years old. That man is his father. He wants me to tell him where my son is so he can make my son like him. I will not."

The woman's eyes close as she comprehends my meaning, my intent. "I understand."

"I'm sorry," I whisper. "Forgive me."

She shakes her head. "There is nothing to forgive. I would do the same."

Rafael has a tool in his left hand, which he tucks under his armpit so he can give a slow clap. "How lovely. How inspiring." He grips the tool once more—a pair of industrial bolt cutters. "How stupid."

He digs in a hip pocket and produces a large, black-bladed folding knife, and from the other pocket a cigar lighter. These he places on the floor at his feet, holds the bolt cutters in his hands, and glances over his shoulders. Two burly men enter and take the woman by the arms. One grips her right hand by the wrist while the other pins her jaw to force her to look at me.

Raffael's eyes never leave mine as he severs her thumb at the first joint with a swift clack of the tool. The woman screams, sags, sobs. The men let her drop to the floor.

Rafael tosses the cutters to one of the men, and then holds the blade in the flame until the metal is red hot. He cauterizes the stump with the flat of the knife, and the scent of boiling blood and seared flesh fills the room.

The woman's screams are breathless and silent.

Rafael rises to his feet, ushers his men out, and pauses in the doorway. "I'll leave you two to discuss things."

Fuck.

Can I hold out? Once, I could have. When I was Inez, fully and truly. When my heart was atrophied and shriveled and cold and empty and calcified in my chest. But now?

I don't know. Even for Little Ren, can I sit here and watch Rafael cut this innocent woman to pieces?

I force myself to sit up straight and stare blankly at Rafael as he assesses me.

He shakes his head. "Women," he grumbles, his tone derogatory and derisive. "Your new bleeding heart will only allow so much, I think. A few more fingers and you'll break." He leaves, locking the door behind himself.

When he's gone, I watch the woman cradle her hand to her belly, shuddering silent sobs. "I'm sorry," I whisper.

She crawls into a corner as far from me as she can get, curls up facing the wall, and weeps softly.

I lay back down and let guilt eat me.

"If you break, it will be for nothing," she whispers, eventually. "You cannot break."

The hate I claimed to have rid myself of erupts from deep within me, white-hot and calculating; it seems I'm not done hating Rafael after all.

CHAPTER 14

THE LAST FIREFIGHT

LORENZO

THE MOOD IN THE ROOM IS MOROSE, BITTER, AND angry. We took a block of rooms at a Best Western just off the freeway in the eastern outskirts of suburban LA. The women, wisely, sensed the collective mood and retreated together into one of the other rooms where they're eating carryout and watching TV, opting to let the men stew in our anger without them.

I scan the room: Sol, Sax, and Si are sitting together with their backs to the wall beside the TV stand; Chance leans in the bathroom doorway, massive and hulking and brooding; Rev and Kane take up one of the beds, Kane with his back to the headboard while Rev perches on the edge, long legs stretched out; Lash and I are on the other bed in similar arrangement, and Scarlett is by herself with her back against the door.

Solomon's phone buzzes, and our attention turns to him all at once as he answers it. "Yeah, hey there, bud… you did? Fucking killer, where? Fuck, that's tricky. Okay, thanks. Bye." He tosses the phone down between his thighs. "So my friend at the NSA was able to track the boat out into the Pacific. That's the good news. The bad news is Rafael's no dummy. He joined up with five other yachts that look identical, from the sky at least, and they're constantly rotating positions and breaking away and rejoining. Playing an ocean-going version of the shell game, essentially, so we have no idea which yacht he has Inez on."

"Sneaky fucking bastard," Rev grumbles. "So now what? Sitting here with our thumbs up our asses ain't doin' her any good."

Kane rubs his face with both hands. "Y'know, I've kinda forgotten why any of this is happening in the first place, other than Rafael is a prick and Pugli is a bastard."

"Sophia and Rafael's son," I answer. "That's why. And also because Rafael is a vindictive prick who won't rest until we've all paid for making a fool of him."

"As for Pugli," Lash says, "he is a sadistic psychopath. He needs no greater purpose than to cause pain."

"Why is he after the Big Boss?" Silas asks. "What's he got to do with anything?"

Lash shrugs. "Who knows? Perhaps to get at us, perhaps Pugli knows our employer, perhaps just out of some perverse sense of vindictiveness. It doesn't matter."

"So we know Inez is on a boat somewhere in the Pacific," Saxon says, eying me. "Why not hit all the boats? I'm done fucking around. Oath be damned, I'm about to start murdering some motherfuckers." He lurches to his feet, scraping his hand over his scalp, mussing his hair. "Fuck this. Fuck Mercado, fuck Pugli, fuck the oath. The gloves are off. Rafael wants to play games? Fucking *fine*. Let's play games." He produces a small folding knife from his pocket, slices open his palm, and paints his face crimson. "The rest of you can do whatever the fuck you want."

"Saxon!" Solomon snaps, shooting to his feet. "You can't just—"

Saxon, his hand on the doorknob, whirls on his brother. "Watch me, brother. Those fucking bastards have chased us all over the goddamned globe. They've kidnapped us. Tortured us. Killed innocent people. And what have we done? Not a goddamn thing but react. And now they have Inez—a-*fucking*-gain. The boss can take care of himself, whatever. Sure, I owe him. And I'll pay up, whatever he asks. But I'm fucking *done* pussy-footing around, missing on purpose, wearing kid fucking gloves while these turd-licking cockroach motherfuckers rape and murder with impunity. Inez is one of us. She brought us all in. Gave us this family. Shed blood for us. Took lives for us. You all wanna sit here and come up with some PG kindergarten cop version of a rescue plan? Be my fucking guest. I won't be part of it. You wanna know why? Because I'm the Bloody fucking Viking."

He goes to jerk the door open, but the chain lock is engaged, and the door yanks against the chain with a loud crack. Snarling, Saxon grips the edge of the door in both hands and rips it open, tearing the chain free of the post, leaving a bloody handprint on the white wood.

We all watch him stride out the door, dripping blood from his hand, leaving a stunned silence in his wake.

Rev stands up, scans the room, looks at the open door, and then swaggers out after Saxon without a word.

Chance follows Rev.

Kane goes too, pausing in the doorway to look back at the rest of us. "I'll carve the brand out of my own arm if the boss asks me to, for breaking the vow. We are who we are. This is what we do. And Sax is right. Enough is fuckin' enough. I'm done bein' a victim. And Inez has been through more than enough."

Sol raises his arm and looks at the broken arrow brand on the inside of his left arm. He stands up, next. "I took the vow because I was sick of the life. I'd seen too much, done too much. Been through too much. I know you're all the same. I wanna get back to a life where the worst thing I have to do is toss a drunk outta the club. Sax is right—sometimes violence really is the only way to get through to people."

"We are going after Inez, I assume?" Lash asks. "Pugli is in the wind, for the moment. In pursuit of our employer, I should think. Or merely recuperating."

Sol shrugs, nods. "I'm guessing the Boss can handle himself. Inez needs us."

Lash nods, rising to his feet. "There is no question. I am with the brotherhood."

Silas stands as well, rolling his shoulders. "Let's end this shit."

That leaves only me. I get to my feet, gritting my teeth against the blaze of pain in my hip, and the three of us file out together.

We find the others two doors down with the women, saying goodbye. Toro, Taj, and Fonz are clustered together by the window, watching.

Taj clears his throat, and the room falls silent. "Toro, Fonz, and myself, we understand that the battle you fight is yours. We will remain here with the women and keep them safe until you have safely returned with Inez."

"You're good men," Solomon says. "Thank you."

Toro just nods, Taj says nothing, and Fonz laughs. "Good men? I dunno about that, but we got you covered.

Ain't nobody gettin' no hands on no bitches." Six pairs of eyes turn to pin Fonz in place at his choice of words. "You know what the fuck I mean, don't get your titties twisted."

Scarlett narrows her eyes at him, her glare cold. "Fonz, you need to learn when to not be funny, if you're going to be part of this group."

Fonz holds up his hands. "May as well ask water to stop being wet, but if ya'll can't take a joke, I'll try an' be a bit more P-C."

"It is not a matter of political correctness, Mister The Fonz," Anjalee says in her soft, quiet voice. "It is a matter of not using insulting and offensive language in reference to people you are supposed to be caring about. We are knowing you do not mean to say that we are bitches, but perhaps it is better to not risk offense, I think. There is a saying in English which I have heard: discretion is the better part of valor. And perhaps in this case, you could substitute comedy for valor. Yes?"

Fonz eyes her. "Even takin' me to task, you're nice about it." he sighs. "I hear ya. Didn't mean nothin' by it, but I take your point."

Anjalee turns back to Kane, kisses him, and then pushes him toward the door. "Go and rescue Sophia. Whatever it takes. Yes?"

Kane palms her ass and yanks her to him. "God, I love you, y'know that?"

She rests her head on his chest. "Yes, I do know. Quite well. And I love you." She wriggles from his grasp and gives him another hard shove toward the door. "Go! Do the violence upon the men who have caused such strife in our lives. It is all they respect, men like those. I do not love you for an oath, I love you for who you are. And I know you would not lightly go against it."

Kane lets her shove propel him into a trot, and he doesn't look back. I watch the rest of the men say their goodbyes, and then I turn to Toro, Taj, and Fonz. "Protect them or die trying."

Taj frowns at me. "Are you quite certain you should go, considering your injured state?"

"Inez is my woman." I shrug. "You could not keep me here even if I was on death's door."

Toro salutes me in perfect parade ground form. "We have the watch, *mi hermano*."

I nod at him, and then turn on my heel and follow the others, gritting my teeth against the biting agony that dogs my every step.

———— ◆ ————

The mini-flotilla of yachts—similar, if not identical—has spread out across several nautical miles, bobbing steadily southward. This works in our favor, as the distance between the boats means we can hit them one by one without sacrificing the element of surprise.

Silas is the somewhat surprising source of our ability to even reach the flotilla—he leveraged a contact in the LA drug scene, a business associate he had extensive dealings with during his time as a major mover of product for the Syndicate. The contact, known only as Crash, provided a helicopter flight out into the Pacific toward the last known location of the small fleet of yachts.

Crash's higher-ups, you see, don't like Rafael's intrusion into the delicate balance of power between the various criminal factions that have divvied up LA; nor do they appreciate Pugli's political interference, and most of all, they despise the extra attention from law enforcement recent events have caused. It's a productive trade-off for them: give us what we need to hit Rafael and rescue Inez, and we do the bloody work of removing their problem without having to risk their own personnel.

Which is how I find myself in the belly of a helo, kitted out in body armor, night vision, with mags for my rifle and sidearm strapped to the vest, and plenty of flashbangs and frag grenades, stomach in my throat as the aircraft skims a handful of feet above the black, rippling surface of the sea. My injuries throb, and my molars ache from constantly gritting them against the incessant ache.

Beside me, Solomon is thumbing shells into a magazine—more for something to do with his hands than because we need more magazines. The helicopter banks sharply, showing the darkly glittering metallic sea at a nauseating angle, the tips of the rotors seeming to nearly brush the waves themselves. The angle of the bank tips me into Solomon, pressing my injured hip against the corner of his holstered sidearm, sending a flare of pain through me so sharp and hot that a breathless groan escapes my clenched teeth.

Sol eyes me. "Dude, you good?"

"Sim," I grit out, "fine."

Solomon barks a laugh and extends his right leg so he can dig into his hip pocket. He produces a handful of single-serving NSAID packets, the kind you can find for sale in a hotel gift shop. "Picked these up at the Bellagio. It ain't as good as lollipop, but better than nothing."

I take several of the packets. "Lollipop? What good would candy be for me?"

Sol chuckles. "It's what we call those fentanyl lozenge things. Ever use one?"

I nod. "Oh, yes. I would do terrible things for one, right now." I rip open packets until I have a handful of blue gel capsules, which I throw back all at once and wash down with a swallow of water. "Thank you, my friend."

Sol nods. "For sure." He glances at me for a moment, and then away. "You know, none of us would think less of you if you—"

"I would," I cut in. "If it was your Scarlett out there and you were in my place, would you sit out the op?"

Sol shakes his head. "Fuck no. Wild horses couldn't keep me away."

I shove the rest of the packets into my pocket for later—I'll need them, I'm sure. "Then you understand. But I appreciate the sentiment. I will be fine. We just have to find Sophia before that monster gets his…." I trail off, my voice shaking with rage. "We *have* to find her, Sol. And quickly."

Sol gently squeezes my knee. "We will." The helo flares to hover over the bobbing shadow of a yacht. Flashlight beams spear the night sky. "Here we go."

I tug my gloves on, tighten the wrist straps, and get to my feet, growling at the protesting pulse of pain. Refusing to limp, I follow Sol to the open doorway, waiting for my turn to fast-rope down. Kane, secured to the interior of the helo, rips off burst after burst at the flashlights and starbursts of gunfire, giving the rest of us time to rope down to the deck.

When it's my turn, I zip down the line, halt myself at the last second, and land heavily on my good leg, dropping to a knee and rolling once to absorb the impact of the landing.

The chatter of automatics greets me, and rounds whip overhead, muzzle-flare brightening the night's gloom. Sol, Chance, and Rev fan out around me as Saxon drops down to the deck, Scarlett next, then Lash, and Silas landing last. Kane stays in the helo, clipped in and perched on the edge, one foot on the skid as he cuts down tango after tango with short, precise bursts.

Unlike every other engagement I've been in with these men, when enemies drop, they do so silently and stay down. Each burst is a kill-shot.

I leave the gunfight to the others and bolt across the deck for the cabin. I kick open the door to a small but well-appointed saloon, dark and quiet—empty. A hand grabs my right shoulder—Silas taking my six. I find the stairs leading down to the rooms—it's steep, more of a ladder, and getting down it without crying out in pain takes everything I've got. Sweating and panting from the effort, I hobble down a narrow, low-ceilinged hallway; I shoulder open each door as I reach it and sweep the room. Empty, empty, empty.

When I've checked each room, I report over comms. "Negative, negative. She's not here. Move out."

Our airborne ride has long since departed, committing us to the op, now. Sol takes command of the yacht while the others dump the bodies overboard, and within minutes of the last shot being fired, we're moving at full speed for the next nearest target. The yacht has a tender, of course—a small boat for getting to shore from an anchored yacht. As we approach the next target, Solomon kills the yacht's engines while Silas and Saxon deploy the tender.

Getting down to it with a bum fucking leg is excruciating, but then, everything hurts right now. The ibuprofen is helping a bit, enough to take the worst of the edge off. Once we're all on board the tender, Chance guns the motor and we cross the dark, choppy sea toward the yacht; it's running dark, so it's little more than a black shadow against the night, but the low throb of its engine guides us. A hundred or so yards out, Chance slows the tender's motor to a quiet chug, and we slide toward the yacht. Right on cue, the chop of helicopter rotors stipples across the sea, echoing and dopplering so it's impossible to determine where it's coming from. Lights wink to life on the yacht's deck, and voices waft across the water. I catch bits and pieces in Spanish. I see the helo skimming the surface like a hunting dragonfly, and then it flares and twists to present Kane, spraying burst after burst at the yacht's stern, distracting them as we approach the bow.

Rev secures a line to the side of the yacht and hauls himself up hand-over-hand, and then helps the rest of us ascend—embarrassingly, it's all I can do to simply hang on to the rope and let Chance use his brute strength to pull me aboard.

Silas and I make for the cabin while the others glide like vengeful ghosts sternward, rifles *TAKTAKTAK*ing. Bodies hit the deck in quiet thumps, and one of them topples overboard with a loud splash that's drowned out by the gunfire.

Another fruitless sweep of the belowdecks leaves me in even more of a blind rage; I'm first back down into the tender, molars gritted so hard they ache, putting a throb of tension behind my forehead. Moments later, the now-full tender is skimming toward our next target.

The process is repeated four more times, and each one is empty except for a handful of Mercado thugs.

The fifth yacht goes down as easily as the first four, also empty.

We approach the sixth and last yacht as dawn threatens the night sky with reaching, spreading, staining fingers of gray and pink and pale orange

Sol grips my shoulder and squeezes. "She'll be on this one, brother."

"She better be," I snap.

My gut tightens as the sleek, low shadow of the yacht creases the horizon. A sour snake of worry curls in my belly, a forewarning I've come to instinctively trust. "She's here," I murmur. "But this...this won't be good, I fear."

"Stay calm, Ren," Solomon mutters in my ear as the tender slows; the helo's rotors thud in the distance, approaching low and fast. "Stay frosty. We've got this. Inez is a survivor—she'll be fine."

A shrill scream of female agony tears across the sea—Solomon's hand on my shoulder is the only thing that keeps me in the tender, otherwise I would have leapt into the sea and tried to swim to her.

As it is, I half rise from the bench, snarling as Solomon restrains me. "Sophia!" I growl. "Sophia!"

"We'll get her, brother," Solomon says in my ear. "Sit down. Wait. Just—wait. Thirty seconds, Ren, and you're up there."

Rev joins the effort to keep me in the boat, and it takes both of them to hold me back. Another scream echoes across the water—female again. I lurch forward, nearly breaking Rev's and Sol's hold on me; they yank me back down by my vest at the last second, and the tender rocks violently.

Another scream.

A shout, male, in Spanish: *"Hijo de puta!"* Another female screams. *"Dime! ¡Dime dónde está!"*

"Jodéte. Come mierda."

A scream.

Sounds carry on the water. Her scream is awful, piercing. Close. Blood-curdling.

I don't remember the ascent to the deck. I hear the helo. Kane's rifle chattering. Silas follows me, hand on my shoulder as we descend into the belly of the beast, toward the screams.

Silas's rifle barks behind me, and I hear the thud of a body hitting the floor. "Got your six, brother," he murmurs. "Get in there."

Gunfire crackles overhead.

I kick the door in and it slams inward as a shout of shocked male pain echoes.

The sight that greets me is one that will haunt me for the rest of my days.

Blood, everywhere.

A woman I don't know slumped in a chair, bleeding from…everywhere. Just…blood. So much blood.

And Inez on her back on the floor in the ocean of blood, Rafael clutched in a leg-lock, his eyes wide, hands reaching, batting, swiping, pawing. Her face is a rictus of hate.

Her thighs clench around his throat, his face going red, heels scrabbling in the slick sea of blood.

I limp into the room. Draw my knife and drop it onto

the floor next to Inez. Stare down at Rafael's gasping, gurgling face, into his desperate, terrified eyes.

Inez snags the knife. Whispers something to Rafael. I see her lips move, reading in them her words to Rafael: "I've waited a very long time to do this, *husband*."

She drives the knife into his belly—slowly, slowly.

CHAPTER 15

BONDS FORGED IN BLOOD

INEZ

I CAN'T STOP MYSELF FROM TOPPLING INTO SLEEP. It's a restless slumber, fraught with nightmares— memories of bygone horrors. I wake screaming, my skin crawling with the memory of cruel greedy grasping hands bruising my flesh as the cot creaked beneath me, hot rank breath on my face, male sweat dripping into my eyes.

I claw back to wakefulness, panting and sweating. Levering myself upright, I see the woman still huddled in the same corner, listless and vacant-eyed.

Her gaze drags to mine. "You have many bad dreams," she says to me.

"Yes." I jut my chin at the door. "Because of him."

"If you do not tell him, then what? He will cut off all my fingers, maybe, or who knows what else. I will die—I know this. My Alejandro has his grandmother and grand-father, so at least I know he will be loved."

"I'm sorry," I whisper again. "You should not be here. This has nothing to do with you."

"You did not bring me here."

"But you are here because of me."

She shrugs. "Perhaps. What is the point of saying it

is your fault, or his fault, or anyone's? I will not get my finger back. I will never see my son again. But when I am no more use to him, what else will he do to get you to tell him what he wants to know?"

"Anything. Everything." I sigh. "I will kill him. If I can save you, I will."

She shrugs as if it doesn't matter and turns her gaze away to the window.

I don't know how much time passes, then. Daylight fades. Evening descends.

I've almost fallen asleep again out of sheer boredom when I hear someone approaching outside the door. My stomach tightens, sours.

Here we go.

The woman hears it as well and shrinks into the smallest ball possible. "No, no, no," she whimpers, "god save me, please no."

It's not time, yet. Instinct tells me I have to wait, bide my time.

The lock disengages, the knob turns, the door swings inward.

"I'm sorry," I whisper. "I'm so sorry."

Rafael enters, dragging a chair. The same two burly thugs enter after him, and they unceremoniously haul the woman to her feet, drag her to the chair, and shove her into it.

They stand on either side of her, each with a hand on her shoulder, holding her down.

Rafael tosses the bolt cutters onto the floor at her feet with a loud clatter that makes her jump with a startled half-scream.

Rafael laughs. "Haven't even started yet and she's

already screaming. This should prove quite…arousing." His eyes meet mine, glittering with wicked delight. "Have you told your new friend who I am? The things I enjoy?" He looks from me to her, expectantly. When neither of us answers, he shrugs. "No matter. I'll find out what I wish to know, one way or another, and I'll have fun in the process." He laughs, a dark, evil chuckle as he crouches in front of the woman in his white linen suit and pale blue silk shirt, wrinkle-free and pristine. "You won't enjoy this very much, I'm afraid. But I certainly will."

Breathing hard through clenched teeth, the woman is growling and keening, eyes wild. "Please…please. Please don't. Please don't."

"Does begging change my mind, Sophia?" he says, his voice a serpentine, slithering whisper.

I stay silent.

He sighs. "Sophia, you are being petty. It's a simple, innocent question." When I remain silent, he slips that same black knife from his pocket, flips it open, and taps the woman's nose with the flat. "It's not me you should plead with, you know. It's her. The second she tells me what I need to know, I'll send you home. Not in one piece, obviously, but alive. So, my dear, I really do encourage you to beg. Beg for your life. Beg her to tell me where my son is."

She considers it. I see it in her eyes, on her face. Her eyes go to mine, searching me. She spits in his face, then, perhaps hoping he'll merely kill her right then out of rage. Oh, my friend, how little you know the monster before you.

He rocks back on his heels, grinning as the gobbet of saliva trickles down his cheek. "I see. Well. I suppose I have my answer, then, don't I?" He whips a handkerchief out of his jacket's inside pocket, wipes his face with it, and then drops it over the woman's head so it covers her eyes. Mostly. Just enough to obscure her vision. So she can't anticipate what he does next.

He glances at the men. "Hold her, my friends. I don't want to tie her up if I don't have to. It's more fun this way."

She thrashes, dislodging the handkerchief, and one of the men grabs her by the hair, wrapping the long mass of it around his fist, and yanks her head backward, hard, and then forces it forward again. Replaces the handkerchief. Keeps a tight grip on her hair.

Rafael crouches in front of her again, knife in hand, and slices the blade up the front of her leggings, making sure to let the cutting edge slide along her skin, drawing a thin cut up her shin from ankle to knee, to thigh, to hip. He does the same to the other side, and then slices away her underwear. Her legs drip blood in root-like rivulets down her skin.

She thrashes again, fighting as hard as she can. She manages to get off a kick that catches Rafael under the chin, making his teeth clack together and knocking him on his ass.

He shoots to his feet, snarling. "I said *hold her*, you useless shitstains!" He spits blood. "Made me bite my tongue, you whore. Chain her legs to the chair. *Now*."

One of the thugs pulls a set of handcuffs from his pocket and secures her leg to the chair, and then produces another pair from the same pocket and does it to the other leg.

"Now hold the stupid bitch or I'll turn you into shark bait," Rafael says.

The men tighten their grip on her, fingers digging into her flesh.

Rafael crouches in front of her again, glancing back at me over his shoulder. "Sophia, please. I know you don't want to see this poor innocent woman suffer. I'm sure there's some silly sisterhood of mothers or some nonsense like that making you think you share a bond. But there is no bond. You will sit there and watch me slice her to pieces, Sophia. Her blood will be on your conscience."

I say nothing; it already is.

He sighs. "Very well. You always were far too stubborn for anyone's good. I know I should just kill you and be done with it, but I too am stubborn, you see."

He wedges himself between her legs and carves the blade up her belly, slicing open her shirt, and then her bra, leaving her naked.

Her eyes go to mine, pleading—just for a moment. And then the blank stare takes over and she drops her gaze from mine.

What follows, over the next few hours, is a waking nightmare to rival those days in the cell. Worse, almost. I can endure pain. I can swallow agony and trauma. But watching Rafael slowly torture this woman by degrees? It's fucking awful.

I think of him—my son. Lorenzo—Little Ren. I think of him watching Pugli blow his mother's brains out. I think of his fear. He is safe—he's with Nick Harris and his men, hidden in a bunker on a private island in the Caribbean, guarded by some of the most fearsome operators on the planet—aside from my boys, I mean.

I think of him, and I know I cannot give him up. Not for this woman. Not for anything. Everything I've been through would be for nothing, if Rafael gets his hands on him now.

No.

I must endure.

I make myself watch.

Every cut. Every plucked fingernail. Every severed finger.

When hours have passed and I've not spoken a single word, Rafael finally loses his temper.

With a snarl of venomous rage, he drives the knife into the woman's thigh, low, near the knee, and begins twisting the blade until she screams.

"*Tell* me, Sophia," he hisses, his voice razor thin and dangerously quiet. "Tell me."

He twists the blade harder, and she screams again. "Tell me!"

"Never!" I snap, the first words I've spoken since he entered.

He yanks the knife free, and blood wells from the hole in her thigh, trails down her calf to form a growing puddle on the floor.

"Dammit," he snarls. "The clock is ticking, now."

I hear something—a low sound, distant, hard to make out over the throb of the engines and the woman's dull sobbing.

In between sobs, I hear it again, and I have to suppress a grin of glee.

It's a helicopter.

They're here.

They've come.

I have to distract Rafael, now. Give them time.

The woman is limp and weak from exhaustion, agony, and blood loss. She's beyond fighting. Rafael turns to me, pricking my throat with the tip of the blade. "Tell…me… where…he…is."

"Somewhere even you can't reach him," I whisper. "You will never have him. He will never know your name. You will never see his face."

With a wordless shout of anger, he whirls, and slams the knife back down into the same wound in her thigh, twisting again. "Son of a bitch!" he shouts. "*TELL ME*! Tell me where he is!"

"Fuck you!" I shout back at the top of my voice, to cover the muffled thumping. "Eat shit."

"Tell me," he snarls, twisting the knife again, harder now, drawing another weak scream.

I hear the crackle of automatics, and I have to fight to keep the currents of energy from showing on my face. "He's with the president of Brazil. They adopted him."

"Lies!" he snaps.

One of the men cocks his head, finally hearing the noise topside. "Uh, chief? You hear that?"

Rafael leaves the knife buried in her thigh and straightens, eying the ceiling, listening. "Oh, yes, now I do. The boys are shooting at birds, I suppose. Go see."

Rafael turns to watch his men exit, and that's when I make my move. Long since having tightened the zipties to the point of pain, I slam my wrists down against my upward-driving knee. The first blow, nothing happens. I try again, and a third time, and on the third attempt, the plastic snaps, freeing my hands.

Rafael hears, whirls, sees me with my hands free, and springs at me.

I roll to my back and lash out with both feet, catching

him mid-jump. My kick flings him backward to slam against the side of the door, momentarily dazed.

I roll forward, toppling to my knees in the slick pool of blood, grabbing at the knife hilt. I yank it free. The woman's eyes meet mine, faint and weak. "Kill me."

I snick the blade through the plastic binding my feet. Rafael groans, stirs, rolls to his hands and knees, shaking his head, and then glares at me. "I don't think so, bitch."

He lunges. The fact that he slips in the blood is the only thing that gives me enough time for my act of mercy.

I drive the blade up under her ribs and into her heart. Her eyes fly wide, locked on mine. "I'm sorry," I whisper again, as the light fades from her eyes.

Rafael slams into me in a flying tackle. The wind is knocked out of me, and I crack my head against the floor. Stars whirl behind my eyes as Rafael clambers atop me, his greater weight pinning me to the floor. His hands wrap around my throat, and he starts squeezing. The dancing stars grow larger, obscuring my vision with whirling white spots. I hear gunfire, closer now. Feet on stairs. A familiar voice. A three-round burst.

Just before the white spots threaten to pull me into nothingness, I kick upward, hook my leg around Rafael's throat, twist and roll like a crocodile with his thrashing body clamped in the unforgiving vise of my thighs. Blood is tacky and cold under me. Gunfire rattles. The helicopter thumps. Rafael gurgles, thrashes helplessly, his hands pawing at my leg, heels kicking in the blood.

Something heavy smashes against the door, which flies open with a loud slam.

Ren.

My Lorenzo.

He's here.

He hobbles into the room, rifle sweeping the space as his eyes land on me, and Rafael struggling in my grip.

He grins, a small, pleased curve of his lips that I doubt he's even aware of. Limps toward me, draws his combat knife—a long, serrated, razor-sharp KA-BAR—and tosses it onto the floor beside me.

Rafael sees it, hears it, and thrashes even harder, gasping for air, gurgling, trying to plead.

I grab the knife hammer-style. "I have waited a very long time to do this, *husband*," I whisper, the words intended only for his ears.

I press the tip against his belly, just above his navel. Apply just enough pressure to slowly—so, so slowly—drive the knife into his belly. It pierces his skin first, and he tries to cry out. I loosen the grip of my thighs so he doesn't choke out too soon.

Sucking in a hissing, desperate breath, he gurgles a plea. "So—Sophia—p-p-please." He wriggles like a worm on a hook.

I slide the knife in another inch. "This is what gets you off, is it, Rafa? This?" I twist the knife a little. "Not so arousing when you're the one in agony, is it?"

He tries to scream, and when he does, I drive the knife in a little further. Twist it. Push it deeper.

I hear footsteps—many.

Flick my gaze toward the door—Lorenzo is just inside, watching impassively; his jeans are dark with blood from a wound to his hip. Silas is just behind him. Chance, Rev, Lash, Kane, Saxon, Solomon, and Scarlett are all clustered behind Silas, crowded in to watch.

Plunging the knife in to the hilt, I grab a handful of his

hair and yank his head to the side. "You see them, Rafa?" I whisper. "My friends. My brothers. My family. We are survivors. Warriors. We beat you."

I yank the blade free, release my grip on his throat, and scramble to my feet, slipping in the blood. He gasps, coughs. "Sophia—"

I whirl, kick his face as if trying to boot a football across the pitch. His jaw cracks and teeth clatter.

I stomp out. "Bring him topside. Do what you want on the way, but make sure he's alive."

Lorenzo grabs at my arm. "Sophia, *meu amor*—"

I jerk my arm free. "Not yet, Lorenzo."

He lets me go.

"What about...her?" Kane's voice follows me.

I turn in place, frantically trying to keep my icy mask in place, to keep my shoulders from shaking. My legs threaten to give out as I look at the poor, dead, innocent woman. "I...she..." I choke on my guilt and sorrow. Turn to Lorenzo but don't meet his eyes—I can't. "Deal with it. Please? He—so I'd...but I didn't. I couldn't. Ren, please. I can't. I can't."

He brushes my cheekbone with a thumb. "Of course. I'll take care of her."

I turn away, leave the room. Ascend the stairs. I hear a dull, soft thud and a groan.

Back under the open sky, dawn is a creeping blush of salmon and tangerine on the endless western horizon. Acid batters the back of my teeth, and I bend over the bow railing and vomit until my stomach curls in on itself, empty, and still I retch.

The scent of death surrounds me, wafting to me in snatches and fragments, and that's when I look around.

Dead bodies everywhere—Rafael had quite a few men on this boat. No way I'd have taken them all out alone, had I tried to escape any sooner. I couldn't have saved her. I could only have died trying.

Each dead body leaks gore from bullet holes to T-boxes, precise and perfectly placed, each one.

A minute or two later, I hear scuffling. Rafael lurches and trips onto the deck, sprawling face-first. His face is a ruin. He's drooling blood, groaning, sobbing. His belly seeps blood. But all in all, I think the men let him off fairly easily.

Kane goes to yank him to his feet, but I hold out a hand to stop him. "Leave him, for now. He'll need what strength he has left."

I turn, spying an orange life preserver on a nearby wall. With curious eyes watching me, I tie the ring to a corpse. Glance at Silas, nearest me. "Knife."

He draws one, flips it to grasp the blade, and proffers the handle to me. I stab it into the corpse's diaphragm and drag it downward in a single, violent yank.

"Um, he's already dead, boss-lady," Kane says.

"I am aware, Kane, thank you." I wipe the blade on the corpse and return it to Silas, and then step back, glancing at Chance. "Toss him in."

Frowning in confusion, Chance does as I ask, dragging the body to the railing and heaving it over the side with a splash. The life preserver prevents the body from sinking while the effluvia leaks out, staining the water.

It doesn't take very long for them to arrive.

Fins, slicing the water. Circling. Tugging. Yanking. The orange ring bobs and dips like an oversized fishing bobber.

"Oh," Kane says. "Oh *fuck*."

The water thrashes wildly, red and pink bubbles frothing the surface.

I turn away to face Rafael. "Stand him up." I glance at Solomon. "Record this, please."

Solomon pulls out a cell phone and begins recording a video, focusing on Raphael.

Chance grabs a handful of Rafael's hair and hauls him to his feet. Rafael can't stay on his feet, however, hunching and curling in on himself. He may have broken ribs. Who knows? Who cares? Not me.

I step into his space. Put my face to his, grab his jaw and force him to look at me. "My father tried to break me. You tried to break me. You both failed." I squeeze his broken jaw until he howls in agony. "Your son will never know you. You die, now, Rafael, and your name dies with you." I shove him away. "Yours is the last life I will ever take."

Chance frog-marches him to the railing and lets him go; Rafael hunches over the railing, a string of bloody saliva stretching down to the boiling, bloody, fin-filled water. "No," he groans, the word more of a garbled sound than speech. "No, no! Please, please! I'm sorry!"

At least, I think that's what he said.

I put my lips to his ear. "Think of all the times people begged you for mercy, Rafael. Think of them while those creatures down there tear you apart."

"Sophia—please—"

"Fuck—*you*," I snarl in English, because the phrase just doesn't have a direct counterpart in Spanish or Portuguese. "Fuck you all the way to hell."

I shove him over the railing.

We all stand at the railing together, watching as the

sharks tear him, screaming, limb from limb; Solomon records the entire process.

The screams stop after a minute, and I watch until the sea goes still and the waves take the red away.

I find Solomon's eyes. "Get us out of here. Burn the ships." I give him a phone number. "Send the video to that number."

"Yes, ma'am," he says. He turns and immediately starts issuing orders, and the others obey without question. Solomon became the leader, at some point.

"Gentlemen?" I call, and everyone stops to look at me. My throat is tight, hot, thick. "Thank you."

No one seems to know what to say, for a moment. Except Lash. He comes over to me, gently takes my arms, and holds me at arm's length. "You are *ours*, Sophia. We are yours. We are a family, we and the women back at the hotel. We would take on hell itself for you." He holds my gaze. "We owe you everything."

I shake my head. "No, you—"

Solomon moves up beside Lash, resting a hand on my shoulder. "Yes. We do. You chose us. You branded us. You gave us new lives when we all had nothing to live for. You dragged us all out of the darkness."

"It was Jakob," I say, knowing the time for secrecy has ended. "Our employer. It was his plan. I was merely the first."

"Jakob," Solomon echoes, tasting the name, sort of. "His idea, maybe, but it was you who was there for us. It was *you*, Sophia."

My eyes burn. Silas joins his brother and Lash, and then Saxon, and then Chance and Rev, and then Kane, and then Scarlett, surrounding me the way the women did back at the club. Except these men...they *know*. They know the horrors of war and bloodshed and death. They understand the bond forged in battle. They know the demons that haunt me, because they haunt them too.

They surround me, and their hands touch my shoulders, my back, my head. I find Lorenzo, beyond the circle, waiting. I reach for him, and he takes my hand, and I let them have it all.

I let go.

My breaking began a long, long time ago. Perhaps, in a way, I was never whole. Never unbroken. I was six the first time I saw my father kill someone. I was already a crack shot with an air rifle by then. I was a cold-blooded killer when most girls my age were dreaming of their *quinceañera*, or their sweet sixteen. I led men twice my age in assaults against rival cartels when other kids my age were discovering sex and alcohol and weed.

While other girls learned the art of getting blood out of clothes because of periods, I learned it from executing people.

I was never whole.

And then came the day when my father told me I was going to marry Rafael Sousa. His protégé. His real heir, since of course the cartel couldn't go to a mere woman. What followed has been covered—no need to go over it again.

I lied to Rafael: Papa *did* break me. Those days chained to the cot broke me into shards and slivers.

Marrying Rafael broke me again.

Imprisonment, becoming his wife—*La Víbora,* the mistress, the cruel queen of his empire. That broke me.

The vile, depraved, violent things he did to me in trying to impregnate me—that broke me.

The birth. The massacre.

Shattered yet again.

But the healing?

I don't know when that began.

When I opened my eyes and saw Jakob's face, stern and severe and brutally beautiful, jet black hair touched with silver at the temples—early graying from a hard life, he later claimed. That was probably the start. His eyes were cold and hard, but I saw kindness in them. Of a sort, at least.

He took me from the detention center and nursed me to health himself. Helped me regain my strength, my fitness. He never pushed me for my story. He just…took care of me.

I expected him to demand the obvious in return, but he never did. I remember the day I tried to give him the repayment I assumed he would expect. He was in his office working—out of a high-rise in Sacramento, back then, the offices of a shell company owned by other shells and subsidiaries, a tangled web of ownership no one could ever decipher. I stripped out of my clothes outside his office doors, knocked, received permission to enter, and went in. He didn't look up until I was at his desk and he caught sight of me in his peripheral vision.

He'd shot out of his chair and turned away. "Put your fucking clothes on, Inez."

Confused, stung by rejection even though sleeping with Jakob was the last thing I wanted to do, I'd dressed again and came back in.

"This is *not* that kind of relationship," he'd said to me,

his tone hard but not unkind. "It never will be. I am your employer. Perhaps a friend. But nothing more. I do not want that from you. If I did, I would have already claimed it."

We never spoke of it again.

That healed me a little more.

Then he brought me his idea for the Broken Arrows. He didn't have the name yet, just the idea. A few men, down on their luck. Operators. warriors, men forgotten by the country they served. Good men dragged down a dead-end road by the vagaries of life. Destroyed by death and war and violence.

"We save them, Inez," he'd told me. "Redeem them."

"Why?" I'd asked.

He'd spent a long, long time thinking about that answer. "Because I needed redemption, once, and there was no one to give it. I had to find it for myself."

"Redemption from what?" It was the closest I've ever gotten to asking him his story.

"My many, many sins."

"Who?" I asked. "Who do we choose?"

He'd looked out at the Sacramento skyline and considered this. "I'll bring you a list and you choose."

The list he brought me, four months later, was extensive. A hundred names. SEALs, Rangers, Raiders, Green Berets, SWAT, FBI, CIA, NSA, men who worked in the shadows and belonged to no one. Each man had a tale of grief to tell in the pages of their dossiers. I spent a week poring over those dossiers. Winnowing based on feel and intuition. Unfair, perhaps, but the only way I knew how.

Eventually, after ten days of consideration, I chose

a man named Rev, and with him, attached at the hip, it seemed, came a giant named Chance.

Then Kane, the Cabot brothers, Lash…

For a while, I felt little more for them than a kind of guarded consideration—reticent responsibility. The idea, Jakob explained, as we designed and built Club Sin and winnowed the list of candidates, was to take men who had been broken by war, by violence, by sorrow, by guilt—the very things that had broken me, and, I assume, Jakob himself, although to this day I still do not know anything about him except his name—and teach them to embrace peace, to embrace life, to shed their guilt and find redemption through brotherhood and belonging and purpose. Isolate them from the world at large, give them—men built to protect—a simple, single purpose: protect the club and the people inside it, and protect each other. Guard their peace. Free them from the bonds of their past.

I was merely the caretaker, I thought. Sort of a zoo-keeper. I am rather embarrassed to admit that "zookeeper" was the word that ran through my head as I thought about the seven men we had chosen. It escaped my notice for quite some time that I was more like them than I wanted to believe. I stayed in the club. I had a single purpose—run the club, manage the men. Ignore the world beyond the club.

Rather like the men, but I didn't realize that at the time.

It escaped my notice that I was the first broken arrow he'd plucked from the battlefield and chose to fix rather than discard. It was just that I was so much more broken than the men that it took far, far longer for me to find my own redemption.

I assumed I was beyond redemption. Beyond salvation. Beyond fixing.

It's only now, as those seven men—and Scarlett, without whom I would never have even thought to reach for my own chance at love—that I truly grasp Jakob's long-term plan.

He used me to reach the hearts of the men. I brought them in. Showed them the rules. Guarded their peace until they were ready to face their pasts, one by one.

Until Solomon's past caught up to him and dragged me, kicking and screaming, out of the myopic and peaceful world of Club Sin and into the dark, violent, and dangerous larger world, where husbands lurked and lovers waited.

These men are *my* redemption. They fought for me. They risked their lives and shed their blood for me. They broke their vows for me.

For *me*.

They surround me. They don't see my past or my weakness. My guilt.

They accept me.

And then there's Lorenzo.

My eyes meet his, and mine water, burn. My throat tightens. A million thoughts flutter through my mind as we lock gazes, but I can't find anything to say. Words are wholly insufficient for the depth and breadth of how Lorenzo's love, patience, understanding, empathy, and resolve have changed me. Healed me. Opened the pathways in my mind and heart. Bled out the toxins of trauma and horror and fear, making room for love and joy and peace.

He held me when I needed to be held. He gave me

space to be angry and difficult, and loved me anyway. He let me be angry. He gave me control when I needed it, and asked for nothing in return except honesty.

He loved me without any reassurance that I could love him back.

That, perhaps more than anything else, has healed me.

Rafael is dead.

It's over.

The book is closed. It's not a blank page in the same old story. What comes next is a whole new book, a whole new story, one yet to be written—a story we will tell together.

Me, and Lorenzo, and this found family, whose bonds have been forged in blood.

CHAPTER 16

A DIFFERENT KIND OF ADDICTION

LORENZO

IT TURNS OUT THAT THE YACHT RAFAEL HAD CHOSEN as his flagship of his ridiculous shell-game flotilla was the one large enough for a helicopter to land on it. We all crammed together aboard the aircraft—putting us dangerously close to the upper weight limit—and flew back to LA.

Inez was quiet, contemplative. You'd think there would be a bigger reaction to Rafael finally being dead and out of her life for good, but for now she seems content to simply be alive.

I don't push. I just sit as close to her as I can, hold her hand, and try to exude calm and peace.

I don't know what comes next.

Returning to the port where our SUVs are parked, we pile in and head for the hotel where the women are. As the building grows larger in the windshield, I feel a rise in tension inside the vehicle—wondering what fresh mayhem we'll find awaiting us.

The parking lot is half-full, with nothing amiss—no blacked-out Suburbans, nothing on fire, no one running screaming from the lobby, no gunfire, no law enforcement descending like a swarm of vultures. Just a quiet hotel on the edge of the desert.

Moving as a group, armed only with pistols—tucked behind waistbands until we're on our floor—we approach our bank of rooms.

We check them one by one in turn—empty, empty, empty.

Sol, as we reach the last room of the ones we've reserved, pauses with his hand on the knob, listening, waiting, the keycard hovering near the reader.

He looks at me, at his brothers. "Am I the only one expecting the worst, here?"

"No," Saxon grumbles. "Just open the fuckin' door already."

Guns drawn, all ten of us—Rev, Chance, Kane, Saxon, Silas, Solomon, Lash, Inez, Scarlett, and myself—surround the door. Sounds from within reach our ears—chatter, laughter, a hysterical squeal.

"Sounds...fine," Solomon mutters.

"Just open the goddamn door, bro, Jesus," Saxon snaps.

"Fuck, fine," Sol mutters.

"*Your* woman is right here with you," Saxon says. "The rest of us are on pins and fuckin' needles."

Sol taps the key to the reader, the light flashes green, and the lock clicks. Sol shoves the door open with one hand, pistol in the other, and slides in, shifting to the side so Silas and Saxon can flow in after him.

A bark of male laughter greets my ears. "*Mierda,*" Toro says, rumbling a laugh. "I almost shoot you, Solomon."

I watch as, one by one, the Cabot brothers lower their pistols. Kane nudges through the brothers, shoving his pistol into his waistband, and the rest of the Arrows follow suit, entering the room.

Sophia and I hang back in the hallway, watching.

"Be right back," she mutters to me. "Gonna clean up real quick."

I peck her on the lips. "Alright."

I enter the room, where all the women plus Toro, Taj, and Fonz are clustered together, half of the women on one bed and the rest on the other, with Taj and Toro on the floor just inside the doorway. Fonz, the strange man, is on the far bed, bad leg stretched out while Myka and Tatiana paint his toenails a violent shade of pink.

Kane, as Anjalee scrambles off the bed to greet him as effusively as if he'd been gone a week rather than less than twelve hours, stares at Fonz over Anjalee's shoulder. "Fonz, buddy, should I even ask?"

"Nope," Fonz says.

"Well I *am* askin'," Rev says. "The fuck, man? Why is my girl painting your goddamn feet?"

Myka giggles, not taking her attention away from Fonz's giant, scraggly, cracked toenail. "Relax, baby. We're bored out of our minds and Fonz is our entertainment."

Tatiana dips the brush into her jar of toe paint, or whatever it's called, grinning at Lash. "Are you jealous as well, Nico?"

Lash snickers a laugh. "Indeed not. I think maybe Fonz is your honorary gay friend."

Fonz, who's had his arm draped over his face up until now, moves his arm away to peer at Lash. "Straight men can have platonic friendships with straight women, I'll have you know. Furthermore, straight men can have their toes painted pink by their straight female friends." He turns his attention to Rev. "And as for you—you jealous, big boy? I'm sure your girl will do your nails next if you ask her nicely."

Rev is silent for a moment, and then, moving oddly slowly, he unties his boots, removes them, peels off his socks, and plants one foot on the bed in a Captain Morgan pose.

His toenails are bright purple. "That's not the issue, jackass."

For a moment, the room is silent.

Myka finishes Fonz's big toe, plugs the brush back into the jar, looks from Rev to Fonz and back to Rev.

She tries to suppress a snicker of laughter, and fails. That snort sets Tatiana to giggling, and soon everyone is laughing except Rev and Fonz.

Sophia, having changed into clean clothes, leans against the doorpost, watching the merriment with a small smile.

Fonz, with partially-painted toenails, stops laughing, eying Sophia. Shimmying awkwardly off the bed, he limps toward Sophia. Brazen as you please, he takes her hand and pulls her into the room.

Stunned by the unexpected move, Sophia lets him pull her toward the bed, the smile vanishing. After a few steps, she halts. "I'm fine where I was."

Fonz gestures at the bed, at Myka and Tatiana. "Boss, just get over there."

Moving stiffly, hesitantly, Sophia shuffles closer to the bed, looks around the room as if for guidance, and then perches on the very edge of the bed, back ramrod stiff, hands on her thighs. "There." She arches a wry eyebrow at Fonz. "Does that make you feel better?"

Myka shifts to sit beside her. Looks at her intently. "Is it over?"

Sophia drops her head, gaze on her hands. "Yes." A pause. "Well, mostly. Pugli is still out there, and last I heard from Jakob, Pugli's men—or at least I assume Pugli's men—have put him on the defensive. He claims to not want or need our assistance yet, however. So, there may be work on that front to do, still, but Rafael is dead."

Tatiana moves to her other side. "Which means you are free, does it not?"

Sophia blinks. "I...yes, I suppose it does." A clearing of her throat. "Free. What a strange feeling." She looks at Lash—Nicolai. "Pugli seems to have shifted his attention to Jakob. Until that is resolved, however, I would still exercise caution."

Nicolai nods. "I will not feel free until I have seen that man's corpse. I'm sure you understand."

A nod. "I very much do, my friend. Jakob was clear, however. He does not want our interference."

"I have questions," Solomon says.

Sophia glances at him. "I know. But I have very few answers for you. I truly do not know much more than you. His name is Jakob—spelled with a K rather than C. I believe he is of European origin, but I don't know for certain. I know nothing of his past. I don't know where, when, or how he acquired his fortune, only that he is very, very wealthy, and a skilled, cunning, and creative businessman. He has contacts in very high places in government—here in the States as well as abroad. He has a sort of..." she trails off, sighing. "Obsession is the only word I can come up with—he has an obsession with redemption. It's what drove him to create the Broken Arrows, and Club Sin."

"So, uh, which came first," Rev asks. "The club, or us?"

Sophia shrugs. "That's a chicken-or-egg question, Rev. The Club was built for you. The two are inextricably linked."

This leaves a ringing silence in the room.

"So he wants redemption for himself, and his way of getting it is…us?" Silas asks.

Sophia shrugs. "Something along those lines, yes. As I said, Jakob has not shared his past with me. I believe he…" She pauses. "I think he fled something terrible in his past. Something bad enough that he faked his own death. That is merely conjecture based on something he said to me recently—'the dead cannot die.' I do not know what that means, except to think that the world at large believes Jakob, whoever he really is, is dead."

"So, lemme get this straight," Saxon says. "You've worked directly with the man for, what, at least three or four years? And you know *nothing* about him?"

Sophia arches an eyebrow. "More like ten. And yes. I know his character. I know that he is used to being in command. He is private, secretive. I know he harbors some deep emotional trauma, like the rest of us. I know that he has great wealth, but spends little of it on himself—he dresses well but simply, keeps to himself, does not own a fleet of supercars or mansions across the world. Is he hiding? I don't know. What could he be hiding from? Again, I don't know. But I know that he cares about each of you. He knows your pasts. He and I…well, I chose you. He gave me a list of candidates and you seven are the ones I chose. Your stories…spoke to me, I suppose. And to him.

"He is…well, kind is not the word. He has no softness. He is all sharp edges, like me. But deep down, there is goodness in him. But it's…how do I put it? A goodness that I believe comes from knowing all too intimately the cost of being…bad. I don't think he was always the man he is now. I think the past he fled was a nightmare at least partially of his own making. But again, that is conjecture."

"We ever gonna meet him?" Chance asks.

She shrugs. "I don't know. Perhaps?"

Silence, then.

"So…now what?" This is from Annika. "Your asshole ex is dead, and I assume that means his goons are gonna be too busy fighting over who's gonna fill the void to worry about his personal vendetta. Jakob doesn't want our help. Pugli is in the wind and seems to have lost interest in us— hopefully, at least, now that he has Jakob as his quarry. The Club got blown up. So…now what?"

Scarlett, leaning her back against Solomon's chest, clears her throat to get everyone's attention. "I know what I want to do next." Everyone looks at her expectantly, and she grabs Sol's arm, lifts it and turns it out so his tattooed brand shows. "I want the brand. I know I'm a girl, but I want to be part of the brotherhood. Whatever that means. Not just because Sol is my man, but because this group of people—" she halts, clears her throat, blinking hard. "You…you're all…ew, fuck, I *hate* getting all fucking weepy. Dammit." She scrubs at her face, and she blows out a sharp breath. "I…I've never belonged. I could never—I never fit. I was never one of the guys. I was respected, feared even, but…" she blinks around at the girls. "You ladies are the first women I've ever been friends with. And you guys—Sol's brothers, blood brothers and brand brothers. You're my crew. My team. My family. So I want the brand."

Sophia lets out a soft sigh. "Scarlett...I hope you know you don't need a brand to belong."

Scarlett nods. "I know. But I want what the brand represents."

"And what is that?" Sophia asks.

"Brotherhood." Scarlett's answer comes immediately. "Family. Taking that brand represents leaving my past behind me and choosing a different kind of life. I went into the jungle to rescue the man I never stopped loving. I found him, and in the process I found way more than I bargained for. I found something worth fighting for. I was given US citizenship for my service. That's great. But I didn't join out of patriotism—I'm not American. Or...well, I don't know. Maybe I am, now. I don't know. The point is, I didn't spend all those years fighting and killing for some noble cause or for a flag or whatever. It was a job, and one I just sort of... ended up in. It turned out I was good at it, and that was that. But these past few weeks, or however fucking long it's been since I got that email...I've...I have a cause: you all. I've fought beside each of you, and I'd do it all again. But I really, *really* hope I don't have to. Because if I'm being honest with you guys and with myself, what I really want is to put my rifle down and never pick it up again."

Sophia nods at her words. "Then you will receive the brand. I must warn you, though—I don't know what's next for The Broken Arrows. Jakob has hinted at changes to come. I have no idea what that means. The brotherhood will never change, however, I *do* know that." She glances at Annika. "What I mean is that I don't know what's next— long-term, at least. I think for now we head back to Vegas and assess the situation. The Club is our home. So...we fix it."

"Wait, wait, wait." Kane frowns at Sophia. "*You* live in the Club?"

She blinks at him. "Of course. Where else would I live?"

He shrugs. "Hell if I know. Until recently, I thought you were…I dunno. An outside employee the boss put in charge. His go-between. You never wanted to talk or hang out. You just appeared when you had something to say to us. You showed up for work and vanished when the club closed. I guess I assumed you lived in the city somewhere."

Sophia looks uncomfortable at best, if not downright unhappy. "I was afraid of letting anyone close, Kane. I stayed away because I…I didn't think I could belong. Much like Scarlett, I never have. I wasn't just a kid, I was the daughter and only child of Bruno de Silva. I was his executioner. I was Rafael's wife. I was *La Víbora*. Then I was…your supervisor. An outsider."

Kane absorbs this silently, and then moves to kneel in front of her. "You're not an outsider anymore, Sophia."

She tips her head back, hissing. "My god, *enough* already. I've cried more in the last few days than in my entire life combined."

"Feelings are meant to be felt, Boss-lady," Kane says, his voice low. "It's all good. You're among family."

She shudders. "Family. I don't know what that even means."

Naomi scooches across the bed to sit behind Sophia, arms locking around her middle. "It means you're loved."

Sophia leans her head back against Naomi's. "You started it, you know."

"Started what?" Naomis asks, confused.

"The great thawing out of *La Reina de Hielo*."

"How?"

Sophia shrugs. "When I spoke to you over the phone, I…I suppose I heard something in you. Fear, but a core of unbreakable iron beneath it. You are far kinder and far sweeter than I'll ever be, but I guess I felt a kinship to you."

"You gave me strength to fight when I was terrified," Naomi whispers. "You were calm. You knew exactly what to do." She hugs Sophia tightly. "And you're kinder and sweeter than you give yourself credit for. You just need practice."

Sophia barks a laugh, bitterly sarcastic. "I am a great many things, dear, darling Naomi, but sweet and kind are not among them."

"I disagree," I say, joining the conversation for the first time. "I think Naomi is right. You have shown me recently that you *can* be sweet. Very, *very* sweet."

Sophia blushes, ducking her head. "Ren, stop. That's different. And *private*."

I enter the room, weaving around bodies, until I am in front of her. Kane shifts away to make room for me, settling back in Anjalee's embrace by the window. "Sophia, my love. *Meu Amor. Meu coraçao*. I don't mean *that* kind of sweetness, as sweet as you are in that sense."

"Ren," Sophia protests.

"Hush, my love. Listen." I take her hands, gazing down at her; with my injured hip—which Kane patched up before we left the port—if I went down to a knee, I'd never get back up. "What comes next, no matter what it looks like for you and for us, will not be easy. I am a soldier. An operator. You are…well, you. Our lives have been extraordinarily unusual. Violence and death are the norm for us. You in particular, darling, have lived with fear and in isolation—emotional if not always physical—your whole life. That doesn't just go away. Even with all of the break-throughs and such that you've had lately, you are not just going to wake up one morning and find yourself Susie Homemaker. I do not say that to mean being a homemaker is a bad thing—it is not. It is a wonderful, beautiful thing with many challenges which not everyone is cut out for. All I mean is that you are not that woman. You *can* be, if you wish. But to become that kind of woman will take work and time and patience. Even just learning how to be Sophia once more, how to let go of everything Inez is and has had to be—that will be hard. You must be patient with yourself, my love. You must show grace to yourself."

"Susie Homemaker?" Sophia says, barking a sarcastic laugh. "I will settle for simply not being Griselda Blanco."

I pull her to her feet, sighing sadly. "You are not that, my love."

She shakes her head. "I can't just forget who I have been." She stares into my eyes, and then looks around the room, from face to face. "No matter how much I may wish to."

"See, that's where you're gettin' stuck," Chance says. "Thinkin' you can or should try to forget who you been. I can't forget who I was, Sophia. I *am* an addict. I'll always *be* an addict. I won't ever touch drugs again, but I'll always be the guy dying in a gutter that you rescued. I *can't* for-get and won't ever *try* to forget that guy, Soph. Can I call you that? Soph?"

She smiles at him, wry and dryly amused. "I suppose after all that we've been through together, I can allow a certain degree of familiarity."

Chance continues. "If I were to forget that part of who

I am, I could be tempted to think I'm fixed. I'm cured. I could try a hit now and then to calm down, to relax and have fun. No harm, no foul, right? I ain't that dude no more, so what's the problem? Once in a while ain't a problem. I can control it, this time." He gently eases me aside, and I let him take my place in front of Sophia. "You see the problem with that line of thinkin', yeah?"

She nods. "Yes, I do. But I am not a drug addict, Chance."

"Maybe not, but it still applies to you. See, you may not be addicted to meth or coke or booze or whatever, but you *are* addicted to something else."

Sophia frowns, puzzled. "And that would be what?"

"Thinking the only way for you to be safe is if you push everyone away and keep them away." Towering over her small, slender frame, Chance exudes compassion, resting one giant hand on her shoulder, staring down at her with obvious affection. "Everyone in your life up, until you met Jakob and the rest of us—*everyone* betrayed you. Hurt you. You suffered unimaginable pain, emotionally, mentally, and physically. The only way you could survive was to shut everyone out and become hard and cold. It protected you against the world, which you understandably see as brutal and violent and full of pain. I turned to drugs. Annika turned to drugs. Kane turned to booze. The others did like you—built up walls and turned into turtles, living inside their shells and pretending they didn't need or want anyone to ever get close."

Sophia blinks, refusing to meet his gaze. "You're not wrong about that, I suppose. But how is that an addiction?"

"Drugs didn't fix my problems. Booze didn't fix Kane's problems. Isolation didn't fix Solomon's. But even though it was obvious that what we were doing didn't do anything but fuck us up worse, we kept doing it. In my case, it nearly killed me. Isolation may not kill you physically, but it ain't healthy. And you *are* addicted to it, in a way. Different kind of addiction, but addiction nonetheless."

Scarlett nods. "He's absolutely right, Sophia. I'm still working on it. I have to fight the urge to run all the time—literally *run* from how Sol makes me feel. It's fucking scary. I'd rather face a dozen armed tangos with my bare hands than be vulnerable with him, most days. *Still.* Even though I know down to my goddamn bones that Sol is the best thing that has ever happened to me. Letting him love me is the hardest fucking thing I've ever done. Showing him my broken, shitty, weak, selfish, pathetic self is absolutely terrifying. It would be easier and seem safer, emotionally, to go back to my handler at the CIA and ask to be put back on a team. That's where I'm comfortable. I *know* that world. I know how to navigate the toxic fraternity bullshit as a woman. I know how to...inoculate myself, I guess, from the guilt of doing morally gray shit for morally gray reasons. Just obeying orders, right? I know how to pretend I'm okay with going back to barracks alone, or a cold empty apartment, alone."

Sophia turns away, shoulders rising and falling rapidly as her breathing comes fast and ragged. "Stop—just—just stop."

Scarlett circles Sophia and grabs her face with rough affection, refusing to let Sophia hide. "No, hon, I won't stop. *Every fucking day*, multiple times a day, I have to let Sol see the *real* me, broken and fucked up and scared and drowning in PTSD. It feels like standing in front of a firing squad without a blindfold, Soph. But I'll tell you this: it's worth it. Because Sol *gets* it. He gets *me*. When I try and fail to be open for him, he doesn't get mad. He gives me space to figure it out. He loves me. He accepts me. And nothing—*nothing* in this world feels better than letting someone see the worst of you and being totally loved anyway. It's better than any high, better than any win, better than sex, better than medals or money or whatever else there is in the world."

Annika moves up beside Scarlett, and Naomi takes the other side. "You think you're not sweet or whatever because you've never felt safe enough to let yourself *be* sweet," Annika says.

"Same with kindness or displays of affection," Scarlett says. "It feels like weakness to be those things because in the life you've lived up until recently, they were. But they're not anymore."

Naomi leans forward and kisses Sophia on the cheek, softly, sweetly. "That's where Chance is right about addiction. You're not addicted to a chemical, you're addicted to thinking the only way to survive is being tough and alone. And that's just not true anymore. What we're saying is that it will take time and consistent effort to move past that."

Sophia nods, letting out a shaky breath. "You're all right. I know you are." She turns to me. "All I can promise you, Ren, is that I'll try. I do love you. I do want a life with you. I don't have a clue what that's gonna look like, but I want it with you, whatever it looks like and however we get there."

A burden falls from my shoulders, a weight sloughing off my back. I pull her into my arms and crush her against my chest. "That's all I want, Soph. It's all I care about. Let me love you. Let me see the real you. I don't care what comes next, as long as it's with you."

She literally, physically seems to soften in my arms. Tips her head back to look up at me, chin on my chest. "God, Ren." A sniff. "You need me to love you, too, though. It's gotta go both ways."

I smile at her. "I absolutely need you to love me. And you do. You will. I'm not worried."

She presses her forehead and nose against my chest, breathing in deeply, holding it, and letting it out slowly. She steps back, and I see her reach a decision. "Let's go home."

CHAPTER 17

THIS ENDLESS HEAVEN

INEZ

REV, MYKA, KANE, ANJALEE, CHANCE, ANNIKA, Saxon, Terra, Silas, Naomi, Solomon, Scarlett, Lash, Tatiana, Taj, Toro, Fonz, Lorenzo, and I stand in a wide semi-circle outside Club Sin.

The scene has been cleared. Black and yellow crime scene tape still criss-crosses the opening of the door down to the Arrows' quarters. The grenade caused pretty significant damage, but not as bad as I'd expected—the core structure of the stairwell is intact, but the door was blown off its hinges by the detonation, and the stairs, walls, railings, and drop-tile ceiling are all badly damaged. Some of the infrastructure above the drop-tile has been damaged as well, meaning the quarters are without lights and plumbing for the time being—the plumbing being damaged means flood damage, with water ankle deep throughout the lowest floor. The electricity has been shut off to the whole building. The SUVs have been removed, and the bodies. The side of the club is bullet-riddled, as is the interior.

"It's a fuckin' miracle you all made it out alive," Rev says. "Fuckin' *thirty* of 'em? And it was just the *five* of you?"

Lorenzo and I share a look. Ren nods. "They came in

arrogant. They expected the women to be alone and unprotected. Figured they would just waltz in, kidnap the girls, and get away clean. They also assumed they'd be backed up by the element that was supposed to have arrived from Mexico, which Sophia and I, um…eliminated."

Rev shakes his head. "Respect, ya'll." He scans the dozens of bullet holes in the side of the club. "So, big-ass fuckin' firefight, automatic gunfire and fuckin' frags and flashbangs…plus we all obviously know about the security footage. How are we not wanted by the cops?"

I shrug. "Jakob has long had an understanding with local law enforcement."

Rev frowns at me. "A look the other way sorta deal?"

I shake my head. "No." I pause, shrug, tip my head to one side. "Well, sort of. First, the club is one of a very few legal, licensed brothels in the state of Nevada, so that part of the business is unequivocally legal. The understanding is that Jakob, through you seven, enforces rules and laws meant to keep our patrons safe. The girls in Hel are protected. Our clients and customers are safe. And unless we call them, law enforcement leaves us alone to take care of our business our way. In this case, we were defending ourselves. Any footage from the security system will confirm this. The weapons we used are, technically, not legal for civilians to own, but none of us are exactly normal civilians. We are all highly trained professionals. Additionally, the men we killed are all criminals wanted in several countries for a wide range of violent crimes."

Rev laughs. "I see. That's pretty thin reasoning. What it amounts to, far's I see it, is that Jakob shelled out a certain amount of grift, and in return, the law leaves us alone as long as we don't cause problems and keep the people inside the Club safe."

I snort, nodding. "That's about it, Rev. If you would like to contact law enforcement on your own behalf, be my guest, but I would request you leave the rest of us out of it."

Rev chuffs a sarcastic laugh. "Not fuckin' likely. I'm perfectly happy with the arrangement. Just wanted to be sure I understood how shit stands."

"Well, that's how it stands," I say. "Now. We have a lot of work ahead of us. I'll need to contact contractors to handle the skilled repair work. In the meantime, Solomon, I'd like you to coordinate the clean-up."

Sol eyes the mess. "On it. First thing is pumping out the water and getting shit dry, and then assessing any mold issues or water damage."

◆

The repairs take weeks to complete. We do as much of the work as possible, leaving only the skilled work for the professionals. Sol arranges for pumps to get the water out of the basement, and then an inspector goes through the structure and identifies problem areas and recommends solutions.

The electricity is repaired and restored. Plumbing as well. The floors are dried out, water damaged walls are torn out and replaced and repainted. The site of the explosion requires the most extensive rebuilding, leaving our staff entrance off limits for quite some time.

The Club remains closed during the repairs, obviously.

Jakob is incommunicado the entire time.

While the repairs are underway, I arrange suites for everyone at a hotel close to the Club.

It's a weird time, to be honest. We all work from sunup to well past sundown, as the damage to the interior from the gunfight is more extensive than we'd originally anticipated—most of the appliances in the kitchen need to be replaced, all of the drywall, most of the flooring, most of the drop-tiling…all of the furniture. The amount of work to be done is staggering, and every day that passes means the club is closed and not bringing in revenue. We work side by side, sweating, cursing, telling jokes, and laughing together.

Once upon a time, I would have remained apart, separate, aloof—"supervising". Now, instead, I'm down in the grit and the grime with my crew, my family, ripping out drywall and painting walls and backing up stairs with water-stained, bullet-riddled sections of couch. I sit, sweaty and filthy and exhausted, eating cold pizza with dirty hands and swigging water from crinkly plastic bottles while sharing a joke with Kane, or listening to Terra tell stories of her life as a street kid.

When the work is done, we all head upstairs to the club floor and share a drink or six, sitting together in one of the VIP booths with the lights on, crammed in together into the U-shaped booth hip to hip and thigh to thigh, and I feel, for once, a sense of belonging.

I tell my own stories—war stories every bit as wild and gnarly as the ones told by the real military combat veterans.

Scarlett and I become particularly close—she's the only other woman I've ever known or met who can rival my training and experiences. We share a sort of experiential shorthand. We're both Latina. We're both warriors. We've both suffered sexual abuse. She can take one look at me and just know, without being told, when the past is bubbling up near the surface, when a flashback threatens to drag me under. She doesn't need to ask what I need. She just knows.

We're so busy, spending every waking hour working our asses off, that by the time we get back to our hotel rooms at the end of the day, Lorenzo and I have no energy for anything but showering off and falling into bed.

But this too is cathartic, this time with Lorenzo without the added complexity of sex.

I discover, very quickly, the bone-deep comfort of sleeping in his arms, hearing his heart beating under my ear as I drowse and droop and drift into sleep, feeling the strength in his arms, the powerful shelter of his body behind mine as he spoons me.

I learn to show him affection without being self-conscious; more importantly, perhaps, I learn to accept his physical affection without hesitation or demurral or cringing. I learn to smile freely. Laugh easily. It turns out I have a dry, sarcastic sense of humor.

Who knew?

◆

Nearly three months after our return to Vegas, Club Sin is once more open for business. Or, it will be, tomorrow evening.

Today, we officially move back into the Club.

And I officially move out of my private quarters below Jakob's floors—which are the uppermost two levels.

I don't have much to move—a few armloads of

clothing, mostly black slacks, leggings, and blazers, solid-color T-shirts and sensible blouses, a few pairs of jeans, and some mismatched loungewear.

Lorenzo is the only one I allow up with me past the security floor to my rooms. There is only one elevator in the building, and it's tucked away in a corner near the security booth on the third floor, and it only goes to my rooms and to the two floors that comprise Jakob's business offices and personal living quarters; the elevator is biometrically secured, accessible only to the two of us.

The elevator opens directly into the living area of my rooms—a large, open space bathed in sunlight from the one-way, floor-to-ceiling windows. All in black, white, and gray, the suite of rooms is industrial, spare and spartan and modern. There's a single bedroom, a well-appointed bathroom, and a kitchen open to the living area separated by a large island.

Lorenzo looks around, nodding. 'This is very nice, Soph. Remind me again why you want to move down into the Arrow quarters?"

"I have lived apart from them for too long. This is very nice, yes. Spacious. Luxurious, even. But it's the apartment of someone I no longer am, or want to be. Jakob can do as he likes with the space." I look up at him. "I'm sorry, Ren. I know it would be far more comfortable for us to live up here, but I just…I can't anymore. Not if I want to keep moving forward."

He just waves a hand. "Bah, nothing to apologize for. Wherever you are is home. One small room, or a whole floor, doesn't matter."

I shake my head. "Ren, you don't have to be

understanding and supportive literally every moment of every day."

He snorts at this. "Yes, I do. That's how it works."

"Well, yeah, I just—" I sigh, try again. "I just mean that it's okay to want and need and expect things from me, and to be upset or disappointed that you haven't gotten it."

He nods, eyes flicking up and away as he considers this. "That's true, I suppose."

"I also would like to point out that I'm not as emotionally fragile or on edge as I was even a few weeks ago."

He nods again. "I have noticed."

"So, I just…" I blow out a breath. "Be real with me. I feel like you've been…I don't know, holding your breath, sort of, for a while. With us. Giving me the time and space to work through things. Finding a new…equilibrium." It took a moment to dredge up the correct English word.

"Have you?" he asks. "Found a new equilibrium?"

I nod. "Yes, I think so. Knowing that the club is opening tomorrow, that helps. It means we're getting back to normal, or—or maybe a new normal is more correct to say. Regardless, it feels good to know we can resume operating the club." I lead him to my bedroom, and start pulling my clothes from the closet and draping them onto the bed. "What will you do now, Ren?"

He shrugs. "I've been considering my options."

"And?"

"I haven't decided yet. I don't think the Club is the right fit for me, long-term, work-wise. I hope you understand that."

I collect an armload of clothes and stack them with the rest on the bed. "Of course, Ren. The club is my home, my career. I love it here. I like the work. I like watching the customers. I like the challenge of running such a complicated business. But it doesn't have to be your job. I just hope you don't decide you have to go back to Brazil." I turn away from him and hurry back into the closet, scraping hangers together, studiously and determinedly not looking at him.

I have my arms around the load of clothes and I'm about to lift the hanger hooks off the bar when I feel his presence behind me. I go still, breath snagging in my lungs like a burning, bursting balloon. My skin pebbles all over, my nipples harden, and I involuntarily press my thighs together.

"Ren," I whisper.

"Mmmmmm," he hums in return, his nose pressing against the back of my neck, inhaling my scent. "Sophia, my beautiful, sexy, delicious darling."

"Delicious?" I echo, the word barely a breath.

"Mmmm-hmmm." I feel his fingers slide down the short, thick column of my braid, catch at the hair tie at the bottom. "Sweeter than honey. Every…last…inch of you." He punctuates each phrase with a soft, delicate kiss to the back of my neck, each one ripping a quiet gasp from my lips.

I clutch the clothing in trembling fingers. "Ren, I…I want…" I squeeze my eyes shut as desire ripples through me, at war with my long-ingrained habit of ignoring my desires, of suppressing my needs, of dousing my passions.

Ren sidles up close behind me, and his hips press against my backside, the thick hard ridge of his erection pressing between my ass cheeks, and his chest is at my back and his hands roam down my sides and come to rest low on my belly.

"Tell me what you want, my love, so I can give it to you." He tugs the hair tie off, and his fingers rake gently down through my hair, loosening the braid so my hair falls in kinked waves to brush my shoulders.

"It's hard to say it, Ren," I whisper.

"Try. Please. It's just you and me. And we have all the time and privacy in the world." He lifts the mass of my hair aside and kisses my nape, behind my left ear, behind my right, and each kiss pours jet fuel on the fire of desire burning inside me. "Tell me what you want, Sophia. Please."

"I want you to make me feel good," I say, the words so quiet I can barely hear myself.

"I can do that," he answers.

The closet we are in is large, an expansive walk-in with floor-to-ceiling racks for hangers, cubbies for purses, and shelves for shoes; I've used less than a third of it, as clothing and fashion have never been a priority for me. To our right is a full-length mirror. Ren pivots us away from the rack to face the mirror.

"Watch," he breathes. "Watch me make you feel good, my love. Don't look away."

He towers over me, his broad shoulders occluding the world behind him, his eyes holding mine in the reflection. Dressed in dark blue jeans and a plain black T-shirt, I look short and slender against his tall, broad, hard, bulky frame. His thick arms wrap around me like steel bands. I reach up and stroke my fingers down his biceps, barely breathing as I wait for him to make his move.

He keeps his eyes locked on mine, a small, eager grin curving his lips, and his beard, thick and unkempt from weeks of neglect, tickles and scratches my cheek. I scrape my fingers over his beard, along his jawline.

"I think I like this," I say, realizing belatedly that I'm speaking Portuguese. "The beard. Perhaps trimmed a bit and brushed, but…I like it longer."

His grin widens as he answers in the same language. "Then trimmed and brushed it shall be for you, sweetest one."

His fingers dance inward and downward from my diaphragm to the waist of my jeans, pausing at the button. He slips the button free. Pinches the tab of the zipper. Lowers it slowly, gradually, centimeter by centimeter, until my fly sags open, baring a wedge of my white cotton underwear.

His teeth snag my earlobe, and his breath huffs hot and noisy against my ear. A kiss to my cheekbone near my ear. Fingertips slip over my belly, dance beneath the elastic of my underwear; I suck in my belly, anticipating his touch where I want it most, where I need it most.

"Ren," I gasp, aching for him, for more, for the intimacy of his touch. "Please."

I watch the reflection, rapt, as he eases his hand inside the cotton, over my mons pubis, and then a shrill whimper escapes my gritted teeth as his long middle finger rests over my seam.

"I—" another whimper emerges from my throat, a high, tight, wordless noise of need. "I want to…"

"What, Sophia? You want to what?"

"See." I push my jeans down until they catch at my hips. "I want to see. I want to watch you touch me."

"What do you know?" He teases in English. "So do I."

He drops to a crouch behind me, fingers hooking in the waist of my open jeans, and pulls them down; I help by wiggling my hips, shifting my weight from foot to foot as he tugs the tight denim down until they're piled around my ankles. He lifts my foot and whips the jeans away, and then I lift my other foot and they're tossed aside, leaving me in my panties and T-shirt.

Remaining crouched behind me, Ren grasps my hips, nosing one side of my bottom over the cotton, and then the other. He curls one finger into the elastic and tugs my underwear down an inch or two at my right hip, and kisses the exposed upper swell of my buttock.

"Ren, please—my god, I—I need—I want you to—"

He rumbles a quiet, amused laugh. "Did you think I wouldn't take my sweet damned time with you, Sophia?" he asks. "You'll be a quivering puddle by the time I'm done with you, I promise. It just won't be quick getting you there."

He runs that finger inside the elastic from right hip to left, lowering my underwear a bit more, another inch or two, baring more of my bottom, and he kisses flesh as he exposes it.

Left to right now, kissing, kissing—the upper swell, the hint of the cleft. Right to left, more kisses dotting and peppering here and there, here and there.

And now, all at once, the tight white cotton briefs droop past the bubble of my backside, clinging and catching where my thighs press together. I shift my thighs, and the panties drop to the floor. Ren tosses them aside. Rises to his feet behind me.

His fingernails scratch up my sides, bringing my T-shirt up with it; I'm momentarily blinded as he tears the garment off and tosses it aside to join the growing pile of my clothing. Now I'm clad in only a simple, tight, compressive white sports bra, unattractive, unsexy, and a real bitch to peel out of.

"Would you ever consider wearing lingerie for me, Sophia?" he asks, his palms roaming my belly, my hips, down my thighs, teasing near my core but never quite touching me where I want him to.

"I don't own any fancy underwear, Lorenzo," I answer.

"I have a fantasy," he whispers, trailing his fingertips along the thick band of elastic at my diaphragm.

"Tell me," I whisper back.

"You, in nothing but a few scraps of red lace." He tugs the band upward until the lower swell of my breasts spills out, slowly rolling the tight undergarment up and away. "Like the most perfect present, all wrapped up for me."

"I think…" I breathe, pausing to swallow the lump of hot nerves in my throat, feeling my belly flutter with the wingbeats of a billion restless butterflies. "I think that could be arranged." I gnaw on the corner of my lower lip, breath lodged in my throat as Ren peels the sports bra up and up, past the sticking point so my breasts tumble free, swaying heavily. The bra joins the rest of my clothes on the floor, and now I'm nude while Ren towers behind me, fully clothed.

"My fucking god," he breathes, his gaze hungrily raking over my curves, lingering at my breasts before dropping to my sex. "You are exquisite, Sophia. Breathtaking."

My heart squeezes, melts, and I hold my breath and meet his eyes in the reflection. "Ren…god. The things you say to me."

Reaching around me, pinning my arms to my sides, he cups my breasts in his big hands, calluses scraping rough against the tender skin. Thumbs brushing over my erect, sensitive nipples, Ren watches me in the mirror, watches me gasp and press my thighs together at his touch, watches my jaw drop open as I whimper when he tweaks my nipples with a sharp, pinching twist.

Needing to touch him, to feel the reality of him, the solidity of his skin and muscles, I reach up and frame his face, rake my fingers through his beard, lip caught in my teeth. I arch my back, push my breasts into his hands.

He kneads the tender weight of my tits, growling a sound of appreciation.

"Have I ever told you that your tits are fucking incredible?" he murmurs.

I shake my head. "No, I don't think you have."

He lets them go, and they bounce, sway, jiggle. "Look at them, Soph. Goddamned magnificent."

"They're just boobs," I protest. "Nothing special."

He shakes his head. "To me, they are perfection." He scoops them up again, scraping a fingernail over my nipples until a thin, shuddering gasp slithers out of me. "So sensitive. I love the little sounds you make."

One hand still toying with my breasts, his other drifts down my belly to cup my sex. His middle finger rests over my seam, and I whimper, mouth hanging open in anticipation of the touch I desire. I press my thighs together, and then force them relax, to soften, to allow him access to my soft, wet center.

"Please, Ren," I breathe. "Please. Stop teasing me. Just—touch me. Please."

He tweaks my nipple rather hard, making me jump and squeal. "I am touching you," he says, grinning.

I fit my hand over his where it covers my sex. Align my middle finger over his. Press those matched digits against my seam. "Please."

"Tell me what you want, Sophia."

"My pussy," I hiss, the words escaping, bursting out of me, bold and daring. "Put your fingers inside me, Ren. Please. Make me feel good." I slide my feet apart, widening my stance. "Give me an orgasm. Please, Ren. Please. I need to come."

Growling, grinning, lip curling in a pleased, aroused snarl, he presses his finger between my lips, spearing the thick digit slowly inside me. I whimper long and low as he fills my channel with his finger, curling it deep inside me, pressing deeper, deeper, and then withdrawing until his slick fingertip smears against my clit.

"Oh fuck!" I breathe, as lightning immediately sizzles through me at that first touch. "Ren, god yes. Yes. Please, please. More, my love."

He gives me more. He fills me with his touch again, slicking his finger deep inside me and pulling it back out again slowly, circling my clit once, twice, three times—a quake ripples through me, a precursor to climax that leaves me shaking and gasping, hips flexing, pushing, driving.

He nips my neck with his teeth, and then breathes hot on my ear, and then nuzzles my cheek, kisses the corner of my mouth; he fingers my clit again, circling it slowly, his touch delicate and thrilling me to quaking, shuddering, shaking, and when I gasp, he slashes his mouth against mine, claiming a hot kiss. My knees tremble as he speeds his touch, and my tongue finds his and he growls into our kiss. Heat builds in my belly, pressure swelling, and my knees dip, threaten to give out, and his swirling, smearing fingers drive me to the aching, shuddering cusp of climax. Seconds before I topple over the edge, he hooks two fingers inside me, and for a moment my legs do give way, and I'm held up only by those probing fingers inside me.

I grind against his hand, reaching up to cling to his neck, and then I find renewed strength to keep my feet, and now Ren uses those fingers to fuck me, slicking them in and out fast and hard, driving my breath from my lungs and ripping a series of ragged, hoarse, panting gasps from me. I buck against his touch, eyelids drooping as ecstasy shivers and shudders through me as if I've grabbed a live wire. I watch our reflection, watch greedily as he fucks me with his fingers, and my breasts bounce and sway wildly as I buck in time with his drilling, driving fingers, and I pant and gasp and whine as climax swells and expands and builds deep inside me.

I can't form words as I reach the edge, and he hooks his thrusting fingers deep inside me and his palm presses perfectly against my clit and my mouth hangs open, shuddering as my breath lodges in my throat and orgasm detonates inside me, a hot quivering at first, a quick wave of release making my knees give out and my breasts heave.

As the climax spreads through me and builds up to a crescendo, Ren slips his fingers out of me and strums my clit in a light, fast, up-and-down stroke. The spreading climax erupts like a volcano, and a scream rips out of my chest and I quake all over, and Ren has to hold me upright, taking my weight as I lean back against him, dipping at the knees into his touch, legs spread wide open.

I watch, head resting back against his chest, as I ride his fingers, buck against their speeding, flicking, swiping, circling, knees apart and legs working. I look wanton, erotic—sexy. For the first time since I can remember, I feel beautiful. Truly, down to my bones, into the darkest corners of my heart, I feel beautiful, sexy, and desirable.

I let myself scream and cry as the orgasm shatters me,

and Lorenzo's eyes soak up every quiver of my body, every thrust of my pussy against his flying fingers, every jiggling heave of my tits as I gasp and whimper and cry out.

He brings me through the orgasm to the point of feeling boneless and jellied, slicking his fingers back into me, plunging them deep and exploring inside me.

I expect him to turn me, to bend me over or push me to my knees or lift me up to cling to his waist.

Instead, he drops to his knees in front of me, broad back hunched, and his shaggy black hair tickles my thighs and then I can't help but scream in shocked delight as he fuses his mouth to my sex and tongues my clit until the scream shivers into a whimpering gasp. He thrusts his fingers back inside me, pinky and forefinger pressed against the lips of my pussy as he curls his fingers to scrape against my inner walls. I can only clutch at his head and grind my pussy against his hungry mouth, tongue driving against my clit, thrashing side to side, flicking up and down. I have to almost crouch to keep my balance, leaning back with my legs planted wide apart, hunched over him as he devours me, and I drop and dip and grind and thrust in time with his thrashing tongue and thrusting fingers, and now the orgasm I thought was over swells back to life, ramping up into a new explosive release hotter and wilder and louder than the last.

"Oh fuck, fuck, oh fuck, Ren!" I cry, chin on my chest as I buck and thrust into his touch.

My legs—well, my everything—gives out all at once, and Ren catches me, eases me down to my back on the floor of the closet.

Instead of relenting, giving me a chance to catch my breath, Ren renews his manual and oral assault of my pussy. He slows the thrusting of his fingers and softens his mouth, fusing it around my clit—I can only describe it as making out with my clit. It's slow, loving, hungry, gentle, erotic…and all the while his fingers are slicking and sliding inside me, filling and withdrawing, curling and probing and spreading and exploring my channel, and the orgasm doesn't fade, but rather hovers and builds just beneath the cusp of climax. I'm writhing beneath him, my thighs cradling his head as I arch my entire lower half off the floor, hands knotted in his hair, screaming, screaming, screaming.

The climax wrenches me into blissful oblivion, breathless and wildhearted.

As I descend from the mountainous peak of orgasm, greedily gulping gasping breaths, Lorenzo gingerly removes his fingers from inside me and releases the suction of his mouth, and begins kissing his way up my body. Hipbone, hipbone, pubis, inner thigh, navel, back to my other thigh, beard brushing my labia, ticklish and scratchy, and then up to my navel again, and then he nuzzles the underside of my breast, draping the heavy weight of it on his face and he kisses, kisses, finally rolling his mouth over my nipple and suckling it between his teeth, licking it, flicking it, and then the other, back and forth and back and forth. Still quaking with the aftershocks of two monster orgasms, his mouth on my nipples has me mewling and writhing all over again.

Teetering on the edge of a third very unexpected orgasm, I grasp at his face, pull at him. "Ren, please. I need you."

"I'm here," he growls, and then returns to sucking hard on my nipple while tweaking the other.

"I want—oh! Oh god, Ren! Jesus, Ren, fuck." I snarl

my fingers in his hair and yank his head back so he has to look at me. "I want you inside me. I don't want to come again unless you're inside me."

Beard glittering with my essence, he grins. "As you wish, my love."

Before he can do or say anything else, I unhook my legs from his shoulders and sit up, reaching for his shirt. Yank it off, toss it away blindly, already fumbling at his zipper. I push him to his back and rip at his fly, yank his jeans roughly past his hips and down to his knees—he kicks them off while I slide his tight black briefs away from his erection, and then with another scissoring kick, Ren has removed them as well, and he's naked for me.

There's no thought but my need, no fear of anything except not having Ren inside me as soon as possible. I just need him. I need his heat, his hardness. I need his aggression and his love, his wildness and gentility.

Acting on pure desire, I have his thick, hot, hard cock in my mouth before I realize what I'm even doing. His shocked groan is hoarse, and he arches, hands diving into my hair.

"Oh my fucking *god*, Sophia!" he gasps. "Oh god, your mouth, my love…"

His stunned ecstasy is far more than worth the price of entry—all I feel as I slide my lips around him and open my throat to take more of him is pride that I'm giving him this pleasure, that I'm making him feel this good.

I slather my tongue against his shaft as it slides through my mouth, and I swallow around him and gasp raggedly through my nose and cup his balls and massage his taint.

And then, before I know what's happening, I'm on

my hands and knees in front of the mirror and Ren is huge and hard and all rippling muscle and bronzed, beautiful skin behind me. He has his cock gripped in his fist and his other hand reaches between my thighs to feather fingertips against my pussy. I feel the thick round plump squishy head of his cock nuzzling my seam, and then I'm groaning as he feeds himself into me ever so slowly. Once he's sliding inside me, he grabs my ass with both hands, caressing the broad, curving spread of my ass. His hips bump against my ass as he bottoms out inside me, but then he pulls my cheeks apart and thrusts even deeper, and I cry out in a shrill, tight-throated, keening whimper, so full I ache with it, my pussy stretched around his huge cock.

"Ren!" I gasp, as he pulls back, hesitating. "Oh god, you feel so fucking good inside me."

I don't know where the dirty words came from, but I like how they sound, and I love the effect they have on him: he snarls wordlessly and slams back into me, pounding deep, hips slapping against my ass.

"Sophia," he growls, drawing back slowly, only to drive back in right away. "Fuck—you feel—ohhhh, shit, my love. I can't…I need to…"

He trails off, his fingers digging into my ass in a harsh, bruising grip that has my pulse racing and my core tightening.

"Tell me," I pant, pushing back into his thrusts. "What do you need, Ren?"

Thrusting slowly, I feel him shaking, feel his grip tighten until I know I'll have fingerprint bruises on my ass. "I'm trying to be…to be—" He growls again, and, as if his thread of control is slipping, he drives another hard thrust into me.

I lengthen my spine and press my chest to the rough carpet of the closet floor, arms stretched out in front of me, and I sink my ass backward into his thrust. "Let go, Ren," I breathe, looking over my shoulder at him. "Let go."

"I—I don't want to hurt you," he says, his voice a low growl.

"You won't. I promise you won't hurt me, Ren. Just let go. Give me everything you've got." I push back into him, arching my spine as he pulls away and then driving back into his thrusts once more. "Fuck me, my love. Fuck me as hard as you can."

"Oh god, thank fuck," he snarls from between gritted teeth.

He draws back, palms roaming in soothing circles over my ass cheeks, and then rams into me, once, hard, growling in primal ecstasy—his hand cracks against my left cheek, a sudden, shocking, but not exactly painful smack that has me squealing and jerking away, only for him to grip me by the hips and yank me into his thrust, fucking so deep my eyes cross and my squeal of shock dissolves into a low, feline snarling gasp.

"Ren!" I cry. "Oh *god*, I love that. I *love* it. Do it again, baby. Spank my ass. Fuck me and don't stop. Please, Ren, please, fuck, fuck, please fuck me!"

"You beg me for it?" he demands in Portuguese, teeth gritted as he rears back.

"*YES!*" I cry in the same. "I'm begging you, my love, please, please—Ren, my love, please, oh god fuck me, fuck me harder."

I hear the words I'm saying but I can't believe it's me saying them—but I love it. I love the freedom I have, the safety I feel with Lorenzo to give him every last part of me, my wildness, my intensity, my need, my desperation, and I can trust him to take it and hold it and protect it and cherish it.

Any last shred of self-restraint my Ren may have had left is gone, then. One hand sliding up my spine, the other grips my ass cheek, and he fucks into me, a hard, fast thrust that leaves my ass quivering and my pussy spasming around him. Another, and then another, and then he's finally giving it to me with unrestrained desperation, grunting with each hard thrust, pushing firmly on my back to press my chest to the floor. I lengthen again, giving him the angle he seems to want. And my fucking god, the angle is incredible. His cock strokes deep inside me, hitting me inside just right, at the perfect angle to hit the G-spot I always thought was a myth, and now the spasming of my pussy around him becomes wild and frantic, and I use it to make it better for him, squeezing around him with each violent fucking thrust.

I watch us in the mirror, holding Ren's eyes in the reflection. My tits sway and bounce and jiggle with each thrust, and my ass quakes, and my whole body is rocked forward. Ren's abs ripple as he moves, his arms flex and shift, his muscles sheened with sweat, his chest anvil hard and his shoulders broad, and my god, my man is so damned gorgeous as he takes me.

I'm overcome with love, watching Lorenzo fuck me. Tears flood my eyes, threatening to spill over, hazing my vision, and I cry out hoarse and raspy as yet another climax swells within me, titanic and crushing, dwarfing the previous ones he's given me even before it's reached its zenith. He picks up the pace, grunting as he fucks me harder and faster, deeper and deeper with each thrust, and I can't move with him anymore—all I can do is claw at the carpet and take him, take him, take him, screaming until my throat is raw, never looking away, never breaking our locked gazes.

And then, again without warning, Ren bends over me, lifts me up to my knees as he sinks back to sit on his shins. I'm sitting on his thighs, now, and he's impaled deep. I lift up, kneeling tall, reach back and bury my fingers in his hair, and he cups my tits in his hands and drives up into me.

And my god, my god, what a view. I can watch his cock slide up into me from this angle, I can watch my pussy stretch around him, lips thinning as he spears into me, inch by inch, until he bottoms out inside me.

He palms my face and pulls my head around, claims my mouth, sucks my tongue into his mouth, growling in his chest as he kisses me, as we meet each other's thrusts—I lower myself onto him and he drives up, and each thrust goes deeper than I thought possible, until my entire being aches from the depth of him within me. Cupping my cheek and kneading my breasts, he moves into me, moves with me. This isn't fucking, anymore—it's not even just sex or making love. This is beyond understanding, deeper than description, it's something more than merely physical connection or sexual union. It's metaphysical. It's spiritual.

Now, in this most unlikely of moments, I feel…how do I even put it? I feel my soul unfurl and open, feel the weight of trauma and torment fade, dissipate, and dissolve into nothing, feel my Lorenzo rising to meet me, feel each second expand into minutes and minutes into hours and then hours become weeks and weeks become millennia, and my physical form seems to fall away as his mouth and mine mate and move and meld, and our bodies connect, become one—a phrase heard often but never grasped until now. He fills me—yes, physically, driving into me and crashing through me and crushing his heat inside me and I clench around him and even our screams and grunts commingle and become a symphony, a susurrus of sighs. I breathe his breath and taste his tongue and gasp into his mouth and move with him, delving down onto his frantic thrusts, and we watch our lovemaking in the mirror, eyes locked and wide and fraught with love and wonder, and we are sweat-sick together, skin sliding and slipping and clapping and cracking and sucking and squelching.

Have I come once? Twice? A dozen times? A thousand? I don't know. I've lost count of the spasmodic eruptions of heat within me as I move with Lorenzo. Perhaps each scream is a climax, each gasp an orgasm.

Perhaps I've died and gone to heaven.

If so, I'll gladly stay in this endless heaven with Ren forever.

CHAPTER 18

FIRST DAY OF FOREVER

LORENZO

SOPHIA TREMBLES UNCONTROLLABLY, SIGHING and screaming and writhing as we move together. I'm utterly lost in her. How I've held off my release for as long as I have is a miracle I can't explain—and I still don't want to come. I want this to last forever. I caress her soft cheek as she stabs her tongue into my mouth, claiming a searing kiss in between gasps of ecstasy.

She's come at least three or four times since I first slid inside her, here on the floor of this closet, each orgasm wracking her to shuddering pieces, wave after wave of spasming ecstasy that leaves me breathless with wonder, awed at her lush, sensual, erotic beauty.

Her curves take my breath away, and I am cognizant of the privilege of having this woman in my arms, of getting to be inside her, to hold her, to kiss her, to make her come, to taste her, to topple together into oblivion.

She's crying wordlessly as I plunge up into her, spine arching as I drive deep, thrusting her perfect, heavy, teardrop tits to the ceiling.

I need more from her.

I press my lips to her ear and fit my fingers to her

clit and send lightning searing through her body. She screams, arching and shuddering spastically, coming at the first touch. "Say my name, my love."

"*LORENZO!*" She screams, hoarse and gutted. "Ohhhh—*FUCK!*"

And then her shuddering becomes something else as the orgasm cracks her open and shreds through her. Arched and shaking, sobbing my name in a chanted prayer, she seems to lose all control over her body, writhing helplessly.

I roll backward until I'm flat on the floor, taking her with me, keeping her above me, on me. I plant my feet, knees bent, fill my hands with the hot silk of the backs of her thighs and pull her legs against her belly and fuck into her, lips in her ear. "Keep coming for me, my love. Touch your pussy for me."

"C-c-can't—" She pants. "Can't—can't come any—anymore. Mercy, Ren. Have mercy!" She reaches down between her thighs to where we're joined and strokes my slick shaft as I spear thrust after thrust into her tight wet heat, and she cups my balls, stretching to find my taint and massaging me there. "I want you, Ren. Come inside me. Fill me, Ren. Please, my love. Let go. Give it to me. Give me everything. Now, please, please, please!"

Her words act like a trigger.

She strokes the base of my cock as I fuck her, and she fingers herself, and I feel my orgasm finally swelling inside me, fueling the wild desperation that's driven me thus far.

"Sophia!" I shout, pounding into her unrelentingly.

"Yes! Ren!" she pants, undulating on me, trying to

move with me, "now, my love. Come inside me, Ren. Come for me, baby."

My climax swells, rises, burgeons into a pulsing wash of heat and crushing pressure and I can't even consider holding back. I turn my face to hers and find her mouth waiting for mine, and I kiss her deeply, desperately.

"Please, Ren!" she begs, cupping and stroking me desperately as I move in her, adding a wild new level of ecstasy to this already life-changing release.

And then it shatters me.

I make a choked, hoarse cry as my orgasm boils out of me, balls tightening and pulsing and throbbing, and I fuck hard into her, bury myself as deep as I can go, and she mewls in gleeful bliss, feeling my cum pour out of me.

"Yes, Ren! Yes! Oh god, you feel so good inside me, baby," she chants, lips moving against mine. "*MORE*! More, baby. Don't stop, my love, never stop."

Whatever vestiges of control I may have had left flee me, then, and I fuck her through an orgasm that leaves me seeing double, dark spots dancing across my vision and light bursting behind my eyes, and she's screaming silently against my mouth, lips shuddering as she comes with me.

Wave after wave smashes the breath from my lungs, the words from my brain, and I can do nothing but ride through it, cupping her heavy breasts and feeling her pussy clench me with vise-like strength. I'm shouting her name as the waves crash through me, chanting my love for her, gasping breathlessly when the intensity erases everything else in the world but Sophia and me, our united bodies, our merged souls.

After an eternity, I can come no more. My thighs burn and my abs ache and my lungs are on fire, and I'm flushed and sweaty and gasping for breath.

Sophia is quivering endlessly, an occasional violent shudder wracking her.

My cock slowly goes slack inside her, but neither of us seems to want to move, to lose our connection.

Finally, I become aware of how hard and uncomfortable the floor is. I pull out of her, and she whimpers at the loss. Turn her to face me, cheek to my chest, and stand up with her, cradle her to me, carry her to the bed.

A small mountain of clothes is in the way, but I kick them away, shifting us beneath the blankets.

She burrows against me, as if she can't get close enough, and I wrap my arms around her, squeeze her tight. Roam her back, her waist, her ass, her neck, her shoulders.

We lay together like this in blissful silence for a long, long time.

Eventually, she whimpers unhappily. "I have to pee so bad, but I don't want to move." With an irritated groan, she rolls away from me and sits on the edge of the bed. "Stupid bladder."

I just laugh.

Watching her walk away from me is delightful; watching her return is even better. She trots back to me from the bathroom, which does truly awe-inspiring things to her tits, and then crawls in bed as fast as possible, wriggling back into my arms and burrowing against my chest with a happy little sigh.

This makes me laugh out of pure joy and

unadulterated affection. "I didn't know you could be so damned adorable."

She rolls one shoulder. "Me either." She lifts her chin and looks at me. "I'm adorable?"

"Mmm," I hum. "Very. Especially when you do that."

"Do what?"

"That little wriggle and sigh."

I can almost feel her blushing. "Ren, stop."

"No! I love it."

"I'm a badass warrior queen, Lorenzo. I am *not* adorable."

I give her ass cheek a squeeze, a smack, and a jiggle. "You can be both."

"Do you have to do that?" she grumbles.

"Do what?"

"Make my ass jiggle like that."

I laugh and give it another hearty smack that sets it to quivering. "Yes, I do. I happen to be obsessed with your ass, and making it jiggle like that is one of life's small joys that make it worth living."

She snorts at this. "Ridiculous." A quirked eyebrow. "I thought you were obsessed with my boobs?"

"Those too, equally. But they're pressed against me in a way I'm rather fond of, so an ass jiggling is what you get."

"Ren," she scolds. "You're making me embarrassed."

"About what? Having a killer fucking body that I'm absolutely, insanely in love with?"

This keeps her quiet for a moment. "I'm just not used to..." a small shrug follows her trailed-off statement. "I don't know."

"Being loved," I fill in. "Being shown affection. Being adored. Being treated with respect."

"Yes," she whispers, her voice tiny. "That."

"I promise you, Soph, I will spend every waking moment for the rest of my life showing you those things."

Another long silence—this one is thoughtful on her part. "Ren?"

"Yes, my love?"

"What if I can't ever have kids? What if I don't ever want to? What if I can't give you the life you've dreamed of?"

"How do you know what life I've dreamed of, Soph?" I ask, gently scolding. "I'm a career soldier, my love. I've never considered…domesticity. I don't know if that life is what I want, either. Maybe I just want to enjoy a few years of peace, you know? Figuring out how to live a life where I'm not being shot at or chased."

"Don't just…" she sniffles. "Don't just say things, Ren. Not if you don't mean them."

I roll her to her back and lever over her on an elbow. Cup her face. Brush a tendril of hair away. "Sophia Bruna Santos de Silva. I love you. I spent so many years without you, dreaming of you, missing you, needing you, not knowing if you were dead or alive, if you were suffering, if you.." my throat closes and I have to pause to breathe, to let the heat dispute, the tightness relent. "All I care about—*the only thing*—is having you in my life, in whatever form that is, however it looks. I love you with all that I fucking am, Sophia. I'll never tell you something just because it sounds good or I think it's what you want."

"Ren, I—"

I gaze down at her, holding her gaze. "Hold on. Just listen, please."

"Okay," she whispers.

"I'll tell you a few things. They may scare you. You may not be ready to hear them, but…" I exhale, choosing my words carefully. "I want to marry you. I want you to be my wife. I want to belong to you in every way there is. I'm not sure about kids. But I do think Reninho…" I pause again. "He should know his mother."

"She died. Pugli murdered her."

"No," I answer, tapping her nose. "He didn't. He deserves to know you. How that looks, I'm not sure. But you're his mother. Beatriz was his mom. She loved him. She gave him the life you wanted him to have—safe, innocent. She's gone now, but he still has you. He just…he doesn't know you, yet."

Her eyes fill with tears and she blinks them away, only to have more take their place. "Ren, god. I…fuck. Fuck!" She covers her face with her hands.

I wrest them away, dip down to kiss her tears. "Don't hide, *meu amor*."

"I don't know," she whispers. "I don't know. I carried him and I gave birth to him, but…that part of my life seems like a dream…a nightmare, honestly, sort of fuzzy and half-remembered, mainly because I want to forget it. I don't want to remember. I…I don't feel like his mother. I don't…I don't know how to *be* a mother. I don't remember my own since she died when I was so young. What do I know about children, Lorenzo?"

I brush her cheek with the backs of my fingers. "Sophia, darling…I don't think *anyone* knows *anything* about raising kids. Everyone is just sort of doing their best and making it up as they go along."

She frowns at me. "That sounds sort of cynical."

I laugh. "It's not! It's hopeful. There's no handbook out there that everyone got except you, Soph. Maybe someone who's raised a bunch of kids already will have some knowledge or advice, but…does it apply evenly to everyone? I don't know—-I don't think so. We're all different. How someone parents a child is subjective." I rest my forehead against hers. "And I'm not telling you that you should move him in here and have him start calling you Mom. I don't know what you should do about Reninho. I just mean that you *are* his mother, and you *do* have love to give. It can look however you, or we, want it to look. It doesn't have to be traditional."

She shakes her head. "No, no, no." Rolling away from me, Sophia leaves the bed and goes to the window, breathing in slowly, holding it, and letting out slowly through pursed lips—box breathing, to counteract panic. "It's too much, Ren. Too much too soon. It hasn't even sunk in that Rafael is really dead. That…that it's really over, that I'm really free of that monster." She scrubs her face with one hand, shakes her head again. "I'm really, truly, finally free to make my life look however I want. For the first time in my life, I can *choose* my own future."

I leave the bed and move behind her, frame her with my arms. "Sophia, I only—"

"I know, Ren," she interrupts. "I know what you meant. But you have to understand—as a child, my father determined who I was. I was allowed no input over any aspect of my life. What I wore, who my friends were, where I went, whether or not I went to school, what I ate, the color of the walls in my room, the cut of my hair—Bruno de Silva decided *everything* about me. And then Rafael—as his wife, I had some leeway, of course, but at the end of the day I lived in *his* world. Everyone around me was employed by him and was loyal to him. I was, at best, considered first among equals with the rest of the estate staff. My every movement was watched and reported to him." She clings to my bicep, rests her cheek against it. "Even after I escaped, he still controlled my life to a degree. He was waiting and watching for me to show myself. He never forgot. Never forgave. Never let go. Never stopped looking for me. For Reninho. I couldn't choose my life. I was hostage to him even though I wasn't physically his captive or wife. It is only now that he's dead that I can even really let myself think about…who I am or what I want." She turns in my arms, presses her back to the glass and looks up at me. "I barely know who the fuck I am, Lorenzo. How can I think I could take care of you, be your wife, be Reninho's mother?"

I kiss her temple. "Take care of *me*? Soph, I? I don't need you to take care of me. *I* am going to take care of *you*."

"But Ren, you're missing the point. I *want* to. I just…I'm not sure I know *how*." She looks up at me. "I actually feel kind of…adrift. I've spent so long being controlled and afraid and hiding that I don't know who I am."

I pull her against my chest and hug her close. "You have all the time in the world. I am sorry if I overwhelmed you. I just…I suppose I want you to be excited about the future with me, that's all."

She sniffles, sighs. "I will be, Ren. I think I just need some time. There's a lot to process." A long silence. "I would have, back then, you know."

"Would have what, back then?"

"Married you."

"I wonder what our lives would have been, if we had been able to stay together all this time?"

She shakes her head and shrugs. "Who knows? We probably would have been very poor, and we would never have left Brazil." She pulls away enough to look up at me. "I do want to be with you. I want to marry you. I *am* excited about our future together, Lorenzo. I just need time. And, really, I can't marry you until Jakob is back. I owe him so much, and he deserves to be there."

"Of course. I mean, I would marry you right now. Go downtown and have one of those Elvises marry us. Come back here and have a grand party with our friends."

"Family," she corrects.

"Right, yes, family." I kiss the top of her head. "But you are right—Jakob brought us all together. When we marry, he must be there."

She smiles up at me. "You don't mind waiting?"

"Of course not. I have waited for you for years. I have you. That is enough. We can say vows and exchange rings at any time—my love for you and commitment to you will not be changed or lessened."

She rests her head on me again. "I love you so much, Lorenzo Oliveira Araujo."

"And I you, Sophia Bruna Santos de Silva, more than I can ever say."

"Could we..." she hesitates. "Lay down again? I think I would like to try to take a nap."

I laugh, scoop her up in my arms, and carry her to bed. "You're the boss-lady."

"Not of you."

I settle us in her bed and cover us with the blankets. "You're welcome to boss me around anytime, my love."

She giggles—actually giggles. "I might just try that out, sometime."

We drowse together, then. I'm not sure either of us actually falls asleep, but we enter a kind of twilight, neither fully awake nor fully asleep.

I rouse slowly and then all at once. Slowly at first, because I must have been more asleep than I thought; all at once because as soon as I become aware of being awake, I become aware of a certain sensation.

I look down my body, blinking against the crimson-orange glow of late evening desert sunlight bathing the room. the blankets are twisted at the foot of the bed, and Sophia is laying on my stomach, softly caressing my cock. Petting it, really.

"Mmm," I mumble, "hello there."

"Sssshhhh." She doesn't look at me. "Don't move. Don't talk. Just…be still and be quiet."

"As you wish, my love."

"This is for me," she murmurs, "although I have a feeling you'll enjoy it."

I know what she's about. "Soph, my love, all I will say is that you have nothing to prove—certainly not to me, and especially not about what I think you're about to do. If some part of sex triggers bad feelings or memories for you, we don't need to do those things. But if it's important to you to reclaim what was taken, then I will gladly help you reclaim it, however that must happen."

She doesn't reply for a while, though I know she heard me. "I did it to you earlier, during sex, and I liked it. I really did. I liked how you responded. I liked knowing I could give you that. And I want to be able to give it to you."

"I don't need it, Sophia. I enjoy it, obviously, but there is no reason for you to intentionally trigger yourself. Making love with you is all I need. You are enough, exactly as you are."

She has me fully erect, now, and grips my cock loosely in her fist, slowly caressing my length. "I'm not sure how else to say this, Ren." She hesitates. "It's not entirely even about *you*, exactly. He took things from me. Fear and memories of what he did and made me do have kept me as much a prisoner to his control even after I was out of his direct control. I am determined that he will not have any control over any part of my life or our relationship. He is dead, and so his influence over me will die with him."

"As long as you understand—" I start.

"I do, Ren, I really do. And I appreciate your understanding and compassion more than I can say." She pauses, rolling her thumb over the tip of my cock, smearing the pre-cum leaking out of me. "But now what I need from you is for you to shut up and let me suck your cock." My cock twitches as her words send arousal blasting through me. "I see he approves of this plan."

"He's a selfish little bastard, so yes."

"Excuse me, Ren. There is nothing little about him."

"I stand corrected *OHGOD*…holy shit, Sophia!"

Her mouth suctions around the head while her soft, small hands pump my length. "Jesus fuck that feels incredible."

I hold absolutely still, fisting my hands in the sheet at my sides rather than risk upsetting her by grabbing her head. She releases my cock with a loud, sucking pop, watching as she caresses my shaft a few times, and then covers me with her mouth again. This time, she goes slow, sliding her lips down my length inch by inch, tongue swirling and sliding. I groan, arching my back as she backs away, only to plunge her mouth down again, further this time, taking more of me.

Her thick black hair slips with her movement, drifting across her cheek. She brushes it away, and then fumbles blindly—finding one of my hands, she brings it to her head.

"Just…don't push," she whispers.

I gather her hair in my hands, bunch it up and out of the way and hold on—I can grip the slippery mass of black locks as tightly as I want.

She takes her time. I fight the urge to thrust, gasping and groaning as she pleasures me with her mouth, stroking my length and caressing and kneading my balls, never taking very much of me in her mouth before backing away again. Long, glorious minutes later, I feel my climax rising, feel desperation filling my veins, replacing blood with the boiling lava of need.

"Fucking god, Soph," I groan. "I'm close."

"Mmmm," she hums, pulling away and letting me drop out of her mouth. "Come for me, love. Don't hold back."

And then her mouth is on me once more, sliding down my length—more and more, deeper and deeper.

I hear her swallow hard, gasp for breath, and then she's taking even more of me and she gags a little, backs away, mouth open and gasping.

"Jesus, *meu amor*," I murmur.

Another long, slow, wet slide of her mouth down my shaft, lips stuttering, tongue swirling and licking and fluttering. A helpless groan leaves me, and I arch again, crush-gripping her hair as my climax boils through me.

"Oh fuck," I snarl, desperately resisting the urge to push her lower, "Sophia, fuck, fuck. So good, my love. I—I can't—oh god, I—I'm...ohhhhhhfuck I'm coming!"

She hums a breathy, pleased, shocked sound as I unleash my orgasm, and then she's gulping audibly, sucking hard as she slides her mouth down my length and takes as much of me as she can. Stars dance and burst in my vision and my entire body tenses and trembles as lightning shatters me, pulsating heat billows through me. I can't produce a single sound as my orgasm wrenches me and ravages me, and still Sophia doesn't relent.

She sucks and slurps and bobs, and my feet scrabble at the bed as I come and come. Pulling away so I pop out of her mouth, she gasps raggedly, panting, gulping. I let go of her hair and smooth it away, pulling her up to me.

She has other plans.

She takes me in her mouth yet again, palming my balls in both hands, and swallows her way down my length, sucking hard enough to rip the breath from my lungs, forcing me into an arching, gasping, paroxysm of ecstasy, drawing the last dregs of my orgasm out of me, leaving me boneless and breathless.

And *then* she brings her head up to rest on my chest.

I'm incapable of speech for a long time. "Soph," I

whisper, when I can form words again. "You—that was—holy mother of *god*, Sophia."

She giggles again, and the innocent, pleased joy in the sound brightens my soul. "It was okay, then?"

"*Okay*?" I laugh in disbelief. "I don't have words for how incredible that was." I palm her cheek and kiss her, tasting myself on her breath. "And you…how are you… are you okay?"

She nods. "More than okay. I *liked* doing that for you. I liked how you responded. It makes me feel…I don't know. It's hard to put into words. But I'm good. Very, very good." She yawns. "Although I don't know that I have the motivation to move my things downstairs, anymore."

"I must admit, Sophia, it would be pretty nice to have this place to ourselves. Privacy. Space. It would be nice. But I will go with whatever you decide. I understand your reasons for the move."

"I worry I would feel…self-conscious," she murmurs. "About being…loud. If we were down there."

"I do like making you scream," I say.

"Ren," she scolds.

"What? I do! I love making you scream. Especially when it's my name you're screaming." I roll her to her back and kiss my way down her body. "Just…like…this."

I spend the next thirty minutes with my face buried between her thighs, doing just that—making her scream my name again and again.

Only after a long shower do we finally leave the room and head down to see what the others are up to.

CHAPTER 19

THE GANG'S ALL HERE

INEZ

REN AND I ENTER THE NEWLY-FINISHED BROKEN Arrows common room—which some of the girls, led by Terra, have taken to calling the Quiver. Terra calls the new moniker "A multiple entendre," although I can only find two meanings.

The floors are epoxy, as before, but this time the finish is a pale, dove-gray with red flecks. The walls are the same shade of gray as the base layer of epoxy, which would have made for a lot of boring, unrelieved gray, but the women have collectively put their own stamp on things. Art lines the walls: black and white photography ranging from Ansel Adams' landscapes to Fan Ho's portraits of Hong Kong from the 50s; prints of famous pieces by painters from across history, such as Renoir, Degas, Klimt, Rembrandt, Picasso, and other masters; simple water color still-lifes from a variety of artists I've never heard of; and a few wild mixed media pieces. There's a new sectional, black leather again and just as massive but strewn with a profusion of colorful throw pillows and fleece blankets draped over the back and stuffed in wicker baskets. The kitchen is pretty much the same as before, just with the newest industrial appliances. The overall effect of the women's touch is homey, cozy, and inviting. It's no longer the sterile man-cave it used to be. Only the gym and the bedrooms escaped mostly unscathed, although a few stray bullet holes had to be patched and obviously the floor had to be totally scraped away and redone throughout the entire level.

The men are clustered around one of the long cafeteria-style tables, cheering and clapping and shouting encouragement as Chance and Kane arm-wrestle. Bottles of booze litter the other table, along with two liters of soda, cans of sparkling water, bowls of potato chips and tortilla chips, and smaller bowls of various dips. There are also casserole dishes containing homemade Mac 'n cheese, chimichangas, and what appears to be chicken breasts slathered with thick layers of cream cheese and melted cheese. More baking dishes contain brownies, some sort of multi-layer brownie-marshmallow-ice-cream concoction; there's a platter of fat chocolate chip cookies, a platter of small white balls of baked dough doused in powdered sugar, and a small bowl of what looks to be homemade gummy candies off by itself to one side.

The women are on the sectional, a reality dating show featuring ridiculously attractive and vapid young people on TV with the volume off and the subtitles on. Bottles of nail polish and polish remover litter the coffee table, intermixed with red Solo cups each marked with a different color swipe of polish. An ashtray sits off to one side, a huge, hand-rolled joint smoldering. The women are painting each other's nails, cackling and screeching and squealing just as loudly as the men, although I'm not immediately certain what they're laughing about.

"SOPH!" Terra shrieks, spotting me.

She wriggles with comical awkwardness to the edge of the couch, drying nails held ridiculously out in front of her, and then stands up on the couch and leaps over the back. She's a bit tipsy, though, and her landing is sloppy, ending up with her doing a Paul Blart-style tuck and roll across the floor; I came down here once, a few years ago, while the men, all single then, were hammered together and watching that movie, and ended up standing out of their sight line, watching some of it with them, unbeknownst to them. It was…certainly memorable, if nothing else.

Terra hops to her feet, fingers still held out. "I'm fine!"

Saxon cackles. "That was smooth as silk, baby girl."

Terra does a silly yet sensual belly-dancing hip-roll move. "I know." She trots over to me—with a lot of wholly unnecessary bouncing, if you ask me. When she reaches me, she whispers in my ear. "Is he still watching me?"

I frown at her. "Who? Saxon?"

"Yes." She tries to suppress a giggle and fails. "I'm trying to see how long it'll take me to seduce him back to our room. Annika and I have a wager going. If I can get him back to our room before midnight, Annika has to wear any outfit of my choosing every day for a week. If it's after midnight, she gets to put me through three of her most brutal workouts. And girl, lemme tell ya, I'm gonna win. Because number one, Saxy can't get enough of this ass—" and here she glances over her shoulder to make sure he's watching, and then gives her ass a vigorous shaking, "and number two, I hate working out."

"Saxy?" I echo.

She snickers. "Yeah, he hates it. Or, he loves to hate it. A bit of both, maybe." She pushes me around the sectional away from Ren. "I'm stealing your girl, Ren. Go play with the boys."

I glance back at Ren over my shoulder, mouthing *HELP ME*. He just laughs and gives me a finger-wiggle wave. By the time he's reached the table—where Kane has Chance held to a stand-still, their mammoth arms shaking at a 75-degree angle toward Kane—Rev is handing Ren a Solo cup, slinging an arm around his shoulders, and wedging him into the circle of men watching the arm-wrestling contest.

Terra guides me to the couch and playfully shoves me backward so I land seated between Anjalee and Naomi. Anjalee has a cup to her mouth, but she's giggling uncontrollably into it, while Naomi's shoulders shake in silent laughter.

Annika is on her feet, cane hooked over her forearm, several Solo cups pinched between her fingers, which she passes out. "Tequila and Sprite for Myka, vodka soda for Tati, whiskey neat for yours truly, and red wine and Coke for Anj." She shoots me a look. "Whatcha drinkin', Soph?"

"Um." I shrug. "I...I've never been much of a drinker. Not having control over myself and my surroundings, in my life, has most often presented a significant risk."

Annika nods, eyes full of understanding. "I get it, babe, I really do. But you're safe, here. No one's coming after you, or Ren, or any of us. Your ex-dick is dead. You're good. You can cut loose with us. No pressure, though. You don't wanna drink, hit that J. Or don't. We don't care. We just want you to unwind with us and have some fun."

I inhale, hold it, and let it out in a long, slow sigh, nodding. I point at the smoldering joint. "Let me try that, please."

Annika hands it to me. "All yours." She scans the group on the couch. "Anyone need anything before I sit down?"

No one does, and she lowers herself to the couch on the other side of Anjalee, who has finally managed to stop her giggles.

"So, Sophia," Scarlett says—she's lounging in the corner of the sectional, dressed in a pair of very tight, very short black workout shorts that leave the lower swell of her butt exposed, her long legs bare, with a midriff-baring, hand-cut, white muscle shirt over a black sports bra. Her hair is loose for once, and she's sipping from a Solo cup, glancing at Solomon over the rim; judging by their private smiles. They're sharing some wordless, amusing secret.

"So, Scarlett." I puff on the joint, hold it, blow the smoke out…and dissolve into coughing, immediately going lightheaded as the THC takes hold.

"For the daughter of a drug kingpin and ex-wife of another, you're pretty straightlaced," Terra says.

I shrug, nod. "Yes, I suppose so. I grew up watching my father's men get drunk and act like smooth-brained cavemen, and I saw firsthand the effects of the products we produced and distributed. So drinking and getting high have never held much appeal for that reason alone. And as I said a moment ago, my survival frequently depended on my reaction time and situational awareness." Already feeling myself slowing down and loosening up, I shrug and smile, wave the joint. "This, however, seems to hold promise."

Annika takes the joint from me. "If you're new to it, I'd let that hit or two you've taken kick in all the way before you go for more."

I nod, letting out a breath that seems laden with the

myriad stressors I've harbored for so long. "This is quite the party."

Terra cackles. "This isn't a party, babe. It's just a... celebratory hangout."

I glance at Ren—Saxon is murmuring in his ear, indicating the small bowl of gummies. Ren takes one and eats it, and Saxon claps him on the back.

"Those are not just regular gummies, are they?" I ask.

Naomi shakes her head. "Nope. I didn't realize it at first and ate two." She holds up her cup. "This is just Diet Coke because I...am...high...as...*fuck.*"

Silas's gaze goes to her as her shouted statement rings out. He grins at her, laughing and shaking his head.

I eye her. "Naomi, my goodness."

She sticks her tongue out at me. "I'm a big girl, Sophia. I can curse and do drugs if I want."

"Cannabis gummies hardly count as drugs," Terra mumbles into her cup. "It's recreationally legal in the State of Nevada."

Naomi's eyes widen comically. "Really? Even better!"

This gets a laugh out of me. "Oh, Naomi. You're too cute."

She pouts. "Cute. I don't want to be *cute.* I want to be a badass like you and Scar."

Scarlett snickers at this. "Nay-Nay, you *are* a badass. Myka and Anj told me about your run-in with those dudes at the motel."

Naomi nods seriously. "That was pretty badass, wasn't it?" She frowns, then. "Is Nay-Nay cute or badass?"

"Both," Myka, Terra, and Scarlett say in unison.

"Oh. Okay." Naomi peers at my feet—I'm wearing

my slippers, black fuzzy, furry, comfy Ugg clogs, barefoot. "TOES!"

I rear back in surprise at her shouted non-sequitur, following her gaze to my feet. "Toes?"

She points at my feet. "I've never seen your toes. Nakey feet time, bitch." She stares at me, eyes wide. "I called you a bitch. But I was just teasing, okay?"

I splutter a laugh and lean into her. "I promise not to cut your heart out and eat it, Nay-Nay." I pretend to glare. "This time."

She shrinks away from me. "Eeep!" She actually says the word. "I'm not tasty!"

"DISAGREE!" Silas shouts from across the room.

This whole exchange has Anjalee off into another fit of giggles. Keeping her cup against her mouth, giggling, Anjalee leans precariously forward, stretches out a hand, and yanks one of my slippers off, tossing it wildly to one side; it nearly brains Tatiana. Giggling so hard she's about to hyperventilate, Anjalee yanks my other slipper off and hurls it the other way; the sole of my slipper thwacks the wall and drops to the floor, leaving a black shoe print on the freshly painted wall.

"Oops," she whispers, and she points at my feet. "Nakey feet."

Annika shakes her head, looking at me. "Lightweights." She juts her chin at the swarm of polish bottles. "Pick a color."

I frown at the dizzying array. "Um." I look at my toes, wiggling them. "I don't know."

"Pink!" Naomi says. "Barbie-barf pink. Because you would normally *never*, and this is the new you."

My eyebrows go up at this. "I agree, as a matter of

fact." I point at the bottle labelled Cotton Candy Dreams. "That one."

Annika grabs my feet and suddenly I'm laying across Anjalee with my head on Naomi's lap, and the joint is pressed to my lips and Annika is expertly swiping pink polish onto my toes.

I look up at Naomi. "I don't eat hearts, Nay-Nay. That was a joke."

She sputters behind her hand. "I know. It was funny. You're scary sometimes, but not, like, serial killer cannibal scary."

"At least there's that," I deadpan. I turn my attention to Annika. "You're very good at this, Annika."

She shrugs, focused on the task. "I did a lot of travelling for volleyball. Lots of girls, lots of downtime on buses and in hotel rooms. We did each other's nails a fucking *lot*."

"Do you miss it?" I ask.

She nods, gaze fixed on my toes and her hands. "God yes, every day."

"What do you miss most?"

A tip of her head to one side. "All of it. The bus rides— although that's a love-hate thing. You really get close to your girls when you spend hours and hours together on the bus, especially those fucking interminable overnight trips across the Midwest. I miss crashing out on sugar and adrenaline in the rooms after a game. Watching tape. Practices." She pulls back, dips the brush into the bottle, hesitates. "The games, though. *Fuuuuck*, I miss that shit. The rush. The crowds. The way everyone would lose their minds when I got a gnarly kill."

I blink at her. "Kill?"

"Spike," she clarifies. "That's what I was best at—where

you jump up close to the net and hit the ball really, *really* fucking hard."

I nod. "Ah, yes."

She shrugs again. "I miss it all. But…I wouldn't go back. Is that weird? That I can miss something like crazy but also not want to go back to it?"

Tatiana shakes her head, pointing at Annika with her cup. "No, it is not so strange. Not to me, at least." A sigh. "I miss Tata. I miss Zagreb. I miss my business and my girls. But like you have said, I would also not return to that life. I quite like my life here, with you all, quite a lot more."

Annika finishes with my other foot and twists the top onto the bottle. "Now. Fingers. Pick a different color."

I shake my head. "Surprise me."

Someone takes the joint from me, puts it to my lips—I puff, and it's gone. I exhale, head spinning, light and floaty and loose.

I hear a chorus of shouts from the men, followed by groans and laughter. "Who won?" I ask the room at large.

"Kane won one and Chance won one," Annika says. "This is the last of three, and I think my man's gonna get the W."

"Oh no," Anjalee says, "Kane is going to win. He is the…oh my god, I have forgotten the word. Down dog? No, that is yoga. Something to do with a dog."

"Underdog?" I offer.

"YES!" She exclaims. "He is the underdog."

I open my eyes and realize Tatiana is painting the nails of my right hand a pale, sea foam green, and Terra is painting my right hand a garish yellow. "Wow," I mutter. "That is a hideous shade of yellow, Terra."

She cackles. "I know! Isn't it marvelous?"

I lapse into a hazy, contented silence, eyes closed, listening to a half-dozen different conversations wash over me. I hear a door click closed, followed by howls and wolf whistles from the men. I crack open one eye and see Terra sauntering toward us, grinning ear to ear.

She plops down on the couch next to Annika and smacks her thigh. "I win."

Annika frowns. "Um, you two were in there for like five minutes. No way in hell that man plowed you that fast."

Terra pretends to huff on her nails and buff them on her shirt front. "What can I say? I've got a magic poonani."

Anjalee splutters at this. "Magical poonani? What is this poonani?" Her accent has gone rather pronounced as she gets drunker. "Is it your yoni?"

"Yoni?" Terra echoes.

Anjalee points at her crotch in a broad gesture. "Yes. Your lady cave."

Terra covers her face with her hands, cackling. "Lady cave! Anj, fuck me, I love you. Yes. Poonani means pussy. Which I assume yono or whatever you said does too."

"Yo-*ni*," Anjalee corrects. "It is the Sanskrit word for the vulva, or the womb, but really, it means the feminine energy as a whole."

"So then, what's the word for dick?" Terra asks.

"Lingam."

Terra nods. "Well, there you go, Anni." She pronounces the nickname *AH-nee*. "I have a magical yoni which Saxon's lingam doesn't stand a chance against."

Annika frowns, shaking her head. "No way! Less than five minutes? Sorry, darlin', I call bullshit." She whacks the back of the couch with her cane. "Saxon!"

"Yo!" Comes the shouted response.

Terra lunges off the couch and tries to clap a hand over Annika's mouth, but Annika has the reach and the strength advantage, and easily wrestles Terra's hand away.

"Did you just fuck Terra in under five minutes?"

"Hell to the fuck no!" Saxon answers, indignant. "Under five minutes? When I was fourteen maybe."

Terra is still trying to out-wrestle Annika, and Annika is cackling as she fends off the smaller woman. "Not another word, Saxon Cabot!" Terra screeches. "Or I swear to god I'll never suck you off again!" She immediately goes limp, flopping away and smacking herself in the forehead. "Fuck me."

Annika smacks the couch cushion with her cane again with a loud thwack. "You blew him?"

Terra shakes her head. "Nope!"

"Terra!"

"FINE!" Terra groans dramatically, stomping her feet like a toddler having a tantrum. "Fine! I sucked him off."

"The wager was fucking," Annika says. "That was the deal. Oral doesn't count."

I watch the exchange, puzzled. "Why are you wagering on this?"

Annika snorts, shrugging. "For fun."

"But you discuss these things...openly?" I ask.

Terra pats my thigh. "Sure we do. Those walls aren't exactly thin, but they're not soundproof either." A shrug. "We're all adults, we all have a lot of sex, and so yeah, we talk about it, and sometimes tease each other. Why?"

"I..." I close my eyes again. "I couldn't talk about... that."

Naomi, surprisingly, answers me. "I felt the same way when I first came here. Myka, Anjalee, and Annika openly discussed their sex lives with each other. It made me very uncomfortable at first. Where I came from, such things were not discussed—at all. I...I felt like it was private. Personal. Sacred, even."

I blink up at her. "Do you not feel that way anymore?"

"Oh, no, I do. It *is* personal and sacred. But my relationship with these girls..." Naomi looks around, eyes misty. "It's very...intimate. And I..." she blushes, ducks her head. "I was very innocent about sex when I met Silas. Talking to women who have more experience than me has helped me in my relationship with Silas. I can ask questions. Share things. I never had friends, let alone girlfriends. We joke and we laugh and we tease, but we do know how sacred it is for all of us. It is very liberating to be able to talk openly about it with the only other people on the planet who can understand exactly how I feel. What it's like belonging to this group."

"So..." I sit up and turn to put my back to the couch back, holding my hands out to admire the color, although I hate the yellow with every fiber of my being. It's a fun kind of hate, though. "You tell each other things? Personal things? Details?"

Annika shrugs. "Sure. Not, like *every*thing."

"You told me you queefed, Anni," Terra says. "And why. That's pretty personal."

"Because it was funny." She snickers. "It's still funny."

Terra can't help dissolving into snickering. "Queefing is always funny."

"Tell us something, Soph," Scarlett says, leaving her corner and joining the group crowded together at the opposite end of the sectional. "Just jump in with both feet. Trust us."

I look back over my shoulder at the men and find Lorenzo's eyes. He smiles—I may be reading things into it, but the smile seems to communicate how happy he is to see me with the girls like this, bonding, unwinding. Letting my guard down.

"I..." I feel a million thoughts percolating, and struggle to put one into words; my brain feels foggy and disorganized, as if my thoughts are a billion fluttering moths and I have to catch each one in order to create a sentence, but when I catch one, another flies out of my net.

Or something.

"Rafael was a hideously depraved man. The things he enjoyed—his sick peccadillos would horrify even the Marquis de Sade." I stretch out my hand, and someone reads my mind, fits the joint into my fingers; I take a puff, inhale, hold it, exhale. "One of the things he enjoyed doing to me was violent oral sex. It was...traumatic, painful, shameful, degrading. He would hold my hair and..." I shake my head, blowing out a sharp sigh. "You can imagine. So, after I escaped, I avoided all sex. I avoided people. Jakob, the man who owns this building and put the Broken Arrows together...my relationship with him has always been purely platonic. Boss and employee—friends. Perhaps even older brother and younger sister."

I puff again and try to catch the fluttering thoughts whirling in my brain. "I held much shame and fear about sex. But Lorenzo...he...when I am with him, I forget all of that. I felt desire, sexual desire, for the first time in a very, very long time when he and I reconnected. The desire made it easy to forget what I'd been through. Until it became time to...do things. To allow him to touch me, to try and touch him."

Naomi slides an arm around my shoulders and pulls me into a side hug. "I am so, so sorry you experienced that, Sophia."

"Thank you, Naomi." I let her hold me—and I find it comforting. These women support me. Accept me. Understand me. "Today, earlier, Lorenzo and I…" I blush, duck my head, roll a shoulder.

"Got it on like Donkey Kong?" Terra suggests.

Annika elbows her. "I don't think she's at the teasing stage yet, Ter."

I shoot Annika a grateful look, because I am assuredly not at the teasing stage. "Yes. We…connected, physically. It was very, *very* intense. Emotional…in a way I didn't know it could be."

Naomi rests her cheek on the top of my head, which rests on her shoulder. "That's the best kind, isn't it? Where you feel like…gosh, how do you even describe it?"

"It's not just a physical connection," Myka says. "It's your souls…merging. Having grown up in a spiritual, religious family, to me, I still think of it as…touching a part of the divine, I suppose."

"Making love with your bodies," Tatiana says. "But the deeper connection is from heart to heart. Becoming one flesh, as your Christian Bible puts it."

"Exactly," I say. "That's how it was. And it was so beautiful. But…" I trail off, wondering if I'm really going to share this with them.

"But what, honey?" Terra asks. "C'mon, now. Don't be shy. No matter what it is, I promise you, we'll understand."

"We took a nap. And I woke up…" I trail off again, start over. "I woke up wanting to…to do something for him."

Myka grins at me over the top of her drink, which she's been nursing. "Ohhhh *girl*, I know that feeling."

"You…do?" I say.

"Sure. If Ren is anything like Rev, let's just say I'm gonna assume he gets off almost as much from giving as he does getting." She glances at me for confirmation. "Makes sure you come several times for every one time he does. And you wake up and you wanna show him how grateful you are, and he's naked and his big, beautiful cock is just *right there*, begging you to pay attention to it?"

"And all of a sudden, you've got that thang in your mouth," Terra says, picking up where Myka stopped, "And he's waking up like, what's even *happening* right now?"

I stare from woman to woman. "Yes that's….yes."

"But you've got to have some pretty major hangups about giving head, considering what your evil ex did to you," Annika says.

I nod. "I do. Even thinking about…" I hesitate, and then find the words pouring out. "Even thinking about putting his…putting him in my mouth, I…" I shake my head. "It scared me senseless."

"Of course it did," Myka says. "And I don't know him that well, but I can't imagine he'd ever try to make you feel pressured."

"No!" I protest. "No. Not at all. The exact opposite. He made it clear that was something he'd *never* push for. He knew what Rafa was like. He worked for him, after all. He saw things I know he'll never talk about."

"So what'd you do?" Scarlett asks. "Because I don't know how I'd be able to get past that."

"Well, I…" I shrug. "It was made a little easier by the fact that up to that point, every other part of sex that I had fears about—which was everything—turned out to be nothing to be afraid of." I frown. "I'm not certain if that made any sense. It feels rather convoluted."

"We follow you," Tatiana assures me.

"I…earlier, during sex," I drop my voice. "I did it. A little bit. Just for a moment, before he stopped me. Used my mouth on him, I mean. But that was in the middle of things, you know? It's much easier when you're already aroused, is it not?"

"Hell yeah it is," Terra says. "Going down on a guy, especially a well-endowed one? It can be a little intimidating. The first time, at least. You don't know what he's gonna do, how he's gonna respond."

I blink at her, curiosity overriding politeness. "Him being Saxon? Or him being all men?"

She smiles at me. "Meaning it sounds like I know that from experience with a lot of different men?"

"Well…" I say, hesitating to admit that she's right.

She just laughs. "Oh, Soph. You know the boys' backgrounds, but you clearly don't know ours. I was a ho."

"Terra, I would never pass judgment," I say.

"Oh, I know. Me either—that's not a judgement call on myself, it's just facts. I went through a phase in life where I was pretty fuckin' promiscuous. I got no problem talking about it. Ask me anything, babe."

"Can I ask why?" I say, after a moment of thought.

"Why was I a slut?" She shrugs. "Psychologists and therapists call it hyper-expression of sexuality in response to sexual trauma during one's formative years."

I frown. "English is not my first language and I'm kind of stoned."

"I was raped when I was really young by a couple of

my father's friends. It fucked with my head hard." *Hahd.* "I spent a few years hating men and hating myself and hiding my body and cutting and all that shit. And eventually, with my best friend Emily's help, I was able to move past all that. Discovered self-pleasure first, and then eventually sex with dudes. And once I started fuckin', it was off to the races. Couldn't get enough. Provin' somethin' to myself, I guess." Her South Boston accent is more pronounced as the evening wears on. "An' now I got my Saxy-boy, and I can't get enough off him and his giant, magical lingy-whatsit."

"Lingam," Anjalee corrects.

"Yeah, that."

I nod. "I understand. I…well, I never went through a hyper-expression phase. But I can understand how such a reaction would occur."

Terra nods. "It's different with Saxon, though."

"How?"

"Well, it's…deeper. When I was sleepin' around, it didn't mean nothin'. It was for me. It was…I guess partly to prove that I had the power. I could choose who, when, where, how, how long, and what we did. When we stopped. I'd play with 'em, y'know? Tease 'em. Fuck wit' their heads. I followed through, because I ain't a bitch, but it was fun to play. It let me feel comfortable to have that control. With Saxon, there ain't no games. It's just him and me. My heart and his. My body and his. It *means* somethin'. It means fuckin' *everything*. But…" she grins, shrugging. "It don't *always* have to mean somethin'. I took Saxon into our room and sucked his brains out through his dick just because I wanted to. I enjoy it. It's fun. I thought I had Anni here fooled, but I guess not, and now she's gonna try an' murder me through exercise. Maybe she can do what I never could, though."

Annika frowns, puzzled. "That being what?"

Terra stands up, facing away, grabs her admittedly rather large bottom, and gives it a good shaking. "Tighten up this Jell-O."

Annika cackles. "I can do that. You won't like it, but I can do it. The real question is how Saxon will feel about it."

"Saxy-baby?" Terra calls, glancing over her shoulder. "Yo!"

"How'd you feel if Annika helped me tighten up my giant, flabby ass?"

"FUCK NO!" Saxon shouts back. "Don't ruin the magic!"

Terra laughs. "See?."

"Saxon!" Annika calls.

"Annika?"

"What if it's not *smaller*, just *tighter*?"

"Acceptable!"

Terra flings her arms out, palms up, and then slaps them against her thighs. "Dammmit. Saxon, you suck! You were supposed to get me out of my end of the wager."

He crosses the room to the female side, steps up, onto, and over the couch without breaking stride, and presses up against Terra from behind. "Terra, babe, I was just fuckin' with you, you know that, right? You are fuckin' *everything* to me, exactly as you are. You wanna work out with Anni, get your ass all tight? Great, baby. Love it. You don't? Perfect."

Terra sighs, turning in his arms. "I know, I know. I just lost a bet and now I have to let Annika kick my ass in the gym."

"What bet?" Saxon asks.

She gives a cutesy, aw-shucks shrug. "Um, well, when I pulled you into our room, you were supposed to stop me before you blew your load so we could screw, but I sorta got carried away."

"That doesn't explain anything, babe."

She pushes him back toward the guy side. "Don't worry about it. Go back to the boys so we can keep having girl talk." She sits back down and turns to me. "Look, Soph. There's no right or wrong to any of this. My journey is mine, yours is yours. Life experience is subjective. If going down on Lorenzo is hard for you, don't do it. I like it. I enjoy doing it. I like how he is when I've got him right on the edge, you know? All gooey-brained and stupid. But that may not be you. And that's fine."

I shake my head, smirking. "I did it. I went down on him. And...I..." I drop my voice. "I liked it. Like you said. I was scared to start it, scared I'd have a flashback or something. I knew Ren wouldn't be like Rafa was, but the fear doesn't know that."

"No," Terra agrees. "It sure the fuck does not." She grins at me. "So, you liked it."

I bite my lip, nodding, not quite hiding an embarrassed grin. "I did. Like you said, it was...I...I really got into it, way more than I was expecting to. Obviously, you don't get any, like, physical pleasure out of it, but with Ren, it didn't hurt. I didn't feel degraded. I felt powerful. I felt... in control."

"Knowing you have agency and control during sex is a big-ass mothafuckin' imperative," Terra says.

"God, yes," Scarlett agrees. "But, also, speaking as a strong woman with a big personality and a need for control, there's something to be said for trusting and loving your partner enough to be able to give up that control and surrender to him. To just…let go, not be in control, *at all*. It's scary as fuck at first, especially for women like us, Sophia. I don't even like being a passenger in a car because I'm not in control."

"*That* I understand," I say. "For me, my struggle has not been with trusting Ren, but trusting myself and overcoming my fear. It's one of those strange things, you know? I spent years projecting this image of being a tough, frightening, powerful authority figure with no vulnerabilities. But really, inside, I was scared and lonely and hurting. Trusting Ren to not hurt me wasn't the problem. Letting go of the image of myself as indestructible and impervious was the problem. Admitting my fears to myself, facing my fear of Rafael and the things he did to me and the things my father did to me, that was the problem. Trusting my own body to not respond badly to Ren touching me and such was hard. But once I did, once I let Ren touch me, I discovered that he understood my fears and was patient enough to help me overcome them." I laugh, somewhat bitterly. "Even now, it's rather difficult to admit to you girls that I was afraid."

"Of *course* you were afraid," Anjalee says. "I think you would have to be a sociopath or some such thing if you were not afraid of intimacy, after what you have endured."

I sniffle, nodding. "To be even more honest, I was concerned that I was, in fact, sociopathic. How could I have killed all those innocent people, if I was not? I cannot ever forgive myself for that. I will not." Holding my breath, I lift the back of my shirt to show them the tattoo, which so far only the artist and Lorenzo have seen.

Soft, cool hands pull my shirt down. "Sophia," Naomi's

voice says, whispering softly in my ear, full of compassion. "You *must* forgive yourself for that, for everything. Nothing devours joy so swiftly as guilt, deserved or not."

"It *is* deserved, Naomi."

"Perhaps," she agrees. "But who can judge you? Not us. Not Lorenzo. Not the other Arrows."

"If there is a God, surely he judges me for it," I whisper.

"Perhaps he does. But Sophia, you cannot live with that guilt forever. It will eat you alive."

Scarlett kneels in front of me, takes my hands in hers. "It's *done*, Soph. Right or wrong, you did it. It happened. You can't take it back. You can't atone for it. Good actions don't erase bad ones. That's just not how life works. All you can do is move forward. Forgive yourself and live your life. Does punishing yourself by reliving that day and clinging to your guilt bring those people back to life?"

I shake my head. "No. Of course not."

"No, of course not," she echoes. "So who does your guilt serve?"

"No one," I admit.

"Right. No one. Of course you can't forget. I can't forget my family dying in the jungle. Naomi can't forget the awful things her father did to her. Terra can't forget what her father's friends did to her. Myka can't forget her ex cheating on her and gaslighting her. Anjalee can't forget being controlled by her parents and being forced to marry someone she didn't even know. Tatiana can't forget her friends being murdered. Annika can't forget the accident that ended her career, or being an addict. The guys all have their shit they can't forget. But carrying around guilt and shame isn't the answer. That just fucks you up and leaves you isolated and hating yourself. And I don't think that's the answer. I *know* that's not the answer."

I close my eyes and breathe. Think about guilt and self-forgiveness.

Forward progress.

"I think it's time for me to leave the past in the past," I say, as much to myself as out loud.

"You're damn right it is," Scarlett says.

I get to my feet and spin in a slow circle, taking in the room, the people in it.

The guys ended the arm-wrestling contest at some point—I have no idea who won, nor do I care—and are now sitting at the tables in a close-knit cluster, sipping drinks and passing around joints; Kane eschews both, a can of flavored sparkling water looking tiny in his giant hand. The girls huddle together on the couch around me, a few murmured cross-conversations happening.

Slowly, eyes land on me and conversation slows, and then stops. I let the silence breathe for a few moments.

"It's time," I say, and pause for effect. "Scarlett has expressed her desire to take the brand and swear the oath of the Broken Arrows. We will all go together and witness her take the oath. If any of you wish to join Scarlett, you may. There is no obligation. You are welcome and you are part of this family, brand or not, oath or not." I turn and face the men. "Gentlemen, it did not escape my notice that you chose to take lives in the mission to rescue me. After all that has happened over the past few weeks, I understand that choice, and while I cannot and will not speak for him, I know Jakob would agree. And while there is no cause or benefit from re-doing the brand, I think there is value to re-newing your oath against the taking of life. It is my greatest hope that in the weeks, months, and years to come, all of us will be able to put down our arms and live in peace."

I pause, considering my next words.

"With Jakob absent for the foreseeable future, the burden of leadership here falls to me. Jakob has expressed his intention that there should be some changes to the Arrows, but he never shared what those would be. In his absence, I take the responsibility for that decision. I chose each of you—Rev, Kane, Chance, Saxon, Silas, Solomon, and Lash. I brought you to Las Vegas and presented you with a choice: continue living your life as you were, or choose a new path. With me, and with your brothers. You all chose the brotherhood." I let out a breath. "Club Sin will always be your home. You will always have a place here, no matter what, and no matter how much time may pass. That brand assures you of that. But..." I scan their faces. "You have faced your pasts. Your enemies. Your guilt. Your trauma. You have partners. You have futures, now. And should your future take you away from Club Sin, that is your choice to make. You can stay here as long as you want, and should you and your partner decide it's time to start a life together elsewhere, so be it. We will see you off and wish you well. I am not telling you what you should do or should not do—I am merely explaining your options."

Silence greets this—stunned, perplexed.

"The original ceremony took place way out in the desert," I say. "I see no reason to go so far, this time. We will convene outside in ten minutes, and we will hold the branding ceremony in the hills just beyond the parking lot. Any questions?"

More silence.

"Very good. I'll see you all outside in ten minutes."

Solomon gets to his feet. "This isn't a question, Sophia, more of a statement on behalf of all of us. Lorenzo was telling us that you were considering leaving your personal quarters upstairs and taking a room down here, to be more of a part of the group. And while I—and we, speaking for everyone, I think—appreciate the thought, that's fucking stupid."

I blink, barking a stunned laugh. "Excuse me?"

He grins. "Sophia, you have a whole-ass condo up there. You'd be an idiot to leave that for an eight-by-eight box." He shakes his head. "Look, I wouldn't give up my room for anything. Not yet. I'm not ready to go anywhere. That's just me, and I know Scar feels the same."

"I just got here," Scarlett says. "I'm not going anywhere."

"Exactly," Sol says. "Soph, you're one of us, no matter where your bed and clothing are. You have absolutely nothing to prove to anyone. Not to us, and I hope to god you understand that you don't have shit to prove to yourself, either. The best-case scenario, to my way of thinking, is that now that everything is over, our lives go back to normal. Just…with Lorenzo around." He glances at Toro, Taj, and Fonz. "And you fellas."

"Regarding that," I say, addressing the three men. "The choice to bring you in as Arrows cannot be mine alone. Jakob must have the final say. I hope you understand. But please know that you are, at very least, honorary members, and you are welcome here in the Common Room. Your duties, privileges, responsibilities, and pay will be adjusted to reflect that new reality. Once Jakob returns, we will bring you in and hold an official ceremony."

"It is my greatest wish to bear the brand," Toro says.

"I have watched your closeness with no little jealousy in the time that I have been employed by Club Sin. To even be considered for membership in a fraternity such as the Broken Arrows is an honor."

"I feel the same," Taj says.

"Samesies," Fonz says, and then sighs. "No joke, you all are the shit. You've got my loyalty for life, oath and brand or not. But obviously, given the choice, I'll take the brand and swear the oath all fuckin' day long."

Emotions running high inside me, I duck my head and clear my throat. "Very good. Ten minutes, at the top-side entrance."

CHAPTER 20

TAKING THE BRAND

LORENZO

THE MOOD AROUND THE BONFIRE IS SOMBER, serious. The branding iron is in the coals, glowing a bright, vivid orange-red.

We stand in a wide, uneven circle around the bonfire, which rages and flickers a good ten feet high—courtesy of Kane. Everyone is holding hands with the person on either side of them—only Scarlett stands alone, inside the circle, facing Sophia.

"Scarlett Gutierrez," Sophia starts.

Scarlett holds up a hand, and Sophia stops. "I…" she sighs, and starts over. "I have considered this long and hard over the last few weeks." She looks hard at Sophia. "I've watched you. You have chosen to leave your alter ego behind—we all call you Sophia, now, instead of Inez. I…I think it's time for me to leave Scarlett Gutierrez behind, and this seems to be the best time, the best place, and the best way to do so. When you brand me, I'm choosing to go by the name I was born with—Maria Consuela Rodriguez."

Solomon looks on with pride, beaming at her. Grinning ear to ear, as a matter of fact.

"Maria Consuela Rodriguez, then," Sophia says, starting over. "Today, you take the first step in a journey. You are leaving behind all that came before. We do not forget the past—we can't, and we should not, as you told me just a few minutes ago. But the past must remain in the past. We cannot carry it with us everywhere. We can't cling to it. Scarlett is your past. The Maria who was—she is your past, as well. In taking this brand, you choose to put everything you used to be behind you and choose to belong to this very exclusive club. We are your brothers. We are your sisters. We are your mother. We are your father. You belong to us, and we belong to you. The brand..." here, she wiggles her right hand into a thick, heat-resistant glove and pulls the iron out of the fire, "seals your membership into this family. No matter where you go or what you do, you belong to us. It is irrevocable. Permanent."

Scarlett—Maria, I should say—peels out of her black T-shirt, standing before Sophia in a pair of black jeans and a dark green bra. "I am ready."

"Maria," Sophia says, holding Maria's left wrist with her arm turned out and extended so the inside of her bicep faces forward. "Repeat after me: "In choosing this brand, I swear to never take another human life, and I swear my undying loyalty to my brothers and sisters in the Order of the Broken Arrows."

Taking a deep, bracing breath, Maria repeats the oath in a slow, solemn tone. When she gets to the words "I swear my undying loyalty," Sophia gently, quickly, and firmly presses the orange-glowing brand to the inside of her bicep.

A hissing sound erupts from her skin, along with the unmistakable scent of scorched flesh. She screams through gritted teeth, head flung back, eyes squeezed shut.

Removing the branding iron, Sophia shoves it back into the coals without letting go of Maria's wrist.

With a broad smile, she turns to Maria and pulls her into a hug, careful to avoid contact with the fresh brand. "Welcome to The Broken Arrows, Maria Rodriguez."

Cheers rise from the gathered circle, loudest of all from Solomon, who breaks from the circle to pull her into his arms. He hugs her tightly for a long time, while she, somewhat awkwardly, hugs him back one-armed, holding the other out and away. Eventually, he lets her go. Takes a half step backward.

Shoves a hand into his pocket.

Drops to one knee in front of Maria, who claps her right hand over her mouth.

"Scar—Maria…" he grins, laughs, shakes his head. "Gonna take me a second to get used to that." He kisses her knuckles and then starts over. "Maria, I love you. I can't picture my life without you in it. I've been thinking about doing this for a while now, and this seems to be the best moment." He holds up the ring he took from his pocket. "This was my great-grandmother's. She and my great-grandfather were married for sixty-two years. Before I left for Harvard, my mother gave it to me. Told me that if I ever met someone I loved enough to marry, that I should give her this. So, here it is. Maria, will you marry me?"

Nodding, she drops to her knees and cups his face, kisses him. "Yes, Solomon. A thousand times yes." She shows him her left hand, and he slides the ring on. "Holy shit, it fits?"

Solomon laughs. "I didn't think it would. I was assuming we'd have to get it sized."

The cheers erupt louder than ever, and everyone

surrounds the couple, slapping Solomon's back, hugging Maria, congratulating both of them.

I meet Sophia's eyes from across the scrum—she looks happy, but perhaps a little wistful.

Until Solomon pops up from the center of the crowded huddle and reaches for her. "Get in here, you." He shoots me a look. "You too, Ren."

We close in, and the group condenses, pulling us into the chaotic huddle.

I'm the first to pull away. "So, it's my turn, now."

Sophia blinks at me in surprise. "You too?"

I nod, shrugging. "Of course. Did you think I would not? I may not choose to work within the club, but I do wish to take the brand."

Taking a deep breath and nodding on the exhale, she steps back to her place near the iron, close enough to the massive bonfire that the heat billows her loose hair.

The circle reforms with me on the inside with Sophia. She repeats the speech she gave to Maria, albeit a bit condensed and not precisely word for word. Her eyes are misty and her voice is shaky as she asks me to repeat the vow— which I do, loudly, clearly, proudly.

The pain when the iron hits my flesh is unbelievable—a deep, searing sensation so intense it almost feels like intense cold. I clench my molars so hard the ache in my jaw registers through the pain in my arm, and then the iron is gone and the pain subsides to a dull, throbbing burning ache.

Before the crew can surround me, Terra steps forward. "I'm next."

Sophia nods. "Very well."

Terra, being covered in a tapestry of tattoos, places

hers in a blank spot on the back of her left shoulder. Unsurprisingly, from what little I know of her, she accepts the brand without any more fuss than Maria—a teeth-clenched, high-pitched snarl.

"I got next," Myka says.

Sophia blinks at her, then scans every face one by one. "Do you all intend to do this?"

Everyone nods. "Then I think you should induct each other. Terra, if you are agreeable, you will induct Myka, and Myka, you will induct the person after you."

And so it goes—the iron passing from Terra to Myka, Myka to Tatiana, Tatiana to Annika, Annika to Anjalee, and Anjalee to Naomi—who is the only one, male or female, to not make so much as a hiss when the brand hit her skin.

Taj, Toro, and Fonz stand apart, together, watching.

Sol glances at Sophia, at the three men, and then steps up to the fire and takes the iron from Anjalee—after putting on the glove. "Soph, this ain't right. These guys risked their lives for us. For *you*. They shed blood takin' our backs. Jakob can talk to me if he's got issues with this, but I'm inducting them, and I ain't asking."

Sophia's chin lifts, and her eyes sparkle. "I happen to agree, Solomon. Seeing the ceremony, seeing all of you—" she swallows hard, here, emotional, "choose this family, it seems clear that Toro, Taj, and Fonz belong to us as well."

Naomi touches Solomon's shoulder. "Please, may I? It would mean a lot to me."

Solomon shoves the iron into the fire, gives her the glove, and steps back. Glances at the trio of inductees. "Who's first?"

Fonz's hand shoots up so fast it's a wonder he doesn't tweak a nerve. "Me. I had to leave the LAPD for reasons I ain't ever shared. I suppose you know, Sophia. For the rest of you…" he ducks his head. "I've always been the class clown. I always will be. But I…I do know that life ain't always jokes and fuckin' games and shit. This ain't the time for a big origin story speech or what-the-fuck-ever, so the short version is that my best buddy on the squad was a guy named Gauge, spelled like the shotgun caliber. Big, beefy Black guy. Just a great, great dude. Solid. Steady as a rock. Loyal as a fuckin' Pit Bull. We went through the Academy together, made the force together, we were partners as rookies on patrol." He sighs, continues. "Our beat was a pretty dicey section of Compton. If you know, you know—an' if you don't, I can't explain. But I was a white cop in that neighborhood, and Gauge…that man kept my ass alive and outta trouble. Showed me…well, I ain't gonna preach about privilege. Anyways. Gauge caught wind of corruption in our precinct. Bad cops doing nasty shit. He reported it. And he got murdered for it. Made it look like a drive-by. But I knew it wasn't. I've got evidence it wasn't. And those dudes who did it, they know I've got evidence to put them all away for a long fuckin' time, and they want me dead for it. There's a lot more to it, but that's the basic version."

He's quiet a moment or two, thinking, gaze distant, remembering.

"Gauge was more than my friend, more than my partner. He was family. I was…I got fuckin' lost when he got killed. And you guys, workin' here…seein' the way you guys are with each other, hearin' bits of your stories, I…I finally feel like I belong somewhere. In a way I never have, except with Gauge." He looks at us all in turn. "This is the honor of a lifetime, to be a part of somethin' like this."

He jerks his chin up at Naomi. "Hit me with that shit, Nay-Nay."

Naomi grins at her nickname, adjusts her grip on the iron's handle, eying Fonz as he repeats the vow, and then presses it to his arm. Fonz is stoic through it.

Maria steps up, then. "I'll take that." She looks at Taj and Toro. "Step right up, one of you."

Toro steps forward. "I am not ready to share my history. But this…" he shakes his head. "It means everything to me. I was forced to leave behind a life I loved. No, that is not right. The life I loved was taken from me…by those who should have been my brothers. I was betrayed. I should be dead. They think I am dead. Yet, I am not. And I remember. I should like to forget, but I cannot. I belonged to a fraternal order before—a team. Men I shed blood with. And they betrayed me for thirty pieces of silver. Now, I am finding this place. You people. My heart says to trust you. It is hard, that trust, when it has been betrayed in the past. But I am here. I choose to trust. I take this marking to prove that I trust you, and that you may trust me."

"We've got your back, Toro," Kane calls. "To hell and back."

The others, me included, call our support for him, and he drops his head, shoulders shaking.

When he has composed himself, he looks at Maria and speaks the vow, takes the brand.

Taj singles out Anjalee. "I would be honored if you would do this for me, Anjalee. We are countrymen. You are from different castes, I know, but I do not think such things matter, here. I mean this country, as well as among these people."

Anjalee smiles at him. "It certainly does not matter to me, Taj. It would be my honor."

Without further comment, Taj speaks the vow and takes his brand, and just like that, the Broken Arrows, once a circle of seven men, has expanded by more than double.

It isn't just a club.

It's more.

It is found family. We have chosen each other. We have chosen to do life together. We are bonded by our trauma, by lives lived in violence. We all fought to escape that violence, and in so doing found love, acceptance, forgiveness, and belonging.

For some reason, as we stand together by the fire, I think of my mother. I do not think of her often—she died when I was quite young. She was alone in the world, except for me. I never knew my father, and if she had any other family, she never spoke of them, and we never visited them.

We had each other.

We had our community in the favela.

I think of her now. I remember her in the small, dirty, hot, smelly place we called home, and I remember how hard she worked to make it a home, to make it comfortable. I remember her cooking for me. I remember her leaving in the earliest hours of dawn to go to her first job, coming back to check on me and going to her second job, her third job—all so she could provide a few morsels of food for me.

She fought ferociously for me, my mother. Not with guns, but with love. She was a warrior—all mothers are warriors, I think. I don't really know why she is in my mind right now, as I look around at these people who have so quickly become my family. Perhaps it is the notion of love. I

love Sophia, of course. But with her comes everyone else—
an entire family.

It's a lot for a poor orphan boy from the favelas of Rio.
A lot of love. A lot of people who accept me, who understand the life I have lived. That is a rare thing, to be understood and accepted. Not everyone finds that. Yet here
we are, eleven men and nine women, who have found that
acceptance and belonging in each other.

Seems like a miracle, and not one any of us is taking
for granted.

INEZ

Back in the common room, everyone is comparing brands,
laughing, hanging on to each other, teasing, playfully shoving. Even the Cabot boys, once so cold, shut down, and
reclusive even with each other, are grinning and cracking
jokes and being openly silly.

Case in point: Silas is chasing Naomi around the
room with a piece of sliced ham, which she, for some reason, finds utterly horrifying. So far he's thrown it at her
like a frisbee twice, and she's alternating between hysterical cackles and disgusted shrieks. Solomon and Maria are
on the sectional, facing each other with her legs around
his waist, making out like teenagers. Saxon and Terra are
on the floor of the kitchen engaged in what appears to be
a tickle-fight to the death, and Saxon seems to be losing.

Lash is the only one who seems somber. Tatiana murmurs something to him, a question, perhaps. He shrugs,
murmurs in response, shaking his head.

I leave Lorenzo to a fiery and impassioned debate with Toro as to whether the Flamengo FC is better than Real Madrid and join Lash, standing with my back to the glass wall separating the gym from the common area. "Alright, Nico?"

He lets out a sigh, nodding his head at an angle. "I suppose."

Tatiana nuzzles her nose and lips into his throat. "Tell the truth, my heart."

He rakes his hand over his hair. "It is hard to feel as joyful as they are, with Pugli still out there. I am glad, truly, that all of you have found your freedoms from your enemies and the evils of the past. But I...I cannot rest and I will not breathe freely until Roberto Pugli is in the ground. Until I see the life bleed out of him with my own two eyes."

I hand him a small rectangle of heavy black metal—an exclusive, ultra-rare line of credit. "This traces to a shell corporation which is in turn owned by a nesting doll of umbrella companies. Anyone seeking to trace it will spend years untangling the threads. It is not literally unlimited, but as good as, for all intents and purposes."

He takes the card from me, turning it this way and that. "What is it for, and why are you giving it to me?"

"Because Jakob, so far as I know, is not trained in combat. He is elusive, clever, and an expert at avoiding detection and identification. But evading and combating direct, personal efforts to kill him? That is, perhaps, a different story. He needs an ally out there. He may not be pleased that I am doing this, but I, more than perhaps any of you, owe him my life. And you are, truly, the best and only option. If the dead cannot die, then perhaps a ghost is the only one who can find and protect him." I close his fingers over the card. "If anyone deserves the right to hunt down and kill that man once and for all, it is you."

He nods, slipping the card into his hip pocket. "I thank you, Sophia."

I clap him on the shoulder. "Do what you must, Nicolai. We are with you. And you know, should you need backup…"

He nods again, gaze hardening. "I know it." He glances at Tatiana, his expression momentarily softening. "I must do this alone, Lovely One."

Tatiana nods somberly. "I know it. Do what you must and come home to me."

He kisses her, softly, gently. "I must prepare. I shall depart in the morning."

"I'll help you pack," Tatiana says, and then mutters something to him in Croatian.

A small, private smile drifts across his face, and he answers in Croatian, cupping her cheek and then taking her hand.

Something tells me "packing" is going to take a while.

I watch them go, vanishing into their room, his hands busily clutching at her backside as she fumbles blindly for the doorknob with one hand, tugging at his fly with the other.

Someone wolf whistles, and Tatiana's hand appears from around the edge of the door, middle finger lifted— to much laughter.

I pour myself a drink and take a seat on the sectional next to Lorenzo, who has moved his football debate—now Messi versus Ronaldo—to the couch.

Solomon glances at me. "Going after Pugli?" he murmurs quietly.

I nod. "Yes. He can't be truly happy or free until Pugli is dead."

"How is Jakob, do you think?"

I shrug. "Who knows? He is a bit of a cipher, even to me. I just hope this turns out for him like it has for the rest of us."

"Happily ever after?" Solomon says, kissing Scarlett's temple.

I lean into Lorenzo, who grips and squeezes my thigh without turning away from Toro—their conversation seems to have moved away from football and into a discussion of the finer points of Brazilian versus Spanish politics, or something along those lines; their conversation moves seamlessly between Spanish, English, and Portuguese, which Toro seems to understand but not speak.

"Yes," I answer Solomon, after a moment. "Something which I doubt any of us expected."

Solomon snorts sarcastically. "Not fucking hardly, Soph. Not fucking hardly."

I sweep my gaze over the group. "Yet here we all are."

Maria, now sitting between Sol's thighs with her back to his chest and her eyes closed, a happy little smile on her scarred but beautiful face, speaks without opening her eyes. "We fought like hell for it, though, didn't we?"

"We did," I answer. "But then, some things are worth fighting for, are they not?"

"Love is," Maria says. "And family—however it looks."

Wherever you are, Jakob, I hope you find the redemption you've sought for so very long.

EPILOGUE

A GORGEOUS, MYSTERIOUS STRANGER

BRYS

I PINCH THE BRIDGE OF MY NOSE, WINCING AT THE sharp throb of pain lancing through my skull just behind my eyes. Blue blocking glasses dangling from my hand, I tune out the endless, divisive nattering of the board as they debate the pros and cons of our vice chairman's latest batshit crazy acquisition proposal.

I know he's my brother, but he's a real dumbass.

"Do you have any thoughts, Ms. Bennett?" Chairman Carmichael's voice cuts through the hubbub of cross-chatter.

"Yes, as in point of fact, I do." I toss my frames on the table in front of me with a clatter, pinning a glare on my useless, nepo-hire brother before scanning the now-silent members of my board. "It's a ridiculous notion. That we have spent any time or thought even debating it at all should annoy each of you as it does me. We are, primarily, a telecom R&D company. I am quite well aware of the developments in the AI sector, of course, but that's a Wild West shitshow. It's a circle jerk. Why my brother would even *suggest* we invest in an AI company is a mystery to me let alone, a startup with next to no capital, No VCs or angel investors behind them, and a product that only exists in theory... It's boneheaded, even for you, Bryan."

My brother flushes scarlet in a combination of rage and embarrassment—his usual state of being. "Dammit, Brys," he snaps; pronouncing my name *BREEZE*. "You don't have to be a bitch about it. It was just an idea. Jesus."

I let my gaze go icy. "You may leave now, Bryan. Thank you."

"But I—"

"You are here as a courtesy, Bryan. If Father's will had not *forced* my hand, you would not be here. Bennett Development, Incorporated is *my* company. I am the CEO. *I* am the one with degrees from Yale and MIT. *I* am the one who was interning here before I got my first period." Several of the old white male board members shift uncomfortably at my statement, and I glare at them. "Oh dear god, get over it, you crusty old dinosaurs. Women have periods and I, in case you had not noticed, am a woman. You will not burst into flames at the mention of my having menses." I return my gaze to my brother. "Bryan, you *will not* disrespect me in my own boardroom. You will not curse at me. You will not speak to me with such familiarity and informality in this setting. Here, I am not your sister. Here, Bryan, I am the CEO and president of the company you, nominally speaking, work for—as a *junior* board member. Furthermore, and most importantly, you will not waste this body's time with cockamamie proposals which have less than zero merit, even if we *were* interested in investing in AI—which we are not, and likely never will be. If you wish to invest in..." I put my glasses back on as I hunt for the name of the company in my notes—they're blue blockers and readers; I'm only thirty-six, but a lifetime spent peering and squinting at computer screens has left its mark on my vision already. I find the name and look up at Bryan again. "Acheron AI, Limited...then be my guest. With your own money, on your own time. Are we clear?"

Bryan, seething, only nods.

I arch an eyebrow at him. "You may go."

He shoots to his feet, sending his rolling chair rocketing backward so hard it dents the wall, and storms out, muttering who knows what under his breath.

When he's gone, I let out a breath and toss my glasses down once more. "Now. Do we have any other *serious* business to discuss before we bring our investors on screen?"

No one does, so I wave at Jeremiah, our techie; he begins looping in the investors and putting the teleconference on the main screen.

◆

Several hours later, I kick the door to my office closed behind me, sighing in relief as I step out of my heels and shuck my blazer. Collapsing heavily into my chair, I cover my eyes with one hand and address the ceiling. "Coactum—reduce lights by sixty percent." *Coh-ACT-um.*

Coactum is the AI system—ironically enough—that operates the lighting, security, energy usage, phones, and networking in this building. It's overseen by a team of humans; it's a collaborative effort with another R&D company, and we're their guinea pigs for the office management system—no monetary investment involved.

At my command, the lights in my office dim to a dull orange glow that's much easier on my eyes, and the nascent migraine I feel percolating in my brain.

"Coactum—play music. Classical. Debussy. Volume thirty percent."

The name of the system, Coactum, is a Latin word with multiple possible meanings, all of them variations on "bring together."

The soft, soothing opening of "Clair de Lune" floats through the office, and I turn my chair away from the door to face the windows, which overlook downtown Manhattan. It's the golden hour, when the sun shines a perfect shade of gold that bathes the world in light. I wish I was out there. In Central Park, perhaps. Sitting on a bench, watching couples lounge in the grass and toss Frisbees and stroll the paths.

Yet here I am, at six o'clock on a Friday, with hours of work yet to do.

My phone burbles with an incoming call. "Coactum, identify caller."

In my office, Coactum's voice is male, with a crisp British accent. Obviously. "Charles…Edwin…Danforth… the Third," Coactum announces, his voice stilted and awkward. He's better at listening than speaking, so far. I make a mental note to have the team at Vector Technologies focus on improving Coactum's speech capabilities.

I hiss in irritation at the announcement. "Dammit, dammit, dammit," I snap under my breath. "Coactum, answer. Handset only, on speaker."

My phone chirps twice, and then I hear my ex's voice. "Brys, good evening. How are you, darling?" I tried to get Charles to be the voice of Coactum, as he has the most gloriously archetypal upper-crust British accent you've ever heard, but he wouldn't go for it.

"Exhausted, fighting a bitch of a migraine, and buried in work. What do you want, Charles?"

"My date canceled last minute for a performance of La Boheme at The Met this evening. I'd hoped you would be agreeable to filling in. Drinks before around the block, and dinner after. My dime, of course. Strictly business, I assure you."

"I really can't, Charles. I've been here since seven this morning and if I get home before midnight, I'll feel lucky."

He clucks at me in that teasing, scolding way of his, when he knows damn well that I've been burning the candle at both ends for too long. "Brys, darling. When was the last time you stopped working for more than a few hours of sleep? Have you even *seen* the sun this week?"

"I'm watching it set right now, Charles, and I'm not your darling anymore, remember?"

"In person, Brys, not through that UV-blocking bulletproof glass."

I sigh. "Charles. Really."

"*You* really, Brys. I *know* you. You only get migraines like that when you haven't slept more than two hours a night in the past week. Now, tell me truthfully...if you leave the work you have piled up on your desk until Monday— or even tomorrow—will the company go under?"

"No, but—"

"And will the board suddenly vote you out?"

"No, and they can't. I own the controlling shares."

"You know what I mean."

I sigh. "Charles, I..." I turn in the chair and glance at the reports I have to go through, all sixty-four trillion of them, it feels like.

And I discover that I'd rather stick a hot fork in my

eyeball than dig into them right now. But do I want to get all gussied up and spend the evening with my ex? Not that there's any enmity between us; we merely realized we were better off as friends than lovers, so our romantic split was amicable enough that I do consider him still a friend.

"Anything is better than spending one more minute in this building, I suppose," I grumble. "I'll just pop home and change."

"Wonderful. Pritchard will pick you up outside your building at seven. Is that enough time? You'll have to meet us for drinks."

I glance at the time on the phone screen: 6:07 pm. "Barely, but yes. And Charles?" I pause, and he hums an interrogatory noise. "This is *business*. As friends. Yes?"

"Of course, Brys." He pauses. Clears his throat. "As a matter of fact, my date, the one who canceled…we're, ah…actually rather serious. She came down with a stomach bug this afternoon."

"Does she know you've called *me* to replace her?"

"Of course she does," he says, chuckling. "What kind of an idiot do you take me for?"

"And she's not jealous? That your ex is going with you instead?"

He sighs. "No, no. She knows your and my relationship is…erm…unique."

"As long as she doesn't show up here accusing me of trying to steal you from her," I say, only half joking.

"Shauna isn't like that, Brys. She's wonderful. You'd hate spending time with her, though. You'd say she lacks motivation and energy. But she balances me out. Keeps me calm. Anchors me."

"Honestly, Charles, she sounds perfect for you. We're

far too much alike, you and I. For romantic partners, at least." I'm on my feet as I talk, gathering my things, stepping into my heels, and shrugging into my blazer.

"I think she is. Well, you'd better get going, Brys. And, ah, if I may?" A pause. "The one with the sparkly bits on the shoulder. The one that only has one sleeve, or whatever you call it."

"You're wearing your silver tie, I take it?"

"Indeed. With Grandfather's cufflinks and Father's Patek Philippe."

"Got it," I answer, already mentally sorting out my shoes and other accessories to go with the dress he mentioned. "I'm off, now. See you shortly."

"Thanks, Brys, you're a real gem, you know?"

"I do, but thanks for telling me. Never hurts to hear it."

◆

"….Heard of Acheron, as a matter of fact," Roger says; Roger is the CEO of the tech company Charles is courting this whole evening. "They'll fold in six months at best, I believe. They've no product. Great ideas, and some bankable talent on their roster, but you made the right call, Ms. Bennett."

I force a smile at him—he's been condescending all evening. He's called me 'sweetheart' at least twice, mansplained a facet of my own industry to me—a technical element of recent telecom hardware advancements that I have personally helped pioneer—and 85% of his comments to me are addressed to my cleavage. Which, admittedly, is rather impressive in this dress. But still—rude.

Charles is aware of all of this, and is fighting panic.

He knows I'm not one to suffer fools like this Roger, and can tell I'm about to verbally eviscerate him any moment.

"I appreciate your vote of confidence in my decision, Roger," I say. "Now, if you'll excuse me, I need to visit the restroom."

I do my best to tamp down my irritation—I'm here as a favor to Charles, that's all. I got free drinks, a lovely viewing of the opera, and a rather sumptuous dinner out of it. I can tolerate Roger for a bit longer. I just need a moment to regroup my patience—not a trait I'm overly well known for.

I use the facilities and take my time washing my hands and touching up my makeup. A pair of women a few years older than me enter the bathroom, bitching about their husbands. Which is my cue to make my exit; the thought of marriage or commitment makes me queasy.

I'm nearly to the table when movement on the sidewalk outside the restaurant catches my eye. A man crosses the street at a dead sprint, doing an action movie-worthy vault-and-slide over the hood of a taxi. Four men in jeans, T-shirts, and body armor follow him, armed with full-on machine guns. I stop and watch it unfold, fascinated—New York never fails to entertain, that's for damned sure.

The man is dressed in a tan suit with a black button-down, no tie. The suit, I can tell even from a distance, is impeccably tailored to his stunning Adonis physique. Black hair, a bit too long. A sharp jawline, heavily shadowed with stubble.

Horns blare as the man barely avoids being hit by a cube van. I hear a sharp but muffled rattle, and the windows of the restaurant shatter. People scream all at once, fleeing their seats. Before I can blink, I'm caught up in a crush of humanity carrying me toward the exit. I can't even try to fight it—I can only try and keep my feet and not be trampled. I've left my shawl on the back of my chair, which I feel a burst of annoyance about—it's cashmere, and a favorite. At least I have my Chanel clutch with my phone and wallet.

And then I'm outside in the cool evening air, being elbowed and jostled as the crowd flows out of the emergency exit. Trash stinks in the alley, and horns blare and sirens howl. Another burst of shots rings out, and someone screams. There's a crunch of metal on metal—a car crash.

The crowd carries me away from the street where the action is, thank god, and I find myself on a small cross-street, where orange parking cones block off a truck unloading goods; a vent spews swirling clouds of steam. I can hear sirens and shouts and screams, still, but it's distant.

The crowd has thinned, and I'm no longer being swept along. I stumble back against the stone of a building and catch my breath, let my hammering pulse stabilize.

My phone buzzes; I pull it out, answer it. "Charles? I'm alright."

"Oh, thank the good lord. I lost sight of you in the mayhem. Can you *believe* it? Automatic gunfire on the streets of Manhattan. It's like something out of Hollywood. Where are you? I'll come to you."

"I…" I look around, but I can't see the signs. "I don't know. The crowd carried me quite a way. Look, Charles, I'm really alright, I promise. I'll catch a Lyft."

"Brys, darling—"

"Charles," I snap, letting my voice harden. "I'm *not* your darling. I can take care of myself. I'm *fine*. Go home to Shauna. Take that blathering, chauvinistic dick, Roger, out for more drinks and close the deal. Thanks for the lovely evening, though, really. I mean it. I needed a night out, so thanks for forcing me."

Charles chuckles ruefully. "You're on speaker, Brys, and he's next to me."

"Oh. Right." I clear my throat. "Well, I don't take it back. Roger, you're an ass. But Charles really is your best bet. Cowper and Danforth can take your chipset and really run with it. You'd be a fool to pass on this deal."

"Noted," Roger says, his tone wry. "And since we're being forthright, I can see why he dumped you. You're all hard edges."

I laugh. "Not taking the bait, Roger. Charles, good-bye. And thanks again."

"Of course. Message me when you're home safely, please. With this insanity outside, you know I'll worry."

"I will," I assure him, and tap the red phone icon to end the call, shoving the device into my clutch as I head for the nearest major thoroughfare.

It's calmer here, only the usual traffic rushing back and forth, clusters and clumps of pedestrians flowing past me as I summon a car from my phone—four minutes until Akhbar H. arrives in a black Lexus IS.

I only register the sound of running feet at the last second—too late. A hard body slams into me, sending me flying. Or, I would have gone flying had a powerful hand not grabbed my wrist and kept me from hitting the ground.

The owner of the hand yanks me upright, and I smack hard against a chest, which feels an awful lot like a very rugged cliff face, if said cliff face was warm, smelled of sweat, and had the firm give of thick muscle.

He spins me, walks me backward. I can't even man-age a stammered protest, still stunned from being knocked into so abruptly. Beneath the scent of male sweat is the layered nuance of extremely expensive cologne. Hard hands brace my waist, lift me clear off the ground, and then hard cold brick presses against my back, left bare by the low, swooping lines of the expensive—and somewhat revealing—dress I'm wearing.

Dark eyes find mine, close, large, deep, unreadable. "Play along," he says, his voice a sinister, silky-smooth snarl.

He shifts, and the heavy, warm weight of his jacket settles on my shoulders, blocking out the cool night air.

Shouts ring out. "OVER HERE!"

"HE WENT THIS WAY!"

"CHECK THE ALLEYS!"

I press my hands against his hard chest, intending to push him away. I'm not a weak woman. I lift, hard and heavy, several times a week. I practice Brazilian Jiu-Jitsu. I can take down men several times my size. But this man? I can't budge him. I lean my head back against the wall and take him in for the first time.

It's *him*.

The man from the street. The one being chased and shot at.

A few strands of silver stain the inky hair at his temples. His chest heaves from exertion, and sweat streams down his jaw and sheens his forehead.

He's devastatingly gorgeous.

As in my pulse skips. My mouth goes dry. My legs feel weak.

Footsteps echo on the street, layered with male voices—close and getting closer.

His huge, hot, heaving body smashes into mine,

pressing me into the wall, crushing my curves against his hardness.

My pulse races.

What's going on?

"You're saving my life, that's what," he says, his voice barely a whisper, lips moving so close to mine I can feel his breath.

I must have spoken out loud.

"Saving your—" I barely get the two words out...

His mouth slants against mine, one hand cupping my jaw, the fingers of the other digging into my hip. I taste sweat from his upper lip, but then the shocking depth and intensity of the kiss takes over, and I'm lost in his mouth, in the way his fingers splay over the swell of my ass, the way his thumb sweeps over my cheekbone.

It's a commanding and expert kiss.

A panty-soaking kiss—quite literally, in my case.

The footsteps draw closer, and a light shines on us. I turn my face toward the light, squinting; the man buries his face in my neck, kissing my throat, as if he's too enraptured to bother with the intrusion.

"Do you fucking *mind*?" I snap, burying my fingers in the hair at his nape, not at all faking the way my knees shake as he kisses my throat, my clavicle, my breastbone...

It's them—the men in the body armor with the machine guns.

Who the hell *is* this man? Who are these men? Why are they chasing him and shooting at him?

Why me?

And why, most importantly, is my body responding to him this way?

"Wait..." one of them says, frowning, sweeping the

light on the bottom of his machine gun up so it's blinding me. "That's him!"

"Fuck," The man snarls. "Get ready to run."

Run? I'm in four-inch Louboutins and a six-thousand-dollar Little Black Dress, which is so tight even walking requires concentration and effort.

I have no chance to express any of this. The man pivots to face his four pursuers, putting himself between them and me. He grabs a handgun from the back of his suit slacks, whips it around, and fires off three quick shots.

I'm no expert, but it doesn't look like he knows what he's doing, judging by the way he holds the gun, and the fact that his shots go wide, cracking off the walls nowhere near his enemies.

It does serve the intended purpose, however: they duck and crab walk out of sight around the corner as he fires several more shots in their general direction, all of which go high and wide.

The gun clicks empty, the slide snapping back, and he curses again, hesitating—one of them peeks around the corner, and he hurls the empty gun at the other man. His throwing aim is better than his shooting, as the empty gun hits the man in the forehead, eliciting a howl of enraged pain and a string of curses in some European language I don't recognize, other than perhaps belonging to a Slavic family of languages

"*Run*, goddammit!" He shoves me, hard, and I trip into a run, wobbling on my heels.

He catches me when I wobble, keeping me upright and moving forward—half carrying me, if I'm honest.

"I *can't* run!" I snap at him. "Do you *see* what I'm wearing?"

"So kick off the shoes and hike up the dress."

"They're Louboutins," I argue. "*Vintage*."

"I don't fucking care if they're Cinderella's glass fucking slippers," he snarls. "Unless you want to die, kick them off and fucking *RUN*!"

"Fuck me," I grumble, letting my beloved shoes fling away. "You…owe me, you big…dumb…jackass." I'm gasping already; I'm strong, but I don't do a lot of running, for two rather large reasons.

"I'll buy you…a goddamned…warehouse…full of shoes…if we…if we survive this," he says, panting almost as raggedly as me—that makes me feel a little better.

"*We?*" I screech, jerking him to a halt. "I don't know you! I don't know them! I don't know a single goddamned thing about what's going on!"

He lifts me bodily off the ground as if I weighed nothing, tossing me so I have no choice but to trot, stumble, and keep running. "No, you don't," he growls. "And I'm sorry I got you into this. They've seen your face, now, though."

My bare feet slap against the sidewalk, and he jerks me this way and that, ducking down alleys, crossing streets, weaving through traffic. More than once, he yanks me out of the way just in time to avoid being plowed into by a car.

The shouts of our pursuers have faded. The man, his bare arms, thick and tanned and rippling with muscle, stretch the short sleeves of his button-down. Why I notice that even as we run for our lives, I couldn't say.

Or don't want to, at least.

He glances up at a high-rise as we pass it, and his expression darkens. He pulls me to a halt, shoves me through the revolving door and into the dark, echoing marble cavern of a lobby, yanks me aside away from the doorway and presses me up against the wall next to the revolving door, chest heaving as he peers outside, watching.

"Are you going to at least tell me your name?" I say, once I've caught my own breath.

"I think we've lost them, for now," he murmurs, and he turns those eyes on me—night-black, cold, glittering with cunning and intelligence. "My name is…Jakob." The pause seems significant, for some reason.

"And why does it seem like you're unhappy to be inside this building in particular?"

"Because I used to own it," he mutters, then frowns at me. "I should not have told you that. Not sure why I did."

I shrug, smirking. "I have that effect on people, Jakob…" I trail off, leading him toward telling me his last name.

"Just Jakob," he answers, peeking outside. Looks down at me again. "And you are? Other than absolutely fucking breathtaking, that is."

I can't help grinning at his offhand compliment. "Brys Bennett."

He offers me a smile, and I get the impression that smiles from this man are a rarity, to be savored and appreciated. "Brys Bennett? Any relation to Lawrence Bennett, of BDI?"

"My father. He passed a few years ago. I'm CEO, now." I frown up at him—at 5'9", I'm not exactly short, but he still towers over me. "You know it?"

"You resemble him," he says, and looks down at me. "I almost owned BDI, a long, long time ago, in another life. Larry backed out at the last second and wouldn't come back to the table. One of the only men to ever successfully tell me no."

"I have vague memories of that," I answer. "I was in college at the time."

He frowns again. "And yet again I find myself telling you things you have no business knowing."

"I told you," I say, "I have that effect on people."

His face is close, dark eyes now opaque and unreadable. "You're going to be trouble, I think, Brys Bennett."

"You have only yourself to blame," I whisper, mesmerized by the darkness in his eyes, the anger and sorrow and guilt that seem to swirl around him, emanate from him—along with power and authority and charisma.

And sexual tension.

Lots and lots of that.

"Believe me, I know." He stares at me. "I know I shouldn't kiss you again, but…"

"Fuck it," I finish for him.

I lift up on my toes and kiss the shit out of him, surprising us both.

A beam of light sweeps across the lobby, and Jakob crushes me against the wall. "Go, go, go," he whispers, pushing me into a walk, shoulder to the wall, leading toward the elevator banks and the stairwell.

"Hey!" a male voice shouts. "You can't be in here! How'd you—fucking Greg, never locks the damn door."

Jakob shoves me into the stairwell and I trot up the stairs on aching, hurting bare feet, Jakob right behind me.

We reach the first floor landing and I yank the door open, stumble through it, and then Jakob is yanking me around a corner, into a dark conference room. His hand presses my head down, and I drop to my ass on the floor…

And then he's on top of me, rolling us under a desk as the security guard sweeps his light this way and that.

When we rolled, I ended up on top of Jakob, and his hands grip my hips, his eyes searching my face.

"I am sorry to have involved you in this," he whispers.

I'm not sure I am. He's kissed me twice already, and both kisses have been…

Well…

Pretty damn epic.

"You promised me a warehouse full of shoes," I answer. "I expect you to deliver. And not cheap shit, either."

He doesn't exactly smile, but his eyes communicate amusement, somehow. "If we live, I will. You have my word."

"If we live?" I echo. "Would those men really kill me just for being seen with you?"

"Let's just say you probably don't want to find out."

A few moments pass, and then he rolls us out from under the desk and helps me to my feet—lifts me like a child and sets me on my feet, I mean. "Come," he whispers. "Let's sneak out while the guard looks for us."

"And go where?" I ask.

He scans me, his gaze lingering on my chest before flicking to my eyes. "Your place. If you're going to run for your life, you can't do it in that dress, as sexy as you look in it."

Well, I can honestly say that of all the things I expected to happen when I woke up at five this morning, the events of the last twenty or so minutes were definitely not on the list.

Yet here I am, running for my life with a gorgeous, mysterious stranger who kisses me with absolute mastery, and sets my pulse racing.

I have no way of knowing what's going to happen next, but I find myself hoping it involves more kisses.

And maybe a little bit more than a few kisses.

Or a whole lot more.

As long as I don't get killed in the process.

I'm not sure why, but I'm not afraid. This man, Jakob, exudes competence. Courage.

Somehow, I just know that as long as I'm with him, he'll take care of me.

"You got me into this," I tell him, when we reach the street outside the building he claims to have once owned. "I'm trusting you to get me out of it intact."

"I promise," he answers, gaze locked on mine. "I'll see you through it."

I find myself believing him.

I suppose we'll find out, won't we?

About the Author

Jasinda Wilder is a *New York Times, Wall Street Journal,* and *USA Today* bestselling author of more than 100 titles including the #1 Amazon bestseller Falling Into You, the Audie Award-winning (best audiobook) Alpha, and the beloved, 17-book Badd Brothers series.

She and her husband Jack Wilder have sold more than 7 million copies and have been translated into more than 20 languages worldwide. You can find them at their fairy tale cottage by a lake somewhere in Michigan with their 6 kids, 5 dogs, 2 cats, 2 bunnies, and way too many ducks and chickens.

ALSO BY

JASINDA WILDER

Visit me at my website: **www.jasindawilder.com**
Email me: **jasindawilder@gmail.com**

If you enjoyed this book, you can help others enjoy it as well by recommending it to friends and family, or by mentioning it in reading and discussion groups and online forums. You can also review it on the site from which you purchased it. But, whether you recommend it to anyone else or not, thank you *so much* for taking the time to read my book! Your support means the world to me!

My other titles:

Forbidden Fruit

Wild Ride: Biker Billionaire

Delilah's Diary

Big Girls Do It:

Big Girls Do It
Married
On Christmas
Pregnant
Rock Stars Do It
Big Love Abroad

The Houri Legends:
Jack and Djinn
Djinn and Tonic

The Madame X Series:
Madame X
Exposed
Exiled

The Black Room (With Jade London)

The One Series
The Long Way Home
Where the Heart Is
There's No Place Like Home

Badd Brothers:
Badd Motherf*cker
Badd Ass
Badd to the Bone
Good Girl Gone Badd
Badd Luck
Badd Mojo
Big Badd Wolf
Badd Boy
Badd Kitty
Badd Business
Badd Medicine
Badd Daddy
For a Goode Time Call…
Not So Goode
Goode To Be Bad

A Real Goode Time
Goode Vibrations
A Very Badd Christmas
Badd Apple
Badd Baby

Dad Bod Contracting:
Hammered
Drilled
Nailed
Screwed

Fifty States of Love:
Pregnant in Pennsylvania
Cowboy in Colorado
Married in Michigan
Christmas in Connecticut

Billionaire Baby Club:
Lizzy Goes Brains Over Braun
Autumn Rolls a Seven
Laurel's Bright Idea

Club Sin:
Rev
Kane
Chance
Silas
Saxon
Solomon
Lash
Inez

Blood Heir

Blood Heir

Blood Rising

Blood Bonds

Blood Reign

Three Rivers:

Into the Light

Light in the Dark

The Cabin:

The Cabin

Christmas at the Cabin

Standalone titles:

Yours

The Parent Trap

Wish Upon A Star

Big Hose

Non-Fiction titles:

You Can Do It

You Can Do It: Strength

You Can Do It: Fasting

Jack Wilder Titles:

The Missionary

JJ Wilder Titles:

Ark

To be informed of new releases, special offers, and other Jasinda news, sign up for Jasinda's email newsletter.